Binkie's Revolution

Binkie's Revolution

STUART BELL

SpenView

Copyright © 2002 Stuart Bell

First published in Great Britain in 2002 by
SpenView Publications Limited

The right of Stuart Bell to be identified as the Author of
the Work has been asserted by him in accordance with the
Copyright, Designs and Patents Act 1988.

10 9 8 7 6 5 4 3 2 1

A CIP catalogue record for this title is available from the
British Library

ISBN 0 953 86383 2

Typeset by Palimpsest Book Production Limited,
Polmont, Stirlingshire
Printed and bound in Great Britain by
Antony Rowe Limited, Chippenham, Wiltshire

SpenView Publications Limited
One Old Burlington Street
London W1X 2NL

To Alex and Julian

Contents:

Binkie's Revolution

The first in a trilogy dealing with events within Europe over a hundred years leading to the First President of the United States of Europe.

This volume deals with colliery life and the First World War, the suffragette movement and the Russian revolution, all leading to Binkie's revolution. It introduces such powerful figures as Binkie Fatherley and Pauline Alyson and tells the moving stories of their families.

A mining disaster, the battle of Paschendale, Lenin seizing power in Petrograd, Binkie's revolution that almost overthrows King and country but for Winston Churchill's intervention provide powerful backgrounds to the lives and loves of Binkie and Pauline, and the consequences of their loves.

All these shape the history of a hundred years, told at a breathtaking pace by a superb storyteller that makes the novel one of the best to come before the public this year.

A Note on the Author

Stuart Bell was born and bred in a pit village in North-West Durham.

He left the local grammar school at sixteen to work in the colliery office and subsequently became a newspaper reporter, free-lance journalist, copy-typist to *The Daily Telegraph*, typist and shorthand-typist in the City of London, before going to Paris to write. He worked for an American lawyer, read for the Bar to become a Barrister, and spent seventeen years in Paris before returning to enter British politics. He has been Member of Parliament for Middlesbrough since 1983.

He has published two novels, political pamphlets, and a chronicle of the Cleveland child abuse crisis in 1987 called *When Salem Came to the Boro*. His last published work was a collection of short stories entitled *Tony Really Loves Me*, describing his relations with Tony Blair and other leading figures within the New Labour Party and House of Commons. The collection also describes his early struggles as a writer.

Prologue

They came over in the hard morning light.

They were small and dark and hovered above the cliff. They came in from the sea, low over the tips of the waves, cresting the cliff and speeding beyond the tussocky grass, so low over the tops of the oak trees he thought they might slice into the Hall. The helicopters were now neither so small nor so dark, their engines a steady throb, the grass and leaves ruffled like soft hair as rotor blades stirred the air.

Citizen Fatherley's hands did not leave the balustrade.

The helicopters held their course till they reached the Hall, arching higher, those on the outside of the formation peeling away, eight of them in all, their undercarriages and wheels visible, their markings too, the pilots behind their perspex, their helmets orange, face masks dark against the orange, each pilot giving a respectful salute, the helicopters lost now, arching ever higher, the sound of their engines receding, the fan of air from their rotor blades ruffling the dust on the terrace as it had the grass and the leaves.

1

He felt the balustrade cold so early in the morning.

'They will come from the sea,' he said.

'If they come,' Sigrid said.

'They'll come all right,' he said.

'We've nothing from InterActive City.'

'Even InterActive City have not thought so far ahead.'

Citizen Fatherley left the terrace and entered the Hall.

A butler pulled back his chair so that he could settle at the table; waiters stood by the dining room walls. The silver ring enclosing his napkin had been embossed with his initials; a silver coffee pot and milk jug stood on the table, silver cutlery and platters too. The silver condiment pots were as traditional as the dining room, the long table varnished but without cloth, the walls panelled, the windows high, light slanting cold and dull.

He settled the napkin into his shirt and turned the pages of his newspapers.

Newspapers were no longer printed, all information had been paperless, passing through web sites and Internets and interactive communications projected through a universal canvas. In theory the same inform-ation was available to all at the same time; interpret-ations should also be the same. This meant there were no longer rich or poor, privileged or oppressed, all were equal in their prosperity, in their leisure, and in their health.

Citizen Fatherley enjoyed using centralised data

bases and digital technology. He understood the importance of information that would be automatically synchronised and immediately available through communication platforms, but he had been sufficiently traditionalist to enjoy the printed word. His own newspapers were printed each morning, a financial, international and national newspaper of news and photographs.

The newspapers stood on a stand beyond the silverware.

They were all in colour but with no banner headlines, no by-lines only sub-titles. The photographs were graphic but not sensational, the news-type clear and easy to read, the articles consisting of fact but no comment. Comment had dropped out of fashion a long time ago. Television screens covered the walls, hidden by purple curtains; there were cassettes of the latest television news or colloques or information videos. The same television screens could be used for face-to-face interviews with anyone in the world, in their home or office, statesmen or business men or any individual who might wish to speak to him from a government internet café.

They called it the Cyberspace age.

Citizen Fatherley would either watch his cassettes or read his newspapers over breakfast. The silence in the dining room had been total but for the pouring of coffee by a waiter. There would be no urgent messages whilst he ate, his staff knew he should not be disturbed; but if there were they would be logged in his watch computer to be flashed upon a minute screen on the face of the watch immediately his breakfast was over. A chip implanted behind his ear would also alert him that a message was awaiting him.

Citizen Fatherley ate little.

There were fresh croissants, still warm from the bakery, fruit and cereal and butter whirls. There were jam pots and milk and fruit juice, but his intake would consist of so many calories, so many carbohydrates, so many vitamins that he could not deviate. The croissants and butter were luxuries but he would make up during the day. He had already swam for an hour in the basement pool and there would be another hour on a walking machine in the health centre.

'The European Commission have set the date for the Presidential Election,' Citizen Fatherley said. 'The eighth day of May. The final – ultimate – reconciliation when the whole of Europe shall be as one.'

'A truly socialist springtime.'

'You have been reading one of my history books.'

'You would prefer this to a capitalist summer?'

'Victory-in-Europe Day all over again.'

'The country expects you to announce your own candidacy,' Sigrid said. 'It will be a great honour for the people – the First President of the United States of Europe. That he should be English. The island race won the war, did they not, three-quarters of a century ago? It would be a consecration of their victory – a signal of a new beginning for all our peoples in the knowledge that old traditions shall be maintained.'

'Like having breakfast over a newspaper every morning?'

'And a French breakfast at that.'

Sigrid had followed Citizen Fatherley from the terrace.

A waiter poured her coffee and added a sweetener and she stood by the tureens along the dining room walls. The tureens stood as they had stood in the last century, when lords and ladies had dined in this room; breakfast had always been punctual at nine, with prayers said by the master of the Hall. The tureens were as filled now as they had been then, since if members of the Council of Ministers were to dine after Citizen Fatherley their regimes might be different to his own.

No-one had been allowed to breakfast while he was in the room since no-one was allowed to disturb his concentration. Sigrid had been the exception. She liked to hover if not to speak unless spoken to; this was how it had been in the days of Kings and Queens of old, though the present Royal Family had a more relaxed tradition. She stirred her coffee without the spoon touching the china cup and the only sound to the room had been the slight rustle of a zephyr breeze through the gardens.

She had met Citizen Fatherley when she had been twenty and she was now approaching fifty; she wore a dark trouser suit and yellow shirt, the collar and cuffs showing against the dark suit. She rolled her head to soothe her neck muscles and the blonde hair tasselled around her shoulders; the gold-blonde shimmered in the light. She wore little make-up, a touch of lipstick and blue mascara, and though her eyes were green mischievous lights danced in their recesses.

She felt the warmth of the coffee to her throat.

'I have never had ambition,' Citizen Fatherley said. 'Other than for my country. I come from mining stock, my roots are deep in a coalfield that once was but can never be again; but I live in the Hall of the coal owners – despots all. Why should I wish to be the First President of the United States of Europe?'

'You said you would fulfil your destiny – whatever that destiny might be.'

'You're quoting one of my forebears.'

'Now you will not fulfil your destiny at all?'

'The destiny of my nation, my country, my people. The destiny of the European peoples must be for others. The King wishes to cheat his destiny – if he can. He believes he must provide the continuum between past and future. The people prefer prosperity to continuum. All men and women are equal – there cannot be some more equal than others. The voice of the people shall be heard in the First Presidential Election.'

Sigrid ran one hand across the embossed name of the Townley family on a silver tureen. They had lived in this Hall and on this estate for a hundred-and-seventy years; the Hall had begun as a manor house facing the oak trees and cliff tops. The land ran from the cliffs to a port where coal would be loaded. In more ancient times those who had sought sanctuary in Durham Cathedral would be exiled from there. The manor house had been demolished when the Marquess of Townley had bought the estate and raised the Hall in its place.

'They say Lord Byron stayed here.'

'He wrote his best poetry after pistol-shooting on the beach.'

'He also shot bottles that stood upon a wall at the bottom of the estate.'

'You have been reading in the library again,' Citizen Fatherley said. 'You must spend more time before your personal web. The reading of print is not good for you – it wastes too much time.'

'And fills my mind with little irrelevancies.'

'Soon you will be quoting Lord Byron's poetry to me. *"When we two parted in silence and tears; half broken-hearted to sever for years"*. I know them all.'

The Hall stood tall and white and elegant; it had been constantly painted, the odour of fresh paint strong to the nostrils. The windows had been tall, the doors large, the ceilings high and chandeliered, but the lighting had long since been modernised, soft to the eye, always constant however dull or bright the light through the windows, constant even in twilight or evening. Citizen Fatherley had wanted little changed when he had removed the seat of government from Whitehall to the New London he had created across the Durham landscape.

Sigrid had slightly moved her hand and one of the purple curtains gracefully swung aside to reveal one of the large television screens. On the screen had been the agenda of the Council of Ministers set to meet within an hour. There had been but a single item on the agenda and by a raising of his eyebrows an electronic signal had been sent by Citizen Fatherley to approve the agenda. The extra sensory perception of his televisions had been remarkable even to him.

'You must seek further information from InterActive City,' Sigrid said. 'On the entered co-ordinates it declares that you shall be a candidate for the First Presidency and that it cannot be otherwise.'

'The King thinks differently.'

'The King has his own input into InterActive City.'

'He declares his on-line and off-line data do not coincide.'

'You mean he does not trust what InterActive City is telling him.'

InterActive City housed the government's computer systems linked to all the computer systems of Government Europe and the American Association of Free States comprising the old Canada, United States and Mexico. It was linked with the Russian Federation and the Japanese Archipelago. Each computer was capable of a million billion operations a second. The radical cellular computers had been developed to advance science but governments of The World Order had soon subordinated them to their own use.

'The King believes in Divine Right,' Sigrid said. 'At least he does not believe in InterActive City. He does not believe in computer language let alone software applications.'

'There are others who must advise him.'

'He can only take the advice of his First Minister. It is written into the constitution. He may not understand inter-creative space or on-line information, but he understands the need for human decision. Even InterActive City cannot help him with that.'

'He does not understand history,' Citizen Fatherley said. 'He believes because there has been a monarchy these past two thousand years – saving the head of Charles I – there must always be a monarchy. He does not look to take the advice of his First Minister; he looks to take the advice of others. History has been parochial, war-ridden and pestilential; it is the story of power falling into the gutter. Now it must fall to the people.'

'Monarchs of Europe unite,' Sigrid said.

'The King does not stand alone. He has the King of Spain, the Queen of Holland, the King of the Belgians. He has the Prince in Monaco. Should I call them a coven or a brood? He also has the Pope in Rome. They must stand or fall together – fight and lose together. They cannot ignore InterActive City or the will of their people.'

There could be no place in the United States of Europe for monarchs or even a Pope. Vatican City would be incorporated into the Italian Federation, the monarchs would be exiled to the American Association of Free States. A true republic would be proclaimed. But the monarchs had their establishments; they had their armed forces. A struggle of will between elected politicians such as Citizen Fatherley and the military could not be long postponed.

'The monarchs do not accept that religion and marriage should be abolished,' Sigrid said. 'They say the nature of the state is as important as its form.'

'So long as they are able to sit on their thrones.'

'Alberto di Paoli has announced he shall be the candidate of the Italian Federation.'

'There will be other candidates,' Citizen Fatherley said.

'But none so strong as you.'

Citizen Fatherley rose from the table and setting aside his napkin he strolled back onto the terrace.

His eyes were towards the clouds but there was no threat from the sky, no hostility. He hunkered down among the rose trellises in the gardens as his forefathers had hunkered on street corners, lifting a rose so that he would meditate upon the bud, the first yellow flesh of rose seeking the dew on its green cloak. Each day he would come into these grounds and meditate upon this rose. He felt the air gentler as the sun climbed higher, its warmth strengthening the bud, the cloak coarser, more confident, the yellow to the rose hopeful, anticipating life.

He withdrew his hand from the slim stalk and stood his full height.

He had been six feet tall, his shoulders straight, his frame slim, his small head held back, his features even, sculpted some would say; the nose and eyes were small and the brow quizzical, the smile thin across his lips, shy and reluctant. His power lay in his detachment. He was modest in the knowledge of that power, courteous and respectful, attentive. He reassured those around him even if they were afraid of his detachment.

'The King thinks I am Oliver Cromwell,' he said.

'He too reads history books.'

'The wrong ones,' he said. 'His off-line data serves him a dish of unreality. He believes there is a vendetta between the House of Mountbatten-Windsor and the Fatherley family. History, however, is not a question of personalities but of causes.'

'He does not accept the monarchy must end.'

'The people accept it.'

'Unless he overturns the will of the people.'

'He can only do that by force. That is why, when they come, they shall come from the sea.'

'The King has granted you an audience tonight at Windsor Castle. Members of his Armed Forces Council shall be in attendance. They shall tell you the King shall not be hurried. He shall need a period of reflection.'

'The King has had many years of reflection.'

'The Council shall tell you they have a duty to the throne, to the King and through the throne and King to the people and nation. And to future generations. They shall need to be heard. The whole of Europe is waiting to hear what they have to say.'

'The monarchies of Europe have settled their own destinies upon that of the House of Mountbatten-Windsor,' he said. 'Whatever they decide they shall accept. They are prepared to stain their thrones with blood – the blood of their people. There is to be a United States of Europe. There is to be a First President. The date for the Election has been set. Yet the crisis is not passed.'

'The King believes you have worked all these years to become First President – that your candidature is somehow linked to that of Alberto di Paoli. The two of you together oppose the monarchy and the Church.'

'The two of us together believe in the people.'

An impulse from his watch advised him he must return to the Hall.

This sojourn in the garden would be his one moment of peace, of reflection, before he entered upon his duties. He would bring together all his senses, his sense of touch, of smell, of sight and sound, mingling with the sense of taste the warmth of the coffee and croissants and cool of the fruit juice. The last fragrance from the rosebud lingered to his nostrils and the last touch of wind rustled his hair; he had soft brown hair receded from his brow. He held this stillness to his mind, letting no thoughts intrude, no emotions, settling him like the sight of the landscape.

'You must sign the order of the day,' Sigrid said.

She gestured with her little finger and another purple curtain opened, revealing another television screen. The order of the day had been printed in bold letters upon the screen, but beneath the order stood a single line for signature. Beneath the line stood the words: *Citizen Fatherley, First Minister*. He stood before the screen and blinked rapidly three times. His electronic signature appeared beneath the order. The order had been simple enough:

Abolition of the monarchy.

'The Council of Ministers awaits your attendance.'

The date on the agenda had been 15 April 2026.

'If they do come for you,' Sigrid asked. 'What shall you do?'

'We shall make our stand in Highhill,' he said.

'A hundred years is a long time to go back.'

'That is where it all began.'

He looked again at the clouds but there had been no sign of the helicopters.

Book One:
The Fatherleys

1

Binkie Fatherley sat on a shovel at the stapple bottom.

He read by the light of candles lodged in the stone of the landing. He unloaded full tubs from the cage that came down the shaft and coupled them to the main set that hauled the tubs to the shaft bottom. He uncoupled the empty tubs as they came back and signalled for the cage to be hauled to the stapple top. He saw no-one but the men who worked the seam above, and only when they began or ended their shift. When not loading or unloading, he listened to the noise along the engine plain.

He committed to memory some lines from William Morris: *'Socialism is no dream but a cause. Men and women have died for it, not in ancient time but in our time. They lie in prison for it, they work in the mines; they are excited by it, ruined for it. Believe me,'* William Morris wrote, *'when such things are suffered for dreams the dreams come true at last.'*

A single tub rumbled towards him out of the darkness. Beyond the rumble he could hear along the engine plain the rumble of full tubs, the lighter rolling of empty tubs along narrow tracks, the midway rollers toiling; the tubs clanged into a cage at another stapple top and the cage creaked to another stapple bottom. He pulled himself to his feet and righted the shovel against the landing wall. Candles flickered in the draught along the engine plain. The tub trundled to a halt and Binkie saw the pasty face of the under-manager.

'The first time I've seen you here,' Binkie said.

'Water!' the under-manager said.

'Water's better than gas.'

It had been four o'clock in the morning.

Three datal hands sat with the under-manager in the maintenance tub. Binkie manoeuvred the tub into the cage and signalled for it to be hauled to the stapple top; he fumbled for his matches to relight candles extinguished by the draught. He upended the shovel and settled again with his back against the landing, pulling the book from his shirt. His real name was William, but he had been called Binkie from the time he worked as a stoneman. A prop had collapsed behind him and the foreshift had stopped so that he could be pulled free. The stone that flattened him had taken ten men to lift and the stone had first been broken by the men's picks. When they had stripped from him the last of the canch, or bink as it was called, rather than finding him crushed, ribs and shoulders broken, he had been bruised but unharmed.

'Saved by the bink!' the manager had said.

That was how Binkie got his name.

He set down the book and walked stiffly to the miniature shaft. His eyes had grown weary reading in candlelight. He thought of lighting more candles but they would be extinguished by the draught when the under-manager and his datal hands returned in the maintenance tub. A silence had fallen across the pit. Normally he could hear voices, he could sometimes see the play of a carbide lamp; he could hear the sounds of cutters, the throb of rubber belts on well-oiled rollers. He had left open the top buttons of his shirt despite the cold and poked two black fingers into the protruding hairs of his chest.

He called up the shaft to the stapple top.

'Everythin' all right in-by?'

Not even his own voice echoed back.

He recalled once he had led out his pony at the end of a shift; the pony had been a stubborn Shetland, as far gone as China he used to say. He had smacked its sodden haunches to hurry it along. He recalled the scummy pools, the glint of girders, air cold to his face, the smell dank to his nostrils; the pumps had not been properly working in this part of the pit and the hollows were filled with water. The incline widened to a loading point and there were lights everywhere. The white-washed walls and stone-dusted ways were neat and hoppers glistened with new paint.

They approached a long dip to the engine plain.

Binkie had grown uneasy as he approached this dip. The way out-by had been a narrow pathway running alongside rails and rollers; alcoves had been set into the walls against the speeding set. The alcoves were unlit and smelt of carbide where the men had emptied their lamps. The walls were damp, water seeping down them, but there had been no alcove for forty yards. The steel rope did not move across the rollers.

He held his pony, the pony pricking his ears as if aware of danger.

'There, *gallower!*' Binkie whispered.

He listened again for the singing of steel ropes.

'How's it goin' up there?' he shouted.

'Nowt to worry about,' a voice answered.

Binkie had hardly moved ten yards into the dip when he heard the throaty cough of the winding engine and the distant rumble of tubs, like a death rattle growing louder. He stumbled forward, dragging his pony with him, but not fast enough to avoid the full tubs roaring their way to the shaft bottom. The hairs rose to the back of his neck. He noticed a narrow ledge, luminescent with water and damp carbide, and buried himself into the canch as the tubs hurtled by. He had let go the harness and the pony pounded forward and flung itself into a sump at the bottom of the dip.

The tubs hurtled on and Binkie scrambled down.

The pony lay deep in sour water and he hauled it free.

'Not as daft as I thought,' Binkie said.

The telephone rang in the deputy's kist.

'Is that you, Binkie?' the manager asked.

The voice had been faint with static on the line.

'Have you seen the under-manager?'

'I sent him to the stapple top.'

'Go after him!' the manager said. 'Shout your lungs out!'

'You're busy at four in the mornin'.'

'We need all the men on bank. D'you hear that, Binkie, son? All the men on bank!'

Binkie thought of Ollie Lowden.

Ollie had been his best friend.

They had gone down the pit together at fourteen, wearing the garb of the young pitman: cloth cap and muffler, waistcoat, long shortun's, pants that came down to the knees, safety lamp and token pushed through their lapels. They had called at the time-cabin to leave their tokens and strode over the midway rollers and oiled cable towards the drift mouth. They had been met by the safety officer who searched their pockets for cigarettes or tobacco.

'Survive the first day and you can survive the next fifty years,' the safety officer said.

'Bait, bottle, candle, lamp, matches,' Ollie laughed.

The safety officer led them in-by.

There were no lights from the drift mouth, the wick of Binkie's lamp spluttered and flickered, the ground uneven; the roof had been low and he and Ollie rapped their heads against timber beams. They would be dizzy by the end of the shift. They put full tubs from the face to the engine plain and attached the tubs to the set. Lads less strong were used as trappers, opening and closing the door from the seam to the plain; they allowed men to pass without disrupting the ventilation, working ten hours, stopping with the older men to eat their sandwiches and drink cold water from their tin bottles.

Binkie and Ollie felt sweat damp to their fustian.

They did not realise how tired they were till they struggled back to bank. They decided not to walk out by the drift mouth where they would collect their tokens but clamber aboard the set with other men leaving by the main shaft. The men hunkered in the narrow tubs, tired and surly, but letting the youngsters push first into the cage when the set stopped at the shaft bottom.

Ollie had pushed beyond the shuffling bodies.

The cage door had been open but there was no cage.

Hands reached out for Ollie to pull him back, reached to his shoulders and arms and broad back, reached to the fustian, damp and black with coal dust, but Ollie would be first, showing the hewers and stonemen, and his friend Binkie. The cage crashed down and crushed him to death. Binkie had brought the news to his mother and father; he had brought the news to the village. He had collected Ollie's token from the time-cabin, consoled by the safety officer, and he had worn the token for many a year till he had set it upon the mantelpiece of his home, gazing upon it as he had touched his pockets:

bait, bottle, candle, lamp, matches.

Now Binkie stepped from the kist over a tail rope.

He picked up his bait tin and bottle and pushed them

into his pockets; he stuffed the book into his shirt. He wore the garb of all pitmen: fustian breeches, shabby coat, thick blue shirt. A rush of air extinguished his candles and he groped for his lamp and matches. He heard a rumble, like someone clearing his throat, but there had been menace to the rumble, more dangerous than the roar of tubs.

A flecking greyness surged towards him.

Water came headlong towards the stapple bottom down the engine plain, putrid water that carried everything before it: timber and tubs and winding ropes, the grey-white foam curling upon itself as it tumbled along. Binkie stumbled back towards the deputy's kist, his thighs so weak with fear he had to force himself forward. The water hit him with the weight of a full set of tubs, knocking the wind from him, but giving strength back to his legs as he leapt from the landing into the kist; the water followed and swirled around him. He felt it searing his eyes, pinioning his back and shoulders, above his head, dissolving his mind in a blackness.

This time he had not made it.

Nor had the men in the maintenance tub.

2

The Fatherleys might never have come to Highhill had not their chapel burned down.

Ernest Fatherley had been lay preacher in the Primitive Methodist Church; he worked as a hewer during the week and sermonised on Sundays. He had built his own chapel, but he had been so busy carving a pulpit and pews he had not thought to heat the chapel; the windows froze from the inside in winter and children sat muffled and snot-nosed as their breath turned to vapour. They did not listen to Ernest as the cold rose around their feet but waited for the squeaking crescendo that meant Ernest had reached his peroration.

They rushed for the door.

Martha had married Ernest Fatherley when sixteen and bore him eleven children: eight boys and three girls. Two of the girls died in childbirth. They had lived in a row of colliery cottages built beyond grass and dandelion where the wind blew chill along cinder paths that led from each cottage. A wagon way crossed the cinder paths where coal had been trundled to hoppers. The wagon way had also been the children's playground where lasses built dolls' houses of brick and stone. They would take matting and stools from the cottages, pretending to cook with mud as dough and tin lids as baking dishes.

Lads pushed their girders: hoops of rounded steel propelled by steel hooks. They wore their caps and baggy shorts, their Fair Isle jumpers, their rolled-up stockings and boots, sparks leaping from hobnails as they ran with their girders: gords they were called. Sometimes a joint would fall apart and the lad would run to the blacksmith to have his gord repaired. The blacksmith worked the glowing steel and repaired the joint. For the lad it was back to the wagon way, the grate of the steel hook against the gord, the lad running so fast the sparks would fly again.

Binkie lived in fear of the wagon way.

A two-year-old lost his fingers when they were crushed on the line by slow-trundling coal trucks and his friend Albi Birt almost lost his life when his gord ran away and clattered to a standstill on a sleeper between the tracks. A set of wagons came ponderously along, coal dust dribbling from the wagons. The lines had been shiny with use, the wheels of the timber trucks caked with yellow and red dust from the brickflats. Albi leapt to retrieve the gord before the trucks arrived, but he stubbed his toe and fell across the track.

Binkie pulled him from the line.

Albi Birt had been eight years old.

'I'll remember that,' he said.

'Think on your gord,' Binkie had said.

They looked at the twisted metal the wagons had left behind.

3

Binkie and Albi stayed friends till the Fatherleys left for Highhill.

One of their childhood memories had been of a trip they had made to Newcastle to see Giuseppe Garibaldi, who had visited the city as a seaman. Their fathers had hoisted them upon their shoulders so that they could see beyond the cloth caps and red scarves Garibaldi marching on the deck of his merchant vessel wrapped in a cloak. His hair had been peppered white, his beard too, so that in his childish innocence Binkie had felt the hair and beard had been dipped in a barrel of pepper that must stand somewhere on deck.

Albi had been best man at Binkie's wedding.

Wedding photographs showed Binkie's bride with soft chestnut hair and a mole to the left of her mouth she liked to call a beauty spot; she wore her hair bundled at the back. Bess and Binkie Fatherley danced on their wedding night to the sawing of a fiddle. They were married 7 June 1886 and within four years their family had been complete: Ernie born in 1887, Roland in 1888, Albert in 1889 and Roger in 1890.

Bess and Binkie had both been sixteen on their wedding night and childbirth had come easily to Bess. By twenty-one her womanhood had fled, her features had coarsened, not with childbearing but colliery life. Another photograph showed her over a poss-tub on washing day. The lines had deepened to her brow and her cheeks were as rough as nutmeg, but a genuine smile touched her lips and eyes made gentle by her sadness. She knew she would go the same way as Martha Fatherley, old before her time, but not complaining, enduring to the last.

Martha had been bedridden at the wedding.

'Enjoy yourself!' she had said.

She had lain in a cot-bed in the corner, her face without colour but for the hue of the flames from the glowing fire. Her fingers had been long and fleshless and cold, the smile sad as if she knew Bess's future before Bess knew it herself. She lived long enough to see Bess bring Ernie into the world, but a month later she slipped away. Bess would often see in her mind Martha's sallow face caught in the firelight as her husband skipped and jumped and sawed the fiddle on their wedding night.

She recalled the night Ernest's chapel had burned down.

She had been clearing supper dishes when she heard steps upon the cinder and a tap upon the door. Such steps were not unusual. It might be a neighbour's man asking her to help at a birth, a mangling at the pit, an injured son carried to the cot-bed in the corner, or a family scene where a man had drunk spirit and seen the blue devils. He would hammer his wife's head against the scullery floor. She had rinsed the supper plates and wiping her hands on her pinafore opened the door.

A young lad stood there.

'There's a fire, missus!'

'A fire on a Sunday night?'

God clearly moved in mysterious ways.

The flames leapt high from the wooden chapel.

The chapel had been built beyond allotment gardens and pigeon crees, but the timber frame had been well alight and the flames crackled like a giant bonfire. Bess could feel the heat upon her cheeks and arms and hands. The children stirred in the upstairs room and she knew from the creaks of the bed and tapping at the window that they too had seen the leaping flames; they too were staring wide-eyed at the exploding wood-work. Men ran from the allotments with buckets and bathtubs of water and she could see their silhouettes against the fire.

Ernest Fatherley, spindly as ever, had danced in and out of the flaming doorway, Binkie restraining him as windows melted and collapsed and the blackened pulpit keeled into the aisles. The chapel had been built with timber from the joiner shop, the roof pitched with tar from the blacksmith, but timber and tar disinte-grated and melted. The pews collapsed and the chapel fell in upon itself, embers burning into the night.

Bess gave the lad a farthing.

He darted down the cinder beyond the wagon way to get a better view of the fire, leaping upon a pigeon cree, pulling himself up on its white-painted wooden tails that pointed upward towards the flames. Pigeons fluttered against the wire netting of the crees, startled and afraid as sparks fell around their wings. When the last faggot died all that had been left of the chapel lay in fine white ash, the ash damp in the rain, the timber gaunt and honeycombed.

'You'll be wantin' to build a new one, I'll be warned,' the colliery manager said.

'A fine one of stone that'll last as long as the pit.'

'No stone around here,' the manager said.

Ernest Fatherley had been tall and slim and unkempt, the hairs showing white to his face. He wore his neck open, the stud showing to his shirt, and if he had danced around the fire in his raincoat the raincoat had been covered with ash. It smelt too of smoke. Ash covered his boots and as he paced the manager's office he left white footprints upon the stone. He held his hands behind his back, shoulders stooped, blue eyes disconcerting and unfriendly.

'You've talked to the owners?'

'Their pockets aren't that deep,' the manager said.

'What do you expect us to do?'

'Get yourselves over to Highhill,' the manager said. 'They're sinkin' a new shaft. Families are movin' in from all over the place. That many on them they'll need a church never mind a chapel.'

'How do we get to Highhill?'

'My cousin's the manager. I'll drop him a note tellin' him to expect you. I'll send it over by trap. You'll like Highhill, you and your family, and I'll be shot on you from here.'

'A brand new chapel,' Ernest said.

4

His grandchildren had screamed when they learned their new home had seen a murder.

Slum Alley had been the first colliery row built in Highhill; an open gutter ran between the row and the earth closets and rats ran up and down the gutter. There were outbreaks of jaundice. The manager offered a farthing a tail of every rat caught and the children ran barefoot in the gutter chasing the rats. As the tails mounted on the tables in downstairs rooms so too did the farthings and the jaundice had abated.

Their house in Slum Alley had been deloused the day the Fatherleys arrived and they piled their furniture and bedding on the cinder pathway to be fumigated. Bess did not mind the stoving. Nor did she mind the rats or the jaundice. She had left Bedlington and the wagon way and the dread her children might be crushed. She wanted to leave behind the memory of Martha, worn out before her time. She wanted a new beginning, a new pathway, a freshly-scrubbed doorway, a different future for her children that had been disturbed when they learned of the murder.

Matthew Atkinson had killed his wife when she had come home late from the hoppings. He had been drunk and she had not been there to make his supper; there had been a quarrel when she had stepped through the front door, lifting her skirt above the running water of the gutter. She had rushed back into the row. Matthew had stumbled after her and dragged her back. The neighbours heard her screams; they heard Matthew's shouts, but this had been a family quarrel. They did not intervene till the house went quiet.

Matthew stumbled into the row.

'I've killed me wife!' he shouted.

They hanged Matthew Atkinson in Durham jail.

The rope snapped and he fell fifteen feet.

They raised his body from the bottom of the scaffold and having found another rope they hanged him again. This time the rope held and slowly strangled him. The house had since stood empty. The Fatherley children hid under the sheets and watching the ice on the window wondered who would get them first. Would it be Matthew or his wife? They listened to every noise, every scream from a neighbour's house. The shadows the candle made to the damp walls sharpened their imagination and they were terrified when the candle sputtered out.

'I brought you here to build a chapel,' the manager said. 'Not complain about a house.'

'I've four grandchildren,' Ernest said.

'You're lucky there's only four. I thought all your family was comin' with you.'

'The older ones didn't like the idea,' Ernest said. 'They like the wagon way. They wanted to stay where they were. There's only me and Binkie and Bess and the bairns.'

'You'll be right comfortable,' the manager said.

'It's not the house.'

'You mean you're frightened of ghosts?'

'It's the bairns.'

'The bairns had better worry about diptheria and scarlet fever and pneumonia and tuberculosis – not to mention infantile paralysis and the yellow jaundice that comes from rats that swim in the gutter. If they can survive them things they'll survive ghosts.'

It had taken eight years to build the Methodist chapel.

It would know some fine moments, but none so fine as the day they brought the bodies from the pit after the great Highhill pit disaster. The bodies had been brought first to the pithead and taken to the chapel where undertakers eased them into coffins; the coffins were taken to the family homes, the lids removed and the coffins laid open for family and friends to pay their last respects. Flowers were left on doorsteps or brought to the chapel and settled along the front before the pulpit. Black crepe lined the pews and windows. The silence Binkie Fatherley had known in the pit had now been felt in the village, except the organ played in the chapel and would not stop till the funeral processions ended and the chapel began to fill.

The last to enter had been the preacher Ernest Fatherley.

5

They had found Binkie Fatherley half in the deputy's kist and half out.

They put him in a stretcher tub and a pit pony had dragged the tub along the engine plain still cluttered with derailed tubs and props and rollers; the winding gear and compressors and pumps had been smashed, the fans silent and still. Water ran knee-deep, there were eddies and currents, and all the pit lights had been extinguished. There were voices ahead in a pony stable that had been converted into a loading point for injured men.

Binkie had been unconscious but now he vomited the putrid water that had been seeping from his mouth. The air had been fresher around the pony stable. There was still the smell of hay and a more sour smell of dung, but the ponies had long since been removed, not to the surface but to higher ground within the pit where the water had not touched. Lights had been installed along the stable walls but Binkie's eyes stung and he held them closed. His body had been stiff and damp but he felt no pain, only a sickness from his retching stomach.

'How's you feelin', Binkie, son?' the manager asked.

'Did the under-manager make it?'

'Nor the datal hands,' the manager said.

He wore his helmet back upon his head, his face already black; he had laid his yardstick and knee pads and safety lamp on the straw by his side. A soft yellow cone of light came from his lamp. He had been a small man with a moustache, his skin white as parchment under the coal dust; his blue eyes were moist in the light of the safety lamp. The pit had been his life. He had walked the bank top feeling the solidness of the heap, he had listened to the throb of the winding engine and power station, coal tumbling into the hoppers.

Now the pit had betrayed him.

'We got most of the fore shift men out by the drift,' the manager said. 'We think we'll get you and the other lads out by the Number Two shaft. The doctor'll have a look at you. I wished to hell I could tell you it was good news, Binkie, but it's the worst news in the world.'

'You know how it happened?'

'An explosion of some kind sent water from old boardrooms. It had been there for years – seepin' down from the surface. There were traces of shot. Nobody knows whether they're old or new – or even why anybody used shot in the first place.'

'Who noticed the shot?'

'The surveyors were down with the fore shift. They thought they heard shot but they couldn't be sure. One of them went to check. He telephoned bank. I sent down the under-manager and his lads. The surveyors never came back either.'

'We'll need an enquiry,' Binkie said.

'Believe me, Binkie, son, there's nothin' we could've done.'

They brought the cage to bank and Binkie saw below the headstock the womenfolk; they were white-faced and silent, black shawls around their heads and shoulders. How many mothers and wives and sisters and sweethearts? There were back shift men, too, who would not make the pit that day but who would not leave the pithead till they knew the fate of their *marras*: pitmen who worked the same seams but on a different shift. Horse-drawn ambulances lined the pit yard from other pits and the horses had been as silent as the crowd.

The colliery doctor examined Binkie, but already he had drifted back into unconsciousness; they carried him from the pithead across the heap, scrambling down the bluepost to his house. He had three broken ribs and a dislocated shoulder and had swallowed enough water to make him vomit for days, but when he came to they served him tablespoons of broth and bread rusks dipped into the broth. The front door opened onto the stairs and a cot-bed stood in a corner under the stairs. The doctor had strapped his ribs and shoulder to make him comfortable.

'Better keep yourself warm,' he said.

The doctor did not look him in the eyes, nor did the neighbours. No-one talked of the accident and he drifted again, moving in and out of consciousness, dreaming strange dreams, hallucinating, shouting against the coal owners, feeling pain to his shoulder and ribs with each shout, but not ridding the coal owners from his mind.

'We'll get rid of them one day!' he shouted.

6

'We need a revolution!' Binkie said.

'The people don't want revolution,' Albi Birt said.

'How about a general strike?'

35

'You'll need the railwaymen and dockers and power workers and transport men – as well as the miners. But the men would have to decide – to make it legitimate. Then the newspapers might back you and the government would give in.'

'First we need a new Mines Act.'

Binkie rose from unconsciousness.

His thoughts had still been on the coal owners.

The Marquess of Townley and his family were the real coal owners. They owned the land where the coal had been drawn and were paid a royalty on every ton, but for those who worked in the pit, who lived in the village, the real owners were the Derwent Valley Coal and Iron Company. They owned the iron works and railway line that took the coal to the river staithes; they owned the pit where the men worked. They were the dreaded coal owners, the hated coal owners, the focal point of every grievance: working conditions, lack of safety, pay and hours.

The Fatherleys had come to Highhill when Binkie had been twenty-six; they had not feared the colliery manager or the coal owners. They sought the protection of God from their chapel. The village folk might attend the chapel but did not have the same faith; they knew the coal owners provided their work and their home; they knew too without work there would be no home. The men might suffer injuries in the pit but never report them, they might be so crippled they could hardly walk in-by; they could work with nystagmus and pneumoconiosis, squinting and coughing black spittle, but they would work till they dropped rather than not work at all.

Binkie had no fear of losing his home in Slum Alley.

But he understood the men would not get fewer working hours, better conditions, more money in their pockets, more education for their children, unless they took on the coal owners. They called him a Federation man rather than a Company man; he believed in the Durham Miners' Federation not the Derwent Valley Coal and Iron Company. He toured the pit villages in a hired trap, fly-posting pitheads, addressing the men as they came out on bank, yet never losing time in the pit, working his shifts like the rest of the men.

Binkie knew the men shared a common bond.

They risked their lives and spilled blood to win coal, yet the owners set them apart with different rates for putters and stonemen and bargain men and trapper boys and checkweighmen and overmen and deputies and under-managers, setting up a class structure within the village, officials at the head of the structure in their own street of houses by the headstock. They were the heads of the class system, the datal hand on bank the lowest class because of his low pay. Only a union man working for unified rates could bring the men together. Only a union man could unite them, not in the danger they faced but in the wages they earned.

Binkie had become lodge secretary and Albi Birt a Member of Parliament.

Binkie and Albi often sat before the fire, the great

range black-leaded, an oven on one side, a boiler on the other; they peeped into the flames as if they were the future. Strangers hovered on the bar, black soot flakes that forecast a visitor to the house. Holed bricks beneath the boiler drew the heat and as they smoked their pipes and cleared their throats, spittle sizzled on the black-leaded range.

Now Albi Birt stood in the open doorway.

The cracked paving and open gutter and pitheap stood behind him, water from the gutter flowing over shale and bluepost, rippling like a stream towards a waterfall, the sound gentle against the silence of Slum Alley. It reminded Binkie of the silence of the pit before the waters had struck; or the silence of the pithead when he had been brought to bank. Or the silence of his own home he had noticed as he floated in and out of consciousness.

Albi's face had been parched in the light, the blue pit scars showing; the sideboards to his cheeks had been whiter than ever, as white as his hair. He carried his bowler in his hand. He had been dressed in black, his shoes polished, his features grave, his head bowed as he entered the doorway, and only slowly did he raise his eyes from the doorstep to the stair corner. He laid his bowler on the cot-bed. He stooped to embrace Binkie and hold him close.

'I've come to lead the mourners,' he said.

Binkie understood now the silence.

Had it been twenty-six years since his children had pressed their hands and noses to the windows and looked for the ghost of a murdered woman or the vengeance of a hanged man? Perhaps the years could be rolled back and they would still be there, clinging together, four boys, all in night shirts, screaming and hugging each other and looking into the night, afraid of the frost to the windows; and he would rise from his cot-bed and shout them to silence so that they scattered to different corners of the bed, threatening them with a raised hand, a hand he had never used, till the silence settled upon the room and house and street, the same silence he felt now.

They opened the door wide to bring the coffin home.

They would bring the coffin into the room and lay it on the table and Binkie recalled they had once operated on that table to remove fluid from his lung. The surgeon had held a bowl by his side and eased the fluid from the lung into the bowl. There would be chrysanthemums from the allotments or roses from the trellises that climbed by the side of the allotment fencing, but beyond the scent of the flowers Binkie could smell again the chloroform and in his mind's eye see the starched faces: his father Ernest, his wife Bess, his other children, Roland and Albert and Roger. They had held hands and closed their eyes in prayer; their prayers had been answered. He had lived and grown strong and mellowed into the fullness of life.

His coffin would be the first to be laid to rest in the graveyard.

'Why didn't He take me?' Binkie wept. 'And not my eldest son!'

7

It had been gas not water that had killed Ernie Fatherley.

He worked in the pit cleaning faces, stone-dusting ways, white-washing walls, repairing belts, clearing boardrooms: old workings in the pit. He stood next to a ventilation fan and let the air pummel his face, but the fan had stopped and he felt the air stuffy. His head rested against the stone of the rolleyway and, his eyelids half-drooping, he stared at the yellow cone of flame in the safety lamp.

The flame hardly flickered.

He sucked the air.

He pulled open his shirt, pulling so harshly the buttons came away, but the air did not cleanse his mind; the air did not make him think clearly. He felt a tightness to his chest as his lungs contracted and he stumbled towards the pony stables near a downcast shaft where the air had been fresher. He moved past old boardrooms, belts and landings, beyond loading points and old workings, thinking not of himself but of his pigs.

He kept his pigs on an allotment near Slum Alley.

The pigs would have to be shot with a gas gun if

anything happened to him. The smell of pigs' dung and manure clung to his clothes and often he brought the earthy odour with him into the pit. He had been the shyest of Binkie's sons. He had never married and spent his time on the allotment with his pigs and carrier pigeons, his leeks and cabbages and potatoes, the white carnations he grew for button holes at weddings and birthdays.

He helped, too, his mother.

Washing day had been known as the devil's birthday and Ernie would poss the clothes with the poss stick and turn the heavy mangle. He would iron, too, pulling soot flakes from the iron heated before the fire; he would smile at his younger brothers as they bathed in the last soapy water. It would have been different had Bess had daughters, but with four sons she would be up at three to prepare breakfast and bait for Grandfather Fatherley. He worked in the pit like the rest of the men, going in-by at four o'clock; he carried out his chapel duties in the evening. Bess would manage an hour's sleep before waking Ernie. His shift began at six.

Roland would come out-by for breakfast and bath; he had started night shift at ten o'clock. Binkie would be seen out of the house and the younger boys chased down Slum Alley to school; they would return for their midday meal. Roland would roll out of bed to have dinner with his brothers and when the children went back to school Bess would prepare for the return of Grandfather Ernest and Ernie. By the time their bathwater was off the downstairs floor the children would be home again. Binkie too would be home, shaking the pit muck from his boots, hands on the outside wall. He would be ready for his tea and bath, but hardly had the water been heated and his tea put on the table, dishes washed and tub emptied, it would be time to begin again, preparing Roland for the night shift.

There had been the quarrels.

'You're as lazy as you're long,' Bess said.

Grandfather Ernest would not clean out the earth closet at the front of the house.

'I cannot do anythin' with this cough,' he said.

'You can talk all right in that chapel of yours. You can eat, I'll grant you that. The cough's not taken away your appetite. You can go to other people's houses when they're bad; you can smarten yourself up for that. But here you smell – and you do no work!'

Grandfather Ernest had pneumoconiosis.

Coal dust lined his lungs and made him cough. The coughing disturbed the family till they had grown used to it, but it had been a brittle, hacking cough and grated on Bess and deprived her of the little sleep she needed. Ernest had always been dirty, caring nothing for clothes; he no longer worked at the pit but refused to bathe, even when his grandsons left soapy water for him. Being in the chapel had been sufficient. Godliness and cleanliness were not compatible.

Grandfather Ernest had also fallen out with Binkie over the war.

Binkie believed this was a capitalists' war. The

politicians had organised the European economies for the benefit of capitalists and now they were fighting for the spoils. Why should pitmen support the war? Binkie elevated his class war to greater heights. It had no longer been a question of wages and conditions; he opposed conscription from the mining communities. The government and the Miners' Federation reached an agreement that there should be a fresh recruitment drive for unmarried miners between the ages of eighteen and twenty-five.

'You'll be lettin' no men go from here,' Binkie said.

'It's the law of the land,' the manager said.

'You keep tellin' us we need every ton of coal we can win.'

'And as many soldiers at the front.'

'I'd rather have blood on the coal than blood on that barbed wire along the Western Front.'

'You'll get a medal from the coal owners, talkin' like that.'

'You have the medal,' Binkie said. 'I'll keep the men in the pit.'

Binkie read books taken from the colliery institute. The more he read the more he leant towards the Darwinian theory of evolution, the more he doubted Adam and Eve. He understood the Christian ethos, the principles of the Sermon on the Mount; he enjoyed Sunday schoolteaching and chapel preaching, but he doubted whether when his life was over he would be able to hug and kiss his mother in an enlightened hereafter. The quarrels had come to a head when Grandfather Ernest had used his pulpit oratory on recruiting platforms. 'You can make all the speeches you like about the Angels at Mons,' Binkie said. 'You can go on about Lord Kitchener's martial spirit, but for me this is a war to make the coal owners rich and the lads work harder in the pit.'

'Socialism's turned your head,' Grandfather Ernest said.

'I don't know if God made man,' Binkie said. 'But man made socialism.'

'I'll be wantin' the money in the tea caddy.'

Bess kept the family savings of coppers and six-penny pieces in a tea caddy that stood on the mantel-piece above the fire place.

'You're not gettin' your dirty hands on that!' Bess said.

'There'll be no war if there's no money.'

'You can have all the money you want,' Binkie said. 'Only not from that tea caddy.'

It had been New Year's Eve 1916.

Bess had always been proud of her New Year's Eve.

Her house had not changed since they had moved in: panelled wallpaper, orange and fawny, brown paint, brass fenders, brass tidies, brass kettles, brass pokers, oil cloth on the floor and mats she and Ernie made from clippings of old woollies, skirts and coats. They would sit for hours on dark winter nights, cutting the clippings, stitching the hessian into mat frames, designing a pattern, using proggers to make the mats. Only one or two mats graced the upstairs room, but the best mats were put down at weekends and lifted again to be replaced with through-the-week mats.

'All Binkie wants is the men on strike,' Grandfather Ernest said.

'There'll be no strikes as long as there's a war.'

'I'll be givin' you war certificates. You can cash them when the war's over.'

'You're a good for nothin',' Bess said. 'You've preached in that chapel of yours over Christmas. Now you come here to spoil our New Year by askin' for money. You bring nothin' into the house; even when you worked at the pit most of it went into the chapel. You've brought nothin' for the bairns. If you had your God-forsaken way you'd see that we'd all roast in hell! And this soft bugger of a husband! He says nothin', he keeps his peace. He says you cannot have the money, but you'll sneak it out anyway when we're not watchin'.'

Pit life had given Bess a shrewish tongue and sharper temper, but this was her night. There was good money coming into the Fatherley household and they ate well: pease pudding and cold mutton and ham and slices of beetroot and teacake and fadge, the teapot already filled, the best china out, and ginger wine too. There were the small glasses bearing the emblem of the 1911 coronation and this New Year's Eve the weekend mats and plush cloth were down.

Three of her sons were at the social club but Ernie had stayed to help.

He had been in the coalhouse filling pails of coal that would be thrown to the back of the fire: banking the fire. The ledges of the back of the fire could hold six full pails, so that the coal would be raked down, keeping the downstairs room warm at all times. There had never been any heating upstairs. The bed corner had been newly white-washed, the steps newly-scrubbed for the first-footer. Bess had used a stone of flour to bake her bread and fadge and teacakes; she had also baked a spice loaf. Slices of the loaf would be offered with a glass of ginger wine.

'You're a heathen and a pacifist!' Grandfather Ernest said.

'Heathen or not,' Binkie said. 'The money stays.'

'I'll take my coat off to you!'

Ernie had left open the door and the cold air flicked across the table and ruffled the lazy flames of the fire. They could hear the grate of the scoop he used to fill the pails, the coal falling loudly, the wind rustling down Slum Alley. Beyond they could hear men singing on their way to the club, the wind taking their voices and tossing them into the air so that they were thin and weak across the pit heap.

'You don't care about the war,' Grandfather Ernest shouted. 'You don't care about lads dyin' at the front – as long as they don't come from this pit village.'

'You'd send them all to die if you had your way,' Binkie said.

Grandfather Ernest raised a chair above his head.

'I'll show you who's boss in this house!' he shouted.

The leather seat fell out of the chair across the table. The seat overturned the bowl of cut beetroot and beetroot juice sank red like blood into the baize cloth. There had been bitterness to Ernest Fatherley's soul: bitterness that his years of toil in God's vineyard had brought him bad health, that his son whom he had loved and brought up in the chapel was now lost to pagans and socialists, that the woman he had married into his own home spoke without respect.

He raised the chair again.

Bess took a knife from the table and jabbed his throat.

There had been a sudden curl of blood as red and dark as the stain upon the baize cloth. Ernest dropped the chair and clutched at the curl. His legs weakened and he grasped the table. He swung around on the mat and stumbled towards the door, coughing and spluttering as if his throat had been cut. The door opened wide to the blackness of the night and a wind rustled down the pitheap. The wind rushed to flare the fire, its sudden gust disturbing the embers.

Ernie Fatherley stood in the doorway, a pail of coal in each hand, coal dust running down the side of the pail onto the doorstep. He had sought the coal wearing neither coat nor collar to his shirt; the stud showed silver in the top hole, his thin neck disappearing into the rim of the collar. He had been smaller than Grandfather Ernest, but his manner unruffled as he moved to the fireplace to fling the coal to the back ledges.

He put down the pails.

'I'll help you with your cut, Grandad,' he said.

'I'll put the chair back in its place,' Binkie said.

Grandfather Ernest looked at the blood upon his fingers.

'I'll never darken your door again!' he said.

Bess still held the knife upraised in her hand.

8

Ernie heard voices and saw the light of safety lamps.

He had moved steadily between seams and districts, looking for the rolleyway that would take him to bank. He knew all the short cuts but he had never lost the fear that one day he would lose himself. He would miss a cut or gallery and die of suffocation and neglect, or his retreat would be cut off by water around his ankles, that seeped to his knees and his thighs, stomach and chest, slimy water that ran cold to his neck. He would feel it to his lips and throat, he would taste its dirt and stagnation. He breathed heavily and quickened his stride till he reached an incline that linked two seams.

All naked flames had been damped and there had been the clatter of hobnails upon timber. He knew the pit had been brought to a standstill and the water he dreaded, brackish water, water as black as the dark, already swirled around his boots. Men splashed towards him, the water had deepened, and despite their blackened faces, holding his lamp high, he recognised the men as they stumbled towards him.

He saw the under-manager and datal hands.

'You've not got a quoit or two in your bait tin?' the under-manager asked.

Ernie played quoits on one of four village pitches; he preferred grass rather than clay. He made his quoit roll and encircle the hob before settling upon it; he preferred the pitch dry so that his quoit would not stick to the ground. He shaped the quoit himself in the blacksmith's shop. It weighed five to seven pounds, shaped like a deep saucer. The hob, a long iron rod one inch thick, would be driven into the pitch till four inches protruded.

Ernie had become the village champion.

'Or a leek from that allotment of yours,' a datal hand said. 'We could do with a bit of leek puddin'.'

'We're tryin' to get to the drift mouth,' the under-manager said.'

'It's this way,' Ernie said. 'I've been workin' this pit these past umpteen years. I know it backwards.'

'It's not backwards we want to go,' the datal hand said.

'The surveyor found shot in some old boardrooms,' the under-manager said. 'He couldn't understand it. He wondered what it was doin' there. He called bank and the manager sent us down in the maintenance tub.'

'He should've come himsel',' the datal hand said.

'Don't take any notice,' the under-manager said. 'He likes to talk. It keeps his spirits up.'

'I heard shot yonder way,' Ernie said. 'I wondered what was goin' on. Maybe some of the lads puttin' detonators on the tails of the rats. You know how they are – even in fore shift.'

'We'll make for the high ground,' the under-manager said. 'It's the only place we'll be safe. And if we do meet any rats with their tails blown off the datal hand's tongue'll frighten them away.'

They moved up an incline, but water poured through the roof. The lights of their safety lamps glistened upon walls and reflected silver upon the mud. They passed a heavy bulwark at the bottom of the drift; the bulwark had been there to halt the course of any runaway set. Halfway up the incline by the heavy bar a space had been hollowed where older men could pause and regain their breath, but this part of the pit had been disused, water poured through the roof, and the hollow had filled with dark water.

The men splashed through the water towards the drift mouth. They manoeuvred the incline without falling, their yardsticks digging into the soft clay, feeling the slither of their hobnail boots as they tried to grip. Another hollow filled with water lay ahead and the water followed as they climbed higher. 'I don't think much of your short cut,' the under-manager said.

Ernie stumbled, the yardstick went from his hand; his knees scraped the mud and he fell with a splash into a pool. The fall knocked the wind from him, his helmet fell from his head, and he felt pain to his neck and shoulders as his head dropped into the water. The water rushed into his mouth and he felt its slimy taste like ice to his throat. He closed his eyes and held them tightly closed and staggered out of the pool as best he could.

The under-manager and datal hands stood on the edge of the pool, looking not at Ernie but the steady yellow cone of flame in their safety lamps. The flames were strong and violent, an inch long, straight and proud, yet filled with hostility and menace. The under-manager raised the lamp above his head and still the flame did not waver. Methane gas had never been a danger at Highhill, but the men had never been allowed to smoke in the pit and to be caught in the pithead search with cigarettes or tobacco had meant instant dismissal. Water breaking through old workings had released pockets of gas that had crept upon the men more stealthily than any water.

The flames to their lamps turned a deep violet blue.

'Black damp!' the under-manager shouted.

The men fell face down into the water.

9

Bess Fatherley never did get over the loss of her two younger sons to the Western Front.

She grieved especially for Roger, the youngest, the spoilt one of the family, the apple of her eye as she would say to neighbours. He had been a ragamuffin, dirty knees and boots, his cap dishevelled, his trousers torn; but he had black hair and eyes, teeth white and even and a smile that lit the eyes, so that Bess forecast one day he would break the hearts of many a woman. In fact, his vice had been gambling. He gambled away his pocket money on Friday evening in the three-card brag schools at the colliery institute.

His mother would take down the tea caddy and give him some coppers to have a drink at the club during the week. He would use the coppers to play pitch and toss by the burn on Sunday morning, his brother Albert keeping one eye out for the local policeman. There would be trips to the races and sometimes, when he lost all his money, he would walk back to the village from the railway station because he could not afford the trap.

Roger had begun to keep whippets when he was twenty and had come across a disgruntled owner about to drown a whippet in the burn. Whippets were raced Sunday morning in a field that had been used for the annual horse show; this particular whippet should have won a race but had lost. Roger had taken the whippet to Ernie's allotment and later to a disused stable and began breeding his own. He trained the whippets on the fells around the village, sold the better ones to pay his gambling debts, and ran the occasional whippet in the Sunday races.

He had bred a whippet he called *Blue Daisy* and he and Albert had trained the whippet by the Tilley drift away from other owners and trainers. Albert had made a mock hare out of rabbit skin; he had staked out an eighty-yard course. He would pull the mock hare on a rope till the whippet, released from his box, chased the hare over the distance.

'It's the fastest whippet we've had in a long time,' Albert said.

'Better not mention it in the club,' Roger said.

'You think Charlie might shorten the odds?'

Charlie Bessford had been another village gambler.

He did bargain work in the pit and had opened his own book. He never did have difficulty collecting bets on the book he opened; his four sons saw to that. Those who did not pay or welshed were taken in the pit and hustled to old workings where his sons kept rats in tiny cages. The rats' eyes would be yellow and evil in the light of candles pushed into the blue post. Sometimes, they said, if they let out the rats into the men's faces you could hear the screams of the men up through the drift mouth as far as the village.

There would be five or six whippet races on the playing field, half the village turning out to enjoy the races and bet on their favourites. There would be semi-finals and a final. Prize money came from each owner putting half a sovereign into a pool and the money divided among the winning owners. There would be winnings to be collected from the bookmakers. Roger had always sold his best whippets and as owner had never been among the winners.

He hardly won a bet with Charlie Bessford.

'What's the odds on *Blue Daisy?*' he asked.

'Tell us its form,' Charlie said. 'I'll tell you the odds.'

'It's never been in a race in its life.'

'You've never timed it on the fells?'

'I never bother over much with whippets.'

'Ten to one bar the field,' Charlie said.

Roger gave Charlie Bessford a sovereign.

'Where'd you get that?' Charlie asked.

'Robbin' my mother's tea caddy.'

'You'd better not be after robbin' me.'

Charlie put the sovereign in his leather bag and handed over the betting slip.

There had been more excitement than usual that day. Someone had let a real hare from a sack and the whippets had chased it around the field till they had caught it. They had torn it apart. This had unsettled the crowd and spoiled the day's racing; it had also excited the whippets. They did not run to form. *Blue Daisy* waited for the mock hare and bounded down the course to win every race.

The crowds had turned away, but they came back to see this phenomenon, and there were as many spectators at the final as there had been for the earlier races before the real hare had been let out of the sack. The odds-on favourite did not win, but the spectators had not been displeased, nor had the bookmakers. Charlie Bessford studied Roger's winning ticket, his hands upon his leather bag, the knuckles showing white, a bowler hat pushed back upon his head as if he were a real bookmaker.

Charlie had been a big man, bigger than his sons, his arms and legs thick, his shoulders heavy. His neck had been as thick as his arms and legs, his hair as dark as Roger's, curly too, hanging over his brow. He had a full handsome face and blue eyes that attracted women. There had been amusement to his eyes and a curl to his lips when he had taken Roger's bet, but now the amusement had gone.

'You're sure you never timed that whippet?'

'The others were off form,' Roger said.

'I never saw a whippet like yours.'

'It was the fellow with the hare. He got them over excited.'

'I'll be makin' enquiries,' Charlie said. 'Me lads'll be on to you tonight. And if I find you've been timin' and trainin' that whippet, I'll be after you for more than my money back.'

'Cross my heart and hope to die.'

'You'll be right about the last bit if I find you've been gettin' one over me.'

Roger decided to join the Army.

10

'I hope you can find a French woman to keep your feet warm,' Albert said.

'They say they dance the can-can and wear them fancy petticoats,' Roger said.

He and Albert walked up the cinder bank from their home beyond the institute towards the Tilley drift. They passed a clump of silver birch trees; harsh tussocky grass climbed on either side and there were patches of gorse and broom, briars and nettles. The sun shone on the yellow heads of the gorse and the broom fronds swayed weakly in the wind that stirred through the grey leaves of the silver birch. The sun sank rapidly, its rays shooting across the sky, the cirrus scarlet and gold. They could see below them the valley floor, the river twisting silver in and out of the oak trees.

'You can give the money back,' Albert said.

'Maybes I can drown *Blue Daisy* and all.'

'Give *Blue Daisy* to Charlie.'

'I'll keep the money,' Roger said. 'You give him the dog when I'm gone.'

'You forget I trained and timed the dog. If he finds out about you he'll find out about me. He'll drown me in the burn – not the dog. Anyway, it's that fast it's useless. No bookmaker'll take another bet – and the other owners'll not let it race.'

'It'll be good for chasin' rabbits.'

The valley spiralled back towards the river source.

Albert felt the pallid strength of the sun upon his cheeks and forehead and the stirring of the wind through his hair. He had been a year older than Roger, but more solidly-built, short almost squat, studious with troubled grey eyes. He was more like his elder brother Ernie, taciturn and observant, never taking sides between his mother and grandfather, nervously flicking the tip of his tongue around his lips.

Albert worried about Roger.

As children they had swum together in the river below; the crags rose steep and sharp and dangerous but the water ran cool beneath. The current ran swiftly through reeds and pebbles past sand banks, guiding the river through the woods to where it broadened in the valley. The two of them would move down through forest pathways to the crags and strip to the waist before diving into the cool water below.

One day Albert had surfaced but Roger had not.

Albert had plunged again, this time from the bank, keeping his eyes open in the murky water. He had bumped against Roger and hauled him to the surface. A branch of oak came with him; the branch had swirled down river and been caught under the crag. Roger's belt buckle had caught in the branch and as he gasped for air, his lungs half-filled with water, Albert had detached the belt and pushed the branch back into the river.

He turned Roger on his stomach and pushed at his

back till water from his lungs retched through his bloated lips. He half-pushed, half-carried Roger to a ledge on the bank, the ledge green with lichen, the lichen gentle to Roger's stomach as he shivered and coughed up more of the brackish water. The branch swirled away, its scraped bark not showing above the ripples. If the branch had still been lodged under the crag and Roger with it, Albert wondered how he would have broken the news to his mother.

'Thanks for lookin' after us,' Roger had said.

Albert had been looking after him ever since.

'I don't fancy rats crawlin', over my face,' Roger said.

'My father'll sort it out.'

'By the time the war's over, Charlie Bessford'll have forgotten us.'

'But not his ten sovereigns.'

'I'll pay him back from my Army pension.'

'Pay him back now,' Albert said. 'You'll find more than French women at the front.'

'Who cares about Charlie Bessford?' Roger said. 'I'm bored with pit work. I'm bored with the village and all this carry-on in the family, with my grandfather kicked out of the house and my father tellin' the lads not to go to fight the war. I'm twenty-six years old. Why shouldn't this be the greatest year of my life, meetin' some French woman and settlin' over there? There's nobody in the village for me.'

'If you hang around long enough you'll find some-body.'

'For you maybe,' Roger said. 'Not for me.'

'Our grandfather'll be happy, I'll grant you that.'

Grandfather Ernest had taken one of the miners' cottages built for those who could no longer work in the pit. If he was seen at all in Slum Alley it had been shuffling in a sodden raincoat up the cinder path towards the chapel. He was thinner, his cheek bones high, his white hair running down his back, but his eyes were sharp, his fingers lean and fragile, the nails broken and dirty. He never did learn to look after himself, but he had been helped by chapel-goers who would make his meals and press his clothes. The cough persisted and so too did the gauntness, and when he did pass the Fatherley door he would spit upon the thresh. His cough had been like a death rattle, traces of blood to his spittle.

'We'll go in the mornin',' Albert said. 'Before Charlie finds out.'

'You'd better stay for my mother's sake.'

'She'll worry less if she knows I'm with you.'

Below them towards the valley they could see other villages and collieries, pit heaps and pasture. The colliery wheels were turning and there were cattle in the fields so distant they were small dabs of colour on the drabness. Midgies darted above their heads, chaffinches sang, and Roger felt life was flowing not as a song, not as a melody, but as a landscape in nature, dark and brooding, bright and sunny, full of the sound of thunder, the flicker of lightning.

He wanted to be all men and no man.

59

He wanted to be ten men in one and one man in ten. Somewhere deep inside he felt that the art of living was to live, but to live you had to take life by the throat and shake it like a cur. That is what he wanted to do with life once he found it. He knew he would not find it in a pit village; he would not find it along the rolleyway or coming to bank and seeing the headstock edged against the sky. He would not find it through the loins of a pit lass.

The sky had been crisp and gold, the scarlet gone, the cirrus morose, not anxious to lose the light; the powdered leaves on the silver birch were sharp against the cirrus and as the wind rustled through the leaves the sky tressed and fluttered like a bird's wings. An empty set came out of the drift mouth and Roger watched it hauled across the fields towards the colliery. Maintenance men were crossing the fields towards the drift mouth.

The maintenance men passed into the darkness

'That's you and me in thirty years,' Roger said.

'They'll give us an aged miners' cottage when we retire.'

'I'd rather the French woman.'

'I don't know how we'll break it to our mother,' Albert said.

11

It had been a rough crossing from Folkstone to Boulogne and instead of one hour it had taken five.

Roger had joined a brag school in an alley by the engine room as the ship had moved into the darkness. They had plunged and rolled and even a prile of threes could not prevent him being sick and throwing up. He had been glad to be off the ship and marching through Boulogne to camp, but the food queue had been long. They had left camp the next day and on their march to the station Roger had seen his first French woman: a stout lady with dark hair and thick red lips. She had tossed biscuits and chocolates to the soldiers.

Roger had been learning French at base camp.

'Vous jig-a-jig avec me tonight, cherie!' he called.

She threw another bar of chocolate.

'Tommy! Tommy!' she cried.

Each freight truck carried forty men.

Each man carried three quarters of a hundredweight of kit and rifle; the rifles stood against the sides of the trucks. The doors had been open and some of the men sat with their legs dangling. They had encamped first in a farm that had a thatched roof and in the farmyard there had been wooden sheds surrounded by a spiked brick wall. The camp had been miles from the railhead and they had arrived exhausted. The officer had given the order to stand-at-ease and they had collapsed, letting their kit fall from them.

Roger ran a hand along a gutter and gashed his palm.

'The first casualty of the battalion,' Albert said.

'They'll not be sendin' you back to Blighty,' Serjeant Amis said.

'You're needed to fill the gap,' Albert said.

'What are you on about?' Roger asked.

'That's what reserves are for – to fill the gap in the front line.'

'We'll not volunteer,' Roger said. 'That's what we said when we signed up.'

'I hope the recruitin' serjeant gave it to you in writin', Albert said.

They moved to the front by foot or rail.

They marched twenty-five kilometres a day, falling out ten minutes in every hour in a clutter of rifles and equipment. Roger slid forward on the ground and slackening his belt used it as a pillow; he would fall asleep instantly and when he woke reel like a drunk. Albert's feet were blistered and bleeding, but the officers' whistles sounded and they moved off again. Messages come soaring from the sky: *coal boxes*, four booms out of nowhere, a rush of air, a noise that pierced their ears.

Roger and Albert flung themselves to the ground.

'I don't know why they call them *coal boxes*!' Albert said.

There had been four explosions among the ruined

houses behind them, collapsing what was left of the walls. The shells had been packed with a hundred pounds of explosives and a sooty black smoke clouded the air. Later they would grow accustomed to the *coal boxes* and not only hear their wheeze but see them coming out of a clear sky. They would follow their trajectory so clearly they knew where to duck, their hands protecting their ears from the muffle of the sound.

'I've lost my bloody shovel!' Roger said.

'The enemy's partial to roads,' Albert said.

'Let's hope the railway'll be better,' Serjeant Amis said.

He would share his first dug-out with the Fatherleys. Their first trenches had been narrow and tightly packed, six feet from the top of the parapet, floored with duckboard but only wide enough for two men to pass. A fire step a foot high ran along each section, the dug-outs little more than shell holes. Their dug-out had been eight feet long by four wide, a bedstead built into one side with wire netting stretched across a wooden frame.

'We'll get our heads down here,' Serjeant Amis said.

He collected empty sandbags and spread them over the top of the bed. There had been a shelf on the other side of the bedstead, a wooden floor, and a corrugated iron roof with sandbags on top. The ceiling had been lined with sacking. The dug-out had belonged to a lieutenant who had gone to inspect a machine-gun position on the rim of a crater. He had stood his full height and being six-feet-six had been cut down by a sniper's bullet.

His belongings had still been in the dug-out when Serjeant Amis moved in: pipe, tobacco tin, watch, letters from home, embroidery, a price list for extras: a shilling and three pence for a loaf, ten pence for sardines and eggs for a half-penny each. Roger had respectfully inspected the belongings. 'He'll not be wantin' any of these where he's gone,' he said. 'And I hope we're here longer than him.'

'A bit swank for the likes of us,' Albert said.

'I've been in the trenches before,' Serjeant Amis said. 'I know the ropes. Settle in and get your heads down – and if anybody asks questions as to why we're in this dug-out leave the answers to me.'

Their section had been quiet.

They heard a gramophone playing, even a few bars of a piano, but when the weather turned and rain settled across the landscape they had been issued long rubber boots they wore to the hips. The front line flooded, communication trenches vanished and sandbags had to be piled on top of the original parapet; the water ran above their knees, colder than pit water but as morose. Roger had fallen into a hole and the water reached his chest. Men following behind had laughed but there were so many holes, the trenches uneven, they all ended waist deep in water before the rain ceased.

Roger and Albert stood guard for the second half of the night, keeping each other awake – to be caught asleep was a court-martial offence that might lead to the firing squad. In the stillness they would fire a flare to stir themselves. They could see the craters and shell holes and barbed wire and pill boxes behind the German lines, but when the light of the flare faded they turned to fire a few rounds at the rats.

There were *rum jars* and *Minenwerfers*.

The *rum jars* were huge bombs like ginger beer hens; they were trench mortars and when they hit the ground they would flatten ten yards of any trench. *Minenwerfers* were steel drums packed with high explosives and scrap iron; they sailed a hundred feet into the air, a lighted fuse trailing like a meteor. They hit the ground with a devastating smack, the explosion blasting the trenches. Men half a mile away would fall concussed, but there had been no *rum jars* or *Minenwerfers* on their section.

'We can survive here all right,' Roger said.

'As long as you keep your head down,' Albert said.

'You should drop a line to our mother and tell her how quiet it is.'

'I've already written.'

'Did you tell her the name of the place?'

'That's censored anyway,' Albert said.

'I call it Durham Alley.'

'Others call it Paschendale.'

12

Bess Fatherley read the letter again and placed it on the mantelpiece.

'They say there's a big push comin',' Binkie said.

'They've been sayin' that for months,' Bess said.

'It'll not worry our lads. They're at the quietest part of the front.'

'If you believe that you'll believe anythin'.'

Bess wiped away the tears with her pinafore.

She sat at the table wearing the same black dress she had worn the day her sons had gone to join up. They had taken the trap from the village and she had seen them off from the railway station on the valley floor. There had been a fall of snow and the trap had skidded its way to the station. When they had moved from Bedlington they had brought their belongings by horse and cart along bridle paths leading from one village to another, using the ferry to cross the river, but Highhill had gone modern, with a trap to take passengers to the station and back.

'The best thing you can think of is to get your backsides shot off by the Germans!' Bess had said. 'You don't want to sort out this business with Charlie Bessford! You want to be away. You think them French lasses'll teach you somethin' you couldn't find out in the village? You think they're different from English lasses? You'll wonder what came over you when you're in the trenches!'

'We'll be back, mother,' Roger said.

'You'll never be back!'

'They'll give us leave,' Albert said.

'And even Charlie Bessford'll not touch a man in uniform,' Roger said.

'It's fear of your father – not Charlie Bessford – that'll keep you away.'

'He'll have us back, mother,' Albert said. 'You know that.'

'Not once you sign on,' Bess said. 'They might bring you back in a coffin, if they bring coffins back from France. He might have you back then, but he'll never forgive what you've done to the family and the village. He'll not curse you, but he'll not be givin' you his blessin' either.'

Bess could no longer see for the tears in her eyes.

She wiped them clear as the train had pulled out of the station. The railway lines had been sharp in the snow and the steam of the engine curled into the white of the snow and cloud. The coachman stood behind her with a rug. It had been early morning; there had been a chill to the air, but other traps and motor vans carrying newspapers and books to the institute had already left.

She wore her black shawl and dress, as if going to a funeral; she knew with certainty she would never see her sons again. She would long be in her grave before they returned to the village, if they returned at all. The tears she had shed had been tears of anger and frustration as well as loss; she was a pitman's wife, she could live with the fear of accident or injury to her men in the pit; but for two of them to leave home, to fight a foreign war, to be cut off from kith and kin.

That was beyond her.

The coachman handed her the rug.

'You look after him, Albert,' she had said.

She climbed into the trap and noticed she held a purse tight to her fingers.

'This is for you, mother,' Roger had said.

In the purse were ten gold sovereigns.

Bess had not changed her pinafore in weeks.

She had walked the village with a vacant stare. She talked more to herself and when she worked through the house she did things from habit. She had seen the fire low and had gone to the coal house for a shovel full of coal, but she had dropped the coal not upon the fire but in the earth closet. Her mouth fell open, revealing stunted teeth, and she had ceased to trim the beauty spot on her chin.

'Tell me what it's all about,' she said.

The plush cloth no longer came out on Sunday.

'You and your pit work!' she said. 'I married you and raised four bairns and I've lived in this house all these years and always you were gettin' us another. I've worked my fingers to the bone. You used to go to the chapel on Sunday night and leave me here all by mysel'. Never once have you asked to take us for a drink. You tell me what I've done to deserve this.'

'I'd have got you a new house years ago.'

'Only with your union work you didn't think it fittin'
to ask. You discovered socialism and said to yoursel'
this was the way you're supposed to live if you want
to be a revolutionary. This house is a hundred years
old. It's only got two rooms. We had to live with your
father and the lads. Not once have you lifted a finger
in the house – not once!'

'Ernie's been a help.'

'But not you, you bugger! All that union work and
chapel – and that fancy woman of yours. No wonder
you've been happy to let me slave my life away over
a stove while you go and enjoy yourself behind the
pigeon crees.'

'I don't have a fancy woman,' Binkie said.

'All the village knows about you and the school
teacher.'

'The village knows wrong.'

'I've never had a holiday,' Bess said. 'When did
we catch a trap to go to the coast and breathe a bit
of sea air? When did you say to put your coat on
and we'd have a run out? As long as your bath water
was ready and your meal on the table. When did you
give us a kiss and a cuddle? D'you know when you
stopped doin' that, Binkie Fatherley? After our Roger
was born. Now he's gone to fight the war. You and
that daft union work. Because your back was turned
they went and joined up.'

'I had a word with Charlie Bessford.'

'You mean you borrowed the money from the colliery manager and paid him back the ten sovereigns.

69

Now it's docked from your pay. At least Roger wasn't daft enough to take the sovereigns with him and lose them all playin' brag. But there might be somethin' about that chapel o' yours after all. They say if you pray long enough your prayers'll come true. So I pray for Roger and Albert and I'll keep the sovereigns in the tea caddy just in case they do come back.'

Bess buried her head in her pinafore.

Her shoulders convulsed and Binkie let her cry.

He knew he had failed her and failed his family. They had been married all these years and what could he show for it? What had been in it for Bess? She had gone the way of his mother, old before her time, not yet fifty; he could see the trembling body frail and shard, grey hairs tumbling around her cheeks. Her eyes were vacant when the pinafore fell from her face, the cheeks damp with tears, the beauty spot flared and angry. He had deprived Bess, not of her youth or the best years of her life, but of her pride.

'You'll feel better when Roger and Albert are back,' he said.

'My poor bairns!' she said. 'My poor bairns!'

13

Roger Fatherley climbed to the top of the trench and peered over.

He had clipped a half-broken mirror onto the tip of

his bayonet and dangled the mirror against the trench parapet. The sun reflected from the mirror and what little he could see had been familiar anyway: a landscape of craters and shell holes half-filled with water, trees stark against the sky, their limbs broken. By raising the mirror higher he might see the first German lines, the barbed wire thirty yards deep, and beyond the wire the squat pillboxes with mean-mouthed slits from where machine-gun fire would burst. The line had been no more than two hundred yards away, sandbagged and parapeted, but with no sign of the enemy's spiked helmets.

Roger made the mirror dance on the tip of his bayonet.

A sniper's bullet smacked into a sandbag.

'A rotten shot!' Roger shouted.

He scrambled down the trench wall.

'He got one of our lads the other day,' Albert said. 'He was sittin' on the latrine havin' a smoke. A funny thing to die with your pants down and a tab in your mouth!'

'Havin' a crap,' Roger said.

'You might try shootin' a few of them rats,' Albert said. 'I don't like them nibblin' my boots while I'm makin' breakfast.'

The rats ran in and out of Albert's feet.

They were excited by the smell of bacon and only the heat from the charcoal fire kept them from the pan. During the day Roger and Albert would place cheese on the tips of their bayonets and when a rat came to

71

nibble the cheese they would pull the trigger. Always another rat would take its place. Albert filled billycans with freshly-brewed tea and he and Roger drank the tea and ate the bacon, dipping bread hunks into the grease that simmered in the pan. They pushed the rats aside with their bayonets.

Serjeant Amis came along with their duties and fatigues: weapon cleaning and inspection, pick and shovel work on the trench, fetching and carrying from the rear. Always there would be the sniper, lying hour upon hour with his telescopic rifle, watching for the slightest movement. 'Mebbes he's not in no-man's land at all,' Roger said. 'Mebbes he's got more sense. See that old farmhouse beyond the barbed wire? I reckon he's in there.'

'I'll not be poppin' my head up to have a look,' Albert said.

'We can go over the night,' Roger said. 'Give him a blast with a rifle grenade.'

'I'll be tucked in bed,' Albert said.

Serjeant Amis crept up to take a billycan of tea.

He had stood six feet tall but walked with a permanent stoop; to stand risked having his head blown off by a sniper's bullet. He too came from Highhill and had enlisted at the outbreak of the war. He had been in the Territorial Army and had trained and drilled through winter months. He had looked forward to summer camp. He had slept under canvas, drilled and marched in pallid sunshine, but he had enjoyed the copious food dished out by the field kitchens.

He had first seen active service in the autumn of 1914 when the Durham Light Infantry lost as many men in a single day's fighting as it had in the entire Boer War. The dead and wounded had seemed even more implausible because the regiment had arrived in France only a few days earlier. He had been wounded in the leg and in charge of the battalion depot when the Fatherleys had arrived.

'We're goin' on leave,' Serjeant Amis said.

'We've done nothin' to deserve it,' Albert said.

'Does that mean I can go back to Blighty and see my mother?' Roger asked.

'It means you'll be able to have yourself a French lass if you can find one,' Serjeant Amis said.

'I'll find one all right.'

14

They had been transported back to base in the same flat open railway boxes that had taken them to their trenches. They had billeted in a broken-down barn twenty kilometres behind the lines and had spent the first day resting and cleaning themselves up, delousing their uniforms. Lice had been everywhere: in the seams of their khaki, the furrows of their vests, popping like crackers under lighted candles. Some popped more vigorously than others, spattering their faces, as if they had measles. They had lice powder but the lice had prospered and Albert had thrown the powder over the trench wall.

'Maybe the rats can make somethin' of it,' he said.

They had hitched a lift on the back of a motor transport to the nearest village ten kilometres away. There were signs outside the village homes: *oeufs et pommes de terre frites cinquante centimes.* There would be country bread and cognac in the coffee, and after the meal they strolled up the village street. Terraced houses stood on either side, the women outside their doors making lace. Albert bought a bottle of *vin blanc* for half a franc and they drank from the bottle as they walked, examining the lace, flattered by the smiles of the younger women.

They heard the rumble of artillery fire, but the older women sat quaintly dressed in peasant costume working the lace, cushions on their laps. There would be pins and thread spools, the thread deftly criss-crossed as the patterns developed. Each movement of the pins and spools made a click and in the autumn evening, quiet but for the guns, there had been a mass of tiny clicks from one end of the street to the other. The younger women tried to sell Albert and Roger their lace, but Serjeant Amis told the brothers to keep their money for better things.

They had made their way to the first brothel.

A red lamp hung at the end of a cul-de-sac. They found a mass of khaki before them, men standing along the alleyway and along the walls of the cobbled square, at least a hundred and fifty, singing a French song they had picked up in the trenches: *Mademoiselle from Armentiers*. The song had been around since Napoleon's time. At six o'clock the lamp began to sway and the door opened and the men rushed forward as ravenous as the rats in the trenches.

One man had his leg broken in the rush.

Roger and Albert tagged along but Serjeant Amis held them back and when finally they made their way inside they found a space at the corner of the bar. Heavyweights worked for the brothel. They wore British Army instructors' jerseys but were as French as their black moustaches, their hair plastered, a love curl over their foreheads. They had never been to sea but they wore tattoos to their arms and controlled the queue to the stairs where stood the *Grande Dame* of the house.

She had been an ugly brazen woman in her sixties, her hair dyed a bright ginger, her face thick with powder and rouge, her eyes dark with mascara. She dripped jewellery and cheap rings and trinkets and a necklace and wore a pair of fake silver pearl earrings. She had full splayed breasts with no brassiere to hold them firm and her hips were wide, her legs thick and varicosed, but the legs and varicose veins had been hidden by a coarse bright skirt. The large breasts were barely concealed by a loose lemon-coloured blouse.

She charged two francs, one for her and one for the *mademoiselle*.

'We're not goin' to waste our time or money,' Serjeant Amis said. 'In the mornin' I'm goin' to introduce you to somethin' special. Peg Leg Meg's bound to fall in love with you when she sees your hair.'

Roger's tousled hair had been only partly cut. The sides were closely cropped but the black curls ruffled the top of his head, still awaiting the barber's shears. They had stopped at a farmhouse three kilometres from the front; the farmer lived alone in the basement, but he earned centimes by cutting hair between shell barrages. He had trimmed Albert's hair and had been halfway through trimming Roger's when a *rum jar* whistled over the farmhouse and he had darted into the basement.

He had not been seen again.

'Who's Peg Leg Meg?'

Serjeant Amis had led them the following morning to *La Petite Lilloise*.

Peg Leg Meg hobbled downstairs at eleven. They had heard the tap of her wooden leg upon the boards and down the bare stairs that led to the bar. She wore no make-up, her skin sallow, dark pools beneath her eyes; the eyes themselves had receded and the skin had been rumpled around her neck. Her hips were stocky, her breasts full-blown, and she wore a peasant's smock that ran to her ankles. She walked with difficulty, never accustomed to her wooden leg, weary at this hour of the morning, falling into a chair at the table.

'Henri!' she called.

An old man came from behind the bar with a bottle of *vin blanc* and a glass. He poured a drink and returned to the counter where he rinsed and dried glasses. Peg Leg Meg raised her glass to Serjeant Amis and downed the white wine in a single draught. She had lost her leg as a child in an accident; she had been run over by a cabriolet but the cabriolet had not stopped. She spoke English with a slurred accent, either because it had been too early or the effort too great, or because she had been drunk the night before. She looked at the three of them indifferently as she recounted how she had lost her leg and how she had lived in Arras till it fell under German occupation.

'*Les salauds* can keep it,' she said.

A young woman came into the *estaminet.*

She had been small and dark and shy, no more than twenty, her eyes looking across their table as if in search of someone. She did not find who she had been looking for and moved to leave. A sudden gust blew rain through the open door and she thought better of it. She closed the door behind her and settled at their table, shaking her dark hair, raindrops falling upon the polished surface. Henri came from behind the bar with another glass and another bottle. Roger had paid for the first and Albert would pay for the second. The young woman peeled out of her coat, showing bare white shoulders, running her hands down her thighs in her shyness.

'This is the lass for me!' Roger said.

'You must treat her gently,' Meg said.

The young woman had no money and would come into the *estaminet* for breakfast each morning. She lived on her own in a room without heating. She settled at the table and Henri brought croissants and butter and jam and she ate sipping at the white wine, waiting for Henri to bring her a small cup of stiff black coffee, her eyes still towards the door as if expecting someone. In her shyness she spoke only a halting English.

'*Pauvre fille!*' Meg said.

'She must have a name,' Albert said.

'We call her *La Petite Rose* of No Man's Land.'

'Tell her she's got lovely eyes,' Roger said.

'You tell her,' Albert said. 'You're the one who wants to learn the lingo.'

Rose dropped her coat around the back of her chair.

She spoke rapidly in French to Meg.

'She wants to know who cut your hair?'

'I'm on the General Staff,' Roger said. 'We all have hair cuts like this.'

Meg took Roger's hand and laid it on the table.

'You must treat Rose with respect,' she said. 'Her father was killed in the battle of the Marne – the very first days of the war. Her fiancé went to serve in the same regiment to avenge her father, so he said – but he never wrote, never came back. Maybe he never signed on or maybe he's dead.'

She ran a protective hand down Rose's hair.

'The *Ministère de Guerre* say they cannot be sure. They say he may have deserted – they say he may have been shot. Rose believes he is still alive. She looks for him every day in every *estaminet* in every village. She knows she'll find him one day.'

'Nobody loved me like that,' Roger said.

'Your mother did,' Albert said. 'She loved you.'

'I wasn't thinkin' of my mother.'

'She's gone up and down the front,' Meg said. 'The High Command thought she was a spy working for the *Boche*. They wanted to court martial her and put her before the firing squad. How could they shoot her when she was not a soldier? They put her in prison – but when she came out she came back to the front. Now she must stay behind the lines. She is *une fille misérable*. That is why I say you must be gentle.'

'I'll be gentle,' Roger said.

'She is a love bird looking for a love nest,' Meg said. 'See how sensitive she is? She cannot find her partner – her *petit oiseau* – and so like a bird she breaks her wings against the window as if it were a cage. She is a great tragedy of war – where love exists but cannot express itself.'

Rose did not follow the conversation.

She had been aware of Roger's attentions, but she was indifferent to them, except she saw the black smouldering eyes, the curled hungry lips, the brows as dark as the eyes, touches of red high to his cheekbones. She saw how thin he had been, how young, and if there was desire within him it had been coiled as a spring, ready to encompass her. Her arms showed white with the coat dropped from her shoulders.

Knits of worry had been etched to her brow, her skin had been fine as alabaster, her shoulders as white as her arms, but her dark hair no longer lay bedraggled around her face and her cheeks were flushed as she sipped the *vin blanc*. She wore no make-up, her skin unspoiled, her mouth small, the lips arched and appealing. She smiled rarely but her teeth were white and even, and Roger felt if only he could raise the mask of sadness he would find a beautiful woman.

He took her hand and she did not resist.

'You can fall in love with her if you like,' Albert said.

'The way this war's goin' it had better be love at first sight,' Serjeant Amis said.

'Maybe if we could find a priest I could marry her the day.'

'Ye're forgettin' her fiancé.'

'He'll not be comin' back in this war.'

'You tell her that.'

There had been a noise in the square outside.

Henri left the bar and the glasses and stood at the doorway, towel over his shoulder, tall enough to see over the lace curtain. There had been the rattle of wheels upon cobbles, the sound of horses and the jeers of men. They all left the table to peer beyond the lace. Two British military police stood before the *estaminet* with a handcuffed prisoner. They wore their red caps firmly to their heads as they tied the Tommy soldier to the wheels of a gun carriage and trundled him along the cobbled streets.

'Field punishment number one,' Serjeant Amis said.

'That's what you get for desertin'.' He turned to Roger.

'You can fall in love with Rose and you can marry her the day or the morn for all I care – only you don't elope with her. You don't desert!'

'There'll be no gun carriage for me,' Roger said.

'And no marriage either,' Albert said. 'By the looks of things.'

Roger turned from the window but Rose had gone.

15

They returned to the *estaminet* that evening.

The *estaminet* had been full, there were women and more women, the rooms above the bar doing good business. Tommies were everywhere, Canadian and Australian and French soldiers too, and there had been no way they could make their way through the door let alone to the table they had occupied that morning. They spotted Henri, no longer listless, his shoulders drooping; he stood his full height, his hair freshly-dyed, his face flushed with the heat that sent sweat streaming down the walls.

Henri wore the British Army instructor's jersey and controlled the flow of women and customers around the bar and the tables and stairs leading to the rooms. He recognised Serjeant Amis and Roger and Albert and made a path for them to rooms at the back of the *estaminet* they had noticed that morning. These rooms too were full, the haze of blue tobacco smoke as thick as any fog across the Channel.

'D'you think Rose'd marry us if I asked?'

'She might,' Albert said. 'If she'd supped as many bottles of *vin blanc* as you supped this mornin'.'

'I want to go lookin' for her.'

'She's lookin' for her fiancé.'

'I want to marry her on the spot.'

'Serjeant Amis can be your witness and I'll be your best man. As long as you don't run away with her, like Serjeant Amis said. He'll think we're daft, but we'd better be daft than dead.'

'Sooner or later we'll be both,' Roger said.

'I only hope Serjeant Amis survived the thumpin' he got from Meg's peg leg this mornin'!'

Rose might have left the *estaminet* that morning but Peg Leg Meg and Serjeant Amis had gone too.

Serjeant Amis had followed her upstairs and Roger and Albert had heard the thump of her wooden leg on the stairs and onto the bedroom floor above. They had heard a flopping down upon the bed, the springs sagging under their weight. Henri had brought another bottle but the brothers had not minded. Indeed, he had brought several bottles and the more they drank the less they had minded, as if they had never had a drink since they had left the pit village.

'D'you think he's carvin' his initials on her peg leg?' Albert asked.

Rose of No Man's Land had been seated that evening in a corner of one of the rooms surrounded by French servicemen. She smoked a cigarette through a long black holder and had been hardly visible through the smoke. She wore a white dress that clung to her body, a silver necklace to the cream of her neck; she wore earrings that shimmered and her lips were thin slashes of scarlet. She sat on a French soldier's knee and when she saw Albert through the smoke she laughed and called him over, waving her black holder as Roger stumbled behind.

'Viens, mon brave!' she shouted.

The French soldiers parted a way for them to her table.

'Il cherche un coiffeur!' Rose shouted.

Roger thought she had found her fiancé.

He had been certain when Rose leapt from the chair and taking the soldier by the hand led him to a narrow door at the back of the room. Peg Leg Meg stood with her hand on the door jam and when the door parted they could see the brass knobs of a bedstead; other soldiers lined up before the door and so, too, did Roger and Albert and Serjeant Amis. Cigarette smoke seared their eyes and retched their lungs, but Henri beamed and smiled behind them, carrying a tray of glasses and three bottles of *vin blanc.*

'You'd better pay,' Albert said. 'Since this is your weddin' night.'

Roger turned out his pockets.

'I'll win it back in the next card school,' he said.

Peg Leg Meg looked younger than she had that morning. The tiredness had gone and the eyes were alert as she took five francs from the soldier who went into the room behind Rose. She had been stern and authoritarian and kept an eye on Henri who hovered still, satisfying himself the men were in good humour. There had been laughter as the French soldier emerged and another took his place, his five francs lost to Peg Leg Meg's voluminous palms.

'She has an awful lot of fiancés,' Roger said.

'It's the heat makin' you confused,' Albert said.

They each drank from the bottles of *vin blanc*.

'I'll marry her all the same,' Roger said.

'She's Peg Leg's daughter,' Serjeant Amis said.

'How d'you know that?' Albert asked.

'She told us this mornin'.'

'I thought she was hittin' you with her wooden leg.'

'Henri's her husband. He's Rose's father.'

'You're pullin' my leg.'

'Why d'you think they're all fussin' over Rose, makin' sure she's all right?'

'Which one's the fiancé?'

'She's never had a fiancé in her life,' Serjeant Amis said. 'They go along with the story because it gives her somethin' to hold on to. Sometimes it's a fiancé, sometimes she's a film star in one of them silent pictures, lookin' for a producer who's promised her a part. Other days she's lookin' for her bairn that was took by the Hun. I suppose if she faced the thought what life was about – and what was goin' to happen to all them customers of hers – she might as well go out and face a firin' squad.'

'What shall I tell Roger?' Albert asked.

'Tell him his leave's up the morn.'

'He knows that already.'

'Tell him you've not got a bible and couldn't marry him anyway.'

'Who needs a bible in France?'

'Tell him to turn his pockets out and be sure nobody jumps the queue.'

Roger handed Peg Leg Meg the five francs.

'How d'you say marry in French?'

'For five francs you should be gettin' a vicar!'

Albert gave Roger a push and he disappeared into the room.

'I'll give him a good scrub of carbolic when we get back,' Serjeant Amis said.

16

They moved forward around six o'clock.

The evening had been cold, the sky leaden, a chill wind whipped their faces and what trees there were stood stark against the sky. They were slim poles bereft of branch or foliage, as if nature had given up, and the shell holes were filled with water. The light reflected dull and cold from the mud, but they had begun their approach march several hours earlier, and as the sky darkened they moved forward in Indian file. Each man held onto the equipment of the man ahead to keep to the duck boards and plank roads that lead to the forward positions.

The wind rose about midnight and brought a drizzling rain.

'We'll get nowhere the night,' Albert said.

There had been a plop of gas shells.

'Gas masks!' Serjeant Amis shouted.

Roger and Albert pulled their masks from their haversacks.

'I hate these bloody things!' Roger said.

'You'll hate mustard gas worse,' Albert said.

The gas fell among the ranks for two hours.

The duck boards and roads had been laid by the pioneer battalions before the start of the battle and the ranks moved forward again to their jump-off points. They were wet through and slithered on the boards; German flares lit the sky and cast an eerie light to their faces, chalk in the sudden whiteness, inhuman, immobile, looking upward at the incandescence as other shells began to fall. They were high explosive shells, but the shells fell behind them, throwing up mud that spattered their sodden uniforms.

The mud had become so thick coconut matting had been laid across the duck boards and with neither plant nor shrub nor tree nor cottage nor farmhouse nor chapel to landmark their progress, tapes had been laid to guide them to their jump-off points. Even with their masks removed the men breathed cautiously, aware that if mustard gas blistered their bodies it would scorch both eyes and lungs

'Where is Paschendale anyway?' Roger asked.

'The village on the ridge over there,' Albert said.

'If it's just another village why do they want us to take it?'

'They want to give us home comforts for the winter.'

'The rain'll not help.'

'Nor the mud either.'

'You should've seen the Somme,' Serjeant Amis said.

'We're not on the Somme,' Albert said.

'It wasn't like this when we moved out,' Roger said.

'Think yourselves lucky,' Serjeant Amis said. 'The Hun attacked our dug-out lookin' for prisoners. He must've smelled an attack and wanted to know what was goin' on. It was for the best we got out when we did. Else we'd already be pushin' up the daisies.'

'It was that sniper come lookin' for Roger,' Albert said.

The Germans had been alerted by three days' bombardment and had laid two lines of barbed wire before their front line. The wire had been thirty metres deep and fresh aprons of wire had been laid around pillboxes. The pillboxes were squat islands in a sea of mud and had narrow mouths and machine-gun tongues that belched a static fire; the fire had raked the onrushing troops and the wounded had crawled into shell holes.

Some had made it back to the British pillboxes that

were now being used as casualty stations, only there were no doctors to treat the wounded men and no stretcher bearers to carry them across the mud to the advanced field hospitals. Those unharmed found neither ammunition to continue the fight nor supplies to feed them. Duck board tracks had been left free of troops so that pack mules could bring supplies to support the attack, but some of the pack mules had strayed from the duck board and drowned in the mud.

German snipers were everywhere.

Dead bodies had been piled outside the pillboxes and bullets smacked into the corpses or ricocheted from the concrete. The troops had been pulled back three hundred metres, but even then their position had been precarious. Nor could they be sure of artillery support. The gun batteries had not been able to traverse the mud, their platforms had been unstable, and as the rain fell steadily little advance could be made on the plank roads.

'If only the artillery'd soften them up,' Roger said.

'They'll start just as we get stuck into the Hun,' Serjeant Amis said.

Albert noticed their jump-off point stood between the remains of a brick kiln and a church. He wondered why they had built a brick kiln so close to a church, but it had not mattered; the kiln and the church had been demolished by artillery fire. There were craters beyond the jump-off point and shell holes, too. They were no more than slit trenches where German snipers and light machine-gunners had bedded down, covering the holes with rusting iron.

Roger and Albert and Serjeant Amis had lain on a barn floor on their last night of leave.

Several bottles of *vin blanc* had sent Serjeant Amis to sleep. Roger lay quietly with his eyes closed, his cap across his eyes, but Albert had stared through a hole in the roof. As a child twelve stars had been his friends: the seven stars of The Plough, the three of The Sword of Orion, and Sirius and its sister star. As a young pitman going in-by the Tilley drift he would look to them for assurance. They were his companions, his guides on those dark and lonely nights. He manoeuvred to see how many were visible through the hole in the roof.

'We'd have been better off playin' pitch and toss across the fields,' Roger said. 'Or trainin' them daft whippets. D'you remember when we were in the field and the horse came along and chased us? We ran faster than the whippets.'

'I feel my mother and father that close I can touch them,' Albert said. 'Even though I cannot see them in my mind. It's funny that. I can smell pit clothes and tea cakes bakin' and I can see the fire fallin' in the grate with the coal at the back. But I cannot see their faces.'

'They'll come to you when they want.'

Roger thought little of the past.

He lifted his cap and stirred from the floor; straw stuck to his uniform, listless and dead not yellow, but dark and damp like the days ahead. His head had cleared but the *vin blanc* had rotted his gut and he felt a dull pain as if he needed a latrine; but there had been no latrine, and he raised himself on his elbows and scratched at his knees. He ran a hand through his hair and wondered if it would ever grow.

He too looked through the hole in the roof, but he saw no stars or sky, only a void, a stretch to eternity. If his mind lived at all, it had been in a world of fantasy; that was why he had wanted to marry Rose. They were young and they would fantasise together. If this war were to end, he would seek out Rose and together they would start again, in another village, another country, another world, a world without pits or pitheaps, without red lamps or brothels or peg-legged mother.

'I'm sorry about this, Albert,' Roger said.

'They'd have got us on conscription.'

'Our father could've kept us down the pit.'

'Blood on the coal and all that.'

'All the same we're a couple of daft buggers.'

'You're my brother,' Albert said.

They smiled at each other and held each other close, smelling the straw, the earth to the barn floor, holding each other tightly as they had done as children, arms held firm; held each other for a long while as the stars changed in the sky and the twelve stars of Albert's childhood were no more, lost now to the cloud that would bring the first rain.

'I wouldn't even gamble,' Roger said. 'If I could start again.'

The wind rose and the rain began to fall heavily.

British artillery opened erratic and distant, a sound of distant thunder, but the thunder died and the barrage became thinner as whistles went and the first men advanced up the slopes of the jump-off points. There were four battalions in this attack. The battle plan had been for the first battalion to cut through the wire, to be leap-frogged by the second and third who would seize German pillboxes and advance upon the ridge and village. A fourth battalion would be held in anticipation of a counter attack.

The first battalion heard the whistle of shells, but the shells were off target. They did not destroy the barbed wire entanglements nor the pillboxes but buried into the mud. A turgid spray of mud arced across the German lines. The men advanced as best they could through the machine-gun bullets, some cutting at the strands of barbed wire, but the machine-guns did their work and spat them to death.

The second battalion moved forward.

They too advanced but were bogged down in the mud. Some struggled back to their jump-off points; others fell to snipers and light machine-gunners working in No Man's Land. The wind dropped and the rain became lighter, but the men cared for neither as they looked to the sullen sky. They saw no break in the clouds and heard no break in the machine-gun fire; they cursed and cried for help, but there had been no succour from stretcher-bearers for those who lay wounded.

91

Roger and Albert had been in the third battalion.

17

Serjeant Amis led his assault group forward.

They stayed low, leaping from shell hole to shell hole towards the barbed wire. Smoke lay over the battlefield like a blue mist. German snipers and light machine-gunners were killed by those mopping up behind the infantry, their bayonets poking through the corrugated iron covers, hand grenades lobbed into the slit trenches. No surrender had been offered and the snipers and light machine-gunners were killed where they were found.

Serjeant Amis fell into a crater filled with wounded men.

Roger and Albert followed and Roger scrambled up the crater wall to peer above the rim. Machine-gun fire raked the crater and through the smoke he saw the machine-guns firing from pillboxes or emplacements; a particularly murderous fire came from a blockhouse ahead some hundred metres beyond the barbed wire. There were four machine-guns in the blockhouse firing at will, but concentrating on those infantry who made short advances from shell hole to shell hole as they edged towards the wire.

It rained steadily but the crater had not filled with slimy water and mud. The water ran out of a breach in the crater wall into a massive culvert hidden by the thin blue smoke that lay across the mud. The culvert had been blasted by a raiding party of engineers seeking to get as close as possible to enemy lines; they had dug a tunnel and filled the tunnel with explosives. The explosives had blown a massive mound of earth into the air and had left a culvert that filled steadily with water.

The culvert ran beneath the barbed wire beyond enemy lines.

Smoke drifted across the water and stung his eyes as Roger rolled from the crater into the culvert. He waded thigh-deep, one hand feeling its way along the muddy wall, another holding his rifle above water level. He reached the first thirty metres of barbed wire and hunkering down in the water, rifle above his head, he edged carefully beneath it. The water lay shallow as the culvert tapered upward.

Roger crawled under the second belt of barbed wire, his face in the water, strands of wire plucking his uniform. He lifted himself out of the mud and up the damp embankment so that he could see behind him the barbed wire apron at the front of the blockhouse. There had been no apron at the back and he ran around the side of the blockhouse till he found the door bolted shut. He dropped a Mills bomb at the door front and took cover behind the concrete as the door blasted off.

Smoke poured into the blockhouse and out of the smoke came Germans waving handkerchiefs and pieces of white bandage. Others held their hands on their heads. One ran off to the right. Roger shot him dead. The others fell to the ground and lay with their arms outstretched as Roger lobbed a hand grenade through the twisted door. The blast had been followed by more smoke and more men running out till the four machine-guns ceased their merciless chatter.

Roger leapt into the smoking blockhouse.

He threatened with an unpinned grenade those Germans still lingering there. There had been two storeys to the blockhouse, two large lower rooms and a small upper room reached by a ladder; the machine-guns had been in the lower rooms. Roger leapt up the ladder to the upper room. He found a forward observation officer connected by telephone to an artillery battery. He had been monitoring the grudging advance of the British forces. The officer bounded to his feet and placed his hands on his head.

Roger threatened him with the grenade.

He rushed from the blockhouse and Roger scrambled down the ladder and dropped the grenade upon a field wireless. The smoke and dust of the blast followed him down the ladder and in the daylight he saw Serjeant Amis rounding up prisoners whilst other infantry dragged the four machine-guns out of the blockhouse. They set them up on tripods and Albert fired the first machine-gun into the German emplacements.

A whole platoon now swarmed around the blockhouse, cutting through the wire, bringing out more ammunition belts. They organised themselves in teams so that the gunners were able to aim down the machine-gun barrels, silencing the Germans firing from the ridge. Roger loped off again, skirting the wire that speckled the hillside, moving up the ridge towards the village. Thirty prisoners had been captured, other machine-gun nests were abandoned, more Germans gave themselves up, and the advance continued past the blockhouse to the ridge.

Roger saw Germans running from the village, trotting by the side of the road, their rifles hanging loosely. The village had long since been destroyed, abandoned by its people, the house walls gaunt against the sky, rubble swept into doorways from the road. Windows and doors and stairs were smashed, roofs had caved in, and there had been the smell of dampness and cordite. The rats too had fled and shattered bricks and masonry huddled in the rain.

Roger hunkered in what had been a sitting room.

He found a box of cigars with German writing on the box and chose a cigar from the wrapping paper, the label fresh and bright upon it. He lit the cigar and leant against one of the windows that had been knocked out, glass shards still protruding so that he felt their sharpness against his back. Where there were cigars there were matches and he lit the cigar and inhaled as deeply as he could, so deeply he felt the smoke to his lungs, making him suddenly dizzy.

Roger could see down the ridge to the British lines. There had been only desultory fire from the British artillery, their shells had fallen short, and there had been no machine-gun barrage to cover the infantry. The artillery should have moved closer to the front, but Roger did not know they had been bogged down by the mud. The mud clogged too the British machine-guns, their ammunition belts could not be replaced, and with mud in the men's rifles they could be fired but once and not reloaded.

Serjeant Amis and Albert came stumbling into the village.

They brought with them a platoon who dived for cover as a shell whined above them. The shell fell two hundred metres away and when Serjeant Amis and Albert picked themselves up they scrambled into the ruins where they found Roger, his rifle by the wall, his helmet on the barrel, his hair tousled a muddy-brown, his face brown with mud, but his black-bullet eyes smiling as they smiled when he had a prile at brag or his whippet had won or he had been ahead at pitch and toss.

'Have a cigar,' he said. 'We've liberated Paschendale!'

18

'I thought we said no heroics,' Albert said.

'Enjoy the cigar,' Roger said. 'There's more where that came from.'

The platoon fanned through the village.

'They don't know what to do next,' Albert said.

'Sit tight and hope for the best,' Serjeant Amis said.

He studied the ridge through the shattered window.

There had been a lull in the fighting.

The Germans had lain in wait in their pillboxes and strong points and dry emplacements and let their enfilading fire do the rest. Now their machine-guns had been immobilised, their front broken, but the British first and second battalions had exhausted themselves, the third had struggled through the mud up the ridge to the village, but the fourth was still held in reserve. There came again the stutter of machine-guns and the fall of shells. One high-explosive shell burst in the village street and house walls trembled.

The Germans were regrouping.

'Not enough men gettin' up the ridge,' Serjeant Amis said.

'We should invite them to a party,' Albert said.

'You mean like it was New Year?' Roger asked.

'The fourth battalion should be makin' their way by now,' Serjeant Amis said.

Albert knelt by the shattered door, looking along the street. The Germans were making their way back in two grey-green lines, one at either side of the street, their spiky helmets catching the dull light; shells began to whine, crashing down on the houses; machine-gun fire swept up the ridge towards them, bullets whipping and snarling against the damp masonry. Another shell fell close to the house and Albert scrambled from the door.

A lamp signal flashed from the British lines.

'You can read semaphore,' Albert said.

'It says withdraw,' Serjeant Amis said.

'We've just got here,' Roger said.

'Says withdraw to the startin' line.'

'The Hun's goin' to have the last laugh.'

It had been three in the afternoon.

The British advance had come to nothing.

Heavy rain had turned to drizzle and back to heavy rain, the breakthrough had been too narrow, German enfilade fire had caused heavy casualties on other parts of the three thousand-metre front and senior officers had ordered a withdrawal. An order to move up the fourth battalion had been cancelled and infantry began retreating across the mud in groups of fours and fives.

The platoon in Paschendale moved out too.

German snipers were moving up the ridge.

'Take your pick,' Albert said. 'Snipers or machine-gun bullets.'

'I'd rather a prile of jacks than seven-high.'

'You've got seven-high.'

They made their way back as they had come.

The culvert had been raked with machine-gun fire and the blockhouse trembled under the German shells. They gathered others around them, those pinned in shell holes, those who had been wounded; German machine-guns raked them as they retreated. Some of the men fell into the mud, others took more bullets, more wounds, the Germans moving up more reinforcements, snipers everywhere. The men staggered through the mud from shell hole to shell hole, to crater and back to shell hole till at last they reached their jump-off points.

There were more semaphore signals.

'What do they say?' Albert asked.

'We've got to make another front.'

'You mean we've lost ground?'

'About three hundred yards,' Serjeant Amis said.

'They call them metres here,' Roger said.

Another arc of machine-gun fire swept across them.

A bullet passed clean through Roger's left thigh.

The bullet severed an artery and as the arc swept on all three fell to the ground. Serjeant Amis and Albert dragged Roger from the jump-off point into a shell hole. Bullets spat at the rim of the hole as Serjeant Amis ripped open Roger's trouser leg and a scarlet arc curved upwards and fell back to soak the muddy ground. Roger felt no pain, only a sudden weakness, as he pushed his finger into the wound to stop the blood.

It had been as if the exertions of the day had caught up with him. They had taken his strength, taken too the breath from his lungs, deprived him of the use of his legs. He watched as if he were someone else as Serjeant Amis unloosed his boots and made a tourniquet with the laces, lashing tourniquet around Roger's thigh above the wound.

He felt cold and hungry and for the first time noticed the rain.

The rain fell softly into his face.

'Blighty for you, my lad!' Serjeant Amis said.

'I wish I was lucky as you,' Albert said.

'You see all that blood and you call me lucky!'

'At least we're alive.'

'The Highhill lads are present and correct,' Serjeant Amis said.

There were fewer shells landing behind the jump-off point but snipers were still moving up. Albert carried his brother to a casualty clearing station, Serjeant Amis leading the way, finding the plank road, stumbling along the chastened escarpment. Roger had passed out on Albert's shoulder, the wound still bleeding, but the tourniquet was holding and the bleeding less. The day had been drawing to its close, the firing began to cease and shell fire became desultory.

'They've lovely staff nurses in the hospital,' Serjeant Amis said. 'I remember when I was at Rouen after the Battle of the Somme and before they shipped me back to the battalion depot in Blighty.'

'You've never mentioned staff nurses,' Albert said.

'Not with Roger fallin' in love all over the place.'

Serjeant Amis looked again at Roger's wound where he had cut away the khaki. The blood had been less, the wound congealing, the high colour to his cheeks had faded behind the dried brown mud. As the firing ceased, Serjeant Amis took off his helmet and held it in one hand as they made their way back deeper behind their own line. He too felt drained, the tension easing from him, but feeling a quiet satisfaction that he had brought his charges through. Albert lowered Roger to the ground and his eyes opened.

'Am I back in Highhill already?' he asked.

'You can dream about it,' Albert said.

They made their way past the Red Cross ambulances.

Stretcher bearers were all around, there had been more casualties than expected, the casualty station could not cope, and the walking wounded had stumbled to a halt. They stood four deep waiting for attention, but they would have a long wait. There would soon be thousands at the station, waiting for fresh convoys of ambulances to take them to the railway stations behind the lines where stood the hospital trains.

'You're makin' it up about the staff nurses,' Albert said.

'If only you knew,' Serjeant Amis said.

After his leg wound on the Somme Serjeant Amis should not have been sent home at all; the wound had been slight but he had persuaded the nurse at the hospital he needed constant attention. She had not been able to persuade the sister. There had been tension in the ward on the morning the decision had been made; the sister had met with the medical officer and there had been a low-voiced consultation as he had begun his rounds.

It had been slow progress from bed to bed.

There were wounds to examine, treatment to be discussed, decisions to be made. Serjeant Amis had been wounded in the thigh. He asked the nurse that she remove the dressing. He had taken her hand and guided it to his thigh, only he had held her fingers closer to the short pubic hairs around his testicles, his strength rising. She had smiled and kissed him slightly on the cheek and moved her hand quickly away.

'Just because I come from Highhill,' she said.

'I wish I was back in Highhill,' he said.

'You'll know my family. They run the buses.'

'And the stores too, if I remember rightly.'

'Only you can't remember my name.'

'I've been away a canny bit.'

'Nurse Rutland to you,' she said. 'Barbara when the sister's away.'

'You can put your hand back if you like.'

Serjeant Amis had not come from colliery stock.

His mother and father owned an outlying farm around Highhill. His mother had come from a farming family and his father had served in the Boer War. His son had joined up as soon as war had been declared. He had not regretted leaving the farm or the village, he had no sentimental attachment to either and knew that however the war turned out he would never be back.

Serjeant Amis had short-cut blonde hair and a trim moustache. He had been strong and heavy, massive arms and legs, but he had been agile too, with a sharp eye and a strong sense of survival that had not been weakened by his exposure to the front. His father had lived through the Boer War and he intended to live through this one. He might be less strong now, less heavy, but the sharpness had still been there, even with the wound to his thigh.

'You must persuade the sister to let me go home to Blighty,' he said.

'It's only a flesh wound,' Nurse Rutland said. 'And you're lucky – no infection. A wound like that should have given you gangrene and an amputation. You could have gone home to the village – walk around Highhill without a leg for the rest of your life!'

'Try and persuade her all the same.'

Sister approached the bed.

She carried marked labels, red for constant attention, boat-lying for serious cases, boat-sitting for the fitter men in need of convalescence, and green for those to be sent back up the line when they recovered. Sister had noticed the sudden movement of Nurse Rutland's hand, the slight flush that rose to her cheeks, the way she held herself as if on parade, her shoulders back, her expression confused. She reached down to Serjeant Amis' testicles and gauged his new-found strength.

'Nothing wrong with you, my man,' she said.

The man in the next bed had been unlikely to last the night. Sister had pinned a red card upon him for constant attention, the medical officer nodded and they moved on, but hardly had they been out of the ward before Nurse Rutland changed the cards and it was Serjeant Amis who needed constant attention.

The dying man, should he linger, would be sent for convalescence.

Nurse Barbara had been tall and big-boned, blonde and buxom as Serjeant Amis liked to recall, but she had too an open face and pleasant smile. She had had her photograph taken that day to send to her mother in Highhill and Serjeant Amis would remember the blue uniform of pressed cotton, the white blouse and bold red cross solidly imprinted upon it. She wore a white arm band with the same cross and her blouse had been buttoned at the neck into a stiff collar.

Her long fingers had been as white as the blouse.

'Shall we begin where Sister left off?' she asked.

19

'You cannot fall in love with no staff nurse,' Albert said.

'He's already in love with Rose,' Serjeant Amis said.

Even Rose had become a distant memory.

'Better go and find a doctor,' Albert said.

'Stay together,' Roger said. 'That's what we said.'

'You're all right here,' Serjeant Amis said. 'The fightin's over.'

'All the same I'd feel better.'

'You need a doctor,' Albert said.

The casualty station had been made out of a large

marquee with red crosses blazoned upon the white canvas. There were smaller tents behind the marquee where the wounded lay on beds or stretchers; but when there had been neither beds nor stretchers they had been laid on the ground. Medical arrangements for the battle had been made with meticulous care. There had been advance dressing stations the length of the British line; there had been sandbagged collecting centres behind them. Medical staff moved among the walking wounded and in the marquee there were specialist surgical teams of doctors, nurses and anaesthetists.

An operating centre dealt with the seriously wounded.

Serjeant Amis ignored the advance dressing stations and brought Roger to the casualty station; he threaded his way past stretchers and men milling at the station entrance. He marched through the flap of the marquee. There might have been bombast before the battle, a discipline and will to succeed, but there had been little left in the casualty station. These men had been at their jump-off points only a few hours earlier. There had been sweat to their foreheads, their hearts had beaten hard; there had been a dryness to their mouths, a trembling to their hands.

They had been ready for battle.

Now they lay in shock, their features immobilised, their mouths tightly closed, the beat of their hearts slow and hesitant, their eyes unblinking. Some smoked quietly, some groaned in fear or pain or both; even the stretcher-bearers were recovering from a long day in the field. They had evacuated casualties in the face of enemy fire, in spite of snipers and machine-gunners, of rain and mud. Some were in shock and others wounded. Sometimes it had taken four men to bring a single casualty to a dressing station.

Sometimes eight had been required.

The fire had been so murderous, the mud so deep, it had taken two hours to cover three hundred metres to the station. They had seen their comrades fall, never having fired a shot, but they had continued into the dusk when the fighting had stopped. Now they sat or lay with their shirts open, the colour gone from their cheeks; their uniforms had been unbuttoned, their Red Cross armbands lying loosely in their fingers. They no longer noticed the stretchers or the men or the ambulances. Some kept their eyes tightly closed as if they would never open them again.

'I've no time for a leg wound,' the doctor said.

'This man got to Paschendale,' Serjeant Amis said.

'As long as he got back alive.'

The doctor examined a man lying on his side on one of the beds.

Half the man's face had been shot away. One nurse bathed the wound and another prepared bandages. The doctor prepared a syringe. The nurses spoke softly to the man and offered him a cigarette they pushed into what was left of his mouth. Orderlies bundled among the wounded men carrying screens and operating equipment. The man's breath had been foul, breathing through stale blood; his mouth and passages were still raw, with tubes fed into him to keep him alive. The orderlies threw the screens around the bed and the nurse who had been bathing the wound came out into the fresh air.

'You never know your luck.'

'Serjeant Amis,' Nurse Barbara Rutland said.

'I want you to see Roger. He comes from the pit village.'

'Is his leg broken?'

'Not broken,' Serjeant Amis said. 'The bullet went clean through.'

The doctor shouted from behind the screens.

'He'll need a proper tourniquet,' Nurse Rutland said. 'And I'll give him morphine to ease the pain. We'll need to watch for infection. Like your wound on the Somme. Infection kills as quickly as any bullet.'

'As long as he gets his ticket to Blighty.'

'Everyone's getting a ticket to Blighty.'

'I wish I was havin' one with him.'

'Another time,' Nurse Rutland said.

She stumbled into his arms and when she held herself upright Serjeant Amis saw a sadness to her eyes, a hurt, a lack of comprehension. It had been a moment of weakness for her but for Serjeant Amis it had been a moment of humanity, the first he had known all day; a warmth and affection, a familiarity that had disappeared as quickly as it came, but said that he too might understand because he came from Highhill.

'You should've sent a card,' Nurse Rutland said.

'I'll write from now on, I promise.'

Albert made Roger comfortable against the ambulance wheel.

They had taken to smoking in the trenches with weekly rations of twenty each. They had once tried smoking dried tea leaves but it had not been a success. Serjeant Amis rolled his own cigarettes, using a dark pungent tobacco that had filled the trenches with a rich aroma. Roger had left his cigar at Paschendale, but he and Albert each smoked a cigarette as they watched the comings and goings: the wounded, the nurses, the orderlies, the ambulance drivers, the stretcher-bearers, the prisoners of war, the straggling infantrymen.

The brothers heard the plane at the same time as Serjeant Amis and Nurse Rutland.

'Halberstadt,' Roger said. 'Spotter plane.'

He had learnt the difference between a spotter plane and a fighter, a fighter and a bomber, and depending upon his identification the men in the trench had either stayed or moved to their bunkers. He had a quick alert eye trained on his look-out for snipers and his observation had never been wrong as he picked out the plane no bigger than a gnat in the sky. He had seen the plane even before they heard the drone of its engines.

The *Halberstadt* had been a German single-seater fighter that had two fixed machine-guns firing through the propeller. Their pilots had been specially trained. They had been carefully selected from the officer class and given special courses at single-seater fighting schools in Germany. They had been moved to a more

108

advanced fighting school before joining their squadron close to the front.

Albert struggled from the ambulance wheel.

'Not *Halberstadt*,' he said. *'Kampf.'*

The *Kampf* came from the *Kampfgeschwader* bombing squadron. The plane had been built both for bombing and aerial combat, but it had been too cumbersome for dog-fighting, neither light nor fast nor manoeuvrable, and unable to climb out of the reach of the British fighters. Its pilots had taken to sneaking over at dusk, coming low over the British lines, flying no more than a hundred metres to score direct hits. Their speciality had been ammunition dumps and they had veered quickly after shedding their bombs.

The *Kampf* hovered as if suspended.

The walking wounded around the casualty station fell into craters and shell holes, rolling down embankments, oblivious to mud and water. Ambulance drivers and orderlies and nurses ran too. Stretcher-bearers dropped their charges, German prisoners fled, and those straggling infantrymen found the energy to run and leap into any undulation that would take them. A stillness settled on the marquee, the doctors paused, the anaesthetists too, and even the wounded ceased their frightened groans.

Roger lifted his arms to embrace Albert.

Albert had fallen back to protect him and buried his head in his brother's shoulder; their cigarettes had been lost to the mud. Three spindly specks come out of the *Kampf* undercarriage and drifted idly down. They were in no hurry and had no sense of direction till suddenly their cones pointed down and they crashed into the tents and marquee. The tents and marquee were destroyed, pegs and ropes uplifted by the blast, mud rising in an arc, shell splinters ripping through the flimsy canvas like a hail of bullets.

Serjeant Amis and Nurse Rutland picked themselves up from the mud. They could see the distinct Iron Cross on the fleeing *Kampf.*

Where Roger and Albert had lain against the ambulance wheel there was nothing.

20

'It was as if she had known,' Binkie said.

He had placed the telegram from the Army Council on the mantelpiece.

He had pushed the telegram behind the clock as he might a football coupon or betting slip, or a bill for pigeons his eldest son Ernie might have paid. Yet he had been aware of its presence. He could not imagine his sons dead but he could not envisage the trenches; he had opposed the war and closed his mind to its horrors. He had heard stories but he had not conjured them up in his mind. Better to leave them dormant, to die with his sons, but if his mind would not conjure the dead it would leave him with his past and his failure.

'You cannot sit there forever, dad,' Roland said.

Binkie heard the voice of his second son but paid no heed.

'The neighbours have brought in some pease puddin' and fresh ham – and they've brought a bit of home-made bread and teacake. I've made a fresh pot of tea. I think you should have somethin' on your stomach. There's the funeral the morn, dad. You've got to stir yourself.'

Binkie Fatherley sat in the downstairs room and gazed at the open coffin of his wife Bess.

They had laid her out in the room and rested her in the coffin; the neighbours had paid their final respects with the curtains drawn. Binkie had not moved from the chair. Ernie had kept the fire banked and the room had been like a furnace with the doors and windows closed. Binkie leant forward, elbows resting on his knees; he wore his best white shirt and black tie, a black waistcoat too, pulling on his dark coat he had taken from the back of the chair as if it were time for the funeral.

The coffin lay across the table.

The lid stood against the cot-bed, silver handles reflecting the glow of the fire, the wood meticulously carved by joiners in the workshops because this was the coffin of Bess Fatherley, wife of the lodge sec-retary. If the handles reflected the fire the wood had been as polished as a mirror, but from where he sat Binkie could not see his wife's peaceful face, the eyes closed, the white hairs combed straight by the side of her cheeks. Her arms had been crossed and her wedding ring caught the light from the candles in their brass holders on the mantelpiece.

There were no flowers in the downstairs room, no smell of chrysanthemum or lilac, only the smell of pease pudding and ham, fresh bread and teacake, the filled teapot left to stand. The house had been as quiet as if the grave already called, but the door had opened and closed as more neighbours paid their respects and left again. The fire glowed brighter in the light of the candles, the flames reflecting back from the black-leaded range. The strangers had all been swept from the bars and only when the coal fell and ash tumbled did Binkie lift his head.

'Who'll be holdin' the service?' Binkie asked.

He watched Roland rake coals from the back of the fire.

'My grandfather,' Roland said. 'There was no way we could stop him. And its o'er late to change the arrangements. Besides, he wants to do it – bring the family together, like.'

'Bess kicked him out the house.'

'My mother's dead and so are my brothers. My grandfather loved my brothers as he loves you. It's all because of the war, but the war's still here, only my mother's gone and my brothers are gone and there's little of the family left if we count out my grandfather.'

'We'll have to make sure there's room in your mother's grave for Roger and Albert.'

'Nobody ever comes back from France, dad, you

112

know that. They bury them in Flanders fields to make
the poppies grow. They say they bury them with one
arm in the air beckonin' the Germans to keep runnin',
to keep gettin' shot, so the war'll be o'er before they
know it, and all them that's livin'll be back. D'you
believe that, dad, because I don't believe it, but it'll
keep the lads happy talkin' about it and thinkin' about
it, I'll be warned.'

'They'll need to keep room for me,' Binkie said.

'There's always room in the graveyard, dad.'

Binkie lifted himself from the chair.

He did not look at his wife's face.

He could withstand Bess's wrath, her indignation,
her frustration at the life she had led, but the remon-
strance that seeped from her features, that he could
not withstand: he felt if once he were to catch sight
of her face he would fall into chest-racking sobs that
would have him flinging himself upon her body. He
stood with dignity, feeling the stiffness, the aches to
his back and legs, his eyes on the range, the oven, the
boiler, the banked coal, the table with its green baize
cloth: anywhere but on the coffin or the mantelpiece.

Bess had gone to the fish shop for a vat she would
make into a poss tub and had taken ill on the way back.
It had cost her three shillings for the vat where they
had cooked the fish and chips. She would clean the
fat from the vat and the blacksmith would provide a
hole in the bottom where she would insert the poss.
She hauled the vat up the cinder path to the house.
Ernie might have helped but he had been in back shift.

113

She had fainted at the blacksmith's, but the fresh air had revived her and she had hauled the vat past the allotments to her door.

Binkie had brought down a bed to the bed corner but Bess refused to lie for long.

'I'm not goin' the way your mother went,' she said.

'You need to build your strength.'

'I'll cough my lungs out in my own good time.'

'She's got a patch on her lung,' the doctor said.

'More like gallopin' consumption, you mean!' Bess shouted.

'All you need is rest,' the doctor said.

'I'll never see my bairns again,' Bess said.

'Can you not get them back on compassionate leave?' the doctor asked.

'All the way from the Western Front?'

'It would do her the power of good.'

'He'd not have them in the house!' Bess shouted.

'She talks like that all the time,' Binkie said.

'Gallopin' consumption, I tell you!'

'She's got a fever with it.'

'We'd better get her to the sanatorium,' the doctor said.

The sanatorium stood on higher ground above the village; it treated children suffering from scarlet fever or diptheria and others with tuberculosis. The air had been cold and fresh, the sun good for patients lying muffled on the porch, and because the sanatorium had been surrounded by farms food was plentiful despite the war. The doctors held no cure for any of the

114

diseases they treated; all they could do was to ensure their patients had the air, the sun when it came through the clouds, the rest and the food.

Bess had been weighed and bathed and changed and placed into a clean bed with sheets where she could look out of the window upon fields neither green nor white, but a sludgy yellow after early snows had melted. Her hair had gone from grey to white and whilst she would tie it at the nape of her neck now she let it flow. Her brown eyes had sunk deeper and were as hard as marbles. When she coughed her body convulsed and took a while to recover, but when she settled her head again on the pillow Binkie saw the waste to her cheeks. The fight had gone from her and with the fight the bitterness.

Her fever had quieted and he leant over to take the sweat from her brow.

'You're comin' out,' he said. 'The doctor says for me to bring your clothes.'

She smiled a tired smile.

'You've never been good at lyin' out your back teeth. But you've been a good man, Binkie Fatherley, I'll say that. A good man.'

'I wished I could've done more.'

'It wasn't your fault. Blame my mother for bringin' us into the world in a pit village. My life's been no better and no worse than many another. A couple of daughters would've done no harm, but the new poss tub'll work. Ernie helped – and Roland. And you never did run off with no fancy woman.'

115

'I've never touched another woman in my life.'

'But you have your eyes on the schoolteacher.'

'I want to change things, Bess. So women don't grow old before their time – so men don't get killed in the pit. So there's no more wars. It's not o'er much to ask. Only we have to fight all the way. And when this war's over, it'll all have to start again – the struggles. I'm sorry it took that much out of our lives. I wished to hell we could start all over again – make it different.'

'You'll make it different for others.'

'I'll work for it. I'll fight for it.'

'What's that phrase of yours?'

'A socialist springtime.'

'It sounds grand,' she said.

Bess had been tired and her hand slipped from his.

It had been dark and difficult for him to walk back along the pathways through the fields, but it would be shorter than taking the stony road that wound around the hill to reach the village. He sat a long while with Bess in the sanatorium. He could hear coughing from other wings, distant and detached, as if human suffering could be compartmentalised between those whom you knew and those you did not.

The doctor from the village came and stood by him.

'She was right all along,' he said. 'Galloping consumption.'

'You don't want us to bring her things?'

'She'll never open her eyes again.'

Binkie leant forward and kissed her brow and stayed

with her till the first morning light. He had smoothed her white hairs and had seen the troubled furrows leave her brow; the light stole over her pallid features and she had indeed been at peace. He settled the hair from her forehead and held again her hand. He raised it so that he could see her wedding ring. Not once had she taken it off.

She coughed no longer and her chest ceased to heave.

The nurse had laid her arms by her side and laid the sheet gently over her. Binkie felt some part of him had died with her, a part of his life, his past, some part of his being. He felt a weakness to his legs, a sadness to his mind, a numbness that stayed with him as he left the sanatorium, snow beneath the hedgerows, grass tufts above the snow giving way to green as he walked towards the village.

'She said a nice goodbye,' Binkie said. 'She was her old self.'

The mist had risen from the valley and dampened the mushrooms in the fields. Rabbits were out but they did not move as he passed farmyards and barns and men trudging across the fields to the drift: shapes that came and went in the mist. Their paths did not deviate and soon they were lost to the greyness. A set loomed out of the mist, low and squat, hugging the ground, and he followed its rumble till he came to the small bridge at the top of Slum Alley. A pale sun had been seeking to burn away the mist, but the mist lay like a heavy cloak across the cinder pathway. He felt it clammy to

117

his cheeks and when he pushed open the door to his house he saw the fire still aglow, taking the chill from his hands.

Roland sat before the fire, poker in hand, raking the coal.

'Where's Ernie?' Binkie asked.

'He went to feed the pigs,' Roland said.

'A bit early,' Binkie said. 'This time of the mornin'.'

'There's a stranger on the bar, dad.'

Binkie saw the yellow telegram on the table.

21

'I'll be goin' away soon myself, dad,' Roland said.

'And where d'you think you're goin'?'

'I've got my call-up papers. Everybody has to go now, dad, pit or no pit. It's what you call conscription. You shouldn't worry your head about Roger and Albert. They'd have had to go too – and who knows what would've happened, but they'd have had to go and fight and you couldn't have stopped it.'

'You're not goin' to the Western Front?'

'I've volunteered for Italy. They say there's a bit of action there. And it's no good you sayin' you'll have a word with the colliery manager because I'm needed in the blacksmith's shop. I'm goin' the morn as soon as the funeral's over.'

'Why d'you want to go so early?'

'Because you'll be startin' a new life, dad.'

'There'll be no new life for me.'

'There will dad. You know it and I know it.'

'That's what your mother said. She went to her grave thinkin' I was goin' to marry the schoolteacher – that Pauline Alyson.'

'You will marry her, dad. I know that.'

'You're the one that loves her,' Binkie said.

'You love her too, dad. You've always loved her since the day she first set foot in the village.'

'I've always loved your mother.'

'But it was Pauline Alyson that took your heart.'

'You marry her,' Binkie said. 'You're her own age.'

'Pauline's never loved me the way she loves you.'

'She doesn't love me either.'

'You'll see, dad, now that my mother's dead.'

'Did you get round to askin' her? Is that what she said?'

'She doesn't have to say anythin',' Roland said. 'Everybody knows it – that's why my mother knew it too. She admires you, she loves you for your work in the pit. She's opposed to the war just as you're opposed. And there'll be votes for women when the fightin's stopped. She says the Prime Minister told her mother. So that'll not matter very much. She only lives for you, dad – and you should live for her.'

Binkie Fatherley had now been forty-seven.

He stood short and muscular, with broad pitmatic shoulders and heavy thighs; he had a strong stocky chest and his face had fleshed out. There were jowls overhanging his collar, his dark hair had receded and thinned, but his eyes burned black as the coal he flung upon the back of the fire. Of all his children, Roland had liked to sit on his knee whilst he raked the coals, pulling them into the flames so that they flared and thrust out waves of heat.

Roland, too, remembered how he had sat on his father's knee; he rose and poured a pint pot of tea, handing it to his father. Binkie found the tea hot and strong and sweet and Roland smiled inwardly, for he had only ever seen his father drink tea from a saucer when he had come home black from the pit. Now he moved warily around the room, as if testing the stone floor, sipping at his tea, but not looking Roland in the eyes.

He never could recall his looking him in the eyes.

Roland had always been nervous of his father. Binkie had been spending less time in the pit and there had been more colour to his face, the cheeks heated by the fire, but his eyes weary with the time he had spent reading the Mines Act. Perhaps he had been too preoccupied, perhaps because he brooded and scowled and looked down in his concentration; it had been this that meant he had never raised his gaze to Roland. He felt the same respect, the same unease, the same nervousness he always felt in his father's presence.

'Pauline only lives for the young'uns at the school,' Binkie said. 'And for her paintin'. That one of Albi

Birt still hangs in the colliery institute. She's offered to paint me, too, but I've never had time with the war and the Mines Act and the meetin's at Durham. And all that bother with Charlie Bessford and your brothers. And your mother takin' ill with consumption. I've had a bit on my plate, you might say, but it's the young'uns she cares for and them paintin's – and nothin' else.'

'All the same, I wouldn't hang around, dad.'

'What d'you mean by that?'

'I'd ask her to marry you.'

'I wish you'd stay in the village and marry Pauline. I cannot see Ernie gettin' married. He spends all his time with his pigs and his hens on the allotment – but the hens were worth it when your mother was ill – all them fresh eggs. And them pigs of his keep the village in bacon all through the war. You've got to admit Ernie has his uses, but I cannot see him bringin' a woman to the house and settlin' down and havin' bairns and givin' me grandchildren.'

Pit sounds began to penetrate the walls.

They reminded Binkie that life went on whatever the sorrow: the rattle of stone down the pitheap, the noise from the brickflats, the turn of the colliery wheel and coal down shutes, the rumble of conveyor belts and screens where stone would be separated from coal. Binkie walked around the coffin, his hands behind his back, his fingers rubbing at the palms, yet still his eyes would not look into the serenity of Bess's face.

'Better pay your last respects, dad,' Roland said.

'The undertaker'll soon be comin' through the door to batten down the lid.'

'I paid my last respects at the sanatorium.'

'She was alive then. She's dead now.'

'D'you think if I look at her she'll forgive us?'

'Everyone's forgiven from the grave.'

'Maybe she'll never forgive us with that telegram on the mantelpiece.'

'She'll leave you in peace, dad. She'll not bother you. She might come back to you from time to time, but she'll not reproach you. She was a fine woman, my mother, but she knew the odds were stacked against her. She knew the odds were stacked against us all.'

'She said that at the sanatorium.'

'She always did like your socialist springtime.'

'D'you think she'd mind if I held her hand?'

'She'll not mind, dad.'

Binkie Fatherley paid his final respects to his wife as his sons and his friends and neighbours had done. And it was true, as Roland had said, she forgave him, if not from the grave from the open coffin. The serenity of her features conveyed itself to Binkie. He found his thoughts settling, a tranquillity to his soul. A peace pervaded the room, as if he were in a spiritualist séance where voices of the past communicated through the ether. Indeed, a spiritualist church had been set up in the village and its congregation had swelled as mothers sought news of their sons killed in the war.

Her wedding ring again caught the light.

Binkie had taken the trap to Newcastle from

Bedlington to buy the ring. He had asked the goldsmith to inscribe on the inside the date of their wedding: *7 June 1886.* There had also been engraved their initials. The work of the goldsmith had stood out in the light of the chapel when he had slipped the ring upon Bess's finger and she had shown the engraving to the guests in their wedding party because it had been something different. No other young bride had worn such a ring and she had felt it set her apart, that her life would be somehow different. With the wedding over her she had known once she slipped the ring on her finger it would never leave till her death.

'I paid for that ring with gold sovereigns,' Binkie said.

'Take the ring, dad. It'll mind you on. You'll have something to remember her by.'

'I'll never get it off,' Binkie said.

'It'll come off all right.'

The ring slipped easily from Bess's finger.

'There'll be no Western Front, you say?'

'I'll be on my way to Italy as soon as the funeral's out the way.'

'You take the ring,' Binkie said. 'It'll remind you of your mother and father.'

'I'll send it back one day.'

'I don't want no more sons bein' buried in Flanders fields or the like.'

'The war'll not last,' Roland said. 'They say the Americans are comin'.'

'I hope they get here sharp – before you see action.'

'Even if I do see action I'll live through it.'

'You're not comin' back, are you?' Binkie said.

He looked his son in the eyes for the first time.

He had become aware there had been more to the room than his wife in the open coffin, but as he looked at Roland he noticed how Roland held his gaze: there had been no mischief to his eyes as there might have been with Roger, no humour as there might have been with Albert, no vagueness as with Ernie. Roland had clear blue eyes that did not waver, that showed his innocent strength. Not a muscle moved in his face, the skin had been smooth and flushed, but there had been no grief, no sorrow; it had buried inside.

'I don't want to see Pauline again,' Roland said.

'As long as you take care of the ring.'

'I'll take care of the ring,' Roland said.

'And you're sure you'll not be back?'

'Not when we both love the same woman.'

Always, he reflected, it would come back to Pauline Alyson.

Book Two:
The Alysons

22

Pauline Alyson lay on the narrow plank bed in Holloway Prison.

She waited for the first light through the cell window; she knew they always came at the first light. Her red hair lay across the pillow and she felt the roughness of cotton sheets against her skin. She had pulled the sheets to her chin because of the cold, but the sheets had been too small and her feet stuck from beyond the mattress; they were dull purple in the sullen darkness. She ran her fingers up and down her body, the hips and thighs devoid of flesh, the bone solid where the muscles had wasted. The nipples to her breasts were stark and stalk-like, painful to the touch of cotton sheets.

She could feel her ribs and beyond the ribs the faded stomach muscles. There were sores to her legs and she did not turn on her side but lay flat, drifting in and out of a hazy sleep. She had never learned to sleep in Holloway. The mattress and pillow had both been filled with a shrub hard as stone, the blankets and sheets were too small, and the cold had been intense. Nor had there been quiet to the night: outside her door steps passed and voices sounded, and she could hear the swish of the wardresses' keys and a cry as a prisoner dreamed.

Or had it been a nightmare?

'You are a hysterical virago!' the prison governor had said.

'I believe in women's rights,' Pauline said.

'You bite, you scratch and you shriek. What women's rights are they?'

'I was being attacked by male personages.'

'Police officers doing their duty.'

Pauline had first been arrested for throwing stones through the windows of the Prime Minister's residence in Downing Street. She had humped the bag of stones down Whitehall and thrown them one by one beyond the black-painted railings. She had still been throwing when she had been arrested, but earlier she had been in the House of Commons, seeking a pledge that votes for women would become law. There had been no pledge and she had begun assaulting policemen till ejected from the House and flung upon the pavement.

'We know about your famous mother,' the governor said.

'I have no mother.'

'We know about that too.'

The governor had been so severe Pauline wondered if she ever left the prison. She was called Willit and neither signed nor answered to anything other than her surname. She had been small and stout, her face flat and unambivalent; an accretion protruded below her mouth from which grew strands of waspish white hair. Her grey eyes did not flicker and stared not only at Pauline but the wardress behind her. She held a slim file but did not look down at the white closely-typed pages as white as the light in her office.

'We see many of your type here,' she said.

'What type is that?' Pauline asked.

'Upper-class, leisured, unmarried, unemployed, unpropertied and unendowed. But not uneducated. You attended the College of Art in Kensington – now you choose to spend your days in Holloway prison with common sluts and thieves because you are bloated with your own self-esteem.'

'I think women are equal to men.'

'You think what is put into your head. Only the head will not be so pretty if you disobey the law of the land, make a nuisance of yourself and end in here. We have no special privileges because your mother is famous. Even your mother never ended in Holloway.'

'I keep telling you. I have no mother.'

There had been the visit to the prison doctor.

'Unfasten your dress,' the wardress said.

Pauline felt the eyes of the wardress upon her as the doctor went down a line of prisoners touching each with a stethoscope. She had been marched to a larger room where she had been told not to button her front but to undress. She slipped from her clothes and her skin reflected health and vitality, breasts small and firm, nipples uplifted, curves gracious to her stomach, her thighs rippling as she picked up the cotton chemise the wardress had thrown upon the stone floor.

'I'm Denise,' the wardress said.

'I'm Pauline.'

She put a finger to Pauline's lips.

'You're no longer Pauline. You're *Number Fifteen.*'

Prison clothing had been marked with a broad arrow; there were rough stockings too, black with red rings, and long cotton drawers striped red to match her chemise. There had been a thick petticoat more like a peasant's smock with a broad waistband Pauline tied around her middle to keep the petticoat fitted tight like a corset. Pauline knew they were taking away more than her clothes; they were taking away her dignity as a woman. Anger and humiliation rose within, but years of self-discipline meant she kept it to herself.

She had felt the steel of the wardress's keys against her thigh.

'You're not wearing your stays!' Denise shouted.

'I didn't have stays when I came in.'

'Every girl wears stays!'

Denise struck Pauline with the back of her hand.

'Next time I'll use my keys,' she said.

'You can be so cruel,' Pauline said.

'You be kind to me,' Denise said. 'I'll be kind to you.'

She pushed half a brown loaf into Pauline's hand.

'That's your supper for tonight,' Denise said.

Her cell measured seven feet by five feet.

It had a stone floor and barred window, the window high against the ceiling. There had been a flickering gas jet in an opening of the wall lit from the outside. The jet had been covered by tin and separated from Pauline by a semi-opaque glass pane. A wooden shelf stood under the gas jet and across one corner stood another shelf with a wooden spoon chipped with age. There had been a wooden salt cellar, a pint measure to drink the prison skilly – thin oatmeal gruel – a tin plate, a slab of yellow soap, a scrubbing brush for her hair, a three-inch comb, some cards carrying prison rules, and a morning and evening prayer.

A mattress and blankets were rolled upon a lower corner shelf and on the floor beneath the window stood a dust pan, a water can, a small wash basin and slop pail; also a brush for sweeping and against the wall the famous plank bed with a pillow on top, the bed's cross boards raising it two inches when put down for the night. A thin towel no more than a dish cloth sat upon a wooden stool and hanging on a nail had been a disc of yellow cloth; on the cloth was stitched *Number Fifteen*. Denise took the disc from the wall and attached it to Pauline's garb.

'Suits you fine,' she said.

'You've made me ugly,' Pauline said.

'You have nice pink skin,' Denise said. 'I like the colour of your hair.'

'I need my nightdress. Where's my nightdress?'

'Under the pillow where your mother used to put it.'

'I never had a mother.'

'You're stupid as well as silly,' Denise said.

The gas jet began to lower.

'The light'll soon be out,' Denise said. 'Better make up your bed.'

'I've never slept with nothing on.'

'You'll enjoy the touch of the sheet against your skin. It'll make you tingle all over. Don't you want to tingle all over?'

Denise closed the iron door and Pauline heard the key turning in the lock.

23

She was now on her second remand to Holloway Prison.

'How long has this been going on?' the chief medical officer asked.

'Ten days,' Denise said.

'How many days without water?'

'Five days.'

'What had she to eat before that?'

'A bread bun and a banana.'

'Why did she eat them?'

'They were brought in by a friend.'

'Why doesn't she drink?'

'She doesn't think a hunger strike alone will get the vote.'

'She wants to die instead?'

'Nor die either.'

'Maybe I should let her die,' the chief medical officer said.

'She's not yet twenty,' Denise said.

'Let me tell you what is happening to you, *Number Fifteen*,' the chief medical officer said. 'Your tissues are depleted of moisture. Your muscles are wasting. Your bowels and kidneys are ceasing to act normally. The poisons are unable to pass out of your body so you are retaining and absorbing them. You feel shivery. You have headaches. You have nausea and fever. Soon you'll be jaundiced. Your nervous system will go – and soon you'll be dead. If you don't die you'll wish you had.'

'How is Terry?'

'That's *Number Twenty-one*,' Denise said. 'Terry Kenny.'

'No better than you,' the chief medical officer said.

He had ordered food in her cell: tea, bread and butter, jellies and fruits, but she refused to look at the food. Nor did she dwell upon her thirst. Yet she imagined how she would savour the first taste of water to her lips, how sweet it would be, how cool; she would roll the dampness over her palate. But without water there had been a horrible taste to her mouth, her tongue had dried and coated, her saliva had become thick and yellow, and a bitter-tasting phlegm rose within her. She retched but could not be sick. Her urine grew thick and dark and passed with difficulty.

Her bowels had ceased to function.

She thought of Terry, tall and slender with short blonde hair against a white skin; she had a creamy neck and soft eyes and long fingers. She had been with Pauline at the College of Art in Kensington, a landscape painter, vivacious and beautiful as her eyes, a mind as agile as a doe, leaping from peak to peak in any argument, speaking swiftly, her speech a cascade of ideas and wit.

'I'm forming a suffrage society,' Pauline had said. 'You can be my first member.'

'Who'll be the second?'

'I'll hire a hall. Make a speech.'

'Who will you get to fill the hall?'

'Women, of course!'

'Where will you find them?'

Pauline twitched in irritation.

She did not understand the need for organisation; she knew other students at the College were not interested in votes for women. They worried what would happen to them when their scholarships came to an end. They wondered how they would earn a living. They enjoyed themselves at a College dance every three weeks or organised an annual ball. Their worries stunted their imagination and their creative work suffered.

Pauline hid her own anxieties, she too wondered how she would pay for her artist's material in her first year, but as she had sat through lectures on decorative painting and architecture she could hear the applause of the Manchester Free Trade Hall ringing in her ears.

Her stepmother had brought the suffragist societies together in a new National Federation of Women's Suffrage Societies; she had known there were female trade unionists in Manchester interested in universal suffrage. She had brought Kier Hardie from the Labour Party and had called upon Pauline to speak.

Pauline had sat in the Free Trade Hall numbed by cold.

She wondered if the cold would affect her throat, whether she would be lost for words, whether her voice would carry. Perhaps she might faint before she reached the rostrum. The worst did not happen, she had been alert, her voice clear, the timbre strong, and if she had been tense and expectant the eagerness, the passion – and the impatience of youth – had communicated itself to the audience. The response had been overwhelming and later she would recall how the applause had come down from the back of the hall in a wave of sound, reverberating from the balcony, rolling over the audience till it swept across the platform and reached the rafters.

'I'll be your organiser,' Terry said.

The first meeting had been at Caxton Hall.

'My stepmother wouldn't approve of these rough women,' Pauline said.

'You need women who wear caps as well as veils.'

Terry had filled the Hall by leaving notes in lodging houses and writing on pavements; she offered free sandwiches and coffee after the meeting. There had been ropemakers, waste-rubber cleaners, biscuit packers and chicken pluckers; there had been girls who made wooden seeds that went into raspberry jam. The tenements had emptied when they heard of the free sandwiches. The hall had filled with no-one interested in universal suffrage. They wanted to know why they should pay exorbitant rents for furnished rooms, or why they should earn seven shillings a week washing-up in restaurants yet have to pay six shillings a week for lodgings.

There had been no applause.

'At least women with veils clapped,' Pauline said.

Terry's father had been a London builder.

She had never known her mother who had died when she was a child, but her father had died only a few months before she entered the College and she had inherited his flat in Lincoln's Inn as well as a house in Surrey. The flat had a spacious drawing room and two bedrooms; there had been two other rooms for a live-in housekeeper. The ceilings were low, the outside stairs dusty, the windows too small to let in the light, but there had been a homeliness about the drapes and furniture that made the flat attractive to Terry.

'We can run our campaigns from here,' Terry said.

'We'll have to raise funds.'

'Women can practice self-denial. They can go without tea, milk or sugar – one or two meals a day. They might even get up earlier and walk to work. They might give up some of their evenings. They might take in washing, make or sell cakes, sweets, soap – or give clothing. They might stand in the gutter turning barrel-organs – or sweep crossings. Or become pavement artists.'

'How can we sustain it?' Pauline asked.

'We can have our own magazine – called *Votes for Women.*'

'We'll need our own colours too.'

'Why not green and white? And purple?'

'The colours must stand for something.'

'Green for hope,' Terry said. 'White for purity.'

'What about the purple?'

'That would stand for dignity.'

'We'd never get all those colours in a single dress.'

'The dress could be green and white. The sash could be purple.'

24

Pauline had not seen her mother since she had been six years old.

Her stepmother Ann-Marie would take her to Manchester and they would meet in a square in the city centre. Ann-Marie would treat her to a meal and walk around circular paths bordered by plane trees; she remembered the grass had been finely cut and the remnants piled by the gardener in circular enclosures hedged by privet that stood at each corner of the square. Her mother would come late and one day she did not come at all.

Ann-Marie bought her a sketching pad and pencils and she would sit on a park bench sketching the green daffodil plants; she noticed the yellow patches on the tree trunks where the bark had scaled. Sometimes Ann-Marie read to her because her eyes were weak, and if a wind rustled through the garden square she dabbed a little chloroform to a handkerchief and held it to her mouth.

'To kill the germs,' she said.

Ann-Marie had formed a committee for women's suffrage.

She set down goals and priorities. She defined those she felt had nothing to do with emancipation, such as birth control and free love, for both offended Christian beliefs. She saw nothing wrong with domesticity and childbirth. Motherhood she held sacrosanct, though she would have no children of her own, but she opposed state regulation of prostitution because this might polarise opinion and divert attention from emancipation. There should be emancipation in health and education if women were to attain fulfilment. She believed in the vote, but feminism should not be diverted into arguments on the length of a woman's dress or sleeve.

Ann-Marie looked upon herself as middle-class.

She had been a respectable theorist in feminism who enjoyed committee meetings, happy to expound in her drawing room but not to the outside world. She would not offend her husband, the Reverend Arnold Alyson, by embarking on speaking engagements; she would let others do that. She did not believe women should take part in politics once they had the vote and she would have accepted a suffrage bill that excluded married women if this had been a first step to enfranchisement of all women.

Arnold Alyson dropped in for a sherry at the end of committee meetings.

'You'll need the men for full emancipation,' he said. 'Men have power. They have political parties. Why should they part with power if women don't seek their help? And you must work with all political parties so that you are dependent on none.'

'We're not getting anywhere with the men,' Ann-Marie said. 'Or the political parties.'

'Even Queen Victoria declares she is against the mad folly of women's rights,' Pauline said.

She had been sent to the Manchester School for Girls when she was twelve and had taken to drawing with charcoal. Her old nursery had been converted to a studio where she would keep her pads and completed works. She noticed on the school notice board there was to be a debate on votes for women. Some at the school wanted votes for all women except servant girls, others for spinsters and widows. Others thought married women should also have the vote and some believed women should not have the vote unless they paid taxes. Some felt there should be education before the vote, that women should know how to read and write. Otherwise lower-class women would not know how to use the ballot paper.

Ann-Marie saw the suffragist movement failing.

Support had been dwindling, activist women diverted towards the political parties they had long despised; they were into electoral canvassing. One woman in Ann-Marie's village did stand for a county election but when she won her male opponent went to court to have the electoral verdict set aside. The judge held it beyond the common law that a woman could exercise a public function. Suffragists would petition Parliament to bring in a law declaring that no person should be disqualified by reason of sex or marriage. There might be equality for women in divorce and inheritance, but Ann-Marie knew something else would be needed if women were to be enfranchised.

That is, have the vote.

'I shall speak in the school debate,' Pauline said.

'You shall speak for us all,' Ann-Marie said.

It had been her first speaking engagement.

25

'We need a banner of our own, too,' Terry said. 'For our marches.'

When at the College of Art, Pauline had found rooms in Fulham but where other students shared lodgings she lived alone. The rent cost her ten shillings a week, her scholarship money came to sixty pounds a year, with travelling expenses back to Manchester.

The scholarship had been paid monthly at five pounds a month. She had wanted to make her own way without recourse to Ann-Marie and Saturday mornings she would go into Hyde Park and sell designs she had made for cotton prints. This made her a few guineas but because she lived alone, because she refused to share rooms, because she was a suffragist, she found the staff and students at the College hostile.

She enjoyed visiting Terry to draw and paint at her flat.

'We can use it as a membership card, too,' Pauline said.

'They're not very attractive women,' Terry said.

Pauline had sketched a cartoon of a woman holding a scarf inscribed: *Votes for Women.* Another woman stood holding a baby. There were other women carrying pails or tureens, their faces slab-like and unhappy; they wore long white cotton skirts, shawls around their necks or heads, clogs to their feet and striped dresses; there were no muscles to their arms and their feet were more men's feet than women. The message had been simple: *Women demand the right to vote, the pledge of citizenship and the basis of all liberty.* Across the top had been inscribed: *National Federation of Women's Suffrage Societies.*

'I'm not used to drawing women.'

'You should get some experience,' Terry said.

'How can I do that?'

'You can begin by drawing me.'

Terry removed her clothes.

'If you're going to draw me,' she said. 'You should have nothing on either.'

Pauline used crayons and pastels and charcoal, sketching Terry's back and shoulders, the curves to her body. She tried sideways poses, the chin uplifted so that her face caught the light; the light speckled the dust upon the window and fell in white squares upon the floor. Pauline tried other drawings where Terry held her hand under her chin and turned to face the artist so that the eyes stared back from the drawings. Pauline had her reclining on a leather couch where the antimacassar had been rough to her skin.

Terry complained and shuffled.

'I'm not working too well,' Pauline said.

'You're not concentrating.'

Terry took Pauline by the hand and led her to the bedroom.

'Try painting me against the drapes and silks.'

'I've never used oils before,' Pauline said.

She brought the oils and canvas and easel and palette.

She painted Terry cautiously but with concentration and patience. She had her sitting on the bed, head slightly inclined, eyes cast down; she sat in profile, her rose-red nipples suddenly sharp, a hand resting across her thighs. Pauline made less of the red drapes than she had envisaged, but there had been dabs of red in the blonde hair and orange flecks to the canvas. There had been a suppleness about the painting that surprised even Pauline. She had caught a young woman in repose, the background none too stark, the colours none too ambitious.

'I said you'd paint better with nothing on,' Terry said.

26

When Pauline had been throwing stones through the Prime Minister's windows, Terry had been dropping red ochre, jam and tar and permanganate of pot-ash, varnish or phosphorus into letter boxes along Whitehall. She had been arrested but released with a caution. Later she and Pauline had slipped into the Guildhall during the Lord Mayor's banquet; they had been dressed as charwomen and carried pails and brooms. They had broken a stained-glass win-dow in the gallery outside the Banqueting Hall and shouted through the hole, its glass shards digging into their cheeks.

'Votes for women!' they shouted.

Pauline had waited for the Home Secretary and struck him with a horse whip. She had broken win-dows to his residence and pasted the door with post-ers; the Home Secretary had ordered eight men with hose pipes to guard the residence, but the pipes were cut and the windows again broken. She had been arrested and brought before the magistrates' court, but the case had been dismissed for lack of evidence.

Pauline and Terry stood on the platform at Euston Station.

They sold ginger beer and apples and pears and served tea from a steaming cistern. Pauline wore a small sailor hat of black straw and a shoddy coat that reached to her knees. Beneath the coat she wore a brown skirt with an apron tied at the waist. Strands of red hair were like whispers of fire beneath her hat, but she had rubbed dirt upon her cheeks to give her a common look. Terry had pushed a pillow up her jumper to make her look pregnant. She wore a pinafore beneath a black shawl, a maid's cap to her head, looking as if she were Pauline's handmaiden, brushing the platform before the barrow.

The Home Secretary marched down the ramp towards the train.

He had been on his way to Stranraer where he would take the ferry to Belfast; he would make a speech on Home Rule for Ireland and he would make it from the City Hall. There were a dozen people in his party, including the Lord Mayor fully robed and wearing a cocked hat; the heavy gold chain across his waistcoat attracted the light. There were civil servants dressed in black, wearing bowler hats and carrying red dispatch boxes in their gloved hands; there had been a trail of silk and top hats moving down the platform, a pageant of coloured dresses and coats and evening clothes, snaking down the ramp to where the ticket collectors stood. The gates had been opened to let the official party through.

There had been a commotion around the Home Secretary.

A hawker's cart had been overturned, apples and pears were everywhere, and full bottles of ginger ale were flung above his head to smash into the Pullman carriage. The Home Secretary had been enjoying his cigar and the warmth of the astrakhan to his neck; he had been making a speech in his mind and savouring the peroration. He had supported women's suffrage. He had told a meeting in Manchester that women had a logical case with popular support. Yet he had done nothing to help a Private Member's Bill through the Commons and told a deputation that votes for women would not figure in his election address.

Pauline and Terry barged into his party.

The tea urn crashed and the party leapt from the scalding water; more ginger ale bottles were thrown, striking a policeman. The Lord Mayor lost his cocked hat and umbrellas and gloves fell onto the platform and under the carriage. Dignitaries fell to the ground. Pauline and Terry picked up their flower-patterned umbrellas and laid about them, using the umbrellas as clubs or spears. Pauline jabbed a policeman between the legs and poked at the eyes of the Lord Mayor. His wife had fallen to her knees seeking her hat, her fingers scrambling for the torn veil.

Only the Home Secretary stood his ground.

'Votes for women!' Pauline shouted.

She pushed the Home Secretary with force.

He fell over the Mayor's wife, his cigar and walking

stick dropping from his hands, the stick clattering from the platform onto the track. The gold knob stared back at him. He saw it through the sooty blackness. The stick had been given to him by his wife's brother shortly before he committed suicide and he walked with it as a token of respect. Now it lay on a sleeper beneath the Pullman carriage. The cigar had been of no importance box, upon box were shipped from Havana.

Pauline was still pushing.

The Home Secretary lost his balance.

He grabbed at an open carriage door but missed. He felt his shoulder go; he had last put it out playing polo. Pauline pushed again and his back fell against the carriage. Now Terry had been pushing too, pushing him between the carriages, and although he was a big man he could not resist their pressure. The buffers between the carriages were below. A polished shoe came off and fell upon the tracks, his astrakhan-collared coat half-pulled off as female hands were laid upon him. His top hat fell into the steam, showing his not quite bald head, the blonde hair thin, the skin to his head as soft and cherubic as the skin to his face.

A pillow fell upon the platform.

The Home Secretary looked at it with astonishment.

Pauline Alyson pushed again till Winston Churchill fell under the wheels of the train.

27

They came for her at the first light.

'I've found a gap here,' one doctor said.

'I've found a longer gap,' the other said.

'Better still.'

'We should use the wooden peg.'

'She's resisting too much.'

A steel instrument pressed against Pauline's gums.

'This one's too blunt,' the first doctor said. 'Give me the pointed one.'

There had been a stab of intolerable agony.

Pauline wrenched free her head but there were hands on every part of her body; she had been held again and could not move. The steel cut its way into her mouth, her jaws forced apart, a screw turned, a tube probing down her throat, and though she struggled, though she kept her body stiff, her muscles arched, liquid poured into her and kept pouring till she gave up. She vomited as the tube was removed and they turned her on her side. She raised her fingers to her mouth to push them down her throat, to regurgitate the liquid, to vomit again, but she had been too weak.

'We'll be back tonight,' the first doctor said.

Pauline had been sobbing when the prison governor came.

'You little slut!' Willit said. 'You were brought

here for abusive language, obstruction – and damage to property. Now you're charged with attempted murder! That disappoints you – you'd rather be tried for murder and hanged. And a Home Secretary dead upon the tracks.'

'She should be removed to the prison hospital,' Denise said.

'You think you can get out on licence because you believe in women's suffrage?' Willit said. 'You think by going on hunger and thirst strikes we'll let you out on condition you don't do it again? That we'll play cat and mouse? On a charge of attempted murder there's no way out – not on licence, not on remand. Not on anything!'

Denise helped her to the prison yard.

'Try not to fall over and make a fool of yourself.'

'I want Terry,' Pauline said.

'I'm here,' Terry said.

A hand of bone and no flesh reached to her.

'I'm destroyed,' Pauline said.

'Me too,' Terry said.

'I can't take any more.'

She had been three days in solitary confinement.

'You were always stronger than me,' Terry said.

'Not any more. Do you want to give up?'

'I've suffered so much,' Terry said.

'Did you vomit?'

'All over the doctor's clothes.'

Terry wanted to tell Pauline the doctor had struck her on the cheek and fed her again; he had kept the tube

148

deep in her innards. She had been so jittery the doctor had become alarmed. He had ordered the wardress to lay her on the bed and called the chief medical officer. He had wanted to test her heart, but the chief medical officer spent no more than a second with his stethoscope before moving on. The force feeding had continued. She had lost two pounds for every day she had been in prison and had grown so emaciated she felt pain even when lying on the plank bed. They had taken her to the prison hospital where they had diagnosed mitral disease of the heart.

The beautiful Terry Kenny, not yet twenty years old, would never be the same again.

'We should have killed him,' Pauline said.

'Killed who?'

'The Home Secretary.'

'Why did we want to kill the Home Secretary?'

'We need an ultimate gesture.'

'They'd have given us votes for women?'

'There'll never be votes unless we do something dramatic.'

'We'll burn down his house.'

'Nobody cares,' Pauline said. 'We'll make them care.'

'They frogmarched me into prison,' Terry said.

'Frogmarched?'

'They held me face down by the arms and legs – my face bumped against the steps. They cut off all my hair. My beautiful blonde hair you loved so much. The doctor said I was mentally sick – so he had my hair cut off. I feel like a mental patient. When I went without food and he fed me he said it was like stuffing a turkey for Christmas.'

'I'll make them pay one day,' Pauline said.

'Let us die,' Terry said.

'Only when they've paid for it.'

'Let us die together. We have loved each other and loved the cause. The cause is greater than us all, but we can only prove it by leaving this world, leaving it in our cells, leaving it so that the world will weep and understand. Even the Home Secretary shall repent and give us votes for women.'

'You're my first love,' Pauline said.

28

Ann-Marie stood outside the prison gates.

Rumour had it that a suffragist had died within the prison walls and other suffragists had gathered, pressing Ann-Marie against the railings. No-one knew if the rumour were true or where it had come from; the prison gates had not drawn open and the two policemen holding back the crowds said nothing. There were gas lamps at either side of the gates, notices pinned beneath, but none mentioned death, and if common criminals were being released they were coming through a side door leading into the Holloway streets.

Yet still the crowds gathered.

Ann-Marie wore a Spanish lace mantilla over her soft brown hair; she had been tall and spare and looked older than her years. She had been married to the Reverend Arnold Alyson for fourteen years. She had been his housekeeper and had gone to his bedroom one night and found him praying on the stone floor before an altar in a corner of the room. There had been neither gas nor electricity in the vicarage and candles flickered as she opened the door.

He heard the rustle of her skirts but did not turn; she saw in the light of the candles his deep melancholy and knew that he had been praying, as he would pray every night, for the wayward soul of his wife Mary Alyson. She set her candelabrum by the side of the altar and waited for him to rise. His nightshirt fitted him like a shroud and his nightcap stood next to the bed on a table covered by a lace square, his watch and chain set upon the lace. He slept with the curtains open to wake at the first light and pray again at the altar.

'You have to divorce her,' she said.

'The Church will not allow divorce.'

'The Church will allow an annulment.'

'On what grounds?'

'Blasphemy, heathenism – atheism.'

'I'm fighting a legal battle for the custody of my child,' Arnold said.

'Mary's child,' Ann-Marie said. 'Not yours.'

'How can you say that?'

'Because I know. And God knows.'

151

'I pray to God every day,' Arnold said. 'Every waking moment.'

'Do you confess your prayers to the Bishop? Do you let him know your innermost thoughts?'

'He would banish me from the Church.'

'He would bless your honesty and integrity. Mary meddles in scientific thought. She declares there is no God. You are seeking legal custody of Pauline to save her soul – that she might be protected from such influences – that she might be given a Christian upbringing. That she might be familiar with the miracles and parables of Jesus. You do not seek Pauline for yourself – your vanity or your egotism – but because you are doing God's work.'

'If the Church did annul my marriage – what purpose would it serve?'

'You could marry me.'

'Why would I want to marry again? I have failed as a husband.'

'Mary failed you as a wife.'

'The failure was mine – and mine alone.'

Ann-Marie blew out the candles.

The moon had been full and light flooded the room through the mullioned windows. Arnold stood confused, seeking to turn back the sheet on the single bed, seeking safety in routine. Ann-Marie could see confusion to his face, the skin tight in the light; she pulled back the sheets for him and her hands pressed onto his shoulders as he fell back upon the pillow. She settled him upon the sheet, his head against the pillow, straightening his knees, flattening his legs. He had been so stiff it was as if he had died and she was laying him out.

'You look so sad,' she said.

'I am sad,' he said.

'You spend too much time with the scriptures.'

'Religion is a great enigma – a great mystery.'

'It shouldn't make you sad.'

'Life makes me sad.'

'Not any more,' she said. 'Not after tonight.'

She rolled up his nightshirt.

Moonlight washed his body and she was reminded how Mary had washed Christ's body when it had been taken from the cross. *Yes,* she thought, *you were dead, Arnold Alyson, but now you are alive again; you too have been crucified, but on the Cross of Life, not on Golgotha but in your own heart and mind. And because you suffered in your heart and mind you suffered in your body. Your strength went from your body to your mind, but I shall reverse the process. Your energy shall flow from your mind to your body. My hands and my mouth shall bring you alive again, my body shall be your warmth, and the warmth shall touch your heart.*

'I'm in God's hands,' he said.

Ann-Marie smiled for the first time.

'This time you're in mine,' she said.

153

29

They carried Terry Kenny's body from Holloway Prison.

The carriage had been drawn by a single horse, its black shiny coat already dampened with sweat. The mane had been damp, too, the tail swishing, the nostrils distended as the pallbearers settled the casket bearing her fragile remains. She would be laid to rest in the family plot at her home in Surrey alongside a mother she had never known and a father she had hardly seen. The prison gates had swung open and four pallbearers had carried the black casket draped with the flag of the suffragist movement. There had been nestled on the flag purple irises and crimson peonies and laurel wreaths and white lilies: all laid upon the carriage.

There had been a silence from the crowd as the prison gates swung open.

The silence would not change as the carriage edged into Holloway Road towards St Martin's-in-the-Field. There would be a service at the church and the carriage would move to Waterloo station where a train would take the casket to Surrey. The horse had been nervous as it smelt the crowds; its hooves clattered and pigeons rose and wheeled and squawked and settled again. The crowds did not move as the carriage trundled forward, its wheels like tumbril wheels, but a slight crack of the driver's whip would send the horse forward, the driver dressed in top hat and tails, his collar over-stiff for his neck.

Suffragists would lead the cortege.

They were dressed in the colours of their movement: green and white and purple. How many of them knew that green stood for hope, white for purity and purple for dignity, and that the dress had been designed by Terry Kenny? They had come from her College, from her estate, from her father's business; clergy and politicians and suffragists from all the women's societies and committees up and down the country; those who had filled the Manchester Free Hall and Caxton Hall, who had followed Terry's pavement signs, who had read her newspaper and filled in her membership card.

There would be no banners, no demonstrations, no acts of violence, no civil disobedience, only the simple, solemn march down Holloway Road past King's Cross into Central London. The suffragists said not a word. They carried their own bouquets of purple irises and crimson peonies, but they marched peacefully, models of responsibility, their gaze ahead, not to the crowds of office workers and maidservants perched on window sills, but on the long road ahead.

'You thought *Number Fifteen* might have been on the carriage?' Governor Willit asked.

'I thought the worst when I heard the rumour.'

'She tried to hang herself,' Willit said. 'She was found by Wardress Denise who was bringing her a

155

hot-water bottle. She pulled her down and carried her to the prison hospital. She was able to get some skilly into her before calling the prison doctor. They forcibly fed her again, but only a little – to keep her alive.'

Governor Willit stood by the window of her office.

The office stood in the highest wing and below, in the shadow of the walls, she could see the prison yard where the inmates were exercising. The exercise had been less important than the fresh air; most of the prisoners worked, some in the laundries, others in kitchens; some scrubbed floors or shovelled coal into furnaces. Some polished furniture or dusted. She wondered where she might place the latest inmate who had been charged with living off the immoral earnings of other women and had been sentenced to three months.

'Yet the Lord took the body of Terry Kenny.'

'Had she lived she would have been charged with damaging a picture at the Royal Academy, of being in possession of explosives, of conspiracy to commit damage, window smashing, attempting to burn down the residence of the Home Secretary, damage to more works of art – and attempted murder. If God had been on her side Winston Churchill would be dead by now.'

'She was not yet twenty.'

'Sadly misguided by your stepdaughter,' Willit said. 'Had she recovered she would have been an invalid for life – unable to speak, unable to move. Confined to a wheelchair. Needing to be cared for every minute.

156

That is what forcible feeding does to you. It damages the constitution. It lacerates the mouth. It breaks and ruins teeth. It destroys digestive organs. You develop symptoms from which you can never recover.'

'Why go on hunger strike in the first place?'

'The quicker to get out of prison,' Willit said. 'To reduce the sentence. Some of these feminists – all of them middle-class, all of them comfortable – they go on hunger strike, but they have their maidservants smuggle a drug called *apomorphine hydrochloride* that makes them vomit back the liquid. The beautiful Terry Kenny – *Number Twenty-one* – had such a drug smuggled by her solicitor. Only she was on remand for attempted murder – not a suffragist charge at all.'

'You've not told me how she died.'

'Forcible feeding,' Willit said. 'The tube went down the wrong way – penetrated her lung and not her stomach. They tried to operate to remove the liquid but she was too weak. Pneumonia set in and by the morning she was dead.'

'What is to become of Pauline?'

'She should be charged with murder. She killed *Number Twenty-One* as surely as if she'd taken a knife and cut her throat. She led her into the suffragist movement. She made her a militant. She was a young woman with means – but Pauline Alyson appropriated those means for her own selfish purposes. She paid for a printing press and offices and secretaries – and when that was not enough she persuaded *Number Twenty-One* to embark upon a life of violence the likes of which has not been seen in any woman this century. Yet *Number Fifteen* is alive and *Number Twenty-One* is dead.'

'You said she'll never recover.'

'There are symptoms from which she'll never recover,' Willit said. 'The longest anyone has survived without food is thirty-one days. The longest without food and water is fifteen days. *Number Twenty-One* went beyond that. *Number Fifteen* tried to hang herself, but she's alive and she'll stay alive. The Home Secretary has dropped the charges.'

'What does that mean?'

'It means she's free to go.'

'Free to go where?'

'Free to go home – if she has one.'

'Why has the Home Secretary dropped the charges?'

'One death is enough. He'll have to give votes for women now – *Number Twenty-One*'s seen to that. You saw the cortege – the crowds? Besides, where is the evidence *Number Fifteen* tried to kill him? A melee on a platform – a woman who shouted *Votes for Women!* The Home Secretary fell under the wheels of a stationary train. Was he pushed or did he fall? Where's the evidence for attempted murder?'

'We can't have her back in Manchester.'

The Reverend Arnold Alyson had had a stroke.

He had been paralysed and could no longer speak.

'Pauline has undone the Reverend as much as her mother did before her,' Ann-Marie said. 'The poor man looks to the heavens as if God were about to come down in His chariot and take him personally in His arms. Why must one man suffer so much for two women? There is indeed a curse upon him, the curse of Mary Alyson transmitted through her daughter. Pauline left the paths of righteousness many years ago. She left the legalities of our movement. She has brought death to Terry Kenny. She must find a home, but it shall not be my home – nor the home of Reverend Alyson.'

A silence descended upon the governor's office.

It had been the silence of London, the silence of the docks where ships stood gaunt, where lighter men paused and let their vessels drift as the funeral cortege of Terry Kenny crossed Westminster Bridge after the service in St Martin's-in-the-Field. Parliament had been closed and peers of the realm and elected representatives made their own pilgrimage across the river to Waterloo Station. Big Ben chimed noon and upon its doleful signal the casket was again taken and laid to rest upon the flat-bed carriage of the train, flowers placed carefully around it. The flag of the suffragist movement again draped the polished wood.

The train travelled slowly through flat, hop-growing country. The hop pods hung heavily and beyond the fields lay the hop kilns, the funnel-shaped oast houses listless in the wind. The wind plucked at the flowers that had been laid around the casket. They passed houses where women stood in twos and threes – or had it been fours and fives? Emblems of the suffragist movement had been struck across windows. Some younger women stood at level crossings to fling more flowers upon the casket. The flowers were caught by the wind and swirled above the train compartments bringing other suffragists to the graveside. The crowds had thinned as the train moved into the countryside, its pace quickened and the last of the flowers were flung off. Even the white, green and purple flag of the suffragist movement became dislodged and detached.

The casket of Terry Kenny stood stark and alone as the train finally pulled into the station.

30

Pauline Alyson had been given warm water and two ounces of liquid food.

A nurse had given the dose day after day until she had been able to take spoonfuls of solids. She opened her eyes and did not know where she was, but when she closed them again it did not matter. She had been delirious as her body rejected the food. Her skin had become a fiery red, her pulse throbbed, she felt hot and cold and thought either the windows were open or closed. Her brain raced ahead of her: she dreamt she was writing articles and letters and resolutions for her society. She dreamt she was dictating to Terry Kenny. They were making plans, new exciting plans for the conquest of the world.

Where was Terry?

160

She felt she had been crushed by a steamroller. The more food she took the more the pain increased. She had been too weak even to raise herself on her elbows and the thought of standing made her dizzy; her digestive system had gone on strike, her bowels refused to move and she suffered headaches; eczema appeared on her skin and her toes remained red and swollen, burning like chilblains. She suffered heart palpitations and her nervous system had been so disturbed she started at the slightest movement.

Where was she?

The walls were covered with cheap paper, there had been an etching of a ship in full sail and two colour prints of a young girl at morning and evening prayers; her strength grew and she had been able to raise herself on the bolster to see a church steeple and school belfry through the window. There were tiled roofs and flaking brick walls and new whitewash on some of the backyards below. She had been lodged in a slum and she remembered reading that slums had been built upon rubbish-tips and their bricks and mortar infested with vermin.

There were cockroaches too.

They lay in the pink curtains and ran up and down the folds and when she woke in the early evening she had lit a candle to see them marching on the walls. The curtains had been boiled but still the cockroaches had settled in their folds; disinfectant had been placed in bowls but still they hurried along the wooden boards. Sometimes she found them on her pillow and had been too weak to remove them. One clambered across her brow and she had summoned all her strength to flick it aside.

A flag of purple, white and green had been pinned to her bed, scarlet geraniums in tiled pots lay along the window-sills, and when she had been able to walk as far as the window she had seen a young girl in the whitewashed yard below. The girl had short blonde hair and wore a white bodice and had come to help an older woman possing at a washtub. She heard the scrape of a mangle and seeing only the girl's back and shoulders she thought the blonde had been Terry. Even in the slanting light of the yard she knew she was wrong.

This had not been Terry at all.

Still she did not know where she was.

She thought in her delirium she had died and passed on. She dreamt she had been in Venice with Terry, they had visited an apartment and found it deserted; all the furniture had gone but the windows had been left open. She had to make her own way back beyond the canals and there were marble palaces and curio shops and slim Italian boys looking for portraits to be sketched; and older men, too, smoking long clay pipes, but even in the dream there had been no Terry Kenny.

She woke to find an elderly woman in the room.

The woman knocked cockroaches from the curtains and walls and pushed them underfoot as they scurried along floorboards to hide in cracks in the wood. She pulled the curtains closed. She removed the geraniums

162

from the window sill and placed the pot on a chest of drawers; the drawers had been pushed into a corner. With restless energy, her hands aflutter, the woman did not stop but noticed the prints of the young girl at prayer. She placed them out of sight behind the drawers. She took a broom and swept the cockroaches out of the room onto the landing.

Some returned under the closed door and she brushed them out again.

She wore a buttonless grey dress and light woollen cardigan. Her hair had been grey but not white, the face unlined but shiny with sweat, as if the sweat were cream, and indeed a pearl of sweat hovered above her upper lip. Her eyes were clear but the mouth stubborn; she frowned as she went about her work. She wore a single ring on an inside finger of her left hand. The ring had an emerald green stone set in silver and she ran the fingers of her right hand across the silver. Her hands were milky-soft but prone to sweat and she ran them down the side of her dress or through the folds of her cardigan.

She had lost an earlier thickness to her waist, face and neck. She had lost too the curves to her body, her chest had flattened, her hips bony, but she moved with a powerful grace. Her energy had long since consumed superfluous flesh and hardship had taught her dignity, yet if the clothes she wore were tidy they were not extravagant. She returned to the curtains to look out again and the light fell across her face, the features even, the nose small, the eyes alert, the brows arched.

163

Once a beautiful woman.

She saw Pauline was awake and let the curtain drop.

'I'm your mother,' Mary Alyson said. 'I knew you'd come back to me one day.'

31

'Where am I?' Pauline asked. 'Where's Ann-Marie?'

'Looking after the Reverend Alyson.'

'What's wrong with him?'

'He's had a stroke. Left him speechless.'

'I should go to him,' Pauline said.

'All in good time,' Mary said.

A man came into the room.

He too peered out of the curtains.

'They've found out she's here,' Mary said.

'I can see with my own eyes,' Albi Birt said.

'I'm sorry about the cockroaches,' Mary said.

'She'll have to be moved,' Albi said.

'Moved to where?' Pauline asked.

'Detectives have bribed a woman in the flat opposite. They've hired a room so they can spy on you. They think we don't know – but we know everything. Don't we, Albi? Even the money they're giving to the woman. We'll see it's passed to us. You'll have to move all the same. One step into a meeting hall and they'll arrest you again.'

'Why do they want to arrest me?'

'Called cat and mouse.'

'The arrangements are goin' along nicely,' Albi said. 'I've dropped a line to the Home Secretary and had a word with his private secretary. He sees no objection – as long as she leaves London. But she'll have to go within twenty-eight days. They'll not be extendin' her licence. And if she doesn't leave London, if she does anythin' daft, them buggers over there are waitin' for her.'

'What have I done wrong?' Pauline asked.

'They can trump up charges,' Mary said. 'They can say you stood on a street corner and made a speech. Printed a pamphlet. Ran one of them through with your umbrella – hit one with a handbag. What does it matter? They can trump up any charge they like to suit the occasion.'

'I've spoken to friends of mine in the North-East,' Albi said. 'There's a pit village called Highhill. She'll like it there. They need a schoolteacher. She has a College education – and they'll not be lookin' for any fancy diplomas. And she can paint and draw. She's bound to get on with the young'uns.'

'Do they all talk like you in Highhill?'

'Aye,' he said. 'But you'll find the bairns bonny enough.'

'Will they let her settle?' Mary asked.

'They don't know anythin' about votes for women in a pit village,' Albi said.

'We can only have the room for a day or two,'

Mary said. 'It belongs to a shoe maker – and they're on strike. He's sleeping under the arches while I pay his rent. I've told him I want the strike over by the weekend. I want them all back to work for the sake of their wives and children. I'm sick of standing on their picket lines and haranguing the masses. One strike after another. When do you think it'll ever end?'

'When the men get their just desserts,' Albi said.

'Another who believes in a socialist springtime.'

Mary had led a delegation to see the Prime Minister.

They had worn their darkest hats, their longest skirts, their most severe clothes; only one had worn osprey feathers to her hat. Mary had long ceased wearing dresses with hems torn off and solid brown boots for tramping the cobbled streets, but there had been no veils this day at Number Ten. They had met outside the House of Commons and marched across Parliament Square to Downing Street.

There had been photographers and reporters, but they had not averted their gaze nor slowed their gait; they were there to represent women and the working class and were not to be trifled with. A reporter who came too close, a photographer who pushed his lens into their faces; they would be caught with a handbag to their shoulders. Mary had explained to the Prime Minister not the cause of men on strike nor the starvation of their children but the privations of poor women.

'Women leave their children to the mercy of the

street,' she said. 'Only last week a child was run over and killed by a motor bus. And in a strike it's the mother who does the ferreting. Husbands are killed by accidents and overwork. What good has the poor law done? It is hated by every woman. Out-relief is denied to the widow and the deserted wife. Only the workhouse is offered – and separation from the children. Even when out-relief is given it is surrounded by humiliating conditions.'

'You have reinforced the point with your own individual experience,' the Prime Minister said. 'It is a moderate and well-reasoned presentation. I will give it very careful and mature consideration. I am right in saying that the substance of the case presented comes to this. That we cannot get substantial and intelligent reform unless women themselves have a choice in choosing representatives for Parliament.'

The Prime Minister had taken Mary aside at the end of the meeting.

'There'll be a war, Mary,' he said. 'In that war I shall need your help.'

'You're already at war with the militant suffragists.'

'A real war with real enemies,' he said. 'We'll need the support of the trade union movement. We'll need men and women to work together for their country. There needs to be a truce in the political and social fields. I need all the women of the country behind me – even those who chain themselves to railings. I suspect they'll be the greatest patriots of them all.'

'And when the war's over?'
'Your daughter shall have her votes for women.'

32

Mary had brought Pauline into the world on the factory floor.

Her own mother and father came from County Kildare and Mary had been born in Shoreditch; later they had moved to St John's Wood. She liked to say her father had been a gifted surgeon who had cut himself one day whilst operating and had died; he had been in fact a failed medical student who attended operations. One patient died from consumption and either he passed on the baccilus to her father who had cut himself in the autopsy or he had developed the baccilus on his own.

Mary had been very young when he died.

All she recalled had been the death bed scene when she had lain her favourite doll upon the bed. Her mother had aged with shock; she would never be young again. Her husband had died leaving her little, but she had two children to bring up. Her son William would attend Harrow school and she moved the family into a house near the school. She took in other boys as well as a house tutor and Mary recalled the drawing room of the house, the half-window half-door where she tore each new frock on a nail.

Mary had been eight when they had moved in.

She would live there till she was nineteen, except with so many boys in the house her mother sent her to stay with Aunt Mabel at Wimbledon. She would teach her to read and write and later Mary would recall how much she owed to Aunt Mabel, not only in knowledge but the love of knowledge. Mary spent her holidays with her mother, reporting on progress and walking the rooms of the house as if she had never left.

She learnt the Epistle of St James.

She learnt parts of the Old and New Testaments, swinging from a branch on the tree in the garden, reciting what she had learnt, moving from childhood to teens determined there would only be one life for her. That would be a religious life. If she could not marry the Church she would marry a man of the Church; she took communion, she fasted, she scourged herself to prepare for sainthood. Christ had become a living being, an object of passion and devotion.

Mary attended a mission church in South London.

She decorated it with primroses and violets and wild daffodils; their yellow bells preened themselves in the light through the stained glass windows. She had met Arnold Alyson one Easter when he had come to serve as deacon at the mission; she had fallen in love with Jesus during Holy Week and had sought to live in the times of Jesus. She had sought to walk with the Son of Man, to live as he had lived, feeling the pain of those last days and hours and minutes of his earthly life.

She knelt before the cross on Good Friday.

She stood before the empty sepulchre on Easter Day.

If she loved Jesus she would love too this clergyman who had been God's messenger. They had gone on holiday with a group of believers. They had walked and ridden and talked in the trap across the cliff tops of the south coast; they had not touched hands nor looked into each other's eyes; but Arnold had proposed and she had accepted. They had spent their wedding night in the same hotel, on the same cliffs, feeling the same draught through cracks in the window frames. Only now they were together, not in separate cots in separate rooms, but close in a double bed.

They prayed in the night but did not make love.

'I've never known affection,' Arnold said.

'We are married to the Church.'

'Even the Church should come second to you.'

'We are joined in love,' Mary said. 'We need not be joined of the flesh. The Church should come second to no-one.'

At the mission she had also met Charles Wheatley. She had been married three years.

33

'What are you writing?' Mary asked.

'Notes on the service,' Charles said.

'Not the service. The language.'

'Phonetic shorthand.'
'I've never heard of it.'
'Invented by a man called Pitman.'
'Can you read it back?'
'As if it were plain English,' Charles said.
A free meal had been offered daily at the mission.
Charles had been middle class and neither drank the soup nor ate the bread but made notes of the religious service that preceded the meal. He drank the tea Mary poured and warmed his hands on the stone mug. He scribbled his notes, his pencil ahead of his thoughts. His fingers had been white through the half-gloves, the wool heated by the mug, the steam from the tea rising into his face as he bent over his notebook.

It had been cold in the mission away from the soup canisters and tea urns. There had been no heating and the windows were open to let out the smell of those who had come to avail themselves of the free meal. Charles wore a long scarf tumbled around his neck and a hard-peaked cap he removed to scratch his curly blonde hair. He had fine features and light grey eyes and flared nostrils and thick lips Mary might consider sensuous if she thought of such things. He had been desperately thin, wearing stove-pipe trousers, tall and ungainly, his shoulders hunched, embarrassed by his height, seeking to pull himself down to her level.

'Religion is the opium of the masses,' Charles said.
'What's that mean?' Mary asked.
'Religion fulfils a people's spiritual needs, but it dulls their senses. It prevents them from thinking.'

171

Mary sat quietly at the table watching Charles work.

She liked to write herself and had been fascinated by Charles writing a language she did not understand: a series of strokes, some hard, some light, dots and dashes, some forms above the line others below, yet the outlines well-formed, articulate, neat and well-spaced. Charles kept his thumb at the bottom of the page and turned the page without a pause in his writing. His pencil had been sharp and as the room quietened she heard the scrape of fine lead upon the paper.

'You said it prevents them from thinking,' Mary said.

'Thinking of how their lives might be – not as they are. I can tell by your dress you live in a fine house. Why can't these people live in fine houses? Why can't they wear fine clothes? You are fit and well – by the looks of things. Why can't they be fit and well? Historians take the world as it is – the point, however, is to change it.'

'Sounds as if you're quoting.'

'From a philosopher. Called Karl Marx.'

'I'll not find him in the Epistle of St James.'

Mary had been uneasy on the omnibus back to Pimlico.

Arnold had become vicar of a church in Pimlico, the vicarage only a hundred yards from the church and open fields. The church stood compact, red brick and tiles and latticed windows that held the shadow, a weather vane perched upon the tiles. The vane squeaked with each turn in the wind and Mary heard the squeak as she walked from the omnibus that had brought her from the mission.

She recalled how she had analysed the scriptures and found so many discrepancies. She saw how people lived, the brutality, the coarseness, yet if the mission offered bread and tea and soup, if the Church catered for their spiritual needs, how could they move out of filth and grime and squalor, and how could they defeat the hunger that drove them to the mission, the gin that drank away their wages, the disease that carried off their children?

If God looked down what did He make of all this?

'I don't believe in the sacrament,' Mary said.

'The body and blood of Christ,' Arnold said.

'Wafer and some wine,' Mary said.

'Symbolic of the Last Supper.'

'I don't believe in the Last Supper.'

'What do you believe?'

'I believe the Church established by law is transforming me into an unbeliever and an antagonist.'

Mary had been converted to socialism.

The zeal that had carried her into the arms of Jesus now carried her into the arms of Karl Marx. She had entered into a world of real people, people with no set purpose, no set religion, lucky if they survived from one day to the next, but Mary might help such people by marrying her religion to her socialism. She gave gospel lessons at the mission, speaking strongly, holding a bible, but when she became bolder she stood

173

on the corner and shouted to those who would hear her, raising her bible in the air.

Only Charles Wheatley listened to her message.

'How can I meet Karl Marx?' she asked.

'I know his daughter,' Charles said.

'Meeting his daughter will do,' Mary said.

34

Mary felt Charles deep inside her.

Her body arched and she felt her stomach muscles tight; her thighs were damp with sweat and love juice, her nails deep into his back. He held her by the shoulders, steadying her body, but her head moved from side to side upon the pillow, blonde strands across the dampness, his lips seeking her out. His lips were firm and hard and warm, his tongue exploring between her teeth, and with her eyes closed she trembled and cried and sighed and trembled again as pain and pleasure surged through her in mystic waves.

Charles lived in a single room in Long Acre.

'As close as I want to be to Bloomsbury,' he said.

'You should be as close as the British Museum.'

'The intellectual air would kill me.'

'All the intellectuals are in Bloomsbury,' Mary said.

'And that is where you want to be?'

The room had been small and narrow with a single

gas fire and ring; the bed had been small and narrow, too, against the wall. He had no bedstead, but the room faced east and light came through the curtains hanging over the window sill, and only when shadows began darkening the dust to the sill did Mary realise the day was passing, there had been neither food nor drink, but still her body succumbed to the exquisite thrusts of fire from Charles Wheatley.

'I should have met you years ago,' she said.

'You would not have understood.'

'What is there to understand?'

'Love is different from sex.'

'It seems like sex to me.'

'The secret is to know the difference.'

Mary had to make money as best she could from the room in Long Acre. Her brother had qualified as a solicitor and offered her an allowance, but she needed to make her own money for her self-esteem; she tried needlework and accepted stitching at four shillings and sixpence a week. She wondered if she should join a Birmingham firm who wanted her to sell cruet stands and pencil cases.

'Can you see me selling cruet stands and pencil cases to Eleanor Marx or Bernard Shaw?'

She and Charles Wheatley laughed together.

'I've never known what it is to laugh,' she said.

'I never knew a married woman could be a virgin.'

'I was in love with the Church.'

'I am your Christ incarnate.'

'I am now a heretic.'

175

'Not to be burned at the stake.'

'I am still married to Arnold.'

Mary had gone to church for the last time.

She had dressed in a black satin dress and bonnet. She had not felt depressed; she had held her ground with Arnold. She had moved away from dogmatism and would not be beaten back into a faith she had abandoned. She had explained to Arnold she would not take Holy Communion again, that she no longer believed in the truth as laid down by the Church. He had pulled himself to his full height. His housekeeper Ann-Marie had stood in the hall, holding his cloak and arching it around his shoulders.

'I cannot accept Jesus as a deity,' Mary said.

'I forbid you to speak of your disbelief,' Arnold said.

He had picked up the communion plate and carried the plate and wafers from the vicarage to the church vestry. It would be carried to the altar with the wine that was the blood of Christ. Mary sat in her pew at the front of the church. The congregation steadily filled the pews and there had been a rustle of dresses and creaking of more ancient bones as the communicants knelt.

At the appointed moment, when the wafers were ready, when the deacon held the wine, when the procession formed before the altar, Mary Alyson stood to leave the Church for good. She bowed to the altar but did not cross herself; she held herself upright, her hands together. She stared towards the back of the church and ignoring the congregation she walked steadily, renouncing God and his works, accepting from this time forth she was a heretic.

The congregation did not stir.

There had been no curiosity.

A slight smile played around the corners of her mouth. The congregation watched her progress from the pew to the aisle, thinking she had taken ill and had left the church for fresh air; it would be weeks before they realised she would not be back. They would remember the smile, the moisture to her eyes, the steady gait, the thickening waist, but few noticed that if there were tears they were not tears of regret but tears of happiness.

She alone knew she was pregnant.

35

'You have brought my white hairs with sorrow to the grave,' her mother said.

'I love truth, mother,' Mary said.

'You love yourself.'

'I have found the way to truth is the way to peace.'

'Truth will take you one step forward and two steps back. I know all about truth. It exists only in the mind.' Her spindly fingers moved to her temple. 'Up here.'

'She cannot last the night,' the doctor said.

'What is it, doctor?' William asked.

'A valve has gone in her heart.'

'What can we do?' Mary asked.

'Nurse her to the end.'

She thought of Charles Wheatley and how she had heard the news.

She had lain on the bed, her hands on Charles' hips, holding him steady, feeling his thrusts, the spasms through her thighs to her toes. She no longer resisted his full mouth and let his tongue probe beyond her lips; she had held her head steady and the warmth of his body melted into her own. Her mind had been elsewhere. She had cast off religion, but she could link her new faith to mankind. In her youth she had wanted to be a saint. Now she wanted to lead a new movement of social righteousness, a true Commonwealth, a bond to bring aid and relief to the oppressed.

Who were the oppressed?

Women who were paid half-a-crown to make a dozen pair of shoes, finding their own polish and thread. Others who made fancy-best shirts ten-and-a-half hours a day and were paid from ten-pence to three shillings a dozen; they found their own cotton and needles and paid for their own gas and towel. There were mantel finishers paid two-shillings-a-week and sixpence for their materials. There were other women who could not make ends meet and who put their heads into a gas oven.

Mary let her legs wrap around Charles.

In her mind she had been in the East End visiting factories, looking for the brotherhood of men, the sisterhood of women. She felt his body convulse and collapse heavily upon her. She did not mind his weight as his breathing deepened; his head buried into her shoulder and her hands moved from his hips to hold the soft blonde hair. He slept soundly but over his shoulder she could see shadows cast by gas light beyond the window, the lemon flare of each lamp as the lamplighter tipped his way down Long Acre.

There had been a tap upon the door.

She eased from Charles.

She could see her swelling belly in the lemon light through the window and felt her skin warm and firm as she dragged a nightgown across her shoulders, pulling her arms into the sleeves. How many months to go? Perhaps three. Perhaps more than that. She had not kept a proper count. The nightgown fell loosely around her and she felt bloated and slattern as she opened the door. The light had been stronger on the landing where the gas lamp stuttered and flickered.

Arnold Alyson stood in the lamplight.

He wore a cape around his shoulders and held his gloves and walking stick. His black hair had been pomaded to his scalp and the lemon cast to his features accentuated his thick lips. Pauline stood back and let the dressing gown fall open. Arnold looked at the distended belly. His gaze travelled to the tired face and ruffled hair. Mary let the door swing open but Arnold did not move; nor did Charles stir in the bed. Arnold stiffened, protruding his chest, rising on his toes to give him height. He did not lose his self-control. There had been a slight bow, his lips parted, but there had been nothing sardonic about the smile; rather tragedy and sympathy curled the edges.

'You're mother's dying,' he said.

Yet she had clung to life.

Perhaps it had been the sight of her family around her, perhaps the last flickering will to live; or perhaps her body had been stronger than her ailing heart. She wanted to lift herself up, she pulled at the pillows, she grasped the hands of William's children. She wanted to speak to Arnold, to plead forgiveness for Mary; she wanted to embrace William's wife. Silken dresses rustled in the room, shadows roamed the walls whilst her eyes smiled upon those who had gathered there. Her shard frame relapsed again. Dropsy set in and her strength began to fail.

William asked Arnold to administer the last sacrament.

'Mary will have to leave the house,' he said.

'Her mother is dying.'

'She has renounced God. She has renounced the sacrament.'

'You cannot let me die without the sacrament,' Mary's mother said.

Mary had gone through to the scullery.

She had taken her mother's best silver tray from the cupboard; engraved upon the tray had been scenes from the coronation of a young Queen Victoria. She polished the surface with a wash leather and could see her reflection as if she were back at the vicarage on a

Sunday morning. She set the tray upon the table and took a loaf from the pantry; the crust had been hard, the bread firm, and she had sliced the bread, holding the loaf to her chest; she had pealed the crust from each slice before kneading the fragments into wafers. She rolled the wafers flat with a rolling pin so that each wafer had been as round and delicate as a snowflake.

She laid each wafer upon the tray.

She had converted a communion plate and carried the plate through to her mother's bedroom. Arnold had been ready to administer the sacrament, but she ignored Arnold and went through the service with William. Her mother could no longer be bolstered with pillows and took the thin wafer on the tip of her tongue. She lay on her side and a hand reached out to touch Mary. Her eyes never left her daughter. They said that all her life she had done her duty by God; this sacrament had been her act of worship. It had been a symbol of her unity with Christ.

Why could it not be a symbol for Mary?

'Take communion with me,' she said.

'She wants you to participate,' William said.

'I swear I cannot,' Mary said.

'It will make her die happy.'

'I will forgive you,' her mother said.

'Perhaps God will forgive you too,' William said.

Arnold stood impervious beside her.

'It is God's will,' he said.

Mary Alyson took communion for the last time.

When her mother died her jaw dropped.

Everyone noticed the wafer had not dissolved upon her tongue.

36

Mary walked with her brother in the garden of their childhood.

'You are with child,' William said.

She watched the dead autumn leaves scrape along the roots of the cherry trees.

'You must return to Arnold,' he said.

'Arnold is not the father.'

'One of your socialist friends?'

'I have only one socialist friend.'

'Does he love you very much?'

'We share the same ideals.'

'You once shared those with Arnold.'

'I am at one with reality,' Mary said. 'Now that I am with Charles.'

'As you see reality.'

'I want justice for women. I have suffered enough – yet I see suffering in others. I shall not rest till I have formed a League for Female Labour. Those who join shall be women of standing. They will only buy goods from those shops I have certified to be clean from an unfair wage.'

'What about the baby?'

'My mother is dead. We are talking about renewal.'

'There will be difficulties with my wife and children,' William said. 'We are a Christian family. We dwell in the ways of the Church. They are no longer your ways, but the pathways of God shall guide us all. My family might feel tainted.'

'I shall not darken your door.'

'Not everyone sees the world as you do,' William said. 'There is convention – settled marriage, churchgoing, children. Atheism and socialism are contrary to our teachings. They bode no good for the world – nay, they bode ill. They bode darkness and evil. There are many who find them offensive.'

After the service Mary had held back in the church when the mourners had gone to the graveside. She had climbed into the pulpit; she had held its sides, she had closed her eyes and delivered her own sermon. Words filled her mind. She wanted to pay one final respect to the altar. Her destiny had pushed her forward, the empty church had grown wider and higher, and she found her speech no longer in her mind but on her tongue. Her voice boomed from the vestry walls; self-confidence mingled with defiance. Her voice grew stronger till she reached her peroration.

She collapsed in the pulpit.

When she revived she found Arnold and William each holding a scented handkerchief to her nostrils. They helped her to her feet and brought her slowly down the aisle to the church door; the fresh air struck her face and when her eyes fully opened she saw the mound of ignominious clay where her mother would lie buried. The service had gone on without her. She had said goodbye from the pulpit to her mother and husband and brother; they had ignored her ravings and laid her mother to rest. Mourners assumed she had been seized by melancholy and had looked from her as they left the graveyard.

'I shall never set foot in church again,' she said.

'You must go home to Arnold,' William repeated.

'The child must have a proper home,' Arnold said.

'I shall fulfil my destiny – whatever my destiny may be.'

'She's still delirious,' William said.

'God has forgiven her,' Arnold said. 'He has forgiven her through her mother. He has punished her enough.'

A soft mist clung around the graveyard.

The clay lay damp in mounds around the grave where gravediggers were now throwing the first clods upon the oak casket. Mary saw the dull glint to their shovels, she heard their damp scrape upon the clay. She felt stronger, the scent from the handkerchiefs overpowering her nostrils; she settled her hat and adjusted her dress and coat and moved from the church past the open grave towards the gates. She did not turn for one final look. She heard only the turn of shovels and the soft fall of clay.

'Her single-mindedness brings her happiness,' William said.

A single tear ran down Arnold's cheek.

He had been overwhelmed by the spirituality of it

all. Perhaps his own faith had been too rigid. Had he really understood the workings of God's mind? Had he not understood God could interpret man and his works not over the length of a day or week or month but over an eternity? Mary might leave his life through the mist, she might not know her future, her destiny, but God would know. His omnipotence sprang from such knowledge. There could be no such thing as rigidity in faith. The mist-filled air freshened his lungs and his uncertainty passed. Sternness settled again upon his features.

They were dampened only by the solitary tear.

'You are crying for Mary?' William asked.

'I am crying for the child,' Arnold said.

37

'Is this a summons?' Charles Wheatley asked.

'You've never had a summons in your life,' Mary said.

'It looks like a summons.'

'It's a contract,' Mary said.

'What kind of contract?'

'Between you and me.'

'A marriage contract?'

'An understanding between us. So we know each other's rights.'

'Why should we have it written down?'

'Not only written down,' Mary said. 'Signed too.'

'Isn't my word good enough?'

'I'd rather your love,' Mary said.

'You've got that already.'

'Your new favourite's Eleanor Marx.'

Mary had taken the lease of a house opposite the British Museum. She had become part of the Bloomsbury set. Her mother had forgiven her long before her death; she had provided for her in her will. She had taken in other Harrow boys and a house tutor long after William had left to do solicitors' articles and the money she had saved she had left to Mary. She had enough not only to live comfortably but to fulfil her life's mission.

That mission included Charles Wheatley.

'We have to have piano duets on Monday evenings?'

'And one-act plays on Tuesdays.'

'Why do we need one-act plays?' Charles asked.

'We can keep up our culture.'

'There's a regular holiday at Broadstairs?'

'You wouldn't want us to return to the hotel where Arnold proposed?'

There were other details in the contract: who was to cook, what they were to eat, who would do the washing, how they would spend their Sundays. Mary would never forget the state of Charles' room in Long Acre: grime to the windows, letters and manu-scripts, half-finished articles, books, envelopes, writ-ing papers and pens intermingled with butter; sugar, apples, knives, forks, spoons, the cup of cocoa or half-finished porridge; clothing on the floor or chairs or bed. The smell, too, with the windows closed. The sourness and staleness had been like a dry flannel to Mary's face.

'We shall need an organised life,' Mary said.

'You want me to spend Saturday afternoon in the Reading Room of the British Museum – to strengthen my mind and have ideas for articles. You want me to give *you* the money I get from the articles.'

'I want *you* to write more articles and get more money so *you* can fulfil your potential,' Mary said. 'We can continue our mission. Don't you see – we are equals. I cannot subordinate my will to yours. You cannot make me a slave to housework or cooking or darning or needling. Our destiny is shared – for the benefit of mankind.'

'It says which meals I am to cook and which dishes to wash. I shall iron my own shirts. I shall turn off the gas at night. I must sit in the library of my own home.'

'I don't want porridge on our books.'

The house had high ceilings and large windows.

A chestnut tree stood in the avenue and in springtime Mary would enjoy its white phlox. She disliked dark curtains and had bought curtains of silken yellow; the sun streamed in and she would stand by the window and, looking across to the British Museum, project herself into the Reading Room where Bernard Shaw spent his time as had Karl Marx before him. She paused with her hand upon the curtain. She reflected there were so many books to read and so little time to read them.

There would be one bedroom for Charles and another for herself. There would be a third for guests or friends who wanted to discuss atheism, socialism or feminism, and where she could bed them down for the night. A piano would be installed on the second floor where she would house the library. The library would be shelved to the windows, but there would be a fireplace and three sets of shelves so that there would be no library like it outside the British Museum. Meals would be taken downstairs in the basement, except when there were guests they would take them in the library.

She made no provision for her child.

'I thought there was to be a nursemaid?' Charles said.

'I'll make up a bed in the basement.'

'You should see a doctor. At least a midwife.'

'Nature will take its course.'

'Sometimes nature needs a helping hand.'

'The ones who need help are the match girls,' Mary said.

38

'The match girls want to make me secretary of their new union,' Mary said.

'You should think of the baby,' Charles said.

'I have more factories to visit tomorrow.'

'You should rest and make yourself comfortable.'

'My match girls will know what to do.'

They had given Mary an office at the factory.

The girls worked for a match-making company in the East End. They paid dividends to their shareholders but not much to their employees; these were fifteen and sixteen-year-old girls employed as piece-workers. Rose Basten had been such a girl. She had waited for Mary outside the graveyard where her mother had been buried and together they had taken a train to London. She had been one of a family of eleven; her mother was illiterate and took in washing. Her father had worked from the age of ten, first as a page boy and then as a pot boy before earning himself enough to be apprenticed to an engineering company.

Rose lived with her sister in a single room.

'I get four shillings a week,' she said.

'What of your sister?'

'She works for the same company. She gets eight shillings because she's older.'

'How much is the rent?'

'We pay two shillings each.'

'How do you live?'

'We get bread and butter and tea twice a day. We save up and once a month we treat ourselves to a proper meal in a corner house – coffee and bread and butter and jam and marmalade – and real loaves!'

'Seems like white slavery to me.'

189

Mary wrote an article condemning the match company.

They threatened her with libel and sacked Rose.

The other girls came out on strike.

Some fourteen hundred girls left the factory, but with no money they soon became destitute. Mary called for a public subscription. She registered the girls for strike pay, wrote more articles, roused the socialist clubs, held public meetings; she wrote to Members of Parliament and they put questions to Ministers across the floor of the House. She even wrote to the company's shareholders:

'Do you know the match girls carry boxes on their heads until their hair is rubbed off and their young heads are bald at fifteen? Do you know they suffer from chemical poisoning? Country clergymen with shares in the company, draw down on your knee your fifteen-year-old daughter, pass your hand tenderly over the silky, clustering curls; rejoice in the thick shiny tresses. Imagine that she works for the company where you have shares!'

Mary gave each girl a rose to place in her bonnet.

She sent the girls marching down Whitehall to Westminster. They must always be polite, always humble. She cleared the march with the Metropolitan Police so that there would be no violence. She set up a club in the East End. She found an old house not far from the factory and renovated the house with money left by her mother. There would be a hallway and in the rooms a piano and newspapers and magazines, tables for games. The club would be an alternative home; most of the girls had no real home. She wanted it lit and cheerful, but there would be no stern discipline, no prim behaviour.

The girls had yet to win their strike.

There had been pressure from the press and from the government and from shareholders. Not everyone had been a clergyman but enough of them had fifteen-year-old daughters. The London Trades Council agreed to act as arbitrators; the strike would be settled and the girls went back to work with no fines and no deductions. Their wages would be improved and a new union established: *The Matchmakers' Union.* It would be the strongest women's union in England.

All fourteen hundred girls signed on.

But if there had been suffering among the match girls, there had been even worse suffering among the box makers. They had lost their jobs through no fault of their own. They had not gone on strike. They had not been upset with management. Yet when the supply of matches had ceased, the match girls on strike, they had been made redundant or locked out. Their pay and conditions were as bad as those of the match girls. They were paid two-pence-farthing per gross of boxes. They bought their own string and paste, but whilst two-pence-farthing had not been a living wage it was better than destitution.

'What is the cure for sorrow?' Mary asked.

Hardly had she helped the box makers than the cry went up from the tin-box makers; they were sometimes mutilated by machinery that had not been fenced. They were illegally fined. There were illegal fines, too, upon shop assistants and legal defences to mount. There were more factories to visit: the furriers, the capmakers, the tailors, the tramwaymen and housepainters. There had been her campaign for a free meal for children, fair wages from all public bodies, and if she had no interest in a seat in Parliament her name had been put forward for the school board of Tower Hamlets.

She had come top of the poll.

A new manager had been appointed to the match factory to see the girls' grievances would be met. Mary would meet him within half an hour, but she could hardly stand. Contraction pains made her so weak she settled upon the couch. The couch had been badly worn, the leather torn, the springs uncomfortable, the arms bare with small spelks that impaled her skin. Charles had told her she had lost the art of smiling. There had been only a pensive frown to her features, a brittleness to her gait, her mind always turning around some dispute with an employer, some argument with a magistrate, some tirade with a newspaper reporter.

'The girls would like you to have the baby on the factory floor,' Rose said.

'I've never had a baby before,' Mary said.

'We can carry the couch through and put up a screen.'

'Who'll bring the baby into the world?'

'There'll be an almighty cheer when it arrives.'

'What of the manager?'

'He says we can all have time off till the baby arrives. He's summoned his own personal doctor and a midwife from the local hospital. The girls can look after you too – and the baby.'

'Socialism pays after all,' Mary said.

39

Her brother William had come to see Mary in Bloomsbury.

'My wife's with child,' he said.

'That should please you,' Mary said.

'She looks upon childbirth as a great joy.'

'Not me,' Mary said.

'Not everyone has their baby on a factory floor.'

'The company doctor looked after me.'

'It is a matter of good fortune that you both survived.'

'I shall never make love again,' Mary said.

'At least Pauline is well.'

She had in fact been a sickly child.

She had caught whooping cough when only a few months old. The whooping cough turned to bronchitis and bronchitis to congestion of the lungs. Mary had placed her in the spare bedroom and lit a fire; a screen had been placed around the bed to make a tent. The tent she had kept filled with steam to ease the child's breath. She sat alone with Pauline day and night. She discovered that rather than giving her to the care of a nurse, she had loved her from the first labour pains, the first birth pangs, and when she fell ill all the things that mattered suddenly did not matter at all.

She had even been tempted to pray to God to save her.

Because she could not pray she fell back upon the steam-filled tent. The doctor feared that paroxysms of coughing would kill Pauline and Mary found even a drop or two of milk would bring on a convulsive choking. It seemed cruel that the child should live. Perhaps she should be allowed to die to ease the pain. Perhaps she should take down the tent, cease placing milk drops upon her tongue; her eyes were still closed, her small fists bunched. Her body had swelled and the retching cough seemed to be the child's last.

'She cannot last the day,' the doctor said.

He took a bottle of chloroform.

He put a drop into a handkerchief and held it near the child's face till the drug soothed the convulsive struggle. Pauline's body suddenly relaxed, a peace settled upon her features, and Mary thought it would be the peace of death. She had seen the same peace in her mother's face when at last life had escaped her body. The chloroform worked some kind of miracle; it had done more than ease Pauline's suffering.

It had saved her life.

Pauline would never know how ailing she had been, how much attention her mother had given her. For years to come there would always be a bottle of chloroform by her bed so that whenever she had a coughing fit or convulsive attack, when she suffered exhaustion, there would be a touch of chloroform upon a handkerchief to induce sleep that would be a prelude to her recovery. Mary had collapsed and spent a week in bed. She had not seen Charles Wheatley in all the time Pauline had been ill.

Nor did he move into Bloomsbury or sign the contract.

'I can't keep up with you,' he said.

'All you need is confidence.'

'I was better off writing my shorthand notes on sermons at the mission. I'm burnt out already. You'll be burnt out too if you're not careful.'

Mary had wanted Charles to stand for municipal elections. She had written a pamphlet for him: *Facts for Londoners.* She would reveal the private and public interests of all those who controlled life in the capital. She wanted political novelty but no revolution. She wanted democracy and government machinery used for socialist ends. 'All the things you said to me at Long Acre.'

Charles went instead to live with Eleanor Marx.

'I should never have given him the contract.'

'You gave him the contract to be shot of him,' Bernard Shaw said.

'I didn't want any more children,' Mary said.

'Once he goes through her money he'll be gone soon enough.'

'I didn't know Eleanor had money.'

'All revolutionaries have money.'

Bernard Shaw had been an Irishman who lived in London with his mother. He had been at the heart of the so-called Bloomsbury set and organised drawing room socialists into something called *The Fabians* after a Roman general called Fabius, though why this should be so no-one knew. He wore all-woollen outfits and knee breeches and stockings. His features had been lean but not ascetic, his red beard untidy, his limpid eyes softening the rest of his face.

Shaw studied the contract Mary had offered Charles.

'You were to have Indian corn for dinner.'

'You like Indian corn too.'

'Not on Wednesdays and Thursdays only.'

'You survive on Sundays with broad bread and cheese.'

'And a glass of milk and an apple.'

She took the contract from Shaw and placed it in the roll-top desk.

'You should write plays like Frederick Ibsen.'

'I write novels instead.'

'What do you do with them when they're written?'

'I put them in a cupboard where the mice can eat them.'

'Even the mice can make little of your novels?'

'At least I have you smiling again,' Shaw said.

As Mary's confidence had grown so her love for Charles Wheatley had diminished. He had caught her at a vulnerable moment. She had never been enamoured of his looks, but any spiritual attraction had long since waned in her satisfied body and she had seen him for what he was, a philanderer who preferred the attentions of many women rather than one woman. He had been casual with money and when his articles were published she never did see the income.

She would no more think of Charles Wheatley than she did of Arnold Alyson.

40

She poured William tea and offered him a watercress sandwich.

'I'm on official business,' William said.

'How can you be on official business when you visit your sister?'

'I've come from Arnold. He's settled in the Wirral outside Manchester. You remember Ann-Marie? She was your housekeeper in the years you were married. She's looking after him.'

William sipped his tea and nibbled his sandwich.

He had a carriage waiting for him in the street but he had set aside his top silk hat when he had entered the house. He wore a dark waistcoat with a gold watch chain, a dark bow-tie and a frock coat he lifted carefully before seating himself in his mother's old armchair. He had taken a gold cigarette case and sought for matches; his black hair had been turning a premature white and there were white tufts interspersed with his dark locks. The hair had been receding and if Mary noticed the impressive appearance she thought he lacked dignity.

'You sent Arnold a letter about a match girls' strike and chemical poisoning and hair falling out of the heads of fifteen-year-olds. He and his fellow clergymen were most put out. So too was the Bishop. They all received the same letter.'

'I hope it pricked their consciences.'

'Arnold had a modest investment, but of course he wrote to the company. The Bishop wrote too, but he was obliged to tell the Bishop you were his wife. The Bishop suggested you join Arnold in the parish, but he signified this was out of the question. The Bishop asked if there were children of the marriage. Arnold could not tell a lie to his Bishop. He said there was one child – a daughter.'

'The child bears only his name.'

'In law he is the father of the child.'

'Even Arnold would not wish to take Pauline from me.'

'The Bishop and Arnold acknowledge that the child should stay with its mother. That is good for its welfare. Arnold has made it plain to the Bishop that the split between you is irrevocable. It is not his desire to start again. He says being married to you has been as injurious to his health as you have been to the Church.'

'You speak just like Arnold,' Mary said.

'Arnold knows how you have looked after Pauline, saved the child's life – how you set aside your work to nurse her and care for her. He does wish to exact from you a promise – and he does so with the full concordance of the Bishop.'

'What might that be?'

'Pauline should have a Christian upbringing.'

'How can he ask me that?'

'The child should learn the teachings of Jesus. Later she should be able to make up her own mind.'

'Who should take Pauline to church so that she should hear such teachings? Who will read the bible to her on Sundays so that she might learn the Epistle of St James?'

'She could come to church with us,' William said. 'We are a happy family. We would take her for the day and she could read the bible and learn passages by heart as you learnt with Aunt Mabel. She could run in our garden, as you used to run, and she could be happy in the knowledge that Jesus loves her as she loves Jesus. Surely you would wish that happiness for your child?'

'You wish the tyranny of my own childhood to be imposed upon my daughter?'

'Since when has it become a tyranny?' William asked. 'It was never a tyranny when you loved Christ and fell in love with him spiritually, when you fasted to become a saint. You cannot re-write your own history to deprive your daughter of the love of Jesus you carried in your own heart.'

'A tyranny, I say, that cost me years of my life.'

'It is so little to ask,' William said.

'It is easy to ask,' Mary said. 'Impossible to give.'

'You cannot impeach the Christian religion before your own daughter,' William said. 'You cannot inculcate in her your own disbelief. You cannot have her young head turned by the views of the Reverend Malthus – and yet block from her mind the stories of the scriptures – the parables and the Sermon on the Mount. The miracles wrought by Jesus. The goodness and beauty that comes from each page of the bible. Pauline shall be entitled to understand such things. She deserves these images in her childhood.'

'What is wrong with the views of the Reverend Malthus?'

'Malthus has argued that population should be limited. He has argued for early marriage because he believes in the purity of social life; but he warns that early marriage between persons of small means leads to a large family. Large families lead to pauperism. You have espoused these views, Mary. You have made them your own. You have said mothers should be taught to avoid childbirth. For that you might be prosecuted.'

'I have seen the misery of the poor.'

'You wrote an article linking population law to the gospel of atheism.'

'The two are linked through scientific materialism.'

'The court might take the view it would be prejudicial for a child's well-being – and prejudicial to its

200

well-being in the hereafter – if a child were to be brought up an atheist. A child of yours brought up with such views would be an outcast in this life and condemned to Purgatory in the next. A court would hold that your guardianship would be detrimental to Pauline's future prospects – to say nothing of her eternal prospects.'

'Pauline's eternal prospects are safe with me.'

'You believe in an after-life after all?'

'In some after-life,' Mary said. 'I have yet to decide.'

'Would you allow Pauline to read the Old Testament?'

'There is too much coarseness in the Old Testament.'

'A judge might uphold you on that – provided he is a gentile judge.'

'No court in the land can say that I do not care for my child, that I do not love my child, that my standing in the community is not good. No matter what your views may be on the law of population or the gospel of atheism I have not been prosecuted. There can be no attacks on my personal character. No judge will remove my child once he has heard the evidence.'

'He might find the gospel of atheism blasphemous.'

'Blasphemy is no reason why a mother should lose her child.'

'Arnold is concerned for the child's future, Mary. Born on a factory floor, a mother who does not believe in God and proclaims her atheism. A mother who has

201

deprived her husband of his conjugal rights and driven him from the marital bed. An unmarried mother for all intents and purposes. No fatherly hand to guide the child through its early days. You will say we had no father either, he died when we were young; but there is a father for Pauline, respectable and loved in his community, who cares for the child's soul and its well-being.'

'Charles Wheatley is the father.'

'I have a letter from Wheatley,' William said. 'He states that he has heard rumours of an affair between the two of you, but they are baseless and grounded on common gossip. He proposes to marry Eleanor Marx. To his mind, there is no doubt that the lawful father of your child is Arnold Alyson.'

'Arnold saw us together in the same bed.'

'He saw you in the doorway in your night gown. He did not see any apparition behind you – lying on the bed or otherwise.'

'You must have paid Charles well for that.'

'Even Charles would not sell his daughter for a fee.'

'I shall fight Arnold in court,' Mary said. 'I shall not have my daughter taken from me.'

'It will cost you all that you have.'

William handed Mary a copy of the petition:

That the said Mary Alyson is by addresses, lectures and writings, endeavouring to propagate the principles of atheism, and has published an article entitled The Gospel of Atheism. She has associated herself with the views of the Reverend Malthus in giving lectures and in publishing a pamphlet entitled The Law of Population. That there shall be removed from the custody of Mary Alyson a single child, Pauline Alyson, with all future rights of access to be barred.

The petition had been in the name of the Reverend Arnold Alyson.

'No judge will deprive me of my daughter.'

William set aside his cup and sandwich plate.

He replaced his top hat, hiding his white hairs; he had regained some of the dignity he had lost when he had removed the hat and settled into his mother's chair. His blue eyes had been apprehensive. This was his sister whom he had lost many years ago, her stubbornness a wonder to behold, but backed by limitless energy. Nothing would change her mind. He dreaded for her future.

'Long suffering is a splendid school for the teaching of endurance,' William said.

Mary knew what he was thinking and touched his hand.

'Even if Pauline were taken from me,' she said. 'She'll come back the moment she is free.'

41

Mary had taken Pauline to the factory where she had been born.

'Ann-Marie showed me a book of cuttings.'

'Did she tell you how I fought and struggled to keep you?'

'I waited for you in a park in Manchester,' Pauline said.

'I was banned from seeing you – lest I taint you with my ideas.'

'Ann-Marie didn't ban you. That's why we waited.'

'I once lived in a house in Bloomsbury.'

'You're good at losing things,' Pauline said.

She had been four years old when she had gone to live with Arnold and Ann-Marie.

She recalled the vicarage with its gate posts where stood stone lions already green with moss. The drive had been dishevelled, pink flowers in the black border soil. There had been two windows to her nursery, one large, the other high and narrow; it had been from the second that Pauline would peep when she heard Reverend Alyson's footsteps on the drive as he left to visit his parishioners. Sometimes she would flatten her nose to the glass, but the Reverend did not lift his head, even when he reached the gate and turned to close it behind him.

She remembered the prayer book always clasped in his hand.

Ann-Marie had been at home in the kitchen, making her own butter and bread, jam and pickles. She laundered and sewed and one Christmas made Pauline a pantomime dress of pink tulle with a stiff ballet skirt so that she could play Cinderella in the village hall.

Ann-Marie would bring Pauline from the nursery for cake-making; she would let her plunge her hands into the dough, the flour running to her elbows. She would stick orange pips into simmering apple tarts as they were removed from the oven.

She had been given a doll's house.

The dolls had been dressed in white calico, their limbs daubed with a garish paint. She remembered one of the dolls so limp and ugly she had placed it at the back of the doll's house so that she would not see it when she opened the door. She remembered playing with Ann-Marie, running around the dining table with its claw-feet, running as fast as her legs would carry her, laughing and giggling, so dizzy she had run into the fireplace, her head crashing into the smouldering coal.

There had been burns to her arms and legs.

She had been taken to church each Sunday.

She could recall only two of Arnold's sermons: in support of imperialism and the Queen. She thought imperialism had been some kind of gift for the Queen, and she thought the Queen a fairy who wandered the globe dressed in white with a magic wand. She remembered seeing from her window the open countryside, but beyond the grey stone walls and odd bloom of heather there sat above a blue ridge a swirl of soot and smoke.

Ann-Marie told her this was Manchester.

She had not seen her mother since she was six years old.

'That makes it fifteen years,' Mary said.

'I'm here because Reverend Alyson is ill.'

'You're here because you're a suffragist. You wanted to show the world what your mother could do you could do better.'

'I did it for the cause.'

'You did it to show your mother.'

'I have no mother.'

'So you told the governor in Holloway Prison.'

Mary showed Pauline where timber would be brought through the wrought-iron gates. The timber would be sawn into lengths by circular saws that sent sawdust in a flurry across the yard. Machines peeled tissue from the logs and thin veneers came out of the machines; the veneers were folded and piled ready to be sliced by a guillotine that would split the veneers into match lengths. Some fifty thousand matches would be cut every minute and to make them burn well the matches would be boiled in a solution.

Splints were forced into tiny holes on a flexible iron band. The band passed through a paraffin wax bath and over a roller coated with a composition that gave the match its striking red head. The matches travelled up and down in endless bands after dipping till their heads dried and they were ready to be packed; the boxes were made from the same veneers, only thicker, cut into short lengths called skillets. The skillets were taken by the machine, folded and stuck together with adhesive paper, an endless conveyor carrying them to the drying room.

'You've been secretary of the Union all this time?' Pauline asked.

'It concentrated my mind after I lost you. It was also my only income. My brother cut me off. The house had to go to pay legal bills – but the match girls were always good to me. They were good to you, too. They saw you into the world. The doctor is the same who treated you after your hunger strike. The nurse is the factory nurse. They've looked after me all these years – and I've looked after them. Not a single strike – not a single day lost.'

'You've lived among them these past sixteen years?'

Mary had organised a trade union in Ireland when she learned girls of fifteen were working twelve hours in a linen factory for a ten-pence wage, that embroideresses were paid two-pence for nine hours' work, and others who embroidered twelve cushions were paid two-pence three-farthings. They had gone on strike when the management reduced the rate to two-pence farthing. Mary persuaded British trade unionists to send food through Dublin docks so that the striking girls were not starved into going back to work.

She had met Albi Birt.

He had been the first Member of Parliament to support her view that socialism and suffragism were one and indivisible; he had even threatened to leave the Labour Party if his view did not prevail. The first Labour Party Conference had been held in Belfast. Albi told the Conference that he had thought his pioneering days were over, but he had felt with increasing intensity the injustice inflicted upon women. The Conference had not been impressed and a resolution to extend the franchise to women fell by a large majority.

Albi Birt had not resigned.

42

He waited for Mary and Pauline in the room.

'I've presented a petition on behalf of thirty women's suffrage societies,' he said. 'They've a membership of a hundred thousand. There's women's workin' class organisations with a membership of forty-two thousand. I'll work for a new Private Member's Bill. We can add a *Votes for Women* clause in committee and refer it to the full House.'

'We can only have votes for women when the government decides on votes for women,' Pauline said. 'Not by a Private Member's Bill. It has to be a Bill on its own. We can only have a Bill when I organise a People's Army who want to fight for women's freedom.'

'There'll be fighting soon enough without joining your People's Army,' Mary said.

Pauline had fallen upon the bed and slept in her clothes.

She dreamt she had been back in prison, only it

had been a different kind of prison where the cells were large as drawing rooms with casement windows. The prison had really been an ordinary dwelling where inmates came and went from one room to another, but there had still been bars to the windows. The prison had been bright and she had the yard to herself. The furniture had been that of an ordinary room and rather than prison garb she had been entitled to dress like a peasant, except without clogs or bonnets.

Wardresses oversaw the prisoners but there were no guards overlooking the yard. The prison had been so enjoyable, so agreeable that lying in her clothes she had been disappointed when she woke and looked not at a barred window but closed pink curtains where light filtered, and where Albi Birt and her mother were looking down upon the white-washed yard across to the flat opposite.

'We could get her out through the fish curers' yard,' Mary said.

'Possibly among the herrin' boxes.'

'She's so weak,' Mary said. 'The smell of fish might finish her off.'

'I want to go back to Holloway Prison,' Pauline said. 'I want to see the wardress – and I want to see Terry Kenny. Did the Home Secretary pardon her too?'

'All in good time,' Mary said.

'Why can't I see the wardress?'

'Her name is Denise,' Mary said. 'She has been to see you, but you were unconscious and she sat on the bed and held your hand and cried a tear for you. She has been dismissed for misconduct – saving your life, I believe. She wants to join your movement. Only I don't think it's good for her. She's been a disciplinarian in a disciplined service. I shall find her work and you shall never see her again.'

'What about Terry Kenny?'

'I've written you a pledge for your People's Army,' Mary said. She read it aloud: *'I promise to serve the common cause of justice and our comrades under our duly elected officers. I will be a friend to all and a brother or sister to every member of the People's Army. I am a sincere believer in a vote for every woman in the land, propertied or unpropertied, married or single.* How about that?'

'Terry would have done it better.'

'I'm sure she would.'

'Why can't I see her now?'

'I shall bring her to you,' Mary said.

Pauline settled back upon the bolster.

She felt comfortable, her strength returning, aware she had still been dressed, feeling the warmth of her costume. Yet her mouth still ached from the forcible feeding, the laceration to her gums slowly healing; her teeth had been loosened by the steel instruments, and when she took food she masticated slowly, as if each mouthful would set her mouth bleeding again. Her gaze had yet to focus as she looked again at the pink curtains.

It would take two years for Pauline to recover from her hunger strikes.

Her vision would clear and her mouth hurt less, her digestive system would return to normal; but she would lack energy and motivation, her stomach pains might go but she would be unaccustomed to food, so that she would eat little and drink often. She would sleep badly, tossing and turning through the night, not all her dreams friendly of Holloway Prison; she would wake with her night shirt damp with sweat and if there had been a recurring nightmare it was that she had breached her licence and strayed back to London; she had been recognised and arrested.

She was back again before Governor Willit.

Mary left the room and returned with a large parcel.

She stood the parcel against the window.

The curtains were still drawn, the geraniums back on the sill from the chest of drawers. The parcel had been no parcel at all but a gilt frame wrapped in a woollen blanket. Mary removed the blanket and it fell upon the floor to drape the boards. The light in the room caught the frame around a portrait, but the colours to the portrait were more subdued, the artistic taints and flecks obscured by dust speckles.

Mary stood back with her hands on her hips.

Pauline allowed herself a smile of curiosity.

Her eyes had yet to focus and a grey mist settled over her vision. Her mother stepped aside, hands still on her hips, and Pauline saw beyond her mother the portrait of a young woman sitting naked in profile, head slightly inclined, the freshness of her body reflected in the

211

canvas: the rose-red nipple, the hand across her thighs, the blonde hair, the suppleness of life flowing through the taints and flecks.

'The most beautiful painting I've seen,' Mary said.

Pauline knew then that Terry Kenny was dead.

43

Pauline had been twenty-one years old when she came to Highhill to teach at the infant school.

She had her photograph taken on the first day with her class, the boys in cloth caps and hessian blue shirts and grey-knit cardigans, short trousers, long stockings and boots with shiny toes; the girls had worn long stockings and boots and long-sleeved dark pullovers over clean white dresses. She had kept the photograph on the mantelpiece of her front room. There were others of herself, the tints not showing the high colouring to her red hair, the hair parted, her features regular if narrow, the eyes blue, the gaze steady.

There had been another photograph taken before the school in winter; the snow had lain upon the trees and yard and roof. The school had been built by the coal owners on a field open to the wind so that the snow banked in the yard. There had been a photograph where she stood between Binkie Fatherley and Albi Birt, a rose between two thorns she liked to say, taken on Albi's first visit to Highhill socialist club.

212

Binkie would unveil a portrait Pauline had painted of Albi.

He might have almost lost his life crushed by a slow-moving line of trucks; he had moved from coal face to the House of Commons and had supported votes for women. He had worked for a national minimum wage. He lived in makeshift rooms off Fleet Street, his wife and children incarcerated in their pit village. Yet in his vanity he had sat on a cracket before the fire with hope in his eyes that Pauline Alyson would paint his portrait.

'Them detectives might say you should've given them twenty-four hours notice that you were leavin',' Albi said. 'They might arrest you again. They'll not think of lookin' at the home of a Member of Parliament. Your licence'll be up in two or three days. We have to make for Highhill before they start lookin' for you proper.'

'I've arranged to send your belongings from Terry's flat,' Mary said.

'I don't want anything,' Pauline said.

'You'll want your letters back?'

'No letters.'

'I'll send them anyway. And the scrap books.'

'I'll lock them away.'

'Surely you'll want the painting?'

'It belongs to Terry Kenny.'

'It belongs to you,' Mary said.

One day the painting would be hung in the National Gallery as a testament to victory over adversity; women would have their vote. It showed beauty in defiance, the portrait of one young woman painted by an artist who loved her; the whole of youth and art and history had been found in the flecks and tints. That is why, in the words of Mary Alyson, the painting would one day be famous and hang in the National Gallery.

'You keep it,' Pauline said.

'I'll set up an easel,' Mary said. 'You can paint Albi.'

Not all her paints had been there, but she had oils and charcoal and pencils. There had been no feel of a studio in Albi's rooms, no sense of intimacy or artistry or creation, but she had felt comfortable with the glowing fire. She had never the confidence to paint the face of Terry Kenny; she had been afraid she would not catch her beauty. Nor did she have time to paint Albi Birt full-length, frock coat and all. She had been mindful that the painting had to be large enough to be framed and hung so that his world might see and respect.

She had settled Albi on the cracket before the fire.

He held a coal fossil in one hand and a battered brass lamp shield in the other, not because she proposed painting them but because they would keep him still. She had tilted his face upward and asked him to survey the mantelpiece. She had crossed his legs, again to settle him down, so that by the end of the sittings his thighs and arms would ache, but sadness would be lifted from his eyes.

The sadness of his unrequited love for Mary Alyson.

Albi's rooms had been no more than a large single room partitioned by curtains into a living room, a bedroom and a box of a kitchen. The woodwork had been painted dark green, there had been a window seat and a high old-fashioned fireplace with hobs on either side. There were engravings on the walls framed in polished rosewood: a portrait of a franchise demonstration – *votes for women* – and another of the socialist William Morris set in a circular frame. By the door on a polished table stood a collection of brass and wicks that had once been miners' lamps.

Albi lived frugally, he cooked his own food and did his own housework. He blacked his own boots but did not take it amiss that Mary should bustle through his rooms, tidying as she went, her fingers picking up cushions and re-arranging them. A duster would appear from nowhere to dust at the brass and wicks and picture frames; she would light the coal fire and come from the kitchen with bread and butter and scones, heating a saucepan of water to make tea. Mary showed affection for Albi, but she rationed it as she rationed the bread and butter and scones so that, if thankful for the cleaning, he had been thankful too for the touch of a hand to his, her lips against his cheeks.

Pauline would see the sadness of that unrequited love.

She would hold Albi's face in her hands and kiss him on both cheeks; she would let her fingers run over the tight skin, tracing her fingers across the blue scars of past mining cuts. With her easel set up and her paints

215

laid around her, she thought she was back with Terry in Lincoln's Inn as she angled the light onto Albi's head and uplifted face. She had asked him neither to smile nor breathe through his mouth and she had been able to concentrate without distraction until the painting had been finished.

'At least I can see the likeness,' Albi said.

'It captures you exactly,' Mary said.

'I'll need time to finish it,' Pauline said.

'You artists are never satisfied,' Mary said.

Albi's worn face had been gentle in the painting. His brow had quizzically puckered, perplexed by the problems that confronted him, yet his eyes gazed a clear blue from the painting, not afraid of the future, aware of the mistakes of the past; there were scars etched into his forehead and soft grey hair fell by the side of his face into his whiskers. This was not any man, the portrait seemed to say, but one who carried his identity stitched into his skin in blue anthracite veins, one who wished to control events, but who even in his sternness had not been sure they could be controlled.

'It'll hang well in the colliery institute,' Mary said.

'You'll be in Highhill come Saturday?' Albi asked.

'They say it rains a lot in Highhill.'

'I have a hansom cab downstairs,' Mary said.

Pauline adjusted the large black pins to her hat in the reflection from the glass door. She held her mother by the shoulders and a tremor passed through them. Mary held her daughter close so that she could feel her heartbeat through the thick cotton dress. Images passed through her mind: the child in the steam tent, the child she had fought to keep through the courts, the child she had seen under lime trees in a park in Manchester, the child they had brought from Holloway Prison and carried into the shoemaker's room as bone within rags. She did not permit her thoughts to proceed. Otherwise she would crumble into tears, her will breached, and she would never be the same again.

'All my life,' Pauline said. 'I've never called anyone mother.'

'I've loved you all these years,' Mary said.

Pauline kissed her mother on both cheeks.

'It's the first time I've kissed you too,' she said.

Book Three:
The Rutlands

44

Barbara Rutland had met Pauline Alyson in her last year at boarding school.

The Rutland family had been one of the few Catholic families in the village. This set them apart and made it certain that Barbara could not marry anyone from the village. The pitmen were Methodists but the manager and officials were Church of England; the runnels ran deep but only raised to the surface when it came to marrying off-spring. Because there had been no Catholic school, Barbara had been sent to a boarding school run by nuns, returning to the village at weekends or holidays.

'I know all about Terry Kenny,' said the girl in the next dormitory bed.

'How do you know?' Barbara asked.

'Terry Kenny was my cousin.'

The beds had been laid out as in a hospital ward.

Each bed had been set in a cubicle of faded blue curtain. Sometimes the curtain had been stained, sometimes torn, but with the curtain drawn the pupils were never allowed to see each other undress. Each pupil had been allowed a single religious portrait to hang above her bed, a Virgin Mary or the portrait of a Saint, or the depiction of the twelve stages on the way to Golgotha. Barbara had hung a Virgin Mary that had not been changed all the years she had been boarding. She kept her rosary beads and cross by the side of the bed and would say a prayer each night, holding the rosary beads and kissing the cross.

The pupils retired early.

On summer nights with the light strong they would hold feasts, oranges and cakes smuggled into the school by day pupils. Even in winter they would light candles and pull aside their blue curtains and climb two into a bed to keep themselves warm. Discipline had been strict at the school during the day, but once the dormitory doors had closed and the corridor lights extinguished the night-duty nun would leave them to their slumbers.

'How did she meet Pauline Alyson?'

'At the College of Art.'

'Terry Kenny told you this?'

'She told the servants when she came home to Surrey.'

'And they passed it on to you?'

Alma Kenny had not been unlike her cousin.

She had been tall but not ashamed of her height. She held herself well, slim and willowy, small breasts but large nipples; her body had been well-curved, the thighs firm. She had blonde hair she allowed to rustle around the back of her neck, her skin as pale as her hair, but she had poise and assurance not common among other boarding girls. She found them coarse and below her and if she spoke to them at all she had been haughty and ill-mannered.

She had set Barbara Rutland apart.

She might come from Highhill, but her family lived in a private house on the outskirts of the woods that swept from the village to the valley. The house lay beyond a coppice of chestnut trees and copper beaches that kept it hidden from view. There had been freshly-painted gates and beyond the gates a road of red shale hemmed by white stone wended upward through the coppice and down into the hollow where stood the house, the shale washing up to the white-painted walls.

Barbara's father Tom had been son of the colliery under-manager.

He had been promised an opening in the pit, but he had preferred to make his own way and had built a row of shops in the village. He had built other shops in other villages. He also ran the first traps from Highhill to the railway station. He carried newspapers and medicine and preparations for the chemist; he carried the post too. Soon he would bring the first bus into the village. He had been in his early twenties, tall and thin, so embarrassed by his height that he stooped; his dark hair had already thinned, his cheeks had been thin, too, and a slight moustache had graced his upper lip. Tom had met his future wife Rosemary touring the village streets with his bus when he had wanted to show it off to would-be passengers.

Rosemary's father had been a hewer.

She had lived with her mother and father in a cluster of cottages on Bone Hill reached through a gateway of whalebone brought to the village by a wayward sailor. Tom had been determined the whole village would see his bus, but the rise to Bone Hill had been steep; the bus had heaved and grunted and steamed its way to the cottages, clipping the whalebone because the entrance to the cottages had been so narrow. Rosemary had gathered around the bus like other children.

She had been fourteen years old.

Some of the children had tried to clamber aboard the bus from the back, others through the side; still others had thrown themselves onto the cabin roof. Tom had brought the bus to a halt at the top of the row, but the incline had been so steep it had rolled back as he pulled the handbrake. The children had scattered. Those on the cabin roof rolled off. Others sought to hold the bus back but they, too, scattered when they failed.

Rosemary had fallen behind.

Her attention had wandered as she picked her way among stones and weeds and ash to follow the bus up Bone Hill. She looked up and saw the bus rolling towards her. She had lifted her skirts and turned to run, but the back of the bus caught her between the shoulder blades, spinning her from the track onto rough ground. She twisted as she fell. Her head hit one of the stones. The sky and the clouds had swung and the stones and weeds and ash seeped as darkness into her mind and the swinging ceased.

Tom Rutland finally mastered the bus.

His foot had been on the brake, his hand heaving at the handbrake; he had swung the solid-rubber tyres inward, shouting at the children. He had ordered them to place stones behind the wheels to prevent further lurches. He had pulled again at the handbrake. He had leapt from the cabin to find Rosemary unconscious on the tussocky grass. A silence had fallen upon the children as they looked down upon her expressionless face, her cheeks and brow as white as the roadway stone.

Tom had carried her home in his arms.

Rosemary had been unconscious for three days.

She would remember nothing of the accident, not even the bus climbing the hill, but because she had fallen badly she had been left with a limp. Her right leg would not straighten. There had been talk of amputating the leg and the kitchen table had been prepared; but there had been no surgeon, the doctor refused to operate, and though he had done all he could to straighten the leg, her right foot would always curve and drag.

She had been crippled for life.

Tom came to the house every day.

Rosemary had not moved in the cot-bed. Her breath had come in deep sighs, her breasts rose and fell, her blonde hair had lost its colour; sweat ran down from her head to her neck and the colour would not come back to her cheeks nor lips. Tom had found her hands warm, the fingers soft, and so long as her breasts rose and fell, so long as her chest heaved, he knew there would be hope.

One day he found her sitting up and tasting broth.

'I love you,' he said.

He had never thought of it before.

'You mean the knock on the head made me beautiful?'

'You were always beautiful,' he said.

Two years later they were married.

Nine months later Barbara Rutland came into the world.

45

'What did the servants tell you?' Barbara asked.

'Do you feel an ache sometimes?' Alma asked.

'Every night before I go to sleep.'

'I feel an ache too,' Alma said.

'And the servants?'

Alma recounted how Terry Kenny had been indifferent to clothes till she met Pauline; she wore her hair long and it straggled her back. She had ambled around the College of Art wearing a cardigan, only two buttons fastened, hands in the cardigan pockets; she had worn no make-up. She had been brought up at her father's country house in Surrey and Alma recalled the four bedrooms, the billiard room, the large garden with its own bowling green.

'Not very exciting to me,' Barbara said.

It had only been when Terry had wanted to please Pauline that she had taken an interest in her appearance; she had cut short her hair and plucked her eyebrows. She had begun to wear make-up. She bought coloured dresses from the new Liberty store along Regent Street; she had thought of buying woollen clothes from Jaeger because this would make her more attractive to Pauline and more healthy. The wool would supposedly dispose of the poisons the body exhaled through the skin.

'How could Pauline be interested in anyone so dull?'

'She began to eat less sugar and pastry,' Alma said.

Terry's figure had slimmed and hardened and she had pushed back her shoulders and stood her full height. She had set aside the cardigan and wore loose-flowing red or blue blouses, white buttons to the cuffs. She found by changing her clothes and her looks she gained confidence and became more abrasive; she had been thorough in her lectures, but her heart had not been in her studies. She had no intention of being a painter, a decorator or a teacher.

She would devote her life to suffragism.

'Did Pauline Alyson live with her?' Barbara asked.

'She lived at Fulham.'

'You're holding something back,' Barbara said.

'I once met Pauline at Terry's flat. She dressed above her station. After all, she was only a vicar's daughter, but her stepmother sent her bonnets that gave her a grander look. When she removed the bonnet a bundle of red hair shook around the whiteness of her neck. I can remember it still. There were high colour spots to her cheeks that reddened and deepened as if she were shy. It was so exciting. Her eyebrows arched and there was something about her fingertips as they touched my hand that made me blush.'

'Why did you blush?' Barbara asked.

'It comes back to the ache.'

'Did she make you ache?'

'She made me all weak and damp.'

Barbara slept in a night shirt with high neck and long sleeves and buttons down the front running to her stomach; the night shirt had been of white cotton with red edges to the arms and hem. She had felt the coarseness of the cotton against her skin, but as the years passed she had grown accustomed to the coarseness. She slept with the buttons open, one hand on her breast, feeling secure, comforted, the nipple soft and warm to her touch, sending an ache through her body.

'Do you feel the ache now?' Barbara asked.

'I always feel the ache when I'm near you,' Alma said.

She opened the last of the buttons to Barbara's night shirt. She let her hands run along the line of her stomach. Barbara had felt the closeness of Alma, her cotton night shirt rubbing against her own, her long legs parallel so that she felt her thighs. Alma's mouth followed the fingers and before she knew it Alma was suckling the nipple to the right breast and the ache she had felt permeated her body, lighting her nerves, so that rather than bring her hands around to remove Alma's lips she clasped her head and kept her there.

Alma's hands were now seeking the hem of Barbara's night shirt.

The lips left her breast to follow her hands and her licking tongue moved up her thighs till they found her dampness, so that for Barbara the ache concentrated and sharpened and gathered, the tongue working so steadily, so softly, so patiently, the hands holding her hips so that she could not move her buttocks, the tongue exploring deeper inside her, licking and suckling till the tension could no longer hold, the ache became a pain, a sharp pain, a lingering pain, a pain the likes of which Barbara had never known.

Alma kissed her full on the mouth.

'Don't you find it exciting?' she asked.

Barbara struck her hard across the face.

She struck so hard the smack echoed around the dormitory, stilling half-smothered coughs and the restless moving of pillows and springs. A light went on in the passageway and a yellow beam sneaked under the door, settling on the blue cubicle curtains. They heard the shuffle of the night-duty nun and the scraping of a chair in the corridor. The light extinguished, the chair ceased to scrape, and the half-smothered coughs began again.

Barbara felt the slim body move away from her.

She buttoned her night shirt around her stomach, but her hand fluttered and paused around her right breast. She recalled how she had slept with one hand on her breast, the warm touch sending an ache through her body, a friendly ache soothing her to sleep. She would still be holding her breast in the morning, but she knew now the ache would never be the same again as she gazed at Alma on the bed, her shape no longer visible.

She had been radiant when Barbara had struck.

Alma leant over and kissed her softly.

'You liked it all the same,' she said.

46

'I thought you were the housekeeper,' Pauline said.

'I didn't know you were working,' Barbara said.

'I'm not working. I'm enjoying myself.'

'Looks like work to me.'

'Not when you get the hang of it.'

Barbara had called upon Pauline Alyson when she returned to the village at the weekend.

Pauline had rented from a farmer a cottage halfway between the village and the school. Hawthorn bushes surrounded the cottage and the gate creaked against the prickly leaves. She had her own lane, the land dipping to a sand quarry, the quarry surrounded by gorse, pock-marked where the martens had nested, the windows of the farmhouse beyond the fields darkened by shadow. There had been crazy paving around the house, violets at either side, the path leading towards the quarry.

She had converted an upstairs room into a studio where she painted, more watercolours than oils, depicting some of the landscapes, not the pit but the sand quarry; she had painted the farmhouse and fields, the yellow corn dull in the cold light. Sometimes she would take her easel and canvas and pencils and charcoals to the river, painting the waters rushing over pebbles between the fir trees.

She had filled out in her twenties.

She had still been thin with lack of food, her breasts firm and upright, her buttocks hard, her hips thicker, but she walked slowly, as if tired and disorientated, heads turning in the village, children stunned by the colour of her hair. The girls asked permission to brush the hair in their playtime, the boys asked if they could run their hands through its softness as reward for good work. The country air put roses into her cheeks and the light came back to her eyes.

Pauline Alyson had all the poise and beauty of her womanhood.

She dressed well, too, green and blue or white costumes sent regularly by her mother, gloves and shoes to match. She had been conscious as she stepped out carrying a coloured umbrella, her polished shoes avoiding puddles, that nothing had been bought in the village. She had thought this would cause resentment, but there had never before been a village school-teacher, and the village folk showed her respect. She had not yet become part of the village, but she was young and attractive. They might have preferred an older woman, a spinster, even a crippled spinster as they had in the next village, but she kept to herself and the children loved her. She taught them well: reading and writing, geography and history, even if their future lay in the pit or as the wives of pitmen, with no-one straying beyond the village.

'I'm upstairs,' Pauline had called.

Barbara had found the cottage door open and stepped inside.

The cottage had been sparse but comfortable, red tiles, a wardrobe opposite the fireplace. There had been woodworm in the mantelpiece and with table and chairs standing between the wardrobe and fireplace, the room had looked hopelessly crowded. Higgledy-piggledy. A door led to the scullery and through the scullery windows Barbara could see the gorse bushes sloping towards the sand quarry. The scullery steps were painted white, the sink filled with unwashed dishes.

'You can find your way,' Pauline shouted.

Barbara manoeuvred around a table filled with magazines and school books and more dirty dishes. She set aside chairs with wicker seats, uncertain how she should place them, edging towards the stairs. Dust flared her nostrils. She saw more woodworm on the staircase, dust rising from each stair, but there had been no banister, only a solid wooden wall. She found the upstairs ceiling low, the beams heavy, only a small window set into the roof. She stepped over the square of light that came from the window and pushed open the door.

She found herself in Pauline's studio.

'You can sit over there if you want.'

Barbara noticed a camp bed against the wall.

'I don't sleep here,' Pauline said. 'I sleep in the room next door. But once I start a painting I like to finish it – because once I lose interest it never gets finished. But if I do want to finish it, I lie on the camp bed looking it over; I fall asleep for twenty minutes and then I paint again. Sometimes I paint in the night, but when the light comes through the window the painting is gaudy. You might say garish. I set it aside as ugly. You think I'm talking too much? I hope you understand what I'm trying to say.'

There had been oils and paints and pencils and charcoal everywhere; an easel stood at the centre of the room. Oak beams to the ceiling were as thick as trunks, pock-marked with woodworm, but hanging ponderous and low so that Barbara had to stoop to find her seat. A large window filled one wall, letting in natural light; the light caught dust particles, but through the window she could see again the gorse and the sand quarry. Canvases lined the walls, some straight, others lopsided, some complete, others half-finished, some not painted at all.

Barbara found the smell of paint more oppressive than the smell of dust.

'I've heard about your portrait in the colliery institute,' Barbara said.

'You've not seen it?'

'They don't let women into the colliery institute.'

'They let me in.'

'Only because you painted the portrait.'

'They don't believe in women's emancipation in the village,' Pauline said.

She stood with her back to the window.

She had been dressed in khaki overalls spattered with paint; she wore, too, a black beret with red strands of fiery hair protruding and curling around her forehead. She had been smoking a cigarette in a holder. Her face had been ringed in tobacco smoke and her eyes squinted as the smoke curled upward. Some of the pupils had sneaked cigarettes into Barbara's dormitory and they had opened wide the windows to be rid of lingering tobacco smoke; women in the village not only smoked but stood in queues for their fags, as they called them.

Barbara had never seen anyone smoke through a holder.

'I only smoke when I paint,' Pauline said.

'I want to join your suffragist movement,' Barbara said.

'The women in our movement are giving white feathers to young lads who've not enlisted to fight the war,' Pauline said. 'They want their boys to fight so that the government will honour its pledge to give votes for women when the war's over. Votes for the blood of Flanders fields! Votes for women is a noble cause – even a mighty one – but stained with the blood of young men to fight a capitalists' war makes it dishonourable.'

'You knew Terry Kenny?'

'The world knows I knew Terry Kenny.'

'Her cousin sleeps in the same dormitory at boarding school.'

'How long will you be at boarding school?'

'Only a few months.'

'You can be my secretary,' Pauline said. 'The suffragist movement always needs a secretary.'

'I wouldn't want any money,' Barbara said.

'I'll pay you in kind,' Pauline said.

She took a canvas from the easel and handed it to Barbara.

The painting had been fresh and unvarnished and the smell of the paint more overpowering as she took the canvas and held it to the light. The painting had been of the cottage, the lines straight and stark. There had been harmony to the painting but no warmth, the texture in the grey walls and blue tiles and squat chimney a contrast with yellow sunflowers against dark hawthorn bushes. The hawthorn had been hostile to the warmth of the sunflowers.

Blue cigarette smoke curled across the canvas.

'First payment for services rendered,' Pauline said.

'Do you think this too will end in the colliery institute?' Barbara asked.

47

They had hung Albi Birt's portrait at the entrance to the institute.

Pauline's trap had pulled up outside, the horse nudging its way through men unable to get into the institute. They had climbed the cinder paths from their homes and stood not only four-deep on the pathway but in the shrubs around the institute. Some sat on a joiners' wall opposite, others spilled into the playing field, sitting on the grass. The younger ones sat on each other's shoulders and the sun coming out at the right time fell across Pauline's red hair and cheeks.

Had they come to see the portrait or Pauline Alyson?

She had indeed been the only woman, dressed in a long skirt and dark blouse, dark coat and plumed hat; a shawl draped her shoulders and she carried an umbrella because there had been a shower. She had adjusted the shawl and shaken the umbrella; she had unpinned her hat and let her red hair flow around her shoulders, the sun catching its auburn tints as she handed both shawl and hat to the trap driver. The men parted a way for her into the institute and one of them even gave up his seat before the institute window where the portrait would be unveiled.

Albi Birt described Pauline's talents as a painter.

How her early sketches had been sold in Hyde

Park to pay for her suffragist campaign, how she had painted his own portrait against his wishes. He did not believe in self-aggrandisement. How she had painted the portrait hiding from the police because she wanted to keep her mind from the worry of being caught and returned to Holloway Prison, how the police had played cat and mouse with the suffragists.

'You'll be able not only to attend the institute, lass, but join our socialist club,' Binkie said. 'You'll be the first and only woman – an exception, you might say, but the men'll not mind. And the women neither.'

'I'm too weak,' Pauline said. 'Too tired.'

She knew that Binkie Fatherley had been expected to pull the cord that would reveal the portrait of Albi Birt; that was his duty as lodge secretary. But he and Albi had wanted her to please the men by this symbolic act, her first in the village. She sought to conserve her strength, her energy, so that she could rise from her chair. The portrait stood on a stand before the institute window. A rose trellis had been removed from the outside so that the crowd would have a better view. The portrait stood against a giant easel so that the face of Albi Birt would rise high for all to see.

The institute swung around Pauline as she sat.

Through the large window she could see cloud and sky and to her ears came the strong voices of mining folk, so loud they boomed beyond the cinder pathways to the village. For Pauline they were echoes, accents she did not understand, a dialect she had yet to master. She had been so frail she could not stand. Binkie and

Albi lifted her from the chair and a silence fell upon the men. Pauline had been so young and yet so old, proud and defiant, yet defeated and broken. She had defied oppression and yet she had suffered at its hands.

These men had struggled all their lives for better pay and conditions; they had known the hardship of strikes and lock-outs. They suffered pneumoconiosis and nystagmus, hunched with their work underground; their women folk had learnt to go without – and their children too. None had suffered as Pauline Alyson had suffered. None had deliberately deprived himself of food and water; none had gone to prison for his convictions. None had endured so much physical pain or almost died. Pauline Alyson, so frail and slender, a fleshless hand pulling at the cord, shamed them into silence. The silence lasted till she had been brought back to rest in the chair.

Binkie Fatherley and Albi Birt led the applause.

It had been picked up by the men, all that they had to give, echoing around her, waves of sound reverberating from the institute walls, the kind of applause she had known at the Manchester Free Trade Hall so that Pauline cried for the first time, cried for a mother who was no more, a past that was gone, consigned to the grave of time, a useless thing that could not be resurrected, replaced now by warmth, the devotion of these strong people, determined to respect her, to accept her leadership, because she had suffered, because they had understood her suffering, that she wanted a new home in the security of their village.

'We'll give you a platform, lass, and you can make speeches,' Binkie said. 'When you feel up to it, that is, when you feel less tired and weak. You can help me carry the gospel to other pits, speak at the pit head, catch the men from their shifts, even down the pit if the management'll let you, though I doubt that, but we can try anyway.'

'I believe in votes for women,' Pauline said.

'And socialism too. Don't forget socialism.'

'My mother believes in socialism. She's handing out white feathers in Hyde Park.'

'Only socialism can bring the brotherhood of man,' Binkie said. 'Only socialism can take money from the coal owners and give it to the pit lads. They're the ones that dig the coal. My job's to convert you to socialism – not you to convert me to a woman's vote. You can have all the votes you like, but you'll need socialism first and last. Socialism for our time and socialism for all time.'

'I don't understand the dialect,' Pauline said.

48

'You'll learn,' Binkie said.

The war had brought Binkie and Pauline together.

Binkie saw the war as a capitalist conspiracy to defeat socialism; it had been about markets and trading, not about working men. They had been victims twice over: exploited at home and shot at abroad. They should unite: they had nothing to lose but their chains. Each should receive according to his need and as he campaigned from pit head to pit head he compared the coal owners in their country houses and estates with miners and their families living in single rooms, in homes without electricity, still using lamps and candles, their holders standing on the mantelpiece, the brass regularly polished by womenfolk.

Binkie would drive his trap beyond a country home that had never been used; its walls stood stark against the sky. The home had been built by a coal-owning family for their twenty-one year old son when he had married, but he had died the night before the marriage; the home had been abandoned, its windows broken, stone overgrown with lichen. Yet the coal owners had let it collapse rather than pull it down and destroy the memory of their son.

'Why should there be such riches in the world?' Binkie demanded.

Why should a family have so much money it could leave a house go to wrack and ruin and not repair it? Why not let others live in it? Why did they think morsels of concrete could remind them of flesh and blood? The men should own the pits where they invested their lives. They should break the capitalist cycle of good years, bad years, when the coal owners protected their profits by lengthening the men's working week and reducing their pay.

How could men own the pits?

They could overthrow the state, capitalism would exhaust itself in one crisis too many. The war might be that final crisis, but sending young pit workers to the front was not the way to bring about revolution; rather it would weaken the working classes whose sons had been sent to do the fighting. The men should organise, agitate, disseminate. Then all the working class, not just the miners, would rise as one and strike down the ruling classes, the oppressors, those who had against those who had not. A new proletariat would take their place and create its own dictatorship, but it would be a working class dictatorship where all would be comrades.

In short, Binkie Fatherley wanted revolution.

49

'I'll call you William,' Pauline said.

'What does that mean?'

'It's your proper name. You call me Pauline instead of *lass*.'

She had sat with Binkie in his trap.

She wanted women to be in the vanguard of his revolution. Women needed the right to vote but this was not a maximalist demand; it was the minimum needed so that women could reach above themselves to greater equality. Only revolution would bring equality so that women could have their own careers; family would become a partnership and if there was to be equality in the home there would be equality at work too; women would drive buses or work down pits or serve in the armed forces. Even a revolution would need armed forces, its own guards, its own militia. Only in a revolutionary society would women find their rightful place.

'The womenfolk'll not like it,' Binkie said.

Who would do the washing when the men were in the pit? Who would bake the bread, make the meals, darn the socks or beat pit clothes against outside walls to shake them free of dust, *dadding* as they called it? Parliament had refused votes for women. The state had taken care of its own, a capitalist state had protected family values where women knew their place. Yet there had been so much fire to Pauline, so much red hair blazing from beneath her bonnet, that however unconvinced the womenfolk had been they had applauded all the same.

Binkie became proud of Pauline.

He taught her to drive the trap, flicking the whip to hurry the horse along. They carried their message from one end of the coalfield to the other, making their speeches at weekends, sometimes in the evening if the pit head were not far away, but never once did Binkie lose a shift. Never did he give the coal owners a chance to sack him.

Nor did Pauline miss a day's schooling.

Sometimes their only meal had been sandwiches and tea prepared by the wives of other lodge secretaries, but neither of them cared whether they ate or drank; they were intoxicated by their speeches, so enthusiastic at their revolutionary ideals. They laughed at each other's jokes, they enjoyed the same stories, they reacted to the same events. Each moment became as precious as a rainbow, filled with colour, magical and inexplicable, but like the rainbow their lives were threatened with dark clouds, the clouds of war, of death, scudding ever closer to the pit village, more death than revolution, so that as the crowds gathered at the pit heads their message became more serious. Men listened quietly but attentively. There might be blood on the coal but the blood stained ever deeper Flanders fields.

'We need a single act,' Pauline said.

'What d'you mean – a single act?'

'We should burn down a house – kidnap the colliery manager.'

'Hide him in the pit with Charlie Bessford's rats?'

'A single act would incite men in other villages.'

Pauline explained how she had wanted to burn down the home of the Home Secretary. He had lived by the river and she and Terry Kenny had stolen a canoe and filled it with inflammable oil, pick locks and glass cutters. Only the river current had been too strong, they could not handle the canoe and they overshot the Home Secretary's home. But if they had burned down the home there would have been votes for women and Terry Kenny might still be alive.

'You mustn't upset yourself talkin' of those times,'

Binkie said. 'It's one thing preachin' revolution, it's another startin' one. We need an uprisin' from one end of the land to the other. We need a national strike. We could start it here and make it spread, but there's still a war on. The revolution might come, but only when the war's over and the lads are back.'

'We should make plans for when the war's over,' Pauline said.

50

'No schoolteacher's goin' to marry a colliery black-smith,' Roland Fatherley said.

'You want to be married?' Binkie asked.

'I'll be married some time, dad.'

'Do it before the revolution,' Binkie said.

'People get killed in revolutions, dad.'

'How can one class rise up against another without blood bein' spilled?'

'What about Pauline Alyson?'

'She believes in revolution too.'

'I meant about marryin' her.'

'You want to marry her?' Binkie said. 'You ask her.'

'I've never said a word to her,' Roland said. 'Not even winked an eye.'

'I thought Rosemary Rutland wanted to marry you?'

'She'd be a laughin' stock for marryin' beneath herself.'

'She's a village girl too.'

'And a Catholic to boot.'

'But you love Pauline Alyson?'

'Pauline's a better age for me, I'll grant you that.'

'You'd have a better future marryin' Rosemary.'

Roland had been colliery blacksmith for five years.

His father had brought him out of the pit when he had been twenty-four. He had preferred to be in-by with his friends and feared a charge of favouritism, that his father had placed him on bank, in the fresh air as it were, but there had not been a word of reproach. Besides, Roland had been too muscular; he had been short with chunky legs, squat like a weightlifter. Indeed, he had often thought to enter weightlifting championships at country fairs.

Roland had met Tom Rutland through the blacksmith's shop.

Tom had become master of the local hunt and had built stables behind his house. Roland would ensure his horses were well-shod and groomed for the village hunt. There had been no more stirring a spectacle than the sight of the huntsmen in their red and white, wearing their black caps, their horses shining and sweating, the hounds trotting among their feet, noses into the grass as they moved from the front of Tom's house through the village to the countryside.

Tom liked to say that he could not see the village from his house but he could feel its peace, security and humanity stretching like a hand across the fields and forest. He had opened more shops and his passenger bus service had been doing well, though he had competition from Charlie Bessford who also ran a bus service as well as keeping his own book on the whippet racing.

Tom had been impressed by Roland.

Often Roland ran bus trips to race meetings and on one occasion a bus trip to London. Sometimes, to fill the bus, he collected passengers from other villages; often the passengers were not there and others had to seek them. Seekers were sent after the seekers and it would be an hour before the bus got away on its solid rubber tyres to reach the racecourse in time for the first race.

Roland had never complained.

'I'd like you to run a pub for me on the fells,' he said.

'I cannot leave the blacksmith's shop,' Roland said.

'You can run the pub in the evenings after work.'

'Your pub's gettin' Charlie Bessford aggravated.'

'Because I run my own bus service from the pub?'

'His buses only make money when the pubs come out.'

'I'll worry about Charlie,' Tom said.

'At least it'll make a change from shoddin' horses,' Roland said.

Tom had enlisted in the Royal Flying Corps.

He had sided with Binkie Fatherley in his hostility towards the war; he had a life in the village that he had built for himself. He had shops and buses to run and now a pub. No foreigner had ever set foot in the village except the French onion seller; the only

246

foreign presence had been the whalebone on Bone Hill. Why should he fight a war? But as conscription approached he had enlisted to fly aeroplanes rather than be conscripted into the officer class and the mud of the Western Front.

He had been trained for coastal defence missions.

He had taken with him his leggings and leather jacket. He wore polished brown boots laced to his knees, but with his height he had difficulty manoeuvring into the cockpits of the new planes. He had wanted to join a bomber squadron, but with his height he would not be able to manoeuvre the plane, and he had to settle for aerial reconnaissance. His duty had been to locate every gun and machine gun emplacement along his flight-path. He knew that to miss a single gun a thousand lives might be lost.

Tom also had his private war with Charlie Bessford.

He might have introduced the first village trap but Charlie had introduced the first bus he called *Silver Cloud.* Tom had bought four abandoned lorries and converted them to buses; he had introduced bargain ticket packs and proper timetables and had encouraged his drivers to be aggressive. He had not intended to drive Charlie out of business and had been alarmed when he heard that not only had there been fights among the rival drivers but sabotage of buses.

Tom had wanted to call off his war.

What he had seen flying over the Western Front persuaded him that his bus war with Charlie served no purpose; there was a reality he could not escape.

247

Even as a reconnaissance pilot he was not likely to return. The Germans had new types of planes; they had a single-seater fighter called the *Laberstadt*. The pilots were specially-trained. The Vickers fighters of the Royal Flying Corps were no match for them. Nor were their reconnaissance planes. Tom flew off one day and did not come back. No-one could be certain whether he had been shot down over enemy lines and captured or whether he had been killed outright.

The telegram said:

Missing on active service.

Roland had come to visit Rosemary Rutland when he heard the telegram had arrived.

She stood on the balcony to her bedroom window and smelt the richness of the countryside. There had been a dampness that came with the dusk and with the dampness the odour of flowers and grass, of trees in the coppice. In summer there would be wheat ripening in the fields, carrying its dry odour like pollen in the wind. The sun would never be the same two nights running, one night a brilliant white that changed slowly to a pale deepening yellow, the other a scarlet tinge bursting to a radiance with the glow of its own warmth.

Roland had entered through the front door and waited for Rosemary to come downstairs from her room, pulling herself down with her twisted foot. The news had spread quickly through the village. Roland had hung up his leather apron in the blacksmith's shop and hurried to Rosemary, the sweat still clinging to his back and shoulders as he walked up the drive to her house. The light through the landing window and the reflection from the panes shimmered upon the carpets in the hallway.

The light caught at her poised throat.

She held the banister tightly as she came downstairs, the light catching her wedding ring and silver pearls. Tragedy hung around her face and Roland realised she had become as much a victim of war as her husband, a victim whose life spun backwards as she confronted the reality of the present: Tom had married her from pity not love. He had spent his time on his buses and shops and pub, his hounds and horses, even sending his daughter away from the village to boarding school so that he could be free of Rosemary, not be reminded of her, so that he could forget his foolishness in marrying beneath him.

She fell into Roland's arms.

She held him close and could smell the soot of the blacksmith's shop. She could feel his sweat. She clung to him with the desperation of a child. Had she too not been of the village? Had she not been raised in the cluster of houses around Bone Hill? As she held Roland close she felt she had come back to the village, she had returned to her own. Now that she had found the village through Roland she would not let it go.

Roland felt a stirring within.

His arms went around her shoulders and clasped behind her back. His hands moved to hold her thick blonde hair and he felt her tears commingling with his sweat. He had never held a woman so close. The light caught her beauty and he trembled in his confusion. Life was never going to be the same for either of them; the war had seen to that. Her hands came round to his face and she held his cheeks.

'I wanted to send for you,' she said. 'I wanted to feel your strength.'

'No matter what you think,' Roland said. 'He always loved you.'

'He loved the village too.'

51

Roland began following Pauline Alyson around the village.

In the blacksmith's shop he produced nails from thin bars heated in the forge and bent into shape with a hammer. Roland had been perplexed by the noise, so much beating and pounding, echoing back from the stone walls; the walls were lined with tools or ploughs that required repair; and a sooty black kettle stood on a ledge among cups filled with sparks that flew from the hammering metal. Roland withdrew the hot metal bars from the forge. They were covered by sparks that would shower and burn his skin and smart for many a day.

He left the blacksmith's shop and waited for Pauline coming from school.

Pauline had been indifferent to Roland, but once when there had been snow she had difficulty opening her door. The snow had drifted across her pathway, capped by a sparkling dry ice, so that she slipped and fell, bruising her buttocks. The snow had whitened the quarry and drifted across the road that linked her cottage to the school, but she had battled forward till she reached the school gates. The snow had lessened during the day, but after lessons when she returned to the cottage, she found a pathway had been cleared to her front door.

Roland stood before her gate leaning on a shovel.

'Thank you, Roland,' she had said.

He had been too shy to reply.

'You should tell her for us, dad,' Roland said.

'You've followed her around enough,' Binkie said. 'You might do yourself a favour to say a few words – be polite, like. You're not that gormless. But if you want to ask her to marry you, if you want to be her friend, if you want to go courtin', make her your fiancée like; if you want these things to happen between a man and a woman you'd better tell her yourself in your own way.'

Roland lived above the blacksmith's shop.

Bess Fatherley had furnished the flat for her second son. She had trawled the village sale rooms, buying an iron bed frame and feathered mattress, feather pillows and cream pillow cases to match. There had been brass ornaments for his mantelpiece, lace curtains for his windows, and a chest of drawers so old she had persuaded the colliery painter to give the drawers a coat of varnish.

Bess had fussed and dusted and coughed, but she had made Roland's tea and seen that there had always been home-made bread in the pantry, fadges and tea-cakes, butter and jam, and when the nights had turned cold she would carry down to him a dish of Lancashire hotpot. She changed his curtains when winter turned to spring, taking down heavy blankets she had pinned to the curtain rails to keep out the winter cold, replacing the blankets with flower-patterned curtains that let in the morning light.

He had never been cold in the flat.

The furnace never died in the blacksmith's shop below; its embers glowed through the night. Even when the snow piled as high as the window frames along the street there would still be warmth to Roland's flat. His mother set the table and chairs and cracket in the scullery; there had been an iron grate and black chimneypiece she had insisted on black-leading; but Roland only lit the fire when he wanted to heat a pan of water. Even then his mother would leave the teapot rinsed and tea in the pot.

Now Roland brought from his pocket a ragged hand bill.

'I'll ask her at the Durham Big Meetin',' Roland said.

'She'll be o'er busy. You'll never get a chance.'

'Mebbes I'll feel better askin' her surrounded by people.'

'Suit yourself,' Binkie said. 'There's safety in numbers.'

The hand bill had been crumpled and sooty and torn at the edges.

The hand bill advertised a rally at the Durham Big Meeting where Binkie Fatherley and Pauline Alyson would set out their views on a public platform rather than a pit head. Lodge secretaries would organise buses to bring miners and their families to Durham. Banners would be unfurled and as women and children settled along the river banks, enjoying the sunshine, their menfolk would hoist their banners and wend their way down cobbled streets across Elvet Bridge beyond the County Hotel till they reached the race track.

The names of Binkie Fatherley and Pauline and Mary Alyson and Albi Birt were set in bold type on the hand bill. Seeking further into his pocket, Roland produced a piece of charcoal and underlined Pauline's name on the bill. Why it should be better to ask for her hand in marriage at Durham rather than at Highhill he did not know. Why he should feel guilty about asking Pauline to marry him at all he did not know. It had become a matter not of imposing his will upon Pauline but upon himself.

He had resolved to ask her and ask her he would.

He replaced the charcoal in his pocket.

'It's all the better for her mother bein' there,' he said.

52

'*The Supreme is not really hidden from us,*' Mary Alyson quoted. '*He cannot hide from Himself. To think that He can be hidden from us, who are Himself, is the subtlest of our illusions. He is our innermost Self, the very heart of our being.*'

'It's impressive,' Albi Birt said. 'I'll grant you that.'

'You don't understand it?'

'Nor feel it neither.'

'How about this,' Mary said.

She had written out another quotation on the train:

There is a self that is the essence of matter. There is another inner self of life that fills the other; there is another inner self of mind, there is another inner self of truth-knowledge. There is another inner self of bliss. Happy is the man or woman who by continually eschewing all images and who by introversion and the lifting up of his mind to the spirit at last forgets and leaves behind all images.

'I wish you'd write my speeches,' Albi said.

'You don't understand that either?'

'We've had a heavy week at the House.'

Mary had taken the train north to visit her daughter in her new home.

She would see Pauline for the last time on Durham

Big Meeting Day. She had taken the train from King's Cross Station and through the steam she had looked out upon her country and her people; she had given so much, but she had never replaced God in her soul. She had sought to lose her inner self through working for the poor, through the trade union and labour movements; she had worked with determination to immerse her past in the present. She had not allowed herself to think of her lost child, her self-denial towards men, but the inner self had drifted in search of a refuge.

She had found this in the occult.

She had discovered a superior being that she called Spirit, that lived in all that lived, listening through the ear, seeing through the eye, clinging neither to this nor to that, attaining immortal life. She climbed towards Spirit through attention and concentration and meditation. Only beyond meditation would she find Spirit, not a ripple to the surface of her mind, not a rustle through the undergrowth of her thought. Yet when her personal self had ceased its war with her will, when will and awareness had fused together in an impersonal self, then she had found true Spirit.

It filled her mind with a golden light.

It had given her peace and tranquillity.

She had lived on a higher plain and only when she had begun thinking again, when she had descended the ladder from meditation to concentration and attention, when she had sunk among fouler shapes in inner conversation, simple association, and thinking of moving had she returned to her basic nature, wilful and energetic, but pulled hither and thither by her thought processes. She had sought to describe the Spirit, the golden light, but no words would reach out. It lived beyond words as it lived beyond thoughts.

'You should write articles,' Albi said.

'I'm writing them all the time.'

Occult magazines were publishing articles throughout the world but Mary wanted to write books. She wanted to nurture this new-found spirituality. She thought the secret of life lay in the finding and keeping within sight of the self; she wanted the world to know and never forget. But to write books she had to understand and to understand she had to go to India.

She found that Spirit was immortal.

It could be found in chanting hymns, mantras they were called; it could be found in the Upanishads, the bible of the Hindus. It could be passed orally from teacher to pupil as it had these last six thousand years. It lived in all that lived and could be seen in the rustle of the wind through chestnut trees, the ripples across a pond, in the shadows across the sun. It had even been the basis of the Jewish religion and could be found in Genesis when the Spirit moved across the face of the waters.

She would need to travel in wartime, by a circuitous route, but she would leave as soon as possible. Her travel arrangements were in hand. She had travelled north with a book-bag filled with everything she had found written in English on the Upanishads. She wanted her own personal translation, but for that she would need to learn Hindu, and to learn Hindu she would need to travel to India.

'I wanted you to be the first woman Member of Parliament,' Binkie said.

'My daughter will be the first woman Member.'

'You cannot leave your union work.'

'My union work's left me,' Mary said.

'You can write another of your socialist books.'

'They're only read in Russia,' Mary said. 'And my articles.'

'They read everythin' there,' Albi said.

'I only hope it does them good,' Mary said. 'I want to define the indefinable. I want to write about will and awareness and self – a troika of the mind. If I can write about that – if I can reveal the fundamental wisdom – I shall truly leave something behind for future generations.'

'Binkie Fatherley wants to be a revolutionary,' Albi said. 'I'm tryin' to talk him out of it.'

'How can you talk a revolutionary out of anything?'

'I want him to work through the ballot box.'

'Vote for me and I'll give you revolution! Change can only come through the trade unions. It can only come from a Labour government. Otherwise, you take two steps forward and one step back. Socialism in one country or socialism in all countries? You won't get socialism through revolution – dictatorship maybe, but not socialism. You forget – I've tried it.'

'You've tried most things.'

She and Bernard Shaw had marched together.

Shaw believed socialist change should come through evolution rather than revolution. He believed change had to be by consent, but to achieve consent there had to be argument and organisation. But when revolutionary socialists had taken to the streets to march upon Parliament he and Mary Alyson had marched arm-in-arm under a banner Mary had made when she lived with Charles Wheatley in Long Acre.

They had met at Clerkenwell.

There had been flags and banners at every corner, the flags and banners red; revolutionary slogans and lines from the scriptures had been woven into the cloth. They had marched upon Trafalgar Square and taken over the plinth. Speaker after speaker had declared that all property was theft. They condemned the ruling classes and declared that if the whole of the propertied class had but a single throat it would be cut without a second thought.

'Revolutionaries confuse justice for the poor with envy for the rich,' Shaw said. 'The revolt of an empty stomach will not lead to a baker's shop.'

Police had charged with truncheons.

They came from alleyways around the Square and Mary and Bernard Shaw had been bowled over. Charles Wheatley had been hit with a truncheon and made his own way back to Long Acre, blood running from a cut in his forehead. Their banner had furled and fallen like a colour stricken on the battlefield. Police had trampled over them, their uplifted truncheons swinging right and left, the banner torn by their hobnail boots. Blood stained the corners of the banner where those who had been trampled had cut their heads against the cobbled square.

'We'd better skedaddle,' Shaw said.

Revolutionaries had been skedaddling ever since.

53

'You'll never paint anything better than the portrait of Terry Kenny,' Mary said.

'Or the head of Albi Birt.'

'At least you flattered his vanity.'

Mary had arrived at Highhill by trap.

Rather than making her way to the cottage, she had asked the trap driver to give her a tour of the village. Highhill stood stapled upon the hill. Smoke curled from the chimneys into the afternoon sky; there were women in the streets doing their shopping, men hanging around street corners, all cloth caps and open necks or scarves; the women had their headscarfs nipped tightly beneath their chins. All heads turned towards the trap, some of them smiling, none of them sullen, aware they had a famous woman to their midst.

Word had spread that Mary Alyson would be arriving.

Mary had wanted to feel again that closeness with

people she had felt when she had ridden on top of the bus from Pimlico to the East End, when she had served at the mission, when she had met Charles Wheatley with his shorthand. She wanted to feel again that empathy and sense of injustice with those who needed raising up. She smiled at those who acknowledged her; she felt their closeness, their sympathy, but there had been no stirring within. The time had come for others to take up their cause.

She had devoted her life to it.

It had worn her out.

She had tidied Pauline's cottage as if she were the housekeeper. Her hands had been quick, a concentration fret to her face, putting as much into it as if she were writing an article or the chapter of a book. She cleared away the magazines and school books, disentangling the dirty dishes and placing the dishes in the scullery sink. She set the wicker chairs differently to make more room and finding a duster she swept away the dust from the staircase. But if she dusted the stairs she did not venture beyond the landing into Pauline's studio.

She showed no interest in her paintings.

'I attended my father's funeral,' Pauline said.

Arnold Alyson had died after suffering his stroke.

'The Reverend Alyson was never your father,' Mary said. 'Our marriage was never consummated. Your father is called Charles Wheatley. I met him when I came to work in the East End. Bernard Shaw warned me against him, but it didn't matter. I had so much pain bringing you into the world I swore I'd never let another man touch me.'

'And have you?'

'Not even Albi Birt.'

'You've kept it from me all these years.'

'You've had enough on your mind with suffragism and revolution.'

'But I want to meet my father. It's my right.'

'You'll need to take a slow boat to Australia. He married Eleanor Marx – but it didn't last. Eleanor died from poisoning when Wheatley told her he proposed to divorce her and marry another. Bernard Shaw had been right all along. By that time Wheatley had gone through Eleanor's money – or the money the revolutionaries provided.'

'He didn't need to go to Australia.'

'He never recovered having his head beaten in at Trafalgar Square,' Mary said. 'He thought he should have a new beginning. He joined the Labour Party but they didn't have much time for him – they thought he was a Marxist because he'd run off with Eleanor.'

'I didn't know any of this,' Pauline said.

'It was never in Ann-Marie's cuttings book.'

'Yet in all my childhood she knew and Arnold knew.'

'Ann-Marie persuaded the Bishop to allow an annulment of my marriage, even though you were supposed to be Arnold's child. Typical of the Church to live a lie to save a soul! But having lost Charles Wheatley and having lost you it didn't matter whether – in the eyes

261

of the Church – I'd ever been married. I'd renounced God and the marriage vows. I had renounced the flesh – my work for the people was all important.'

'Were the people worth it?'

'We'll end footnotes to history.'

'Not Terry Kenny.'

'In the eyes of the people, when votes for women come, it will not be because Terry Kenny died – not because you almost died on hunger strike – but because Ann-Marie Alyson eschewed violence and I gained the confidence of the Prime Minister to fight his capitalists' war – as you call it. Will I be remembered for the match girls or for handing out white feathers to young lads at Hyde Park Corner?'

'At least you'll be remembered.'

'We are a long time dead, Pauline, but whilst my active life is over yours is just beginning. You can become the first woman Member of Parliament. You can build on votes for women. You are young enough to battle on with your health restored – young enough to leave more than a footnote. You can stamp your feet on history as if leaving your imprint in concrete.'

'You wish to inspire me, mother – or shock me with the truth?'

Mary had pushed her sketch pad and pencil into Pauline's hands and linking her firmly they had set off to walk across the fields. Mary had set no direction and though she walked quickly she realised her daughter had been unable to keep up. Her health might be restored, but she tired easily and found it difficult to be brisk, dressed as she was in a long skirt. She had been exhausted by her pit head speeches, her trap drives, and she had been nervous about speaking at the Durham Big Meeting.

'You've given me a fright, mother,' she said.

'I thought you were strong enough for all things.'

'Not strong enough for the truth.'

Pauline felt the strength flowing from her.

Mary paused and when her daughter stumbled into her arms she held her there; she let her head bury into her shoulder, feeling the red hair rich to her hands. She felt too the wind to her face as if she and her daughter and Spirit were as one. She felt herself in harmony with the wind and the sky and the farmhouse and cow stall and barn across the field. The summer light fell shiny across the furrows and Spirit moved as the wind through the gorse; the smell of the gorse, the grass and cow-dung and ploughed soil invaded her senses and made her complete with Spirit.

Mary laid Pauline upon the grass.

'I shall always love the Reverend Alyson,' Pauline said.

'You never loved him in your life and you've never loved him since he died. You can respect him, think of him; you can respect Ann-Marie – she set you on the road to suffragism. But when it went wrong there was no Ann-Marie and when you ended in Holloway she refused to have you back. It was only when you needed me that your mother was called – not by you but by the very authorities that took you from me.'

Mary smoothed the red hair around her neck and shoulders, Pauline's face white, the blood fled, the eyes closed, her daughter defeated, frail, vulnerable, stricken by the truth. She took off her own jacket so that she could cover Pauline as she lay, keeping the warmth within her. She loosened the buttons to her neck and smoothed the long skirt around her thighs. She stroked the hairs across her brow and held her hands that were so cold.

'I should draw you, mother,' Pauline said.

'I do not want to be remembered from a sketch pad,' Mary said.

'I should have a sketch of you as you are now – as you once were. Let my imagination trace you back down the years till I see you at my age – suffering all manner of evil. And then bring you forward to this day – when we are together at last. If you are to leave me, let me have this remembrance of you.'

'My photograph is on the cover of my books,' Mary said. 'Find them and read them and whatever you read, however often you read them, there you will hear your mother thinking. There you will see her before you. Perhaps you will not miss the water till the well runs dry, but the well ran dry many years ago. I cannot expect you to miss your mother when she leaves for India.'

'Is it too late to love you, mother?'

'I hope it is not too late for you to love anyone,' Mary said.

54

'She's seein' her mother off at the station,' Binkie said.

'I wish you'd speak to her first,' Roland said.

'They've gone for a walk along the river and a look at the Cathedral. It'll be o'er late for her to come back to the village. She'll need to rest. She'll stay at the County Hotel till the mornin'. I've said I'll come back and fetch her, if she needs fetchin' that is, but I want to get home to your mother.'

'She's still coughin', dad.'

'I'll look after her,' Binkie said.

'Mebbes I should stay the night in the same hotel,' Roland said.

'There's a room already booked for me. You can stay in that. I was supposed to stay for the Federation dinner, but with your mother coughin' the way she is I'd better get back. You stay, though, and go about your business. You know I'd put in a good word for you if I could.'

'Mebbes I should let her be till she recovers from her speech.'

It had been the first and last time Mary and Pauline Alyson would share a platform.

It had been, too, the first major speech Pauline had made since the Manchester Free Trade Hall. She had felt the same intoxication, the same power, speaking with the river behind her, looking across the former racecourse to where the grass undulated towards the road and the traffic, the throng massed before her, no seats, all of them standing so close they could feel each other's bodily heat.

Pauline, speaking without notes, her hands uplifted, her voice stronger than her spirit, had sent her message not only across the heads of the pitmen, not only beyond the road and traffic, but into the future and into history. How had she been able to see so far ahead for one so young? There were those who said she had spoken from the heart, others that she had studied the speech and committed it to memory, but with her red hair flaming around her neck her voice had been carried not by the wind but by the nobility of her sentiments that would inspire not only her generation but other generations to follow.

'I look forward to the day when men and women shall be equal,' she declared. 'Equal in pay and conditions of work, equal in dignity, equal in compassion and understanding. When bringing children into the world is a shared experience, the man looking after his woman, bringing up his children, taking responsibility for them. When a woman can not only become Member of Parliament but solicitor or barrister or accountant; when she can drive a bus, work down the pit – even join the Army. Where she has free will and free expression, not the object of violence, not the victim of attack or ridicule. That day will come as surely as the sun rises or the snow falls. As men will triumph so too will women.'

Pauline had fainted as she reached her peroration.

Her words had trailed like a stranded horse without its jockey on the same racecourse, but the fading words had more impact on the crowd and those on the platform. There had been silence rather than ovation, and the silence had continued as Binkie Fatherley lifted Pauline into his arms and carried her through the parting throng to the County Hotel. Silence had followed his every step until there had come a single handclap from the platform.

Mary Alyson stood to applaud her daughter.

The applause rippled out from the platform to the men and women in the throng, rippled across to the river bank where women and children played by the water's edge, rippled across the Elvet bridge towards the Cathedral. The ripple became a roar and buffeted Mary Alyson and Albi Birt on the platform. It carried on till it engulfed the City and only the Cathedral towers seemed able to resist.

Pauline heard the applause as she held Binkie by the neck.

'It can be done!' she said. 'It can be done!'

Binkie saw colour coming back to her cheeks.

'What can be done?'

'Our revolution. The men and women are with us. They want to rise up. They want a new order. They're looking to us to challenge authority. We shall take a bus to London. You can put me on the bus and they can arrest me and put me in Holloway Prison. I can die like Terry Kenny. Or they can abolish my licence and let us win – not only votes for women, but dignity and respect for all men – and women. Don't you see, William, it's all there for you and me.'

'You can hold your horses,' Binkie said. 'Your mother's goin' to India. Let her get herself away before you end up again in Holloway. And let's have the revolution here first in Highhill and the Durham coalfield before we export it to London.'

'We will have the revolution, William?'

'I call it a socialist springtime,' Binkie said.

Now she and Mary Alyson walked by the Cathedral.

The Cathedral stood tall and majestic, darkened by age, its profile strong against the river and castle and trees; but whereas once Mary Alyson might have seen beauty in its lines, its construction, now she looked upon it as a useless hunk of building stone. Her heart had become as hardened as those felons who had beat upon the door for sanctuary and who, if sanctuary were granted, would be escorted from the Cathedral by the clergy to the coast where they would board a boat and sail into exile.

'You should blow it up one day,' Mary said.

'All I want to do is get back to the County Hotel.'

55

Roland had been shown a room on the same floor as other Federation guests.

A young lad no more than sixteen dressed in a uniform as if he were on the stage showed him to the room and Roland noticed the fez-like hat that sat upon his head. He held out his hand and Roland fumbled in his pockets till he found a few coppers. He had worn his best suit for the Meeting, his shirt tight around the collar, his tie not properly knotted, and if his jacket had been finely-cut the lapels were adrift, pointing upward, his trousers too tight around the waist and thighs.

He moved back to the hotel foyer.

Pit lads were throwing coins into a goldfish pool set in one of the corners, the fish silver and gold, some of them large, others anaemic, some rising to the surface to open their mouths at the pit lads, but most of them diving deeper into the pool as the farthings fell around them. The pit lads drifted from the foyer to the Dun Cow pub in Elvet Road and Roland followed. The pub had been narrow with white-painted walls and lattice-like structures across the front.

Roland settled into a corner.

He ordered a pint of beer and a tumbler of whisky.

He felt trapped by the love he felt for his dying mother, the respect he had for his father; he felt trapped in his own loneliness, his own gaucheness. When he looked back on these events in later life he would put them down to his work in the blacksmith's shop, the noise to his ears, the beating and pounding, the hammering of nails; but if he looked back at all his memories would be happier. On this Durham Big Meeting Day his mother had still been alive and his brothers too.

The sadness of other events lay ahead.

Roland would not leave the Dun Cow.

He stood foot on rail, drinking the beer and whisky, the one chasing the other down his throat, feeling his balance going and his senses, but not moving, not talking, resting his arms upon the counter, feeling morose and maudlin, trying to focus through the haze of alcohol on what he would say to Pauline. He had left no message asking to see her, but he knew her room number from the boy with the fez. He felt overwhelmed by the heat of the pub and the alcohol to his veins and stumbled back into the hotel.

There had been a bar in the hotel opposite the goldfish pond. Roland ordered another whisky chaser. His head had cleared as he left the Dun Cow and walking by the river bank he had regained some of his balance. Still he did not have the courage to find Pauline's room and knock upon her door, but if he could not think what to say he felt encouraged that perhaps his father had left a message and she would understand.

She would invite him in and sit him down.

270

Pauline had been booked into a suite on the third floor and Roland had walked up the stairs rather than use the lift; the only lift he had known had been the cage at the pit. He held the silver rail and felt the plush carpets. There had been less air on the stairs and he felt dizzy. He opened his shirt collar, undoing his stud, loosening his tie, straightening his lapels, hitching at his trousers, aware of their tightness, losing his balance so that he almost fell.

He found Pauline's door and knocked respectfully. There had been no response.

Perhaps he had fallen against the door, perhaps he had stumbled, but his hand went to the door to save himself and the door swung open. He found himself in an ante-room with another door before him. This door too had been open. He pushed through the door and saw that the suite consisted of a living room and a bedroom and a bathroom beyond the bedroom. There had been the smell of freshly-cut flowers and the hazier smell of alcohol. He saw an ice bucket in one corner and the curved neck of a bottle protruding from the ice.

His legs carried him forward but his mind was clearing.

The bedroom door had been open and he saw a bedside lamp, his eyes adjusting to the pink light that came from under the tassels. Alcohol still raced through his bloodstream, but he paused ashamed of himself, aware of his drunkenness, certain he was doing wrong; but he did not turn for the door. His feet settled upon the carpet, his legs like tree trunks, his eyes focused on the pink glow from the bedside lamp. He sought to balance himself, the room steadying, the pink lamp swinging with the furniture.

He saw two women lying upon the bed.

Roland forced his legs backward.

He made his way out of the living room.

He sought to hold himself steady, not stumble or fall, more sober than he had been. His mind had cleared and he did not close the door behind him but left it ajar so that it would be left as he had found it. He paused in the ante-room, the smell of freshly-cut flowers and alcohol behind him; the air had been drier and he felt dizzy. He forced himself into the corridor, again not closing the door, holding the wall to steady himself, moving as quickly as he could till he found his own room.

He fumbled for the key.

He had worn his best suit but he had worn too his cloth cap; he took the cap from his pocket and let it drop to the floor. He kicked it across the carpet till it crumpled against the wall. He opened the door at last and if his consciousness had cleared of alcohol, if it had left his brain, now it attacked his limbs; it weakened his legs so that he could hardly stand. The alcohol attacked his stomach and he felt sick. Indeed he was sick, sick by the door, sick on the carpet, sick in the bathroom, sick till his body rejected the last of the whisky and beer, so sick that he felt he would never be well again.

He had seen Pauline Alyson making love to Barbara Rutland.

56

'I heard the door go,' Barbara said.

'Probably the wind,' Pauline said.

She lay with her red hair in wide strands across the pillow.

The sheets beneath her buttocks had been warm and comfortable, not coarse like the sheets on her cottage bed; she had used coarse sheets as a penance for her past life. She knew in the arms of Barbara Rutland her life was beginning again. The colour had returned to her face, two pink splashes across her cheekbones, but her lips were pale and the skin ran white from her neck to her breasts. She closed her eyes as Barbara ran her hands from her face to her neck.

'Did Terry Kenny love you as I love you?' Barbara asked.

'She was gentle,' Pauline said. 'Thoughtful.'

'But rough too?'

'Not so rough.'

Barbara bit at the flesh around Pauline's left nipple.

'You like that?' she asked.

'Harder,' Pauline said.

Barbara had been taller than Pauline.

She had a pure skin unmarked by sun, as pure as her blonde hair. The valley of her breasts shone with sweat and her breasts were large and flaccid, only the

273

nipples firm, seeking out Pauline's breasts. Barbara had taken control of Pauline. She had dominated her. Her hands and mouth did the work, her words soft in Pauline's ear, her teeth soft-biting, her tongue suckling the nipple, touring the darker softness around the nipple. Her tongue lingered, probing and sensitive and delicate.

There had been no harshness, no pain.

Only a gentle ecstasy for Pauline.

'Terry was my first love,' Pauline whispered. 'You shall be my last.'

'We should live as man and wife,' Barbara said. 'I have heard of couples who live together. They call them spinsters. Do you think we can live together as spinsters?'

'We are too young to be spinsters.'

'All the same we could live together.'

Barbara had left the boarding school and returned to the village.

With her father missing, she had helped her mother with the accounts. She had been surprised at so much book-keeping, so many entries, so many shops and buses to run as well as the pub. She would visit Pauline in the afternoon at her cottage, clearing dishes and books and uprighting chairs. She would even tidy the studio. The order lasted only a few hours and Barbara reasoned that Pauline's untidiness had something to do with her upbringing. There had always been someone to tidy after her, whether it had been Ann-Marie or Terry Kenny.

She would have fruit and groceries delivered from the Rutland shops and make tea when Pauline returned from school. Sometimes she would stay late till Pauline and Binkie returned from speaking at another pithead, keeping the door open so that the light would fall across the pathway. Pauline's bedroom had always been locked, the key hanging by the side of the mantelpiece; Barbara had been aware that this was Pauline's private domain. Pauline never asked her to make up the bed nor dust the room. But Pauline had been delayed, the tidying done, the larder stocked. The key had caught the light from the fire and Barbara had felt its warmth to her hand. She had taken the key and opened the bedroom door.

The red curtains were drawn and she pulled them apart.

The room had been simple, the floor bare, the bed narrow and neatly-made. It had been almost a cot, with hard wooden sides and board, the pillow dour and lumpen as if filled with straw. However untidy Pauline might be elsewhere, she had not been untidy here; there were book shelves lined with books on socialism and the suffragist movement. There had been a bible too and photographs of a Reverend and a gentle woman, and a larger photograph of a woman that Barbara thought she knew but could not place. She deduced this to be Mary Alyson. There had been a safety lamp, her only concession to Highhill, but there had been nothing personal to Pauline: no romance, no exotic scents, no self-portraits.

275

Yet standing in Pauline's bedroom Barbara had felt another presence.

The presence lay in the neatness, in the quiet power, in the unspeckled light through the window. It lay in the firmness of the bed where Barbara had settled, in the low beams, intricate with their woodworm, in the wood panels to the walls. She noticed opposite the window a curtain drawn across what appeared to be another window, but when she drew the curtain aside it had not been a window at all. There had been a portrait on the wall of a young woman, her head turned, the portrait filled with orange and gold tints, the lines curved, the portrait so alive she wondered when the young woman might turn her head and look at her. She had been so startled by the presence of this other woman she had turned to sit again upon the bed.

She noticed a trunk under the bed.

She pulled the trunk free.

The trunk had not been locked and she heaved it open, anxious and nervous, panicking with the other presence in the room, finding letters, newspapers and photographs in the trunk: photographs taken at the funeral of Terry Kenny, newspaper cuttings of her life, letters from Terry, the handwriting so laboriously neat, as if Terry had wanted to please. Barbara laid the letters and cuttings and photographs upon the bed.

She looked up and saw Pauline standing in the doorway.

'Now there are three of us in the room,' Barbara said.

Pauline saw Barbara sitting on the floor with the letters of Terry Kenny around her and the curtain drawn so that Terry's bare back caught the light and came alive before her. Her mother had sent the portrait when she knew she was going to India, but seeing the light striking the back the defences that Pauline had built around herself broke down. She had kept three rings around her inner self all these years to ensure no thought, no reflection, no emotion ever broke through. They had been as rings around the moon.

Now she was confronted by her past and her future.

In that moment she had not been sure she should love or hate Barbara. She had exposed her to herself, she had revealed her past, she had made her feel guilty and regretful and melancholic. She had wanted to relive the past and project it into a future she had wanted, she and Terry alive, both heroines to the cause, that votes for women had come about because of them. That had not come to pass. That is why she had shut the thoughts from her mind and built up her defences.

That is why she might yet hate Barbara Rutland.

But with her defences down and to her own astonishment she felt a sudden weakening to her knees. A tear came to her eyes, a single silver tear to each eye, followed by another and another, till soon her body rose in revolt, her self burst from its three rings and she cried. No: she wept for a past that was gone, wept because she was vulnerable, wept because she had become defenceless, wept because she could no longer hide from herself. She found herself on the floor with Barbara, swimming among the letters, the portrait of Terry Kenny above her head.

She clasped Barbara to her.

'I could hate you,' she said.

'You must turn your hate to love,' Barbara soothed.

Now they lay together in a Durham hotel.

'I don't want to lose you as I lost Terry Kenny,' Pauline said. 'If we lived together I would lose you as I lost Terry.'

'Do you think anyone really cares who lives with the schoolteacher?'

'You have a mother to think of. You have a life ahead. Do you really want to spend it with a revolutionary? Better to be my lover, flesh of my flesh, blood of my blood. Tell me what it is you want, my dearest, and I will give it to you.'

'You must paint me,' Barbara said. 'As you painted Terry Kenny.'

57

'No daughter of mine can live with another woman,' Rosemary Rutland said.

'I want to share my life with her,' Barbara said.

'I can see that my daughter is innocent of the ways of the world,' Rosemary said. 'Boarding school was not the best experience. It's made you too dependent on your own sex. There's another world of men and women where they fall in love and marry. Do you think any man will marry you if he knows you lived with another woman?'

'I don't care about men.'

'That is Pauline Alyson talking. She has filled your mind with tomfoolery. She led Terry Kenny astray. She was a fine girl with a nice upbringing. She came from a respectable family. She died because Pauline Alyson killed her. You want to put yourself in the same position. You want to walk out of my house because of an infatuation.'

Mother and daughter walked around the coppice of chestnut trees and copper beeches near their house, neither feeling the chill, letting their eyes wander from the shale to the leaves. The sound of the village had been remote as they breathed the freshness, the scents of honeysuckle and moss not making them drowsy, rather sharpening their senses. Each walked separately from the other, the distance one of emotion as well as space. The pathway dropped and they found themselves back on the red shale with the large windows of the house staring back at them.

'She's a fine woman,' Barbara said. 'A great woman. She's sensitive as well as strong. She's a painter and a suffragist. She's all that I ever want in life. Even you, mother, can see that.'

Barbara could see Pauline in her mind.

Pauline in her overalls, the cigarette holder between her lips, her eyes squinting, holding the palette, her head uplifted so that Barbara could see only the rim of the French beret, but if she had not felt the coolness of the air walking the coppice nor had she felt it reposing on the cot in the studio. Her naked body had been turned towards Pauline, her head resting on her hand, her elbow imprinted upon the pillow, the blonde hair shaking around her neck and ears. She had held her teeth together to prevent herself from smiling.

Her eyes never left Pauline.

'I have confidence to paint your face,' Pauline said. 'Terry meant so much to me I never could bring myself to paint her face. I caught the radiance of her soul with the flecks of red and orange and gold – and the lines of her back. I caught her beauty – and her youth. She's luckier than me. She reposes eternally and lives forever. You will live forever, too, when I'm done.'

'You'll let others see the painting?'

'All men will admire it.'

'And women too, I hope.'

'I'll let you paint my face if you catch the love in my eyes.'

'And the sensuality of your hands,' Pauline said.

Barbara and her mother came into the living room.

'You are to become a nurse,' Rosemary said.

'You don't believe in the war.'

'Being a nurse is helping mankind.'

'You want to send me away.'

'For your own good,' Rosemary said. 'You'll be over your infatuation by the time the war ends. Seeing real life at the front will make you understand emotions aren't everything. There is a higher plain – the plain of duty as well as love. You must put your duty before your love for Pauline Alyson.'

'I'll never stop loving Pauline.'

'The choice would be yours – but only after reflection, when time has passed, when you've lived a little longer. You can write, of course – but distance will slow your heartbeat, your emotions can settle. Then you can decide.'

'You think my emotions will settle on the Western Front?'

'Your father died on the Western Front. At least he went missing. Perhaps it will help you to understand his life, to understand why he is gone as others are gone. Your father called off the bus war with Charlie Bessford because he understood how meaningless it had become compared to young men dying, throwing themselves on barbed wire, being cut down by machine-gun fire. Only Charlie carries on with the bus war against a woman as lonely as myself. You'll get the message, you'll understand – and when you do you'll thank your mother, as you should thank her, for saving you from mortal sin.'

'You talk like the preacher Ernest Fatherley.'

'And you're still a Catholic.'

Rosemary felt ill with her sense of failure.

She had tired with her walk around the coppice and back to the house. Her right leg had dragged but she insisted on walking normally, ignoring the pain, but because of her emotional state the pain had been more intense. She felt bewildered and saddened. She recalled Barbara's first pony, her first gymkhana, her first gymslip, how difficult had been her birth. She had felt empty when Barbara had been released to the world as she felt emotionally empty now.

'I'm still not leaving Pauline,' Barbara said.

'There's a hospital ship leaving for Le Havre in two days. They'll settle you at Rouen before moving you to Flanders. You'll be on probation, of course, not a full-fledged nurse, but all the training you'll need will come from your common sense. There'll be matrons and staff nurses to help.'

'I'll never leave the village.'

'I love you too much to let you stay.'

Rosemary handed Barbara a long brown envelope.

Barbara's name had been on the envelope.

The envelope had already been opened and a legal document fell into her hand. She had been bewildered by the small print and seal. No-one in the pit village received a summons; the village had been too enclosed to allow legal interference, and if there were disputes they were settled between the parties. She had seen copies of summonses at boarding school when they had touched upon law as part of her course work. She held the rough paper and tried to make out the words.

It had something to do with Pauline Alyson.

She knew that Pauline had still been on licence, that she could not return to London, could not engage in political activity; she wondered if special constables had made a report to magistrates after her speech at the Durham Big Meeting and the magistrates had

282

issued the summons. Strands of the speech had stayed with Barbara and echoed through her mind: how she had talked of her own weakness, how the suffragist movement had been all but destroyed; how sons had gone from the coalfield to fight the war as their fathers had gone to fight the Boer War.

Sons of clay, she had called them. *Caryatids of the earth.*

Why would they want to lock her up for that?

'A special constable brought the summons from Durham,' Rosemary said. 'An information has been laid that you committed an unnatural act with Pauline Alyson at the County Hotel on the night of the Big Meeting. A miner came into the room by mistake. He saw it all. He reported you to the police. The special constable will want a statement from you and from Pauline. If convicted each of you will spend two years in prison. No hunger strike would get you out. There'd be no public sympathy.'

'You wouldn't do that to Pauline?'

'You will see how her revolution thrives in prison.'

'You would send me to the same prison?'

'Not if you leave in the hospital ship.'

'I'd never be able to come back,' Barbara said. 'It will always be hanging over me.'

'The miner will retract his statement if you leave.'

'Why would he do that?'

'Because he too loves Pauline Alyson.'

58

After Bess Fatherley's funeral, Roland walked through the village to the home of Rosemary Rutland.

Roland walked down the pathway, letting his fingers run through the leaves to the bushes, not looking up till suddenly the pathway hit the shale. The house stood tall above him: three storeys with balconies running along each of the upstairs windows and downstairs French windows that opened at the back upon acres of lawns and herbaceous borders. The blue stain of the forest crept to the edges of the estate. The sun had slipped behind the house and the three storeys of windows were black forbidding pools of shadow.

'I thought I might have seen you at the funeral,' Roland said.

'It reminds me too much of my own man,' Rosemary said.

'My grandfather Ernest did us right proud.'

'And your father?'

'Never said a word. Refused to sing a hymn. Never looked at anyone, never acknowledged the colliery manager; but Albi Birt stood next to him and when he felt under strain their hands touched. Two grown men – holdin' hands in a chapel. I never thought I'd see the day.'

'Albi Birt came all the way from Westminster?'

'Somewhere like that.'

'All his life your father'll blame himself.'

'So he says, but he's o'er busy to fret for long. He has his work. The pit'll keep him goin'. And there's Pauline. He doesn't think he'll marry her – but he will.'

'Was she at the funeral?'

'You didn't come. Neither did she.'

'She'd not want to get in the way.'

The black door to the house had been open, its knob and letter box newly-polished.

Roland had moved quickly inside, feeling the tightness to his boots where he had walked through the village. He had felt a chill to his face, he had kicked the odd stone in his path as he had done in his childhood, the stone peeling the leather from the toe of his boot. His mourning clothes had been his Sunday best: dark suit and waistcoat, a silver watch chain, white shirt and starch collar, black tie only worn for funerals, his boots polished and tightly laced. He wore a black trilby pulled deep across his brow; his father had worn a bowler hat leant to him by the colliery manager. His boots had steel-capped heels and tapped back at him from the newly tarmacadamed village road.

Rosemary had taken Roland's trilby and hung it on the hat stand in the hallway.

'They say you're off to Italy?'

'If the boat takes us that far.'

'Only across the Channel. After that you take a train.'

'As long as I get there.'

'As far away from the village you can get?'

'Even that'll not be far enough.'

Rosemary poured Roland a whisky and settled him on a settee in her drawing room.

She had settled beside him, holding herself erect, her skirt covering her knees, a slim woman of forty. Her natural blonde hair rippled over her shoulders, blonde strands fretting across her brow so that she nervously flicked them away. Her blue eyes never left Roland. She listened to what he had to say, treating him as an equal, a hand resting upon his knee, feeling the tightness of his trousers, watching as he drank his whisky, throwing it to the back of his throat, his gaze out of the French windows.

'I read in the papers how the Prime Minister wants to keep Italy in the war. He fears they might retreat before the Austrians. That would release more enemy divisions for the Western Front. That wouldn't please our generals. They want to create a new division for Italy that can be sent from this country. They want to keep all the men they have to beat the Germans.'

'That'll be the day – beatin' the Germans.'

'My husband thought we could beat them.'

'My brothers thought they could do it single-handed.'

'We shouldn't be talking about the Western Front,' Rosemary said. 'We'll not get through the day otherwise. All those thoughts about my husband and your brothers. I thought your father wanted you to stay in the village and take over as lodge secretary?'

'You pick up all the gossip.'

'They say he wants to go into politics.'

'He's into revolution now,' Roland said. 'First in the village then in the county, and after the county the country. First you light a spark, he says, that spark'll light a fire. And the fire'll light the world.'

'Sounds fine to me.'

'Except people get killed in revolutions.'

'There'll not be a revolution here.'

'There might be,' Roland said. 'When the war's over. He wants you to be a part of it – with your shops feedin' the men on strike. He'll need to get the colliery manager to close down the pit. Or let the men strike underground. He's figurin' it all out – even though my mother's hardly in her grave.'

'What about your brother Ernie?'

'He's content to look after his pigs and grow his leeks and throw his quoits. He'll look after the house now my mother's gone. He'll look after my father to see his socks are darned and his clothes dadded. He might be quiet but he's devoted, I'll say that for him.'

'What'll happen to him if your father marries Pauline?'

'If they live in the cottage he'll have the colliery house all to himself.'

'Your father's relying on you to become lodge secretary.'

'My father relies on nobody – except Pauline. I never told him the whole truth, but he's o'er big for the village. He towers over the men. The manager's

scared of him. The owners'd kick him out the pit if
they could, but they know he'd louse out the whole
coalfield. You talk about his family. He's got Ernie
sorted to do his biddin' around the house. He wants
me to do his biddin' as lodge secretary.'

'You could always marry me.'

'I told my father you'd be a laughin' stock of the
village for marryin' beneath yourself. He knows you
look upon yourself as a village girl, born and bred so to
speak, but all that's a long time ago. Would you really
want a blacksmith to keep your feet warm at night?'

'A big strong blacksmith,' Rosemary said.

'I think the noise of the blacksmith's shop turned
my head,' Roland said. There's nobody in the world
I think on more than you, but this village – this life
of mine – it's over now. Nothin's as it was. Nothin's
as it used to be. And nothin'll bring it back.'

'I'll never see you again?'

'I'll not be comin' back, if that's what you mean.'

'Shaking the dust off your feet?'

'Rather the blacksmith's sparks from my nose.'

'Remember the promise you made,' Rosemary said.

'I always keep my promises,' Roland said.

59

He rubbed at the palm of his hand.

When making a cross for the chapel the tip of the

red-hot poker had slipped and bored a hole into his palm. He had finished the cross before thrusting his hand into an urn of cold water. The doctor had added a dressing, but the hand had been bandaged for weeks, and children at the Sunday school where he had taught had been more interested in the hot poker searing his palm than the cross he had made for them. The cross stood on the wall of the chapel opposite the organ, nailed into the colourless walls through holes Roland had bored.

The wound had healed, but when the bandages had been removed there had been a red sore that had turned steadily black with the dust and soot of the blacksmith's shop. *The mark of Christ*, Grandfather Ernest had said. The thought had disconcerted Roland. He rubbed the mark when nervous or preoccupied. Often he would wipe sweat from his face with the ends of his apron, oblivious to the roughness of the leather. He rubbed his hand again as he sat in the comfort of Rosemary Rutland's drawing room, feeling the warmth of the whisky reassuring to his stomach.

Rosemary poured Roland another.

He had not needed another, but he knew from the flutter of Rosemary's hand and the tremble to her lip that she had risen from the settee to overcome her emotion. He had reminded her not only of her husband but of her daughter. There were photographs of Barbara along the top of the piano that stood at an angle in the corner of the room, photographs taken at boarding school, hair blonde like that of her mother, buxom and happy, with a wide, open face and pleasant smile. She had been tall and big-boned and ungainly on the photographs, but she had looked smarter and trimmer in her nurse's uniform.

There had been a more sombre look to her features on the photograph they had taken in the field hospital in Rouen where she had treated convalescing soldiers. It had been a happier photograph before the reality of the front. It had been, too, the photograph Rosemary had enjoyed more than the others. She had arranged and re-arranged them on the top of the piano and letting her fingers ripple over the keyboard she linked the notes to the nostalgia that she felt to her soul.

'I should have asked about Barbara,' Roland said.

'I got a card post-marked two days ago.'

'They say the mail works from the Western Front – if nothin' else.'

'She's a proper nurse now – not a probationary. Only she expects the Americans to be in the war shortly – she calls them Yanks. She's looking forward to them because it'll bring the war to an end. Or so she thinks. They'll get their bottoms shot off just like the British and French.'

'And the Italians.'

'But not my dear Roland.'

She ran her fingers across his thigh.

'She'll know all about Albert and Roger,' Roland said. 'She always looked up to Roger when she was a lass.'

'You were closer to Roger than your other brothers.'

'Nobody was closer than Albert.'

'That's why he went with him to fight the war.'

'I have images floatin' in my mind,' Roland said. 'Like a picture runnin' through my memory. I can see the two of them as lads growin' up. I can see them pushin' their shirt tails in before goin' off to the pit. Daft things like that. I can hear my mother shoutin' at them. She loved everybody, my mother, but above all she loved to hear the sound of her own voice.'

'All pit women are like that,' Rosemary said.

'You're right there,' Roland said. 'Otherwise nowt'd get done.'

'Albert took the stable next to the blacksmith's shop for his whippets. That's how they came to cross Charlie Bessford.'

'It's the first time you've mentioned him,' Roland said.'

'And the last,' Rosemary said.

'I was talkin' about Barbara and how she knew my brothers.'

'Barbara's all right,' Rosemary said.

'You mean she'll not be comin' back either?'

'I've lost you both,' Rosemary said. 'Tell me, Roland, what is there for me to live for? My buses gone, my garage burned down by Charlie Bessford. My husband's gone, my daughter's gone, swearing never to come back. Now you're going too with the same oath upon your lips. I shall sell the stables and the pub on the fell. I'll be left only with my shops. So I'll ask you again, Roland – where will it end?'

'In my father's revolution, I suppose.'

'But if there's no revolution?'

'I do love you,' Roland said.

'Not the way you love Pauline Alyson.'

'Pauline's done for us all,' Roland said.

60

Roland sought out Charlie Bessford in his house at the top of the village.

'I'm sorry about your brothers,' Charlie said.

'I didn't see you at the service,' Roland said.

'The service was for your mother.'

Charlie lay in the cot-bed beneath the stairs.

He had been tall and stocky; now he was thin and shrivelled. Cancer had come upon him quickly and ate away his bowels. He had always been active, but if his body had let him down his brain had not; if he felt pain, though it might deepen the creases to his face, it had been neither to the eyes nor to the lips. There would be no word of complaint. He had been stricken at fifty, in the prime of his life, with his sons, his pit work, his book-making, and his buses; but the cancer had not understood any of these things and ate his bowels as a steady fire.

'I never neglected my pit work,' Charlie said. 'We

kept our coal face clean. All them stories about what my lads did to them that didn't pay their bets – your father knew it was all a load of rubbish. That's why he never said a word. They're fine lads, my sons, they've been good on the face, and if they keep goin' they'll do every job in the pit. Only I wish they'd take a deputy's ticket – or even under-manager.'

'They've as much chance of gettin' killed in the pit than at the front.'

'The chances of bein' killed at the front are greater. No soldier can count on more than three months at the most. The same for officers as for the men. I'd rather they took their chances in the pit than at the front. I'm sure your father would've have preferred Roger and Albert where he could see them comin' in-by than wonderin' how they met their end in some foreign cornfield.'

'Nobody knows how they died,' Roland said.

'They say Rosemary Rutland doesn't know if her man's alive or dead, whether he's captured behind them German lines. All they know is he went up and never came back. Mebbes he's up there still, flyin' about, a rider in the sky. You might write a song about him if you felt up to it.'

'There's nothin' wrong with your tongue, Charlie.'

'It's my bowels that gives us pain.'

'I didn't mean to be funny.'

'You've got some business,' Charlie said. 'Other-wise you'd not have walked up the bank.'

'I've come to find out how Roger and Albert went to the front in the first place.'

'They were daft as brushes. Even your dad knows that.'

'Albert was never daft.'

'Roger was daft enough for them both.'

'It doesn't explain how they left the village.'

'Your father came to see us with ten gold sovereigns,' Charlie said. 'Told us his lads had been trainin' their whippet on the fells, the one that won all the races. They must think us daft, not to know they'd been trainin' a dog like that, but if they won everybody else lost, and our bag was full of money when we left the field. Your mother Bess knew all about it. She stopped us once in the street. They didn't have to fight no war because of a bet. Your mother knew that and your father knew it too, only he didn't want to let on. Else he'd have to admit they went to fight the war to be out of his house and his fights with his own father – and more besides. Maybe they didn't like your father much after all.'

Neighbours came and went, the door opened and closed, but the view from Charlie's cot-bed had been different; it looked out not upon the pitheap but down a narrow street to the colliery institute and joiners' yard and pit head. Charlie would die as he had lived, the institute and yard and colliery wheel turning like a tumbril before his eyes; it would be etched into his mind, those coming into his house not his workmates but the wives of his workmates. They came to see that he had been comfortable and watched for any sign he might make so that any need would be fulfilled.

Yet there had been no sadness in his household.

The village lived with death, a fact like any other fact, a stage on the way, an experience to be lived through, like getting up on a cold morning to go to work, only more definitive, a final retribution, no returning from the grave, no beckoning figure to express regret or remorse, no call to live it all over again. There were those who left this life gracefully, serenely, accepting death, preparing for it, or at least preparing for the funeral that would follow, but there were others who got away badly suffering from cancer.

Charlie Bessford had confronted death as he had confronted life.

He talked to Roland but passed instructions over his shoulder to his four sons, all of them respectful, all of them dignified, standing by the table in the centre of the room, all of them listening: who should run his allotment, his club committees and leek shows, who should take over his book, his buses, which of his sons should live in the house. His wife had long since died in childbirth. There would be no will, nothing written down, that was not the way of the village, but Charlie's instructions were as binding as if they had been signed, sealed and delivered in a solicitor's office.

'Why did you burn down Rosemary Rutland's bus garage?' Roland asked.

'I'm not sure you'd make a good lodge secretary,

son,' Charlie said. 'You're a bit on the direct side. Your father might have gone about that question differently. He'd have sat there for many an hour till I'd have told him the truth to get shot on him. Me and him – we've had many a long chat. He wants me to help him with his revolution. Did you know that? I said I'd give him all the help I could from where I'm goin'.'

'Do you believe in his revolution?'

'I believe in most things,' Charlie said. 'Your father respected us and came to us for advice. He knew he couldn't take on the coal owners by himself, not even the colliery manager, so he came to me and asked what could be done. I said it was like lightin' a match to make a flame that you might cup in your hand. The flame might light a fire – and after that who knows what a fire might do.'

'You were talkin' about the bus garage.'

'Not that kind of fire,' Charlie said.

Roland had slept soundly in his flat above the blacksmith's shop, but on the night of the fire a roar and lick of flames had sent him from his bed to the window. The shop stood behind the Rutland shops and already the flames were high above the rooftops. He dressed and stumbled down the stairs through the shop into the night air. He felt the hot air hitting his face as he turned the corner, ash and soot swirling as in a storm, the heat so intense, the flames so bright he had shielded his face. Petrol tanks had exploded and the blast flattened him against a wall.

Roland had felt an arm slip through his.

Rosemary Rutland had been brought from her home in a trap.

The trap had stopped a hundred yards away by the Cooperative store, the horse rearing with fright, the driver seeking to quieten the horse as Rosemary had dragged her way along the street till she had reached the blaze. Neighbours in night shirts rushed from their homes with pails of water. The reflection of the flames had been crimson to her face and she too drew back as another petrol tank in one of the buses exploded, the flames sucking at the air, rising ever higher, rinsing the clouds an angry red so that she and Roland hurried away.

'I'll take you back to the trap,' Roland said.

'I told the driver to settle the horse and take him back.'

'How'll you get home?'

'I'm not a cripple altogether.'

'I didn't mean that,' Roland said.

'You don't want me to be on my own?'

'I've never liked you bein' on your own since Barbara left.'

He had taken Rosemary back to his flat.

'I'll make you some tea,' Roland said.

'Something has to be done about Charlie Bessford,' Rosemary said.

'Somethin' will be done,' Roland said.

61

'You might think like the rest of the village I burned down the Rutland garage,' Charlie said. 'You might think you're right – but you're wrong. We should've burned it down, since Rutland's drivers were pushin' my lads off the road. There was more danger comin' in and out of the village than there was in the pit. Somethin' had to be done about the Rutlands. My lads said that and I said that – and all my drivers said that.'

Charlie enjoyed Cornish pasties.

He had enjoyed gorgonzola cheese, too, though it reached the village with maggots running from the cheese. He had felt the energy passing from him even before there had been pain. He had not been able to hold his food and his weight loss had been dramatic; his complexion had yellowed and the jowls that overlapped his stiff collar had disappeared. So too had his beer belly. He had felt so weary in the morning he had not wanted to get out of bed, but when he began to count his own ribs, so little flesh to his chest, when he could trace the angular bones to his arms, he had known it was time for him to make his arrangements.

'So you burned down the garage,' Roland said.

'We should've burned down the garage. Tom Rutland was away fightin' the war. He said he didn't want

298

no more aggravation, but his drivers didn't know that, or if they did they took not a bit of notice; and his missus knew nothin' about it. So we figured we'd better hold our horses, think of somethin' else, mebbes get the money together and buy Rosemary Rutland out – when her husband didn't come back, that is.'

He coughed and a neighbour pushed a tin plate before his chin; hardly had he spat into the plate than the neighbour took it away. Sometimes as he spoke his voice would be strong; other times it faded. Sometimes Roland could hear every word, sometimes he would need to lean over in his chair. Charlie Bessford had been one of the natural leaders of the village, as had his father, but if his father had lived for others Charlie had lived for his sons. He had been feared in the village and in the pit, but on his deathbed his sons were around him.

He wondered who would be around the deathbed of his father.

'I know you're Rosemary's fancy man,' Charlie said. 'All the village knows that. And you moonshine over Pauline Alyson. They know that too. I'd put my money on Rosemary, if I was you – but I hear you're daft enough to follow your brothers into the Army. Now that is not smart – even from my cot-bed I can tell that. You don't have to look out at no heap to know that it's all wrong – unless you want to get away from your father.'

'You're wanderin', Charlie,' Roland said.

'It's like the pain,' Charlie said. 'My mind comes and goes.'

'I wished you'd tell us about the garage.'

'Even you'd accept we had to do somethin' about them Rutland buses. They were puttin' us out of business. Even you never charged sixpence in that blacksmith's shop if a shillin' would do. And if the garage did get burned down there'd be insurance money and the like. You'd hardly say she was loosin' out. Only we never burned it down. You know what cancer is? Some say it's a fire from hell that creeps into the body; others that it's a tree that grows inside. You can feel its roots all over. The funny thing is, it destroys the body, but it destroys itself with it. It's got no future in the grave – but it destroys all the same.'

'You're a brave man, Charlie Bessford. I'll say that for you.'

'Not as brave as you,' Charlie said. 'Your brothers are dead, your mother's just been buried, you have a fancy woman in the village that owns the stores. You're snug in the blacksmith's shop with a flat above it. Now you're off to shoot people you've never seen before. Now that's brave – that's really brave.'

'There's conscription, Charlie.'

'Your father would get around that.'

Pain creases deepened to Charlie's face and he moved on his side.

'Bed sores,' he said.

'You were tellin' us about the garage.'

'We never burnt no bloody garage.'

'You mean you paid somebody to do it?'

'It went up of its own accord. Like some act of God.'

'Somebody burnt it down.'

'There might be enough fires where I'm goin',' Charlie said. 'I didn't need any on this earth. The Army wants to buy our buses to carry troops. They say buy but they mean requisition. We're turnin' them over next week. We should've burnt down the garage, but we didn't – because like everythin' else in the village – like everythin' else in this life – it doesn't matter any more.'

Charlie made a signal and two neighbours came forward to help him from the cot-bed out of the house to the water-closet in the back yard. He had been too proud to use a chamber pot. His feet did not touch the ground but he had been so frail they held him easily. He wore a long night gown, but the night gown had hardly been held by the fragile frame, and Roland noticed if there had been yellow to his cheeks there was yellow to the backs of his legs. He had been brought back into the room and laid upon the cot-bed.

His black hair had turned white.

'Don't go yet, son,' Charlie said. 'I didn't let you in here to talk that rubbish. I want you to do somethin' for us – a request from the deathbed, if you like, somethin' you'll have to honour. Will you do that if I ask?'

'I'll do anythin' for you, Charlie.'

'There's conscription, you say, and all the lads'll

301

have to go, but they'll always be needin' coal, so most of the older hands'll stay and only the young'uns'll be sent. I don't want any of mine sent, that's what I'm tellin' you. They're better off at the face.'

'You want us to have a word with my father?'

'A special word about Arthur. He's my young'un. My wife died bringin' him into the world. I know how it broke your mother's heart to see Roger go off in the trap and it's o'er late to break my heart. But I want Arthur to take that job of yours in the blacksmith's shop when you go off to Italy. Keep them bellows blowin', you might say. If you could do that I'd die happy.'

'Everybody should die happy,' Roland said.

'Tommy should stay on the face.'

'Anythin' else – before I go?'

'The other two are old enough to fend for themselves.'

'If there's anythin' at all,' Roland said.

'That'll do for this life.'

Charlie nodded to his son Tommy.

Tommy handed Roland a cotton bag with a cotton string around its neck. Tommy might have been his father in his younger days: heavily-built, full face, dark hair oiled to his scalp, complexion ruddy, eyes clear. He looked at Roland, knowing they would never meet again. There would be no Fatherley as there would be a Bessford succession. Roland caught the gaze as he reached the door and understood and nodded and took the cotton bag, weighing it in his hand.

Washing hung on lines between the colliery houses and hessian shirts billowed in gusts of wind.

Roland paused to take in for the last time the sweep of the village: the institute, the joiners' yard, the colliery headstock, the honey-brick of the colliery houses with their blue-tiled roofs and russet chimneys, the smoke from the chimneys blown sideways across the village. Behind him lay the coppice where his brothers had played pitch and toss and ahead the uneven track that led under the bridge that carried the full sets to the coal hoppers.

Roland felt again the weight of the cotton bag.

He pulled aside the strings and looked inside.

In it were Binkie Fatherley's ten gold sovereigns he had borrowed from the manager to pay back Roger's gambling win.

'He got his gold sovereigns back after all,' Roland said.

62

Binkie Fatherley found Pauline Alyson painting in her studio.

'Come on up,' she called.

'I'll wait down here, if you don't mind,' Binkie said.

He had made Pauline Alyson come to him.

'You got through the day,' she said.

It seemed the whole village had come out for the funeral of Bess Fatherley.

'Now Roland's gone too.'

'He'll not bother you any more,' Binkie said. 'He left the house the night. He had a final word with Charlie Bessford and Charlie told him a few things that put his mind at rest. He had a few messages for me – and I'll take care of them. I owe that to Charlie, at least. But Roland's gone and he'll not be comin' back. You might say I've lost four of my family on the same day.'

'You've still got Ernie.'

'He's a fine man. He keeps himself to himself.'

'You want me to take Bess's place?'

'Nobody can take Bess's place.'

'Not if our marriage had to be measured on the number of times she scrubbed the floors or dadded your clothes – as you call it. Or washing your shirts to hang out on that poky line with the pit heap on one side and the downstairs room on the other. You should think of pulling down Slum Alley and have the people moved out before the pit smothers them all. A bit of rain one day and the bluepost'll be in your room and across your cot-bed.'

'If I want to marry you, Pauline, it's for your own sake.'

'There's a revolution coming,' she said.

Binkie had brought Pauline each night that day's newspapers from the institute and she had read everything she could about the Russian revolution. The Czar had abdicated, a provisional government had been formed; workers and peasants had created their own communes they called *Soviets*. Pauline had wanted to call a mass meeting to celebrate Russian freedom, but her speech at the Durham Big Meeting had alerted the authorities she was active again and no meeting had been called; but if freedom had swept through Russia, if the soldiers were no longer fighting the Germans, she knew that the revolution had been only partially completed.

'The only revolution I want is in Highhill,' Binkie said.

Pauline had been painting and stood before Binkie in her overalls and black beret. She had removed the cigarette holder, since she knew Binkie did not like her smoking. Another woman would have made him tea, but there would be no tea this night, and he settled before the narrow fire and picked up the poker. He poked at the crusts of burning coal, unsettling strangers from the bar, raking away ash as he had been doing all his life. A sadness hung around his shoulders, his mood sombre, but as his eyes delved the coals his mind delved the future.

'I've loved you as a daughter,' Binkie said.

'And I've loved you too, William Fatherley. Perhaps I should have married Roland. Perhaps I should have become one of your family. But Roland never spoke a word to me – never in my four years in the village. How can you marry someone who doesn't talk to you, who doesn't know how to approach you? Someone who never says a word?'

'He might learn a bit when he gets to Italy.'

'All these years you've wanted to run everybody's life. But the only life you couldn't run was your own. You couldn't live your father's life; so he left you. You couldn't live your sons' lives; so they left you too. You wanted to run Roland's life – but he saw through that. Now he's gone. You've never tried to run Ernie's life – and so he's stayed. Now you want to run my life by marrying me.'

'I want to be on hand to help.'

'You want to put your hand on my shoulder?'

'A bit like that,' Binkie said.

'Who says I want a hand on my shoulder? I was born on the factory floor. My mother lost me through the courts. I've lived my own life since I was sixteen. I've been in prison. I would gladly have died. I wished that the good Lord – if He exists – would take me. But He didn't. Instead He sent me to Highhill to recover and be out of the way. But I have recovered and I don't want to be out of the way any more. I cannot go to London because I am banned, they want to arrest me because I made a speech and they say I broke my licence. But if I cannot go to London I can go to Petrograd.'

'It's a long way in war-time,' Binkie said.

'I have a higher destiny, William Fatherley, as you have a higher destiny. Only I'm prepared to fulfil mine. Are you prepared to fulfil yours?'

'Is that why you burned down the Rutland garage?'

'Who says I burned down the Rutland garage?'

306

'Ernie saw you. He was moonin' about his allotment. He thought one of his pigs was goin' to have sows. Only it was a false alarm. He was comin' back through the village when he saw you. You were all dressed in black. You know how he is. He popped into a doorway out the way; he didn't dare come out lest you saw him. He saw you pull open the garage doors. The next thing the whole garage was aflame.'

'You've bred a family of peeping Toms,' Pauline said.

'He saw you come out as quietly as you went in. Only you made your way back to the cottage through the allotments. You've learned your way through the village, I'll grant you that. You didn't seem o'er anxious to walk back through the village with all them flames behind you.'

'You sent Roland to my room so that he could ask me to marry him. The page boy saw Roland leaving my room. He found his cap against the wall. But since Roland was so sick and the smell so bad the page boy came to my room. He found the door open and left the cap on the table in the living room. No questions asked – no answers given. It was Roland's cap all right – he'd followed me around long enough for me to recognise it. I had heard the door go and knew then Roland had been in the room.'

'He wanted a kindly word,' Binkie said.

'You sent him so that he could learn the truth,' Pauline said. 'So that he could be destroyed – because it suited you to destroy your own son. It suited you that he find out about Barbara Rutland and would tell her mother because you knew she was fond of him and he was her friend. You knew Rosemary Rutland would send her daughter away. And with Roland out the way and Barbara too the way to me would be clear for you.'

'You don't really think I would think such thoughts?'

'Roland withdrew the summons once Barbara left. Rosemary Rutland knew what she was doing. She knew she would discredit me, divert me from my task. She knew I could not remain in the village with rumours of a summons flying about and a threat to arrest me because I'd broken my licence. She knew when people found out I loved her daughter they'd say I wouldn't be fit to teach schoolchildren. Barbara didn't believe that – but I did. She knew she would be able to denounce me at any time and send me to prison – yes, William Fatherley – to prison.'

'I can always speak to Rosemary Rutland.'

'The way you speak to the colliery manager and Charlie Bessford?'

'You burned down the garage to get even with Rosemary Rutland,' Binkie said. 'You wanted to sort her out because she sent Barbara away – out of your clutches, you might say. You'd better pack up this business about women. It's time you settled like other women. You'd better settle if you want to be a revolutionary. They'll not bother with that stuff over in Russia, if that's where you want to go.'

'You want me out the way too?' Pauline asked.

'I want to marry you and settle you down, so that you don't do anythin' daft like burnin' down a garage – that single act of yours. I want us to work together for our own revolution – not the revolution of somebody else. But if you want to go I'll not stop you. It'll do you good to let the rumours die. Only you'll always have a place to come back to. We'll have our revolution – and when it comes I want you at my side.'

'You'll fulfil your destiny?'

'As long as you come back.'

'You'll do me a favour before I go?' Pauline asked.

'Everybody wants a favour.'

She left Binkie by the fire and returned to her studio.

The fire had slumped further in the grate before she returned, but when she did she handed Binkie an open carrier bag. He looked inside. There had been a canvas frame shattered and disjointed; there had been fragments of a painting, the fragments jagged and dangerous, as if Pauline had just made them, cutting or stabbing a portrait with a knife. He picked out one of the fragments, the edges sharp but the colours rich. He let his hand run around the inside of the bag and picked up more fragments.

He let them run through his fingers.

'Give them to Rosemary Rutland,' she said.

'Why'd you do a thing like that?'

'It's a painting of her daughter. It's all that's left

of it. She'll know then the past is dead for us all – including Barbara and me. Including Terry Kenny. What was once can never be again.'

'Everybody seems to be sayin' that,' Binkie said.

Book Four:
The Skobolievs

63

Pauline Alyson had made her own way to Petrograd.

She had not applied for a passport, for she had known none would be granted. She had taken the trap from Highhill to the Tyne quayside and enquired of tramp steamers moored at the quay. She had learned the name of the steamer going to Bergen and pulling her skirts around her ankles, feeling the chill as the wind curled from the water, she had marched up the gangway and installed herself in the captain's cabin.

She sat with her travelling bag till the captain arrived.

'A stowaway,' he said.

'A woman with a mission,' she said.

'A revolutionary.'

She looked out of the porthole and saw the water whipped white by the wind.

'The time will come,' she said.

She had paid the captain in gold sovereigns given by Binkie Fatherley, counting some of them from a cotton bag that Roland had given his father before he had left for Italy. The captain had found her a bunk away from the seamen's quarters and from Bergen she had taken a passenger ship to Hemmerfest, the most northerly port in Norway where the sun shone a weak yellow. From there she had crossed to Vardo island. She had eaten little, her stomach had retched its way across the sea, and she had rested two days before taking a fishing boat across the narrow stretch of Arctic to Murmansk.

She had brought a single change of clothing she had washed herself at Hemmerfest and because she had no passport there were telegrams back and forth from the British Embassy before she had been allowed to continue to Petrograd. She had used the time to wash her clothes again, using sand instead of soap, but as she journeyed south by train the grim cold had left the air. The sun had risen higher and stronger and when she reached Petrozavodsk in Keralia she had eaten a thin fish soup with a piece of black bread.

Her first sighting of Russia had been the frontier post at Beloostrov.

Everything had seemed different in this country of revolution. The trees, the sky, the people, even the air she breathed, the air of political freedom. She arrived at the Finland Station in Petrograd and settled in the Europa Hotel. She would remember her first meal, bowing to the waiter in the dining room, who bowed in return; he offered her a potato ball, black bread and a glass of tea. There had been pink-coloured wine in a decanter, but the wine had been raw and harsh, and she had felt its bitter path to her stomach.

She had gone to the British Embassy with a letter from her mother.

'Your mother was a great help to our war effort before she left for India,' the Ambassador said. 'The Foreign Office say I am to be of no assistance to you, not even for your mother's sake; that you left without a passport and should be immediately deported. They say you've been in prison, that you are banned from London and broke your licence when you made a political speech at Durham. They say there may even be a warrant for your arrest.'

'Yet you sent a telegram authorising my entry.'

'The Foreign Office doesn't understand revolution.'

'Not only do I understand it,' Pauline said. 'I believe in it.'

'Except you had better be on the winning side.'

The Ambassador explained what Pauline had known from her newspaper reading, that the revolution had been only half completed. The Czar had abdicated and power lay with the provisional government and *Soviets*. One or the other must prevail. There were constitutional democrats and social democrats and socialist revolutionaries; there were *Cadets* and *Essers* and a Party of People's Freedom. There were internationalists and social patriots, reactionaries and intellectuals.

There were Mensheviks and Bolsheviks.

'Enough to make you dizzy,' the Ambassador said.

'What does Bolshevik mean?'

'It means Maximalist.'

'They are the true revolutionaries?'

'It is for you to find out.'

The British Embassy overlooked the Neva river.

The building had been squat and sullen with large square windows; it stood three storeys high and as wide as the river itself, with long corridors and high ceilings. The outside walls had been gaunt with age or grime or both, the chimneypots stood tall and cracked, smoke steadily rising in the still air; the windows were pools of light or shade depending on the time of day, and drainpipes ran like lattice down the side of the building to the street.

The Ambassador worked from the second floor.

'How will you live?' he asked.

'I'll need a ration card.'

'Two million soldiers have deserted the Army,' the Ambassador said. 'Carriages are disappearing from the streets. There are train robbers and estate robbers. No estate owner is safe in his home. The price of a cab has gone from twenty-five kopeks to five roubles. There are queues for everything – cigarettes, chocolate, flowers. You can hire a soldier to stand in a queue for a few roubles. Soldiers are selling chocolate bars at eleven roubles a bar – and deserters are everywhere.'

Pauline would discover for herself there was no street like *Nevsky Prospekt*, sordid and dilapidated, the houses low and drab, the paint peeling. The street had been wide but haphazardly built, as if unfinished, the shop windows empty, the *Prospekt* filled with soldiers

and sailors and bourgeoisie and peasants and proletariat talking, taking free sheets or buying newspapers,
but all of them good-natured, notwithstanding the first
winter ice that lay in a thin film across the cobbles.

All her life she would remember the dwarf perched
above the crowd at the top of a pole held by a peasant.
The peasant collected kopeks and stamps and notes in
a box that he waved before passers-by. Pauline had
stared at the dwarf and he had caught her staring;
he swore and ordered the peasant to chase her. The
peasant moved towards her as swiftly as he could, the
pole swaying. Pauline had turned and moved quickly
through the crowds, the imprecations of the dwarf
following her till they were lost to the shouts of other
hawkers.

'You must help me find out who are the winning
revolutionaries – and if they will make a separate peace
with the Germans.'

'Why should they fight a capitalists' war?' Pauline
asked.

'If they make a separate peace with the Germans
and the Germans transfer all their divisions to the
Western Front the war might be over before the first
American soldier gets off the boat. A lot more bullets
will be coming the way of our soldiers if the wrong
revolutionaries win.'

'They might be the right revolutionaries for Russia.'

'They will be wrong in the long run.'

'Russia must write its own history,' Pauline said.

'You talk like your mother,' the Ambassador said.

'She had money here from books and articles. The publisher has deposited the royalties in a special account. Your mother says in her letter you can have the money. She has given permission it be given to you. You can live on the proceeds of your mother's labour.'

'How can I meet the publisher?'

'I'll help you if you'll help me.'

'How can I help you?'

'I've told you about the *Cadets* and *Essers* and the Party of People's Freedom,' The Ambassador said. 'There are also the Populist Socialists and the Monarchists and the *Yedinstvo*. Everyone opposed to everyone else. I want to know which group has the upper hand. Perhaps your mother's publisher speaks English. Probably he did the translations. If he can release your mother's money he can also be your interpreter. He can help you find out what's going on in the street. Once you find out you can tell me.'

'You want me to become a spy?'

'They shot the last woman spy in France. Her name was Mata Hari. We want nothing so grand – only information. We're getting it from doorkeepers and journalists and janitors, from the British and French colonies, but it doesn't all add up. Anything you can give will add to our knowledge – complete the picture.'

'Sounds like spying to me.'

The Ambassador stood by the window and looked towards the golden dome of the Church of the Resurrection. He had been a career diplomat with the all the appropriate initials after his name: GCB, GCMG,

318

GCVO. He was also a Knight of the Realm and Privy Councillor. His suit had been immaculate, dark and graceful, tailored in London, and he wore a narrow starched collar and fully-knotted tie. A thin mist rose from the river and he could see the lights of the Church through the mist.

The Ambassador smoked a cigarette he had taken from a silver cigarette case on the desk. He inhaled deeply, recalling his audiences of the Czar when the Czar had offered him a cigarette from his own gold case with the imperial monogram. He had tapped the tip of cigarette on the gold. Often they had sat on the same sofa, but when last they had met the Czar had kept him waiting and received him officially, standing rather than sitting, and there had been no offer of a cigarette.

'Your Majesty must break down the barrier that separates him from his people. His Majesty must regain their confidence.'

'You must tell me, Excellency, how the people will regain *my* confidence.'

'Your Majesty shall see that it is a question of both. Without mutual confidence Russia cannot win the war.'

The Ambassador described what the Czar must have known already, that in Petrograd the people and the Army were as one and that in the event of revolution only a small portion of the Army could be counted upon to defend the dynasty. The Ambassador understood that sometimes in great affairs, where events follow one upon the other, it is often the small event that captures the attention and impresses itself upon the mind.

The people of Petrograd had taken to the streets because they were hungry; workers were on the streets because they were locked out or on strike; a garrison of a hundred-and-sixty thousand soldiers had mutinied or stayed in their barracks. The Czar's government had been incapable either of delivering food or fuel or putting down an insurrection. Half of the Czar's imperial guard had defected.

'Petrograd is central to the conduct of the war, Your Majesty,' the Ambassador said. 'Its location is central to the railway system. You need to send ammunition and troops from Petrograd. You need to maintain morale at the rear if your troops are to fight at the front.'

'The front is not solid,' the Czar said. 'That is why I have left Petrograd to be near my troops. I am here to show by the presence of the Commander-in-Chief that the Fatherland counts for the Czar as it counts for them.'

'The front is not solid, Your Majesty, because your battle-trained troops no longer exist. They have been lost in the retreat across the Polish plains. They have been lost in a strategy that believed the Czar's forces could be divided to wage war against Austria and Germany at the same time.'

'The war is not lost, Excellency.'

'If Petrograd is lost, Your Majesty, the war is lost.'

'We shall win the war with our glorious allies. Do not forget, Excellency, that the Germans and Austrians are now fighting the Americans. The first troops shall be landing shortly. The Fatherland shall be saved. God and the Czar shall prevail.'

'I pray that Your Majesty is right.'

64

The Czar had shown no emotion.

The Ambassador understood he had no right to speak to the Czar as he did; he went beyond diplomatic courtesy or the instructions of his government. He showed lack of respect. His only excuse had been the deep feelings of devotion he felt for the Czar. He recalled the days when the Czar's smile had been tender and shy and slightly sad; his blue eyes had been frank and innocent. 'If I were to see a friend walking through a wood on a dark night along a path which I knew ended in a precipice,' he said. 'Would it not be my duty to warn him of the dangers? Is it not equally my duty to warn Your Majesty of the abyss that lies ahead?'

The Czar's features had always been solemn, he had been aware that his destiny should be borne like a heavy cross. The knowledge deprived his face of character and showed what many thought to be weakness and inadequacy. There had been a lack of boldness or imagination. He had developed an impenetrable reserve of caution and distrust. His mind probed beyond the words of the Ambassador.

'Are you saying I should abdicate?'

'I am saying Your Majesty should return to Petrograd to take charge of his people.'

He had stood before the Ambassador simply dressed in his Army tunic and breaches impeccably-creased folding into the tops of his polished boots. He wore no medals, no epaulettes, and if there had been power it came from his simplicity. He had a thin face and receding hair, his hair as dark as his beard; his hands were small, the fingers podgy, but not a tremble stirred their delicacy. The longer the Czar had reigned the more remote he had become; the more crises he lived through the less responsive he became. He had been an absolute monarch and had the divine right to govern in accordance with his will. He had not responded to the Ambassador because no response could be given. He had no obligation to answer to anyone. The Czar might have kept the Ambassador standing, deprived of his cigarette, so that his mouth parched and his lungs ached, but it would only be a matter of time before the House of Romanov should fall.

The Czar would fall with it.

'As it is Your Majesty's desire,' the Ambassador said.

Now the Ambassador had offered a cigarette to Pauline but she declined. The days of the cigarette and cigarette holder were over. It had been her last promise to Binkie Fatherley. The Ambassador smiled as if he knew this, his reports had told him so, and with the smoke warm to his lungs he returned to his desk and laid the cigarette on the rim of a gold ashtray.

'If you help me your licence will be revoked and the warrant for your arrest shall be dropped. You shall be free to do whatever you like in your own country – even return to London.'

'How can I meet the publisher?' Pauline asked.

'He'll release the roubles from your mother's account. He shall cover your expenses at the Europa. You can come to the Embassy as you please, speak to anyone and everyone, tell us nothing if it suits you. Remember you come from Highhill. They've lost enough of their sons to the Western Front without losing more if the Russians pull out of the war.'

'I owe it to William Fatherley,' Pauline said.

'You owe it to your country.'

'I'd rather owe it to William.'

'Officially, you're here to write.'

'My mother wrote for *The Workers' Dreadnought* and *The Workers' Socialist Federation.*'

'You can write for them too.'

'What does *kivost* mean?' Pauline asked.

'The tail of a queue. The longer the breadlines the more people talk of *kivost*. There'll be more talk in future. The bread ration's being cut. Sweets are costing ten roubles a packet. There's not enough baby milk. The revolution will be completed – but who will win? That we must know. There's no-one else with your credentials. You're the only one I can ask.'

'For William's two sons killed in the war.'

'For your mother,' the Ambassador said. 'Those white feathers she gave out at Hyde Park Corner.'

65

Pauline found her mother's publisher in a bookshop and printing works in a street leading from *Znamenskii Square.*

'My father did the translations,' Nikolai Skoboliev said. 'I did the printing and publishing – and when my father went to the war I did the translations too.'

Nikolai had a round shiny face, blonde hair and blonde lashes and blue eyes. He loped rather than walked, round-shouldered, keeping his eyes down, tucking his chin into his chest, but he would look up shyly, surreptitiously, hoping that the person he was looking at would not be looking at him. He had been older than Pauline but he wore no rings; a single gold cross hovered around his neck that he would finger when nervous. Printers' ink had seeped into his fingers and he had been conscious of this too, rubbing his hands in the folds of his leather apron.

He had been polite and formal, but pleased to come face-to-face with the daughter of Mary Alyson.

'Perhaps you can write like your mother,' he said. 'You can follow our revolution through the eyes of a foreigner. Your writings can be published in London as well as in Petrograd. These are exciting – and historic – days. If you can write about them your name shall last forever.'

'I want to see my mother's books,' Pauline said.

She could not recognise her mother's name in the Russian script, but there had been her photograph on the frontispiece of each book. She would look at the photograph and let her fingers run down the harsh uncut paper. What had her mother said about reading her books and seeing her photograph and being reminded of her thoughts? Now that she was in Petrograd there were the books and there the photograph. Her thoughts began chasing each other into the past, till she halted the chase and moved from the books to the articles.

'I am sure you can write as well as your mother,' Nikolai said.

The articles had been printed on smaller sheets with the date and price upon the sheets: twenty-five kopeks an article. Her mother had written about workers' rights and women's rights and the political struggle of the proletariat so that Pauline asked herself aloud why she had supported the war. *Because she loved you and wanted votes for women* came the reply. There had been articles on the birth rate, on mothers' pensions, an appeal to women to rise against men; articles on independent working class education and the future of schooling. There were even articles on the self-education of workers.

'We had an *International Women's Day* inspired by your mother,' Nikolai said.

'You must tell me about your own family,' Pauline said.

'First I must tell you about the royalties from your book. The Ambassador will collect the roubles and hold them for you. He will see you are paid the equivalent in England. You must write about our revolution without worrying about income. His Excellency wants you to make an account of all the political parties and all the events. You must publish your work for the world to read.'

Nikolai had taken Pauline from the shop across a courtyard into the printing works.

The printing room had been filled with linotype machines but the compositors were all women; they wore headscarves and boiler suits and short-sleeved jumpers so that their arms showed white against the machines. They wore no make-up, their faces as white as their arms, starch in the brittle light. There were more women bundling newspapers and tracts, the printing machines sending copies along their own rolleyways to be bundled on flat silver tops. Telegraph printers ticked somewhere in the noise of the printing presses and linotyping.

'I shall write about the Bolsheviks,' Pauline said.

'You must write about all parties.'

'The Bolsheviks are the party of the peasants and

326

workers and soldiers,' Pauline said. 'They are the party for me.'

'You have noticed the red flag pushed through the hands of the statue of Catherine the Great?' Nikolai said. 'The flag has been there for weeks. You can see it before the *Alexandrinsky Theatre*. They tell you how the revolution will go. All the imperial monograms and eagles have gone. Even the *gordovoye* – our civil servants – cannot bring them back.'

'You're the only man on the printing floor,' Pauline said.

'The Grand Duke Nicholas Michaeolowich let me stay as a mark of respect for my father. Besides, the government wanted me to publish their propaganda. The propaganda has changed as the war has changed. The February revolution has changed everything again.'

'Is your father coming back?'

Nikolai had nudged his chin deeper into his chest.

'My father was a great man,' Nikolai said.

66

Anatole Skoboliev had been a writer at the Court and a retainer of the Grand Duke.

He had written plays and poems and his portrait stood high above the presses in the printing works; he had bought the works to publish his own writing and though his books might have sold in Petrograd they had not sold elsewhere in Russia. He had seen the danger of revolution and his pamphlets had warned of the need to nourish the spiritual life of the working class as unions and workers' parties nourished their economic and political interests.

'His poems and plays were set in the traditions of the Orthodox Church,' Nikolai said. 'He believed in love within the family – in caring and responsibility. He believed guilt weighed down those who did not live by the teachings of the Church.'

He saw the Russian people not through the eyes of the Church but the eyes of the Court. The people must follow and obey their Czar; tradition would save them from revolution. It would give them happiness in this life and hope in the life to come. There had been a languor to his poems and plays, a weariness that reflected Russian life, where the steppes were stitched to the sky, but if Anatole's faith had been strong, his belief fervent in the Czar, he had not communicated this to his readers.

'You translated your father's works?'

'They were unreadable in Russian.'

'And now he is gone?'

The Grand Duke had been Commander-in-Chief at the outbreak of war and Anatole Skoboliev had fought at the battle of Tannenburg. The battle had been lost because of tactical errors; the Russians had lost their guns as well as their shells; but they had lost too a quarter of a million men. The morale of the Army had never recovered. The Grand Duke had sat in his six-car railroad train and Anatole had warned him of the chaos to the rear as transports began to congest.

'You talk of congestion with so many brave men dead?' the Grand Duke had asked.

'You are a military man, sire, not a planner. I shall be your emissary to Petrograd. I shall discuss transport on your behalf.'

'Why do you think transport important?'

'Because, sire, the battle may be fought at the front but the war shall be won in the rear. Those who organise transport, traffic, supplies, food, ammunition. It is there that the war shall be won.'

'You are a tactician as well as a poet.'

Anatole Skoboliev had never arrived at Petrograd.

Some said he had committed suicide because he had been depressed at the death of Prince Oleg, brother of the Czar, the first and last of the Czar's family to die in the war. Anatole had been at his side when his horse had swerved and fallen; the Prince had been killed not by a bullet but by a broken neck. The horse had waited patiently as Anatole had lifted the body and placed it across the saddle and led the horse back to Army headquarters.

Others said Anatole had been captured and tortured to death by the German High Command because he had been a royal retainer; others that he had been stricken with typhus and died in a Vilna hospital. He had been buried in quicklime to kill the typhus before it spread. Others said he had become a poet again, spending his nights in Petrograd wine cellars, letting the candles burn low, drinking his vodka as he wrote.

Poems began to circulate written in his style, but Nikolai toured the cellars and found no trace of his father. He had toured the Vilna hospitals but there had been no trace either of his father or the typhus, and no-one had been buried in quicklime. He had found himself in the six-car railroad train of the Grand Duke where he would be granted an audience. There had been a rainfall as Nikolai had made his way to the Grand Duke's car, but a courtier had rubbed the mud from his boots before he entered the Grand Duke's presence.

'I award posthumously to your father the Cross of St George,' the Grand Duke said. 'He disappeared and probably died rendering a signal service to the Czar. He may never be found but his bravery will live on in your memory.'

The Cross had been pressed into Nikolai's tunic.

The printing works and shop had been released to him and he had brought his father's Cross in a dark case back to his mother, the Cross set in velvet. His mother had placed it on the wall of their front room and Nikolai had hung his father's portrait in the printing works so that his father might live on, in his memory perhaps, but as an image to those who worked the linotypes or bundled the papers and tracts or turned the presses.

'You say he will not be back,' Nikolai said. 'But he is with us all the time.'

330

67

'My mother is mute,' Nikolai said. 'She has been mute since birth.'

Anna Aleksandrovna Skoboliev brought out a heavy-backed journal containing all their transactions for Pauline's mother. The entries were written in a fine hand, in ink rather than pencil, the writing legible and in English, as if she had expected Mary to come one day to inspect her work and collect her roubles and kopeks. Some said she had been born without a tongue, others that a childhood shock had left her mute, but she had never spoken a word in her life and of course she had a tongue.

She wrote a laborious note and handed it to Pauline.

'She wants to be your mother,' Nikolai said.

'I am honoured,' Pauline said. 'One mother a life-time is enough.'

'She thought your mother might have come for *International Women's Day.*'

'She went to India instead.'

'My mother wished so much to meet her.'

'She has the honour of meeting me.'

Nikolai produced a photograph of women in head-scarves standing before a bus, the women close together. They held a placard above their heads and upon the placard there had been written in white chalk:

'If woman is a slave there will be no freedom. Long live equal rights for women!' The wording and the placard had been inspired by Mary Alyson.

'You must come and have dinner,' Nikolai said.

'There is food rationing – and *kivost.*'

'My mother has read every one of Mary's works. She is not emancipated – she will never be emancipated – but she recognises that emancipation must one day come for all women.'

The Skobolievs lived in *Ligovski Prospekt.*

The street intersected the *Nevski Prospekt* at *Snamenskyii Square*; the Nicholas railway station stood nearby and traffic flowed back and forth. There were *droshkies* and *troikas* and embassy and government cars; trams trundled and heaved and screeched, and the china rattled on the shelves. Anna Aleksandrovna had long believed that her husband would return from the front no matter what the Grand Duke had said. She had stored food for that happy event, vodka and fine wines too, but if she had not been able to share these with Mary Alyson neither would she share them with her daughter.

There had been cabbage soup with *kasha* mounds and black bread around the soup bowl; a samovar stood on its own table and Pauline drank the clear tea from a silver-bottomed glass. She felt Anna Aleksandrovna's eyes upon her, conscious of her muteness as she had been conscious of the dwarf upon a pole in the *Nevsky Prospekt*; but she had been conscious too from the stare to her eyes that Anna wanted her to know she had not

332

eaten like this at Court, their lives had been better, and perhaps might be better again when her husband returned.

Anna Aleksandrovna had never believed in the war; she knew it would be disastrous when the Czar changed the name of St Petersburg to Petrograd. She had not left the printing works to see the troops march from the city, the crowds deep along the *Nevsky Prospekt*, the people holding flags above their heads; holding, too, portraits of the Czar and icons of the Orthodox Church. She had surveyed the portrait of her husband on the walls of the printing works and had returned to the printing shop and arranged his poetry and plays and tracts in the window, cleaning the glass and sweeping away the dust.

Pauline had been aware of the uneasy silence.

'What is it the people want?' she asked Nikolai.

'Peace, bread and land,' he said.

'Is that too much to ask?'

'My mother has her own idea,' Nikolai said.

Anna wrote a neat note in bold letters and passed it to Pauline.

Power to the people!

'She has been reading my mother,' Pauline said.

68

Pauline arrived at the printing works to find the narrow street sealed by Army *Cadets.*

The lights were extinguished at midnight in Petrograd and generated electricity served only the gambling halls and brothels and cabarets where those who did not care – or did not wish to know – danced and drank port and brandy as well as vodka till they were ready to pass out like the lights. Nikolai Skoboliev had his own generator, his presses never stopped, and through the night his girls worked to turn out the latest Bolshevik edition of their newspaper *Rabochi Put*. The *Cadets* had shot up the premises. They had turned out the girls, confiscated eight thousand copies of *Rabochi Put*, destroyed the metal sheets and closed the printing works.

Pauline distributed *Rabochi Put* along *Nevsky Prospekt*.

She had an office in a corner of the printing works and would arrive early, *troikas* from the gambling halls still on the street; she dressed as a man because it suited her better when she sold the newspapers. She wore a corduroy suit, a red neckerchief around her throat, a corduroy cap settled on her red hair, the hair crushed beneath the cap, strands straggling around the nape of her neck. She took roubles and kopeks and ran back to the printing works for more copies, feeling the cold to her hands through her mittens; the cold attacked too her throat where the neckerchief unravelled as she ran.

She returned with more newspapers to sell.

There were tracts to hand out as she listened to the silver bells from the horses' manes as *troikas* and *droshkies* moved down the *Prospekt*. Sometimes she sold the newspapers and tracts along the river bank where the ice already lay thin, a grey filament across the water; gas-lamps along the *Champs de Mars* shone through the mist that caught her throat as rough as the Ambassador's tobacco smoke. Once, when she lay awake, she had counted some sixty-five tracts and pamphlets she had handed out as well as the *Rabochi Put.*

'The enemies of the people have taken the offensive,' Nikolai said.

'Who are the enemies of the people?'

'Those who seek to destroy the revolution.'

'Or make the revolution their own,' Pauline said.

She stood in *Znamenskii Square* and stared at the barricades.

Nikolai stood beside her dressed in a sheepskin coat and blue corduroy cap; his blonde hair splintered around his cap. He held his gloved hands deep in his pockets, his chin tucked into his chest; his eyes rolled as he watched more *Cadets* bringing food and munitions, cannon and machine guns to perch upon the barricades. Some of the guns pointed towards the printing works and others across the *Square* to where stood Pauline and Nikolai. Trams ran across the *Square* and the people went about their business with hardly a glance towards the barricades.

'They have closed our printing works,' Nikolai said.

'They have fired the first shots,' Pauline said.

'The revolution shall be completed!'

'But who shall win?'

'The *Cadets* have the guns.'

'But we have the people.'

'We have tracts and newspapers,' Nikolai said.

He removed his gloves and held his warm hands to his cheeks.

'They know we print for the *Bolsheviki.*'

'Even *Cadets* can read Russian!'

'They have turned off the electricity. They have disconnected the telephone lines. They have raised the bridges across the river to cut off the *Vyborg.*'

'Are they defending the Winter Palace?'

'The *Cadets* are piling wood against the Palace gates.'

Pauline found her mittened hand in his as he led her out of the *Square*, not walking but rolling towards the river bank, his head down, his eyes looking up beyond his cap. He pulled Pauline close so that she brushed against him as she sought to keep up, a hand to her corduroy cap. The mist had lifted and the sky was now a frosty blue, but the cold had been sharp as they pulled themselves along the river bank till they reached the *Smolny Institute.*

This had been the home of the Petrograd *Soviet.*

The *Institute* had once been a school for young girls, the building yellow-painted with white pediments and columns; its austerity contrasted with the rococo domes and pale blue buildings of the *Smolny Convent.* The *Convent* had small-paned windows and wrought-iron gates. The *Institute* stood three storeys high and two hundred yards long and upon its façade, above the entrance, there perched the last imperial eagle in the whole of Petrograd. There were armoured cars and field guns outside the *Institute* gates and cars within the courtyard.

They carried small red flags, not of menace but of defiance.

'Thank St Nicholas,' Nikolai said. 'The *Smolny* has not fallen.'

'The *Smolny* has not even been attacked,' Pauline said.

They pulled themselves along till they reached the *Liteiny Bridge* and crossed into the *Vyborg* district. There were *Cadets* on the City side of the bridge but red guards on the *Vyborg*, and neither *Cadets* nor guards took any notice of Nikolai and Pauline. Half-way across a tram passed, rattling upon its iron rails, its electrical points squeaking and scraping, sparks blue in the cold air. The Botanical Gardens in the *Vyborg* were closed and birch trees outside the gardens stood forlorn, stripped of their leaves, the leaves scraping along the gutter, life fled from them.

There were more barricades in the *Vyborg*.

They had stood there since the February revolution, a pathway cleared for trams and cars. The barricades were now flimsy, holed where timber had been pulled away, but some of the boards had been plastered with slogans or fly-posted with bills. All of them were *Bolsheviki*. The *Vyborg* had been the cradle of the February revolution, the home of the workers, like one of the mill towns of Pauline's childhood with Ann-Marie and the Reverend Alyson, the same trams running, the same clatter of clogs upon cobbles, the same grim faces.

A fountain stood at the end of the street.

There had been a street market the day before, iron rails and tarpaulin still standing. Some of the vegetables had turned rotten and cabbage leaves drifted across the cobbles. Old women with twig brooms tried to sweep up the leaves, water running down the gutters, already freezing to a black ice. The smell of cabbage had been as strong as the smell of tobacco, but there had been no wind to sweep away the smell as the women's brooms swept away the leaves towards the back of a lorry.

They entered an apartment building.

Letter boxes lined one of the walls and a single light showed an unpolished winding staircase. The light swayed as Nikolai pushed open the door with his shoulder. The light had been harsh as a tear but as they climbed the stairs the light extinguished and they made their way in the darkness. They reached the fifth floor where three knocks upon the outside panels opened the door and they found themselves in an apartment so filled with natural light they paused, blinking and uncertain. The walls to the apartment had been painted white, the floor polished but without carpets, the rooms filled with sparse woodwormed furniture.

A samovar stood somewhere in a back room and

there were all manner of men and women in the apartment, silent and respectful, watchful, red guards with rifles slung across their shoulders, their caps back upon their heads. There were shabbily dressed functionaries who either sat by a telephone or took messages that were written down to be passed around. There were, too, secretaries with headscarves, some of them as young as Pauline, so that she paused in her surprise. A voice came from the bedroom.

'What have you to tell me, Comrade Nikolai?'

Vladimir Illych Lenin spoke without turning his head.

69

'They have shot up the printing works, Comrade Illych. There is a barricade across the street and reinforcements of *Cadets*. They have raised the *Niolaysevksy Bridge* over the Neva, but the *Sampsoniyevsky Bridge* is in the hands of the red guards. Trams are still running over the *Liteiny* and the people go about their business as if it were the February revolution all over again.'

'Did the *Cadets* damage the printing presses?'

'The *Cadets* fired recklessly,' Nikolai said. 'They smashed windows with their bullets. They pulled down my father's portrait, but they left the presses.'

'And the *Smolny*?'

'The red guards have armoured cars and field guns before the gates.'

'The *Cadets* are guarding the Winter Palace as they are guarding the barricade before your printing presses,' Vladimir Illych said. 'But the Army of the provisional government stays in its barracks. What do you make of it, Comrade?'

'We have no copies of *Rabochi Put* on the streets.'

Vladimir Illych had been trying on wigs before a dressing-table in the bedroom.

Few of the wigs suited him; they sat uneasily on his bald dome. He had shaved off his red beard and moustache and his cheeks were shiny, but if he looked old he had always looked old. He had been bald since thirty. He had been short but lithe rather than squat; his brown eyes were slightly slanted, his cheek bones high, with no touch of colour. His hands too were fragile, his wrists slim, white as his head and face.

Pauline found him no less provincial than those she had left behind in Highhill.

He had been an educated man, an intellectual, a bourgeois brought up in the Orthodox Church, but he had a rough manner, the movement of his hands brusque, his laughter high and nervous. Some thought he resembled a middle-aged tradesman, others a grocer or schoolteacher, but Pauline detected an inner force that glowed like a blacksmith's furnace. He had will, discipline, energy, asceticism and an unshakeable faith in his cause. He might be unprepossessing and coarse, he might be bald, his skin might shine, but she knew he had an impact on crowds once he began to speak.

There had been no aura about Lenin, no sense of history, no strength emanating from him as he took first one wig and then another. He had been in hiding since July, but he had been in hiding or in exile all his life: in Siberia, in Switzerland, in Finland, and now in the *Vyborg*. He knew that power was his for the asking. He could pluck it as he might a feather duster; he might take it as easily as a sweet from any chocolate shop along the *Prospetsky Nadia*. He could place it as a crown on his head as he might any of the wigs on the dressing room table.

'We have no uprising either,' Vladimir Illych said.

'We must not wait, Comrade Illych,' Nikolai said.

'Who must take power, Comrade Nikolai? Do you want power? Let the Revolutionary Military Committee take power.'

'If we wait we shall lose everything.'

'I will dictate a pamphlet. You must publish the pamphlet on some other presses if your own are seized.' A secretary came into the room and Vladimir Illych dictated: *All districts, all regiments, all forces must be mobilised at once and must immediately send their delegations to the Revolutionary Military Committee and to the Central Committee of the Bolsheviks with the insistent demand that under no circumstances should power be left in the hands of the provisional government.*

'I can print this within the hour,' Nikolai said. 'I have a press for pamphlets in my home.'

'An historic moment, Comrade Nikolai.'

'The revolution has truly begun!' Pauline said.

Comrade Illych smiled a smile that said he was pleased with himself.

'You see how history is made,' he said. 'I have found a wig that fits!'

70

He had settled on a dark wig that made him look older still.

'Comrade Nikolai tells me you are to write a book,' Vladimir Illych said. 'You must explain how an alliance – no, a conspiracy – of workers, peasants and soldiers took the Russian state and shook it like a tree. How the autocracy was toppled by the masses, how the provisional government disintegrated before the might of the *Soviets*, how the bourgeoisie fled before the proletariat.'

'I am honoured that you have noticed me, Comrade Illych.'

She had stayed close to Vladimir Illych when Nikolai had left. Messengers and secretaries came and went, the apartment larger than she had imagined, a balcony beyond the windows. The rails to the balcony had been as black as the bread Pauline ate with her cabbage soup, but there were flower boxes filled with irises, the irises deceased, their stamen tongues no more. A comrade wearing a smock and short-sleeved pullover and scarf served tea from the samovar. Pauline settled near a table and wrote her notes.

'I am here because I believe in you, Comrade Illych.'

'You must believe in events too.'

'If I write about them I shall understand them better.'

'You must read my pamphlet on the English situation,' Vladimir Illych said. 'It is called *Left Wing Communism – an Infantile Disorder.* I hope you like the title. I have even devoted a chapter to the views of your mother.'

'I am honoured she is so well read.'

'You shall be too – in your time.'

Sometimes his forehead wrinkled, the wrinkles deep and corrugated, etched into his skin not by concentration but by disgruntlement and anger. Even in his anger he chose his words carefully. He might walk the floor and punch his fist and shout to himself, but he never allowed his emotions to show before those not within his inner circle. When he did speak each sentence was like a road leading to a bridge, perfect in its construction, pausing before the bridge, crossing the bridge with another sentence, so that his logic marched like soldiers till whole battalions of thought had assembled together in his speech. Pauline had been learning Russian and would speak it a little, but she understood his fluency even when he addressed her in English.

'You must write it all down, Comrade Pauline.'

He left Pauline for another room.

There would be discussions behind a closed door, but as they waited for darkness to settle across the streets news came that cannon had been fired from the Peter and Paul Fortress; *Cadets* with fixed bayonets had taken up positions before the closed gates of the central bank; that trams were running on the *Nevsky* but offices and shops had closed at two in the afternoon.

If the *Bolsheviki* printing works had been closed down, the government were turning out their own propaganda on their own printing machines. They appealed against insurrection and addressed their pleas to peasant and proletariat alike, even to soldiers at the front, whilst on the streets deserted soldiers were selling second-hand copies of their own newspaper at fifty kopeks a copy. Nikolai Skoboliev had also printed Lenin's urgent supplication and had been distributing the pamphlets himself along the *Nevski* and down towards the Neva.

'You must go to *Smolny*, Comrade Illych,' Pauline said.

'I shall go at nightfall. You shall come with me.'

They walked out of the *Vyborg* across the *Liteiny Bridge*.

Power had been restored to some parts of Petrograd, telephone lines reconnected, and the *Cadets* around the barricades at *Znamenskii Square* had been subsumed into the night so that the women working night shift at the Skoboliev printing works were able to resume printing. Lumber piled before police stations, three-inch guns had been wheeled out by some *Cadets* but soon abandoned.

Where areas were still blacked out the trams did not run and there were few people on the streets, but the lights were back on in the *Nevsky Prospekt*, the crowds thick and unafraid of those *Cadets* with fixed bayonets. They felt nervous with the onset of darkness, no longer standing to attention on street crossings, lacking in authority, berated even by the bourgeoisie. Men wearing fur-collared coats shouted insults and waved their fists; they had been unaffected by rationing and smoked large cigars, the women on their arms draped in jewellery.

They had yet to hear of the dictatorship of the proletariat.

Vladimir Illych had worn clogs and a pair of baggy trousers, a soiled waistcoat and an unbuttoned shirt, keeping the cold from his neck with a green muffler wrapped around and around, the tail of the muffler falling to his knees. He had pulled his cap across his brow but the fake dark locks of the wig straggled beyond his cap towards his cheeks and neck. He had been more tramp than revolutionary, more dishevelled than any worker, a parody of those he sought to represent, but safe in the knowledge he was so grotesque he would never be stopped let alone recognised.

Two Army deserters approached selling cigarettes and sunflower seeds.

They were more desperate than threatening and Pauline gave them five roubles she took from her mitten; they veered away without a second look at Vladimir Illych. The golden dome of the Church of the Resurrection sparkled in the thin fog. The gambling halls and brothels and cabarets were opening for business, but the red guards had gone from the *Liteiny Bridge* and so too had the *Cadets*. Trams were running into the *Vyborg*, but if the gambling halls and brothels and cabarets prepared for another night of extravagance it would be their last for almost a century.

The lights were on in the *Smolny Institute*.

There had been *Cadets* on the streets around the *Smolny*, some shooting in the air, but cars and motorcycles came and went through the open gates. An armour-plated car left with its siren blaring and sparks rose like fireflies from a bonfire red guards had lit at the entrance. Embers from the fire scorched the wheels of the car and a sudden smell of burning filled the air. Tarpaulin covers had been removed from four rapid-firing machine-guns and more red guards bestrode the machine-guns. They wore dun-coloured breeches and ammunition belts around their shoulders, the cartridges reflecting dull in the light from the *Institute,* their rough hessian shirts buttoned against the cold.

No-one could enter the *Smolny* without a pass.

The colour of the pass had been changed from white

to red, but with the gates still open as the armour-plated car left Vladimir Illych Lenin slipped easily inside. Pauline had paused to savour the moment, the atmosphere, the tension; she knew her own life would never be the same again, that once she stepped into the *Smolny* she too would become a true revolutionary with a purpose and mission. She had no pass. She found herself caught in a throng of red guards at the gates and other guards who leapt from their machine-guns.

One guard struck Pauline with the raised butt of his rifle.

He struck her in the chest, not a massive blow but enough to send her backward, her cap falling, the red hair tumbling around her shoulders. She had seen the blow struck not from anger but from fear, from nervousness, and she had been ready to forgive as a sickness rose inside. She wore her corduroy suit and red neckerchief, slim as any man, and seeing the tumbling red hair the guards fell back in astonishment.

A woman in their midst!

Pauline stooped to pick up her cap, but the throng, the cold, the events of the day, no food except black bread served with tea, the raw-smelling guards, their unshaven faces close to hers: all became too much for her. She fainted onto the cobbles, a blackness settling around her, not the blackness of night, nor the blackness of the soul, but the blackness that came from the hemming bodies and lack of air.

'Make way! Make way!'

A *tovarich* lifted her to her feet.

His hands were under her arms, so that she felt the cold air as a smack to her face. Yet the old weakness had been there, the strength gone from her, the colour too, the cupola domes of the *Smolny Convent* spinning around her head, mingling with the imperial arms carved in the stone above the entrance to the *Smolny*. The *tovarich* settled her upon her feet and she would remember the smell of the earth that came from his hands and face, from his clothes, his face so close, so brooding that she fainted again.

He removed his own cap and fanned her face.

She opened her eyes and saw his black hair falling across his brow.

'Comrade Illych?' she asked.

She spoke a soft halting Russian.

The guards laughed and slung their rifles over their shoulders, but a silence settled upon them as Comrade Illych and his Military Revolutionary Committee appeared at the *Institute* entrance. He had set aside his wig and tramp's garb and stood before her as he would be remembered in history when his beard and moustache had grown; he wore a neatly-cut brown suit, waistcoat, high collar and dark tie. He had been soft-spoken but authoritative so that as he took her hands and pulled her respectfully towards him the guards fell back.

He noticed her cap on the ground.

The *tovarich* noticed it too and picked it up and

348

handed it to Vladimir Illych. He dusted the cap against his sleeve, straightened the peak, and replaced the cap on her head. The red strands of hair ran wild around the cap and her face was peaked from the faint. Her eyes were bright, her gaze steady, but she saw not the golden dome of the Church of Resurrection but a pinpoint of red light that glowed from a building not far from the *Institute.*

Contrasting the pinpoint with the golden dome of the Church, she realised that the dome was the past, the pinpoint the future. It might reflect change in permanence but change there would be. The gold of the dome might sparkle as it had done for centuries; it might shine through the mist, but it would be irrelevant; its time had come and gone. Something new was about to rise in the firmament, a new symbol would take its place.

A crowd had gathered to look at the pinpoint.

Some said it was an *agent provocateur* who would soon fire upon the *Smolny*; others thought it a kind of religious sign. Others more sophisticated, more political, remembered the red flag pushed through the hands of the Statue of Catherine the Great before the *Alexandrinsky Theatre.* They thought perhaps the two were linked. No-one left the crowd to investigate but the red pinpoint glowed and waned through the mist.

Vladimir Illych also noticed the red.

'Comrade Pauline is one of us,' he said.

He raised a finger towards the pinpoint.

'The Red Star shall glow for her as it glows for the rest of us.'

He turned and walked back into the *Institute*.

71

'The *Bolsheviki* have seized our presses,' Nikolai said.

'And I have become a People's Commissar,' Pauline said.

'I am to publish the decree. They say that printing presses are the poisoners of the mind. Can you imagine that? They say that ownership of print type and paper should belong to the workers and peasants. I have become a *petit bourgeois*. I printed Vladimir Illych's pamphlets on my own home press. I have turned out his *Rabochi Put*. I can still print – but only under the control of a People's Commissar.'

Snow had come to Petrograd and when Pauline woke in her first floor suite in the Europa Hotel she found the snow iced to her window ledge. The snow had fallen so thickly it had banked high against the hotel door. When she left the hotel it had still been falling, the flakes stinging her eyelids, her hands and head covered in fur, only the straggles of red hair showing against her white cheeks. She could not see beyond her mittens, the snow pristine, not a single footprint upon the paths, the *droshkies* turned into sleighs, bounding down the snow-ridden roads, the beards of the coachmen frozen white as if they had prematurely aged.

Pauline would pause for tea in a *traktir.*

Her Russian had been improving and the red guards in the *traktir* knew she was one of them, that she was writing a book, plucking a notebook from her corduroy jacket to write thoughts, scenes and descriptions. A table had been cleared for her of teapots and tin cups and ashtrays filled with foul-smelling tobacco stubs. Waiters ran between the tables crying *Seichass Seichass* – wait a minute – but she kept her head over her notebook and felt the warmth, the protection of the red guards, loving the atmosphere, the revolution still swirling around her.

There had been the night processions.

The processions moved along the banks of the Neva river, a band playing, men singing, red banners unfurling, some of the banners now gold-embroidered. The snow and ice sparkled and danced. The cries had gone up: *Long live the revolution! Long live the dictatorship of the proletariat!* Torch flames licked at the night, orange hues cast across the darkness, sparks fluttering from the torches, the sparks settling upon the ice, the ice flaring with the orange from the torches. *Long live the brotherhood of all peoples!*

'Long live the revolution!' Pauline shouted.

Pauline wrote that the revolutionary movement would be international, invincible, that no force in the world could extinguish its flames. As the old world crumbled

351

so a new world would begin. 'There must be world-wide revolution. Socialism in all countries – not just socialism in one. That is the life's mission of Vladimir Illych; that is his life's work. His revolution is just beginning.'

'I have read your articles,' Vladimir Illych said. 'They have been translated and I have ordered their publication in Petrograd. You shall oversee their publication with Comrade Nikolai. But one day, Comrade Pauline, you must do more than write about revolution. You must create your own.'

'The time is not yet,' Pauline said.

'The enemy shall always be with us,' Vladimir Illych said. 'We have always said that when we reach power we would close the bourgeois press. To tolerate the bourgeois newspapers would mean to cease being a socialist. When one makes a revolution one cannot mark time; one must always go forward or back. He who talks about the freedom of the printing presses goes backward and halts our headlong course towards socialism.'

Pauline visited Vladimir Illych at the *Smolny*.

She took her evening meal with the red guards, standing in line to receive a bowl and wooden spoon, taking boiled beef from a pot that stood at the end of a broad table. She would pour cabbage soup into the bowl after the beef and nibble at black bread as she prepared ideas for articles to show Vladimir Illych, sipping the tea she had taken from the samovar on the same table.

'If socialism is to succeed there must be means to an end,' Vladimir Illych said. 'A Bolshevik means to a Bolshevik end.'

If this meant suppression of the freedom of the press so be it; if this meant the elimination of a bourgeois life with the closing of gambling halls, brothels and cabarets then bourgeois life would be eliminated. It might mean the destruction of the country, but a new socialist state would rise from the destruction, pure as the snow that fluttered down upon Petrograd, undiluted, untainted, contaminated neither by capitalism nor the bourgeoisie.

The rich would oppose the power of the *Soviets*.

They would seek to dismantle the government of workers and soldiers and peasants; they would seek to dismantle the Revolutionary Committee and the *Constituent Assembly*. They would halt the work of government employees and those who worked in the Parliament. They would incite bank strikes, bank managers would refuse to hand over their funds to the *Bolsheviki*; they would disrupt the railways, the post, the telegraph. They would prevent food getting through from farms. But if the rich and their *agents provocateurs* did halt food they must be punished; they must be deprived of their own food, any reserves requisitioned and their property confiscated.

'All this must happen as a railway scatters sawdust,' Vladimir Illych said.

'And what is to become of the war?' Pauline asked.

'To save the country from suffering we must make peace. It is the Germans who do not want peace. They want to choke the Russian workers and peasants and return the land to the landlords.'

'They would even bring back the Czar.'

'You are still seeing the British Ambassador?'

'He sends my book chapters to London.'

'It is good that you stay close to the British ruling classes. The better to hang them high. You must tell the Ambassador that he must seek permission from his King that the Czar and his family be allowed to travel to England.'

Vladimir Illych handed Pauline the decree confiscating the printing presses.

'You must give this to Comrade Nikolai,' he said. 'He must not halt our headlong course towards socialism.'

'And who shall be his Commissar?'

'You shall be his Commissar,' Vladimir Illych said.

72

Pauline would not paint in Russia.

She would walk the river bank when the light had been pale and soft and her painter's eye had seen dreamy blues and a sky like a dying rose when evening set in. There had been no melancholy, no regret at leaving Highhill, but the sunset glow, the darkness of the cloud low over the cupolas; they made her think of the village with cloud coming over the hills and woods and Pennines; but if she could not paint she would sketch and she would publish her sketches to illustrate her book.

She thought of the *tovarich.*

She remembered the black hair, the black eyebrows, his cap with its crumpled peak. She remembered the peasant smell so overpowering she had fainted again. Had he worn a moustache or a beard? She wrote her notes in the *traktir,* recalling not only the *tovarich* but her conversations with Vladimir Illych, his thoughts, his reflections, his vision and imagination, yet his practicality, his common sense, his remorseless devotion to the revolution.

Snow blew in from the street and Pauline decided the citizens liked their snow. They walked with heads uplifted so that the flakes fell upon their cheeks; children ran muffled into snow banks, making their own snowstorms, rising again like white phoenixes; but above the snow, above the hovering flakes, there stood the gold cupolas and dark spires where snow had slid to the streets below. She recalled again the brooding face of the *tovarich* and in her mind the domes of the *Smolny Convent* were swinging again and so too were the imperial arms above the *Smolny* entrance.

The door to the *traktir* had opened again.

This time if it had blown in snow it had blown in too a strong peasant smell. Pauline looked up and saw the *tovarich* standing there, shaking the snow from his coat, brushing it from his shoulders, blowing it from his cap, his eyes squinting in the blue tobacco smoke that drifted towards the open door. His cap had been as black as his hair, a new cap uncrumpled, a red star stitched neatly into the black. His eyes had been as black as she remembered them, the lids low, and there had been grey to his moustache where the frost had gathered. There had been too a small black beard under his chin untouched by the frost.

The *tovarich* would come regularly to the *traktir*.

Always Pauline would know he had arrived by the peasant smell that came in with the cold. He would sit in the same corner, beyond the same tobacco smoke; he would smoke, too, his eyes smouldering like the end of his cigarette, the embers glowing towards her, his eyes turning away should she look at him. She wrote or sketched and one evening, on the way out, she had dropped by the door a sketch of the *tovarich* she had made in charcoal.

He had followed her back to the hotel.

She walked in the dry cold, seeking the moon above the thin cloud when the snow had lifted, but if it were really cold she would take a sleigh, feeling the warm blanket across her knees. She would close her eyes and imagine she was on the trap from Highhill to the railway station, feeling the same warm blanket, snow raw to the air, the same cold against her cheeks, numbing her lips, sharp to her eyelids, but she would drive out the memories and open her eyes to the domes and spires of Petrograd.

She had almost completed her book and sketches and now she felt an emptiness. There were fewer meetings of the Petrograd *Soviet*, soldiers were now expected to dig trenches and not debate; peasants were

356

expected to farm land and produce food; workers to make their factories turn out tanks or guns or tractors. With Vladimir Illych's decree, there were fewer newspapers and fewer fly-posters, fewer militia on the streets and less excitement.

Pauline had never thought she could be attracted by a man, but a revolutionary with a red star to his cap, a man with strong hands and face and a moustache as cold as his eyes? She had enjoyed the friendship of Nikolai Skoboliev. She would never have written her book without him. He had taken her to the *Congress of Soviets*, the *Peasants' Congress* and the *Constituent Assembly*; he had interpreted events and provided her with insights.

Nikolai Skoboliev loved her, but she had not encouraged his love; he had held her mittened hand when they had passed the *Smolny Institute* and marched across the *Liteiny Bridge* to the *Vyborg* district, but he had not touched her since. He had stood behind her at the printing works as she proofread the English chapters of her book; she had heard the smooth running of the presses and smelt the printing ink. She had lain a hand on her own shoulder so that he might take it as she read, but either he had not understood or had been too shy; her hand had remained on her shoulder till she had turned another page of her proof.

She heard a knock on the door of her hotel suite.

It had been a firm insistent knock, as if the time had come. Pauline knew it had come too but she was ready. She had never seen the body of a naked man and she wondered if he would have as many hairs to his chest as to his face, how firm and hard would she feel his body against hers? Would she feel the sweat to his thighs? She felt composed and efficient, a stirring to her nerves, so that she felt they singed and smouldered.

She had made a new life in Russia.

She had made a life of revolution, a man's world she had made her own. She wanted to be remembered not as a writer or painter but as a revolutionary; but as Vladimir Illych had perfected the revolution she would perfect her womanhood. She would link body to body as she had linked ideal to ideal. She stood by the window looking at the snow along the ledge; she saw its virgin whiteness, its purity. She wanted to tug open the window and move the snow away with her hand.

She moved to the door and pulled it open.

The *tovarich* stood muffled against the cold, frost upon his cap, whitening the edges to the red star. There was frost too upon his moustache ends as there had been at the *traktir*, and his cheeks were stiff with cold, his lips grey, the fleck dry. He held his coat collar tight to his neck, his hands gloved, the gloves as black as his coat, stooping slightly. His shoulders drooped and there had been frost to his boots as white as the frost to his moustache. A tawny light flickered to the blackness of his eyes.

She held the door wider and he stepped inside.

He sought to open the top button of his greatcoat,

but it had been tight and frozen. She used her long white fingers to undo the buttons, feeling the cold, the frost flaking into her hands, standing close to him, overpowered by the strength of his peasant smell that again almost made her faint, so that she fell forward and felt the rough hessian of the greatcoat, as cold to her skin as the buttons to her fingers.

'Long live the dictatorship of the proletariat!' Pauline said.

'My name is Mihael Zaichnevsky,' he said.

73

'Half a million men transferred by the Germans to the Western front,' the Ambassador said. 'Italy will be submerged by the Germans and Austrians. The war will be lost by spring. Roger and Albert Fatherley have died in vain.'

'Vladimir Illych wants to send all the bourgeoisie to the front,' Pauline said. 'He will send men and women alike if there is no peace.'

'And if they resist?'

'They will be shot as counter-revolutionaries.'

'The Revolutionary Military Committee will give Vladimir Illych his mandate to make peace with the Germans,' the Ambassador said. 'It is the British and French – and the Americans when they arrive – who will pay with their blood.'

'Vladimir Illych fears that Western capitalism will conclude a peace with German capitalism so that together they can destroy the *Bolsheviki* and partition Russia. He feels too exposed in Petrograd – the front is only a hundred miles away. That is why he has moved the government to Moscow.'

The Ambassador had spent his life in the diplomatic service.

His father had been First Minister and he had been born at the British legation in Copenhagen; he had been posted to Vienna and Rome and Tokyo before being appointed Ambassador to the Czar's Court. He had impressed by his elegance, but now there was hesitation to his step. He suffered from vertigo. He would close his eyes to stop the chandelier from spinning, the room turning upside down; he felt his legs so weak he thought he might faint. The vertigo would pass, his eyes open, and his fingers played again with the ends of his moustache.

'Do you think Lenin's a German agent?' the Ambassador asked.

'He's a Russian patriot.'

'The Germans paid for his passage from Switzerland to Russia. They gave him gold for newspapers, gold for agitation, gold to foment trouble among soldiers at the front. So much gold the *Bolsheviki* had twelve daily papers circulating among the troops.'

Pauline handed the Ambassador the last chapters of her book.

She had realised through her writing that power had

360

been seized by the *Bolsheviki*, not from the state for the state had ceased to exist; not from Parliament for the Parliament had died, nor from the government for there had been no government; but from the gutter where it had lain since the fall of the Czar. She realised too that Vladimir Illych had seized power not on behalf of the *Soviets*, not on behalf of the workers, peasants and soldiers, but on behalf of the *Bolsheviki*. He had understood power and knew how it should be used.

'You once asked me about peace, bread and land,' the Ambassador said. 'You asked if it were too much to ask. Possibly not – over the centuries – but over a week or ten days, even a month, it is too much.'

'The *Bolsheviki* had a political programme,' Pauline said. 'They were a minority, but they knew what they were doing. Only Vladimir Illych had a will so powerful he could impose himself on others.'

'The peasants wanted land – not revolution,' the Ambassador said. 'The soldiers had tired of the trenches where they had no food – and no fodder for their horses. Vladimir Illych politicised this agitation and perfected the revolution. You should put that in your book.'

Pauline's book would be more than an account of the revolution, it would be a manual on how revolutions should be organised, the workers made aware; how through organisation linked to events any ruling class might be overthrown. The enemies of the revolution were not the capitalists, nor even the bourgeoisie;

they were those social democrats who seized power and gave it away again.

'They're recalling me to London,' the Ambassador said. 'They say I should never have allowed you to stay. You are a bacillus that will sooner or later infect our own country. I've told them the *Bolsheviki* trust you because you're a suffragist and a socialist. That's why I begged them to pass on your chapters to the publisher.'

'And they agreed?'

'Not to publish would make us as bad as the *Bolsheviki*. Vladimir Illych would accuse us of confiscating printing presses!'

'The book will be called *The Red Sunrise*.'

'Does Vladimir Illych approve?'

'He has written the foreword.'

Nikolai Skoboliev had simultaneously translated the book and it would be published in Russia at the same time as in England. Soon there would be queues before the shop at the entrance to the printing works, waiting not for the latest *Bolsheviki* newspaper or tract but for *The Red Sunrise*. The book would be bound in red calf leather and displayed in the window where once the poems and plays of Anatole Skoboliev had stood.

The foreword by Vladimir Illych would also be printed and magnified and displayed in the window next to his photograph. The window would be cleared of dust, the glass cleaned and polished, the queue for the book straggling back to *Marinksii Square* where the crowds had first gathered to storm the Winter Palace.

Two young girls would sell the book from behind the counter of the shop and when they tired they would be replaced by two other girls from the printing works.

'Even your mother would be proud,' the Ambassador said.

Pauline had warned the Ambassador of the *Bolsheviki* storming of the Winter Palace. The Palace stood facing the Neva River, the Little Neva to the left, the great Neva to the right; the Peter and Paul Fortress stood on an island on the Petrograd side. The Palace had been used as a hospital during the war and when the Ambassador visited there had still been the rancid odour of chloroform and disinfectant in some of the smaller rooms where the more distinguished patients had been housed.

The government had sealed the Palace with sentries and a cordon of troops, but the Ambassador had known that if they might hold back the restless citizens they would not hold back the *Bolsheviki*. The troops had understood this too. They carried wood across the courtyard to stack against the main gate whilst other long-coated *Cadets* drawn up under arms in the Palace square were being harangued by an officer about to send them into the street to defend strategic points.

Servants inside the Palace went about their business in their brass-buttoned uniforms, their collars of red and gold, as if there were a government in residence. One of the *Cadets* had dropped a lump of black bread upon the marble steps; it had not been picked up by the servants and the Ambassador had kicked it away so

363

that it skidded and settled in a corner of the staircase. The Ambassador found another scrap of bread beneath his feet on the marble.

'And thus it came about,' he said. 'That power fell to the people.'

An illumined scroll conferring the freedom of Moscow upon the Ambassador sat against one wall of his office; against the other, also illumined, sat a fifteenth century icon representing St George and the Dragon. A silver drinking bowl stood upon a table in the corner with the helmet of a prince who had fought against the Swedes and Germans in the thirteenth century. The Ambassador's desk had been clear but for a pen stand and blotting paper and silver cigarette case and gold ashtray. The desk had been wide and polished where not inlaid with rich leather.

The Ambassador looked at the cigarette case but did not reach to open it.

'Do you think Vladimir Illych will trust an Ambassador who enjoyed his cigarettes with the Czar?'

'He has a message for you,' Pauline said.

'I shall write a personal note for the King,' the Ambassador said. 'We can get the Czar and Czarina and their family out through Murmansk. A fast destroyer would be there within days.'

'It is Vladimir Illych's wish they leave safe and sound.'

'But shall it be the wish of His Majesty's Britannic Government?'

'It is Vladimir Illych's message to you.'

'I am being recalled because of my vertigo,' the Ambassador said. 'I cannot give diplomatic advice standing on my head. I shall let the Foreign Office and the Home Office know how helpful you have been. There shall be a note on your personal file.'

Pauline had brought her sketchpad to the Embassy.

'I have made a sketch of your wife,' she said.

Pauline had met the Ambassador's wife when there had been a telegram from her publishers and she had brought the telegram to the printing works. She had invited Pauline for dinner at the Embassy and they had dined on *Poltava* borscht, meat fries, cold white fish, veal with fresh greens, roast chicken and duckling, fresh and pickled cucumbers, raspberry sweet dessert, fruit and wine. The Ambassador's wife had explained that the menu had come from the Czar's Palace at Tsarskei Salo.

'They serve you black bread at the *Smolny.*'

Pauline had eaten little, her stomach weak, her appetite small, but she had been struck by her hostess's smooth features, fair hair banked high at the back of her head. She had curved eyebrows and thick eyelashes, and in the chalk drawing Pauline had placed a fur stole around her neck, the smooth skin to her throat draped by the heavy cross of the Orthodox Church. She had robed her in a voluptuous red gown, her arms showing, a gold bracelet to her wrist, an arm draping the arm of the chair, another draped by the stole.

'I shall hang it in the entrance to the Embassy,' the Ambassador said.

'Better than on the front cover of *The Red Sunrise.*'

'And when we return home it shall be in the hallway of our residence.'

The Ambassador suffered another attack of vertigo and his head tilted towards the chandelier; he closed his eyes so that Pauline saw the thin veins to his lids. His hands grasped at the leather upon the desk and he let his head rest upon the back of his chair. The revolution had aged him, there was less colour to his face, the stains under his eyes were darker and deeper, and when he leant forward again and opened his eyes she felt they were less penetrating.

'We shall never meet again, Pauline,' he said.

'You are on the side of the capitalists,' Pauline said.

'You have been kind to me,' the Ambassador said. 'I shall be kind to you.'

'How can you be kind?'

'You are seeing a man called Mihael Zaichnevsky. You know him as a *tovarich*, but he is a left-wing socialist revolutionary. And you know Anna Bobinksy. She has come to the printing works where you are the Commissar. Nikolai Skoboliev has printed her pamphlets.'

'They are both of the revolution.'

'The revolution is a prism through which events are seen differently.'

'They are both allies of the *Bolsheviki.*'

'Not any more. They plan to shoot Vladimir Illych.'

'They are his comrades,' Pauline said.

'I would warn him,' the Ambassador said. 'If it is not too late.'

74

Anna Bobinsky wanted permanent revolution.

She wanted the excitement of the fall of the Czar, the storming of the Winter Palace, not the tedium of administration, of bureaucracy, of seeking to run a country. She did not want Vladimir Illych to make peace with the Germans or that the capitalists who had run the factories and made the profits should be called back to do the same under the *Bolsheviki*.

She had brought her tracts to Comrade Nikolai Skoboliev.

'The revolution has hardly begun, Anna,' Nikolai said. 'Yet you want a counter-revolution. You should join the government – become a People's Commissar – if you want to change things.'

'Vladimir Illych promised world-wide revolution – yet he does not carry the revolution into the heart of Europe. He consorts with the Germans – but he does not rouse the masses against the imperialists. He believes in the dictatorship of the proletariat, a Congress of peasants and workers and soldiers, but he sends soldiers into the villages to take grain from the peasants.'

'The rest of us must eat, Anna.'

'I say Vladimir Illych is a traitor to the revolution!'

'Vladimir Illych does what he can with the clay that is Mother Russia,' Nikolai said. 'This vast soil has gone to waste under the Romanovs. The people have lost their way. A whole continent must face a new direction. The whole of Russia needs time, Anna, but no-one needs more time than Comrade Illych.'

'Will you publish my tracts?'

'Not those that calumny Vladimir Illych,' Nikolai said.

'You do not know the pain, Comrade Nikolai. The *Bolsheviki* have taken over the policies of the Czar. I have worked side by side with the *Bolsheviki*. I have fought on the same barricades. I had hoped to fight the glorious battle to the end. Now the Germans have an Embassy in Moscow. The tears I weep are tears of blood for our beloved Russia.'

'I shall publish your tracts,' Nikolai said. 'Even though it is against the wishes of the People's Commissar. There should be debate and discourse. And you need to channel your energies away from disappointment and violence. You must battle from within the revolution rather than without.'

Anna had been older than Pauline.

She stood the same height but had no colour to her cheeks; her hair had not been a fiery red but a dull brown that had once been blonde. She wore no make-up and her smocks were as dull as her hair; she had been short-sighted and wore a pince-nez; yet she had a way with crowds and when she spoke she held out her arms to embrace the toiling masses and draw them to her as a mother draws her children.

'You are still a child, Anna,' Nikolai said.

As a child she would recall trams running on narrow lines shining like flint embedded into the cobbles, stretching to infinity. The trams ran so close to her home they had rattled the china in the cupboard of their front room and dust that rose from the traffic settled along the window-sills and froze in the early frost. The dust lay white and solid till spring when the thaw washed the dust back into the traffic.

'Your father wishes you to see what happens to revolutionaries,' her nurse said.

She had followed the crowds in *Znaminskii Square* to the Winter Palace. She had shouted their slogans and waved a banner of her own. She had not been perturbed when there had been shooting and men had fallen around her. She had no fear and no comprehension of death, the sound of gunfire had been exciting, less monotonous than the rumble of trams, and often she would slip from her home whilst her tutor and nurse had been with her brothers.

Her father had been appointed to run the Czar's security police, but she had not understood why the Czar's troops had fired upon the crowds before the Winter Palace. She had been so small she had been able to run in and out of the crowds, side-stepping massive thighs and hob-nail boots, the smell of people strong to her nostrils. It had been a sour smell of stale sweat, but she had followed the flow till she had found herself with the crowd before the St Petersburg Technological Institute.

The crowd had paused, bodies all around, hessian breeches and costumes rough as their hands, the crowd standing so thick that Anna had edged carefully through, afraid to be crushed, to be smacked by an irritated protestor, but edging forward till she was moving with the mass into the Institute. Years later she would realise she had been to the first session of what would become known as the Petrograd *Soviet.*

Anna would remember one speaker because he had brushed his hand through her soft blonde hair as he had made his way to the platform. He had been a small man with a red beard and moustache, and wisps of red hair; he liked to speak with his hands on his hips and his voice had been soft, so soft those around Anna had paused and leant forward to hear. Yet if his voice had been soft his thoughts were not and the longer he spoke the more agitated became his audience.

'Let us have permanent revolution!' he declared.

Her father had not been amused.

'Have I disobeyed you, father?'

'Neither your God nor your Czar,' her father had said.

'Whom have I disobeyed?'

'Your nurse and your tutor.'

'Is that a state crime?'

'A crime against the family,' her father said.

Anna had lost interest in the revolution.

The crowds were gone from *Znamenskii Square,*

the Winter Palace had fallen quiet. There had been thousands out to celebrate the signing of a political manifesto, but that had not been the same as bullets ricocheting from buildings, their sharp crack more exciting than thunder. She had been confined to her house with a new tutor and nurse and though she liked them both she had been glad to be again in the fresh air. The air had been sharp to her lungs with the first winter cold.

'The revolutionaries are to be deported,' her nurse said.

She would learn later her father had ordered the arrest of half the members of the *Soviet*. He had seen how they might politicise strikes and radicalise workers; they had been joined by the intelligentsia, by professional workers, pharmaceutical assistants, clerks and book-keepers. Together they might coalesce to bring an end to Czarist autocracy. The leaders would be exiled to Siberia.

The revolutionaries had stood on the station steps looking suitably ruffian in the crisp morning light; their dark beards straggled, their moustaches were untrimmed, their eyes as dark as their beards or moustaches. The revolutionaries wore their fur hats pulled down across their brows and already they were dressed in heavy fur-skinned greatcoats in anticipation of the Siberian cold. They looked morose and threatening and the Palace guards kept their distance as they waited for the train.

Anna noticed there were children and their mothers

too and she envied them the long journey across the plains, the children dressed like their fathers, only more elegantly, with full fur coats trimmed with white fur, white fur to their cuffs, their fur hats matching their coats. The mothers held their children's hands, but their faces were pale, sad, their cheeks runneled where the tears had flowed, yet they stood tall and proud, not hunched or defeated.

'It'll be a nice train journey,' Anna said.

The nurse squeezed her hand.

'There'll be bears on the track. Bears that will gobble up children! You'll be better here with me.'

Anna noticed one revolutionary to the left, not in the front row but effacing himself; he had been the revolutionary who had ruffled her hair on the way to the platform at the *Soviet*. He had seemed the most alone, the most depressed, not at all looking forward to the journey like the children, sad because he had been defeated and because he understood the consequences of defeat. He understood they would not be back for years.

'The children will be grown before they return to see the Neva,' her nurse said. 'The older men will never return – they will die in exile – and those with dark beards and moustaches. They will be as grey as the station platform before they return.'

Anna noticed her revolutionary looked less well off than the others.

He wore neither fur hat nor coat, only a woollen hat and long shabby coat that carried beyond his knees; his

372

hands were out of sight in his pockets but his eyes were downcast, not looking at his fellow revolutionaries nor their guards, nor the police photographer who would take their picture for the state archives. He did not even look at the crowd of onlookers who had come to see them off, who only a few weeks earlier had been with him in the *Soviet*.

'A man should not travel on such a journey without a gift,' Anna said.

A small shop stood next to the station selling religious artefacts. Icon lamps stood in the window, the copper burnished in the light of the sun; some had candles burning within them, the candles weak against the sunlight; other candles stood in boxes, pictures of famous saints stamped upon the front to make them more attractive. The door to the shop swung open as a customer entered.

Suddenly Anna too was in the shop, freeing her hands from her tutor and nurse, in and out of the shop before the shopkeeper knew she had come and gone. She had raced through the open door and grabbed the first candle she could lay her hands on. The candle had stood by an icon on the window ledge at the entrance to the shop. She had run out and raced past the guards and onlookers and photographer up the steps to the revolutionaries.

Anna ran straight into the arms of the man with the woollen hat and shabby coat, the man with the red beard and moustache, the man who had ruffled her hair, the man whom she had heard speak words she had not understood. The man paused, turning on the steps, surprised but not afraid, bemused, bending and opening his arms so that Anna swooped into them, lifted off her feet into the air.

The man replaced her gently on the steps.

'What is this, little one?'

'A gift for a long journey.'

'What kind of gift?'

'A candle.'

'A candle to keep me warm?'

'A candle to keep alive a flame.'

The man took the candle and swept it deep into his pocket.

The revolutionaries had said their last farewells, the last photograph had been taken, their guards were beginning to stir as the train arrived and a wreath of steam from the engine billowed towards them through the archway. Anna's tutor and nurse stood on the steps with the guards as the revolutionaries moved towards the platform, the children holding their parents' hands, lost to view in their fur coats and hats.

The revolutionary had kissed Anna on the forehead.

'The flame of your candle will light the world,' Vladimir Illych Lenin said.

'I want permanent revolution too!' Anna had said.

374

75

'Long live the revolution!' she had cried. 'Death to all traitors!'

Anna had been educated at St Petersburg University. She had entered the civil service and risen to the rank of collegiate counsellor, but she had no aptitude either for medicine or law, and though she did not study politics or read history her instincts told her the land should belong to the peasants. They were the true toilers and they loved the land more than the landlords.

She would recall the shock she had felt when she had seen her first peasant, not on the streets of St Petersburg but at Kazan where her father had taken her on one of his provincial tours. He had met functionaries serving the Empire; he had met merchants with their red beards and black hats and long black double-breasted coats. There had been peasants, too, shuffling down unkempt streets, dragging their goods through the mud. They wore sheepskin coats but their feet were bound in linen rags.

If they were lucky they wore bark shoes.

She had once blurted out her support for the peasants over a family dinner in her father's quarters in the Winter Palace. Her father had left the family home for fear of assassination and lived in his own quarters in the Winter Palace where he not only ran the Czar's security police but the Palace itself. He had been appointed governor responsible for the Palace upkeep, its personnel, its safety and well-being, and he did not mind the strong views of his daughter as she grew up.

'Your head has been turned by the revolutionaries at the Nicholas station,' he said.

There would be Christmas celebrations at the Palace and amateur theatricals, presents had been exchanged with Anna's brothers. There had been a Christmas tree and service in the private chapel, and rides in the *droshki* to *Marinskii Square* where the children had gathered their snowballs and threw them at those lingering in the *Nevski Prospekt.* Once even her father had joined in, enjoying his anonymity. He had kissed Anna on the cheek for the last time. 'I shall never forget the revolutionary with the red beard,' she said.

Years later Vladimir Illych would spend Friday afternoons visiting factory workers on the Moscow outskirts.

His visits would be unannounced but word would pass through a factory that he was there and crowds would gather in the open spaces around lathes and shaping machines. Vladimir Illych would not stand on a box, but he would clamber upon the first piece of machinery, and with his hands on his sides, his head forward, the sun catching his recultivated red beard and moustache, he would speak to the workers. Or rather he would harangue them on the fruits of the revolution.

'We shall triumph or die!' he declared.

Vladimir Illych left the factory and moved through the crowds to his car at the gates.

His chauffeur held open the door but someone fell before him and he could not advance because a woman had tugged his arm and told him about the price of bread. Bread, she said, was being confiscated at railway stations. Vladimir Illych said he knew the price of bread and that he had already given instructions that bread held at railway stations should be distributed. The car door had been open and he had placed a foot on the running-board.

Three shots had been fired.

The chauffeur had tried to close the door and pulled out his own revolver. The crowd scattered and the chauffeur pursued the would-be assassin. He chased her back into the factory but she ran among the workers as once she had ran among the crowds making their way to the Winter Palace. She leapt among the machines, small and nimble, dressed in a boiler suit with a blue scarf around her neck that came loose and fell among the lathes. A cap had been pulled across her brow and the back of her neck had been dull in the factory light.

She did not look back.

Nor did she stop running till she reached the back of the factory floor. The workers had parted for her as they had parted for the chauffeur, but there were no doors at the back of the factory and she was no longer a child running among crowds but an adult exhausted by the chase, her lungs heaving, her legs

377

weak, dropping the gun by her side, leaning against the corrugated walls, afraid now of her own death that would surely come. No-one could be more dead, she reflected, than a failed revolutionary whose father had been head of the Czar's security. She slid to the floor, letting her cap fall, the dull brown hair loose around her neck, lifting her eyes to the chauffeur.

Anna Bobinsky had given herself up.

Her counter-revolution had failed but she had written her name in the history books. She had shot Vladimir Illych Lenin. The chauffeur handed Anna over to others and drove Vladimir Illych as fast as he could to the Kremlin. He was already unconscious. A doctor had arrived. Not a limb moved, his pulse had grown faint, and if the bullets had not killed Vladimir Illych soon he would bleed to death. His breath became low and a death-rattle struggled to his throat.

But Vladimir Illych would not die.

One bullet had struck him in the arm, another between the jaw and neck, a third had missed and struck the woman complaining about the price of bread and its confiscation at railway stations. The doctor staunched the blood flow and Vladimir Illych's breath became easier, the death-rattle ceased. Even when he regained consciousness he would never know, he would never be told, that the woman who had fired the shots had given him a candle when she supposed he had been exiled to Siberia.

Yet it had been Pauline Alyson who had crossed the *Liteiny Bridge* to the *Smolny* with Vladimir Illych on the night the Winter Palace had been stormed; it had been Pauline Alyson who had written *The Red Sunrise* that would be translated and published in Petrograd; it had been Pauline Alyson who had become a People's Commissar. Whose tracts had been translated and published on the approval of Vladimir Illych. It had been Pauline Alyson with her red hair who would keep his flame alive.

Had he not known? Had he not understood?

Anna Bobinsky had loved him more than the revolution.

76

'Anna is in the *Lubyanka* prison,' Nikolai said.

Pauline stepped from the sleigh outside his shop.

Neither the shop nor the printing works had been the same since Anna Aleksandrovna Skoboliev had died. On her last visit she had removed the poems and plays of her husband Anatole in the sure knowledge he would not return or if he did she would not be there to greet him. She had wanted the window left bare, as if in mourning for his passing, for the life they had led that was no more, for those who had died at the front or in the revolution. Or because she wished the emptiness to reflect the memories of her childhood, a life at the Czar's Court.

She had been small and shrunken when she had

visited the bookshop for the last time. She had been
draped in black: black gown, black shawl, black shoes,
a black brooch to her gown, a black string of pearls and
small black-studded earrings. Her noble face had been
framed in white hair, contrasting with the black shawl
around her head and shoulders. She had fine hands that
fluttered when she was anxious. She heard everything
and saw everything, her eyes as alert as her hands, a
notepad close to write down her observations.

She had come to the printing works and given
Pauline her mother's journal where every rouble and
kopek had been registered. She had carried on entries
into the journal for every rouble and kopek Pauline
had made from her own tracts and pamphlets. She had
pushed the journal into Pauline's hands and Pauline
had understood she had wanted her to carry on her
mother's work as it had been carried on in this journal.
There had been something else she had wanted to show
Pauline. She had more roubles and kopeks than her
mother, she had been successful as her mother had
been successful.

She should take comfort from her success.

Anna Aleksandrovna had returned to her house in
Ligorsky Prospekt and setting her face to the wall,
lying in her Czarist bed, dressed fully in black, she
had closed her eyes and her mouth, sometimes lying
asleep, sometimes awake till she died and Nikolai
found her stiff and dry as the carcass of a horse
that had been killed in the revolution and left in
Marinskii Square. She would be buried in the rites of

the Orthodox Church, but quietly, with few mourners, those who remembered her from her days at Court, but ancient as she had become ancient, Nikolai facing her not towards Jerusalem but Tannenburg where her husband had fought his first and last battle.

'She is gone,' Nikolai said. 'And I must go too.'

'The printing works is your life.'

'It belongs now to the *Bolsheviki*.'

'Where can you go?'

'Anna Bobinsky was a true comrade. I printed her tracts. I have been an *Esser* too in my time when my father did not return from the war and before I understood the *Bolsheviki*. You remember her last tract? I should not have allowed it to be published. It called for another uprising, another revolution, the storming of another Winter Palace – in her case the Kremlin – and the shooting of Vladimir Illych.'

'What does this mean, Comrade Nikolai?'

'It means I have become an enemy of the people.'

They walked around the courtyard between the shop and the printing works. The walls hemmed in the sky, the shutters were closed, plaster had pealed from the walls leaving stucco blotches; there were pockmarks from aimless firing when the *Cadets* had sealed the works; and there had been the smell of printing ink and stagnant water from a disused trough at the centre of the courtyard. There had been mould around the trough, still filled with water for the horses to drink, the water frozen solid in winter, too foul-smelling in summer to be removed.

'You are English, Comrade Pauline,' Nikolai said. 'You do things differently in your country. We are used to Czars. We have had Czar Nicholas but we have also had Ivan the Great and Ivan the Terrible. Now we have Comrade Vladimir Illych. He is a revolutionary – and revolutionaries need counter-revolutionaries. They need *agents provocateurs*. They need enemies and they need fear. There shall be enemies enough now that Anna Bobinsky has shot Vladimir Illych.'

'And Mihael Zaichnevsky has shot the German Ambassador.'

'He is with her in the Lubyanka.'

'I shall speak to Vladimir Illych,' Pauline said.

'If you see him again.'

'You are a comrade of the *Bolsheviki.*'

'But not a hero of the people.'

'Where will you go?'

'My mother came from an estate on the Volga. Her parents sent her to Court for her education. It was there she met my father. The Volga is far enough away. Perhaps the estate has been seized – perhaps it is now run by peasants. But there is family – ties, roots, history. I cannot tell you where it is, but you do not need to know. And if you are asked you can say with your hand on your breast, as a People's Commissar swearing by the red star, that you do not know.'

'But your printing works – your machines?'

'My last task is done,' he said. 'I have published *The Red Sunrise.*'

There had always been a queue before the shop,

those who wished to buy back-copies of the *Bolsheviki* papers and tracts, some bringing two roubles, others five and others from ten to fifty kopeks. The shop might still be open but the linotype and printing presses were silent by order of the Petrograd *Soviet.* The telegraph no longer ticked and rats scurried from one linotype machine to another seeking crumbs that might have been dropped by the girls who had eaten as they worked.

Old pamphlets were pinned to the walls, reminding Pauline when Petrograd had been filled with pamphlets and tracts, posters and bills, but now there were only the pamphlets and tracts and posters and bills of the *Bolsheviki*: exhorting soldiers not to stand on street corners, exhorting the peasants to return to their villages, exhorting workers to build the dictatorship of the proletariat.

Nikolai had been dressed in a serge suit with a stiff collar and black cravat, as if he had just left his mother's funeral. A small hat sat upon his head and each time he spoke he lifted the hat slightly, out of respect. There were bags in the courtyard and soon a sleigh would appear and a coachman collect the bags and take them to the Nicholas railway station. There would be no grand exit for Nikolai since the Petrograd *Soviet* had requisitioned all the cars, but the clatter of hooves in the courtyard told Pauline that the sleigh had already arrived.

'We should smear our hands with printing ink,' she said.

There had been no printing ink and she held Nikolai close, his head falling onto her shoulder, his hat in his hand, the serge of his suit against her breasts. She stroked the blonde hair, feeling the sadness to him, the trembling that ran as a sigh through his body. The trembling and sigh came together as tears and she felt them from his cheeks upon her shoulder. Was he crying for his mother and father? Was he crying for Russia? Was he crying for Pauline? Or was he crying for himself because he had to begin again? She could not tell and did not ask, but she had been moved by his closeness.

'I shall go to Moscow,' she said.

'You want to be close to Mihael Zaichnevsky?'

'I want to be close to Vladimir Illych.'

77

'I want to collect mushrooms – only my doctors will not let me walk.'

Vladimir Illych had suffered a stroke that ran down his right side and made it difficult for him to speak. The stroke had carried into his leg and he walked with difficulty. The doctor might have saved his life by staunching the flow of blood, but the two bullets had not been removed and moved steadily around his body. They were poisoning his system. Vladimir Illych had ordered them removed. He wished to be restored to full health, to lose his insomnia.

He wished again to be the man who had led the revolution.

'Did you really push Winston Churchill under a train?' he asked.

'He was saved by others,' Pauline said.

She had moved into a two-room suite in the National Hotel that would later be named *The First House of the Soviets*. She looked out upon the *Okhotny Ryad*, the farmers' market, and beyond the market she could see the Kremlin where they had erected a red star on one of the spires so that its light would shine across the city, shine through fog or damp or hail or snow. She would often walk back to her hotel through a snowstorm, the snow driven by a strong wind, the wind swirling around her feet, blowing the snow from the pavement so that she felt she was caught in a snowstorm of her own.

She dressed as Muscovites dressed.

She wore a long kaftan with a white shawl around her head not only to keep out the cold but to hide her red hair; she felt a touch of the bourgeoisie about her beauty and wore neither make-up nor lipstick, nor let her red hair flow around her shoulders. She kept it short so that it became less noticeable. She had wrapped her shawl more tightly against the snow, but the tighter she wrapped the shawl the less she could see. Lamps had glowed but where were the lamps; people passed but who were the people?

Where was her hotel?

She had looked up and seen the red star glowing

through the snow and despite the storm, the wind, the cold, the numbness she felt to her hands and feet and mind, she had been able to get her bearings and march more strongly till she reached the hotel. She could see the red star from her window and it would be the last thing she saw as she drew the curtains and went to bed. In the morning when she woke there would be the star again, eternal and reassuring, filling her with a determination that would last not only throughout her day but throughout her life.

She had walked the street markets at *Smolenskaya* and *Sukharevskaya* where the people were hungry, impoverished, badly-clothed and pasty-faced. There had been no coal or wood to heat buildings and the food stores were empty. Pauline could understand why people felt the revolution had failed them; they had no patience. But if the markets were empty, if people wondered why there had been a revolution in the first place, if the number of Army patrols increased, the cafes were full. Poets were writing their notes, harlots singing their songs, the cafes smelling of ill-fermented liquor, condensation streaming down the windows, the people talking and laughing and making jokes against themselves, though never against the revolution.

The *Lubyanka* prison had been too close for that.

The streets were not safe for the male bourgeoisie robbed of their gold watches; not safe from the younger red guards who would break plate-glass windows with their rifle butts and steal whatever they found inside; not safe for counter-revolutionaries who might be shot against a wall, a trace of blood in the snow their only remembrance; not safe for those females who wore fur coats, for they would be robbed of their coats as their men were robbed of their gold watches.

Pauline still wrote her articles, using the Kremlin facilities to telegraph them to London, linking the intelligentsia to the revolution, putting forward a view that if Russia were traversing a storm the storm would pass, out of the hurricane true comradeship would be born. There would be peace. There would be the brotherhood of man. Palaces might be sacked, books destroyed, art treasures burned, even the Kremlin might be wiped from the face of the earth, no more Czars, no more Lenins, no more thrones, no more power; but the people would survive and so too would the revolution.

She had been appointed Secretary to the Third International.

She had been given an office in the old *Rossiya Insurance* building on *Lubyanka Square* opposite the home of the new police. It had been one of the biggest buildings in Moscow, with many rooms, many entrances, spacious cellars, and she would have an office to herself with a secretary. She eschewed comfort like Vladimir Illych and her office carried the minimum of desks and chairs and files, with a single telephone to the outside world and another direct to the Kremlin.

The Third International would bring true revolution to the industrialised countries of the west; it would light a flame for backward colonial countries and open a new world for communism. Vladimir Illych would never relinquish his dream of international communism where the Russian revolution had been but a stage on the way. But Vladimir Illych had Russia to run with its policy decisions and its bureaucracy.

How could he organise world revolution too?

Vladimir Illych had attended the first meeting of the Third International that Pauline had opened. She had translated for those delegates who spoke English but no Russian. The comrades had come from all over the western world and in accordance with the ways of the *Soviets* they had talked of credentials and mandates, organisational and procedural matters, but as Vladimir Illych and Pauline knew international communism would be born as if shot by a cannon. Pauline would be impatient of those delegates who talked of revolution but who had little intention of practising it, who doubted the political and doctrinal analysis that showed revolution was certain in their own country, and she had no time for those Latin communists who would end a debate prematurely so that they could enjoy a decanter of Russian wine in a *traktir*.

'There must be no compromise!' she had declared in her inaugural speech. 'We do not have enough brave people in England. They shall need to be galvanised. They shall need to be led. I have participated in the struggle for women's rights. I see the importance of radicalism and bravery in the defence of ideas. I have smashed windows, I have pushed Winston Churchill under a train. I have shown cowardly English males that women will not be downtrodden!'

Vladimir Illych had hardly responded.

Perhaps he overworked, perhaps years with four hours sleep a night had taken their toll, but not only had he been tired, his speeches less charismatic, the rhetoric less flourishing; he had made mistakes when he had spoken. He had talked of two classes of exploiters but had named only one: the bourgeoisie. In fact, he had meant to talk of two classes that had been exploited: the peasant and the worker. She had not thought too much of his incoherence but later she had begun to realise that his health was failing.

The great man was dying.

78

'It is time for your own English revolution,' Vladimir Illych said.

'How can I make my own revolution?'

'You shall return to your own country. Funds shall be put at your disposal – as the German government put funds at mine. There shall be a bank account opened for you in London. You shall be given bills of exchange. You shall be given gold. Gregory Zinoviev shall organise it all. He shall give you a letter. You must infiltrate the Labour Party. You must use it for your own revolutionary ends.'

Zinoviev had been with Vladimir Illych in Switzerland. He had travelled with him through Germany in a sealed train, but he had never had Vladimir Illych's nerve for revolution and had been against storming the Winter Palace. He had supported Vladimir Illych's decision, saying it was better to make mistakes towards the proletariat rather than against them. It had been on his advice that Pauline had been appointed to the Third International.

'You are happy with the Third International?' Vladimir Illych asked.

'I am happy with Article Five.'

Article Five called for revolutionaries to work through their village ties. Pauline knew that Highhill would be the focal point of her revolution. Authority came from the Third International. Vladimir Illych himself had ordered the revolution to work when it came; there could be no refusal to undertake the task or turn it over to undependable half-reformist elements, as Vladimir Illych had said. This would be the equivalent of a betrayal of the proletariat.

Vladimir Illych had called for illegal acts.

Communists in foreign countries did not need to live within the law; they had to make their revolution succeed. This was the essence of revolutionary truth: that any untruth would be legitimate for the revolution to succeed. This too had been important for Pauline. She had lived outside the law till her banishment to Highhill, yet Vladimir Illych had given his imprimatur to her acts. She had not been alone. She had not acted beyond the pale. Civilised society had been wrong to her mother and wrong to her.

On civilised society she would take her revenge.

Only one of the bullets had been removed from Vladimir Illych and his health had not improved. He was to take a holiday in a hunting lodge in Keralia and he had asked Pauline to meet him in Petrograd where the Third International would conclude its proceedings. It had been Christmas and though the *Bolsheviki* had renounced Christ and all his works, Vladimir Illych had been brought up in a Russian Orthodox household and Christmas would always be special to him. He had wanted a Christmas tree with lights, but this would be referred to as a New Year's tree and reports of his convalescence referred to his New Year rather than Christmas break.

Pauline found him sitting in a corner of a second-class compartment in a train in the Finland Station.

His head had been down as if he were sleeping; he had been wrapped in a fur coat, his hands small and white, a fedora pulled well down on his head. He believed by travelling second-class he would not be noticed; but he had always been noticed and there were crowds along the station and platform, workers coming from the *Vyborg*, so that Pauline had to push her way onto the train.

'I've brought you Finnish money,' she said.

She knew Vladimir Illych was forgetful of such things.

'Our revolution took ten days, but yours may take

longer,' Vladimir Illych said. 'Remember – you'll always be a People's Commissar and a hero of the revolution. I am saddened the British Ambassador did not remove the Romanovs but you gave him his chance. History has decided to write their final chapter in a different ink. We tried our best, you and I, but as you say in one of your pamphlets – the revolution lives on.'

'I will need your instructions, Comrade Illych.'

'We have discarded social democracy like a child's shirt. Social democrats are renegades and opportunists – and not genuine revolutionaries. All that social democrats do is crawl on their bellies before the capitalists and lick their shoes. False socialists can be identified by their slogans. True socialists reject such hypocritical freedoms as Parliament and a free press. You are a true socialist, Comrade Pauline.'

'I shall establish a true *Soviet.*'

'You will always be a Communist and a member of our Third International – however often you may be called upon to deny it. You must work within The Labour Party. You must create the conditions for the English revolution.'

'I cannot use those who have attended our Third International.'

The English delegates had been sticklers for procedure. Why had their speeches been cut from the official proceedings? Why were their objections disregarded? Why were translations so slow when speeches had been in German? Pauline did not speak German and could not help. She had told them this was not a debating society but a revolutionary forum to change events in their own countries where the communists were less numerous.

'You must create the event that creates socialism.'

'How can I do that, Comrade Illych?'

'You will need a dramatic act,' Vladimir Illych said.

79

Pauline walked with Mihael Zaichnevsky around the inside of the Kremlin wall.

'I shall not see you again?' Mihael asked.

'Not unless you want to fight the English revolution.'

It had been the first day of a Moscow spring and the light reflected from the Moskva river as if in hope. Pauline felt the touch of the sun to her cheeks and brow and hands and wrists; she had discarded her fur hat and mittens and felt the air warm through her kaftan as it circulated her body. Behind her stood what the British Ambassador had described as 'a curious conglomeration of palaces, towers, churches, monasteries, chapels, barracks, arsenals and bastions'.

Whatever place the Kremlin held in history before the revolution that history had been re-written: red guards and officious policemen were everywhere, no longer friendly to the local populace, insisting within the Kremlin that the newly-covered roads with a white line down their middle should be free at all times for the speeding limousines of the new Commissars. To trespass across the road from a lawn, leaving the shadow of the plane trees, meant a harsh warning from a whistle and the threat of a shot in the back if the whistle were ignored.

The heavy Kremlin walls and gates, whether of ornate iron or brick, facing out as they did to what became known as Red Square, had suited the *Bolsheviki*. To impose a dictatorship of the proletariat they must be free of the constraints the proletariat might impose upon them. Vladimir Illych might have instituted the *subbotnik* for *Bolsheviki* officials – a stint on a factory floor of a Saturday morning – but for the rest the *Bolsheviki* would design and create their new state enclosed in this historic temple behind walls twelve metres thick.

Not only would they stay remote from the proletariat; they would take precautions to stay remote. The more precautions they took the more paranoid they became. In short, the *Bolsheviki* had ranged themselves like the Czars, not enemies of the people, but enemies to themselves. The new regime would build itself upon the remnants of the old, but the Kremlin walls would keep the people out rather than let the people in.

'All power to the Soviets!' Pauline cried.

She had cupped her hands to her mouth and shouted towards the Moskva below.

The great houses opposite stood squat and bourgeois, stained black with centuries of grime; the British
Embassy stood now to the right, close to a bridge, less
squat than the other great houses, but heavily guarded
with soldiers who held their rifles to the ready. If
Mihail Zaichnevsky had done nothing else when shooting the German Ambassador he had assured the safety
and security of all embassies in the new capital.

He had rung the door bell at the German Embassy in
Denezhni Pereuolok at half-past two in the afternoon;
he knew by then the Ambassador would have left his
luncheon table. He had set aside his *tovarich* garb and
worn a suit of heavy serge that had been too small
for him, the shoulders padded; his shirt had been a
starched white, the collar straight, his tie immaculate.
He looked and felt a member of the *nomenklatura*,
the new bureaucracy emerging in Moscow, but for
the Germans he was a counter-revolutionary, a plotter
against the *Bolsheviki*, someone who might take over
the country if Lenin were overthrown.

Mihail had news of an uprising he wanted to impart
only to the Ambassador.

The Ambassador did not know he himself would
be the signal for the uprising, that and the assassination of Vladimir Illych in accordance with Anna
Bobinsky's pamphlet, and only when Mihael had shot
the Ambassador would the uprising begin. What would
be the aims of the uprising? To return power to the
gutter where Vladimir Illych had found it, to create
chaos and anarchy out of which a new revolution

would begin, that would save Mother Russia not from itself but from the *Bolsheviki*.

Mihael had carried a revolver and a bomb in his briefcase.

His nerves had got the better of him, there had been a weakness to his legs. He had felt sweat running down his back, cold like ice, and his arm and hand trembled when he had aimed. The Ambassador had understood immediately and fled up the staircase from the entrance to the Embassy towards his private quarters. The shots Mihael had fired had lodged below the small gold-encased lights on the staircase.

He recovered his nerve and pulled the bomb from the briefcase.

He flung it as high as he could, beyond the banisters, beyond the chandelier that hung like a pendant from the ceiling, beyond the rich carpets with their gold stair-rods. It fell at the top of the stairs and exploded beneath the Ambassador's feet. The blast had blown Mihael across the entrance. It had blown out the large French windows and sliced the heads from the flowers in the herbaceous borders around the Embassy.

Mihael had escaped over a two-and-a-half metre fence and dragged himself to a waiting car.

He had lost his briefcase in the blast and identification had swiftly followed. The Ambassador had died instantly and his government demanded nothing less than the firing squad for Mihael Zaichnevsky. He had been interrogated by the *Cheka*, the new state police; he had been shown the execution ground with its solitary post set in concrete by the prison wall. He had heard practice shots in the night, the ping of bullets from the concrete, the duller ricochet from the post into the wall.

The uncertainty destroyed his nervous system.

He had never recovered from the blast, his hearing had gone, his vision had become blurred. The tremble he had felt to the backs of his legs and in his firing arm would not go away; nor would the steady stream of sweat down his back, now cold now warm, yet running as a river to the base of his spine. He had damaged his leg leaping over the wall. He could not sleep, his lips trembled, he smoked without ceasing, the only amenity in his condemned cell, but the heavy blue smoke curled into his lungs and made him retch.

The Mihael Zaichnevsky Pauline had known in Petrograd would be no more.

'They should have shot me,' he said.

She had saved him from the firing squad.

80

'When will you leave?' he asked.

'As soon as I have my letter.'

'You'll never be back?'

'You'll not want me back.'

'They say no-one will see Vladimir Illych again.'

'At least I saw him,' Pauline said.

'They say when he dies they'll build for him a mausoleum in Red Square. They will embalm him so that the proletariat might forever gaze upon him. The red star shall shine from the Kremlin and he will smile from below.'

Vladimir Illych had had his *yolka,* his Christmas tree even if it were called a New Year's tree. There had been sleigh rides in Keralia, the snow sparkling and bright, not dull and threatening as in Moscow. He had stayed in a hunting lodge, sitting remote in a corner, wrapped against the cold, his fedora down, his hands deep in his fur coat, his head upon his chest. There had been two small strokes that left a twitch to his mouth, but a major stroke had left him only with his speech.

His life had been slipping away.

When she had left Vladimir Illych at the Finland Station Pauline had walked down the *Propetski Neva,* the sky a frosty blue, the cirrus high, ice tufts in the street corners; thin ice had filmed the shallow waters by the river banks. The bourgeoisie had gone from the Neva and Pauline remembered how they had strolled in their black broadcloth coats with their fine marten collars. Their wives had been proud on their arms, smiling at those they knew, ignoring those they did not.

They had all been swept away.

She recalled workers' wives and the wives of the *petites bourgeoisie* and the servants of the great houses queuing at three in the morning for the nine o'clock opening of butcher shops and sugar and tea stores.

Nikolai Skoboliev had told her when she arrived that before the war potatoes had cost fifteen kopeks but now they cost twenty; butter had gone up to one rouble twenty kopeks a pound, and boots from fifty to a hundred roubles. She had walked as far as the end of *Kemonstrov Prospekt* where the bridge led to an island; on the island stood a park, a palace, and what had been the estates of the wealthy.

They were now the homes of the new *nomenklatura*.

The dwarf perched above the crowd had gone from the *Nevsky Prospekt.* So too had the apple-seller who had stood before the British Embassy gates. The Embassy was now the home of the peasants' section of the Petrograd *Soviet*; the apple-seller had been bayoneted to death in an argument with a red guard over the price of her apples. There were red guards before the *Soviet*, standing tall and proud, wearing red arm bands as well as red stars to their caps. They carried their rifles as if they had been born with them, cartridge bandoliers across their shoulders.

She passed the *traktir* where she had written her book.

There were the same waiters, the same bustle, the same atmosphere, the same sweat running down walls, but she had not been recognised, everything the same yet everything changed. She had moved towards the bookshop and printing works beyond *Znamenskii Square*. The window to the bookshop had been filled with the works of Vladimir Illych and the printing works were turning out the Petrograd edition of the new

Bolsheviki newspaper *Pravda.* The courtyard walls had been replastered and the trough had gone. The smell of printing ink had been as fresh as ever, but no-one had heard of Nikolai Skoboliev or his mother.

They had not heard of Anna Bobinsky either.

'Did Anna exist?' Pauline asked. 'Or was she a dream?'

Pauline would seek to conjure Anna upon the screen of her mind, with her dull brown hair and face free of make-up, lips as cold as winter roses, but she would recall only the rings under her eyes as black as her dress, her hair dulled with sweat. She walked as if she were a nun, a woman with a mission beyond the world's comprehension, as if she had her own religion that she wished to articulate but could not, despite her rhetoric and outstretched arms.

'She wore a pince-nez,' Pauline said.

'Not on the day she shot Vladimir Illych.'

'You've seen her again?'

'They took her to the *Lubyanka*.'

'She should never have given Vladimir Illych a candle.'

'She confused Vladimir Illych with Leon Trotsky. Vladimir Illych was not deported to Siberia with the other revolutionaries. He slipped away to Paris and London and Zurich. She believed it was Vladimir Illych because she wanted to believe.'

'Vladimir Illych was exiled to Siberia.'

'Not at the time Anna stood on the platform.'

'She loved the wrong man.'

'She lived with her hallucinations.'

'She tried to kill for them too,' Pauline said.

'I killed for her,' Mihael said.

'And Vladimir Illych gave you a pardon.'

Mihael smelt of fresh soap and starch as they walked by the Kremlin wall.

The sun speckled the grass through the plane trees and struck at the gold cupolas behind them. They walked not as lovers but as friends and companions. There had no longer been the smell of the earth that had so attracted Pauline when he had picked her from the ground outside the *Smolny Institute*. He had been dressed as a lieutenant of Leon Trotsky, the second man in Russia, the man who would succeed Vladimir Illych.

In Petrograd he had been a strong lover, a silent lover, speaking to her neither in English nor Russian, his mouth as cold as his breath. He had thrust into her harshly and she had endured because a woman had been expected to endure even if she did believe in revolution; there had been no equality between the sexes. She had submitted because a woman must submit. There had been in the closeness no deep physical satisfaction.

In Moscow she had wished to dominate him.

She had left open the curtain so that she could see the red star that shone from above the Kremlin walls. She unloosened his hessian shirt and felt its texture thick to her long white fingers; the buttons to the shirt had been white and she had let the shirt fall open to see the hairs on his chest. They had been thick and curled, the odd strand of white, and she had felt the stirring deep to her thighs. She had let her hands flutter till he had been cold and naked before her, the light upon him half-white half-red.

He had not stirred.

The strong silent lover was no more.

'There'll be a power struggle,' he said. 'Who can tell if Leon Trotsky will succeed? It is better you go now while you're still a hero of the revolution.'

'Even though we'll never meet again?'

'There's something I want to show you before you go,' he said.

81

They had met at midnight outside the *Lubyanka* prison.

Mihael had brought special passes to enter the building and they had been met by a Commissar who nodded stiffly to Pauline, his cheeks white and taut in the light, his brow clear as if waxed. He had not removed his cap with its neat red star, and his neck had been thin and frail. He led them through passageways and corridors, the light stark from unshaded bulbs, the cold seeping into them. There had been interview rooms, too, their doors listlessly open, chairs and tables empty, the bars a heavy skeletal black to the outside window.

They reached doors that were locked and guarded.

It had been colder still in the long corridors and the cold had bred its own hostility. She felt a sudden tension, a nervousness as she passed guards who made way for her, shy smiles to their lips, the smiles not reaching their sullen eyes. She had set aside a spring costume of dark serge and white blouse and brooch and wore again her men's corduroy and Lenin cap, her shorn locks tucked inside the cap. The red star shone from her cap as it shone from the Kremlin.

She kept her nervousness under control.

She had come to Russia aged twenty-four and now she would leave it aged thirty. Her body had grown firmer but she had still been slim and fragile; she was pretty, even beautiful, but there had been a hardness that took away the prettiness and beauty and left features that might have been sculpted; they were perfect in form but devoid of emotion. She rarely smiled and like the guards when she did the smile did not reach her eyes.

'They call the inmates at one o'clock,' Mihael said.

'How do they do that?'

'A red guard with a roster will call their names.'

'What have the prisoners done?'

'They are enemies of the people.'

'What happens when he calls their names?'

'He will tell them they are wanted for questioning. They are to be taken to the prison department where they will sign a regulation card. They may read it if they wish.'

'At one o'clock in the morning?'

The Commissar had not traversed the locked and guarded doors, but Mihael knew his way; he took Pauline by the hand and she heard the heavy echo of his boots upon the concrete. There had been no other noise from the night even though the *Lubyanka* stood on a street corner where people passed; except they did not pass after the Kremlin clock struck midnight, not even when winter had turned to spring.

They left the corridors and moved down cellar steps.

The steps had been built a hundred years ago, the walls were damp, the light sharp, harsh bulbs held in upraised sockets so that the light shone towards the roof rather than the steps, catching their faces in a whiter, harsher light. The cellars had been converted into a prison, but the cells had been emptied, inmates standing before open doors. They took off their clothes and placed them in tidy heaps at their feet. If the inmates felt the cold they did not show it. They stood with heads bent and shoulders slanted.

Mihael placed an arm around Pauline.

They stayed back in the shadow.

Pauline saw that the men were frail, old, their hair white, their bodies slumped, as if their bones had collapsed, their ribcages destroyed, their buttocks shard, their private parts shrivelled and irrelevant. They held their heads down against the light and stared at their belongings as if they were memories. They did not know what to do with their hands; some held them behind their back, some clasped before their stomachs. Others let them fall by their sides and scrape at the wasted muscles of their thighs.

There were ten inmates and ten guards.

The guards worked methodically.

They checked the lists before them, some carrying whips, some batons, treating the inmates with politeness but also indifference. They tied the inmates' hands behind their backs, resolving their conundrum, lining them up so that they faced away from their cells towards a door that quietly opened, letting in air that was less cold, still touched by that day's sun, yet sufficiently fresh to ripple at their white hairs. Some of the inmates tried to lift their hands to their heads before they were tied behind their backs.

'They'll be taken into the garden,' Mihael said.

He had his own route to the garden.

He led Pauline back up the cellar steps and along another short corridor that led to another door. The door had been studded by rusting iron, with a small iron grill and black-painted handle and lock. He had pushed at the door and it swung easily open. They stumbled onto a narrow balcony. The balcony stood bare of flower pots or plants or shrubs with a balustrade rather than a rail, the stone cold to the touch of their hands, as cold as the air striking their faces, losing its spring freshness.

The first naked inmate had been brought into the garden.

The cords were released from his wrists and a red

guard ordered him to lie face down in the dirt. He lowered himself gently to his knees. He stretched out his legs, using his elbows to settle himself, sprawling his arms and legs, leaning forward till his nose and cheeks sank into the dirt. He lifted his head as best he could and turned himself sideways so that only a single cheek settled into the dirt.

A red guard emerged from the darkness.

He shot the inmate in the back of the neck.

The sudden shot startled Pauline and she fell back on the balcony. She feared she might faint. Mihael held her hand and she did not fall. His fingers trembled and there had been a tremble to his lip; there had been sweat to his hands but sweat again down his back, cold and running as a river, shivering his skin. Each held tightly the fingers of the other as the second naked man was brought into the garden.

'You fainted on me once,' Mihael said. 'You must not faint again.'

The second inmate had been ordered to lie face down in the dirt. He too was shot. Each naked man was taken into the garden and shot and the sound of the shot was muffled by its closeness to the inmate's neck. The garden had been too narrow to encompass all the inmates and the last inmates were placed on top of those already shot. They had come into the garden slowly, unsteadily, already destroyed, humiliated, and they would leave it for another world.

'If you understand this,' Mihael said. 'You will understand yourself.'

The last naked inmate came into the garden.

Pauline recognised the round face and blonde hair. The blonde had been streaked with grey and lay unkempt and dishevelled. No-one had looked up from the garden, neither guards nor inmates nor executioner, and like all the inmates this night the last went forward limply, resigned, the fight gone, but he did something different. His eyes travelled to the balcony. Perhaps he had known Pauline Alyson would be standing there. Perhaps he had recognised her in the darkness. He walked forward, round-shouldered, his eyes down as they had been all his life, his chin tucking into his chest. He looked shyly towards the balcony but there had been no reproach to the sad diffident smile.

The last inmate to be shot that night had been the printer Nikolai Skoboliev.

Book Five:
Binkie's Revolution

82

Pauline Alyson returned to England as she had left.

She had travelled on false papers and passport and under a false name. She had left Moscow for Leningrad, the new name for Petrograd, and taken a train to Murmansk, the engine burning pine logs, but if Pauline had settled in her carriage she had been wakened by choking, penetrating smoke. The front corner of the carriage had set on fire. She had almost suffocated and been carried from her compartment.

She had breathed the crisp cold air and recovered.

She noticed a balloon-shaped net attached to the engine funnel to catch the red-hot ash from the pine logs, but the ash had escaped the net and caused the fire. The fire had been put out and again she had boarded the train. She would not sleep till she reached Murmansk. She boarded a fishing boat for Vardo and they had set off in the afternoon.

By evening the sea had been choppy and the craft tossed on the waves. She had settled in the forward cubby hole, but she could not stand the smell of mackerel and engine oil, and she had returned to the deck. The sea had surged around her, a tarpaulin pulled close to her body. She had been wedged between the hatchway and a beam and held there by a seaman throughout the night as waves lashed and sought to carry her into the darkness.

From Vardo she had made her way to Oslo.

From Oslo she had taken another train to Bergen.

The *Bolsheviki* had officially renamed themselves Communists and she had been looked after every kilometre of the way. A comrade had offered her eggs and meat and fish and fruit and coffee in the station restaurant at Oslo. Their organisation had fallen away at Bergen, there had been no cabin for her on the outward journey, and the captain of the steamer had settled her in a coal bunker by the top manhole. She had been given a loaf and a five-gill bottle of water; the voyage would last two nights and two days. Firemen in the stokehold shovelled coal from the lower manhole into the furnaces and the more they shovelled the more Pauline slid with the coal.

She wore her men's corduroy and Lenin cap.

She carried her travelling bag across her shoulder and coped as best she could as the height of the coal reduced; odd lumps were left in the upper girders so that as the steamer rolled they fell upon her head. She nibbled at the bread, coal dust to her hands, black finger prints upon the crust. The coal dust lined her teeth and parched her throat, so that she sipped constantly at the water, making it last till she reached Newcastle at midnight on the second day. She slipped up the companionway to look out for the watchman, but there had been no watchman and she left the steamer.

She leapt over the rail onto the quay.

'You're as black as a sweep,' a man said.

She could hardly speak for the coal dust.

'William?' she asked.

A man had come forward from the darkness.

Gas lamps burned along the quay and the lemon light reflected back from the dampness; there had been a shower but if the clouds were low the rain had stopped. The man who stepped forward had been the model of Mihael Zaichnevsky, the same build, the same black hair, the same curl across the brow; he had been dressed in black, his collar turned around his neck because of the cold. The man pulled her to him and held her close and she had been sure now it was Mihael Zaichnevsky sent by Gregory Zinoviev to look after her.

It was not Mihael Zaichnevsky.

It was Tommy Bessford.

Tommy had taken over his father's face work when he died. He had been heavily-built, his dark hair oiled to his scalp, swarthy as Mihael had been swarthy, but more deferential, more respectful even though coal dust clung to her corduroy and obliterated the red star from her cap. She did not remember Tommy Bessford, but she trembled as he held her close, no balance to her legs, balance lost on the vessel, and she did not mind if some of the coal dust rubbed from her cheek onto his.

'You sent a telegram to Binkie Fatherley,' he said.

413

'Where is William?'

'I was in the post office when it arrived. I told the post woman I'd deliver it, only I never did. I remember you from all those years back, with your red hair and your lovely skin; all the village talked about you and missed you when you left. I thought to myself I'd come and take you back. I've got a trap over there – but I never thought you'd be so black.'

'I need to be off the quay.'

83

'I'll take you to a Salvation Army lodge,' Tommy said. 'You'll need a wash and brush before I take you back to the village. It would be a funny sort of homecomin', like, if you were black from the pit. They'd think you'd been hidin' in the old workin's all these years.'

Tommy sent the trap back to the village and he and Pauline edged along the quay towards the centre of the town. He found a Salvation Army lodge but the concertina gates were closed and locked; a half-glass door stood beyond and a light shone through the door. Tommy rang the bell inlaid into a stone pillar by the side of the gate. A lad came out towards the gate but refused to admit them. He took one look at the dark-haired, dark-coated man and coal boy and hurried back up the steps through the door, drawing the bolts and extinguishing the light.

414

'We'll get you bedded down somewhere.'

They returned to the quay and found a seamen's hotel.

The hotel owner had been a fisherman's wife, small and stout, wearing a dressing-gown over her night robes and a nightcap over her hairnet. She showed them to a basement room and brought a dish of cold water and a cloth and some rough towels. When she returned she carried a tray with a pot of tea and two pint pots and a plate of sliced and buttered bread. Pauline sipped at the tea, the first she had drunk in six years that had not been served from a samovar, and as she nibbled she felt the butter mingling with the coal dust to the roof of her mouth.

'I'll take you to Highhill in the mornin'.'

'If I don't want to go to Highhill?'

'Of course you want to go to Highhill,' Tommy said. 'That's why you sent the telegram.'

'Did anyone else read it?'

'Only me and the post woman who took the message.'

'It wasn't intercepted?'

'I don't know what you mean – intercepted.'

Pauline slipped out of her corduroy and undergarments and, hanging her Lenin cap on the brass knob of one of the bed posters, turned her back on Tommy. She washed the coal dust from her pores, leaving the water black in the dish, rinsing the last of the water from the cloth, rubbing the rough towels across her chill body. She felt the cold to the room, the walls damp, the night through the basement side window as black as the coal in the steamer's bunker. There had been no touch of lemon from the gas lamps.

There had been a single blanket on the bed.

'You can sleep on one side of the blanket,' Pauline said.

'You should let the tiredness slip from your bones,' Tommy said.

'I need to get my balance. I'll need clothes too. I want to breathe some air into my lungs – get the coal dust from my throat. That'll take a day or two. They'll have forgotten me at Highhill, but I want to be forgotten. I don't want to be a curiosity.'

'Your book's in the colliery institute. There's no-one forgotten you.'

'You will let me sleep?' Pauline asked.

'What d'you think I am?' Tommy asked.

Pauline had seen the confusion to Tommy's eyes and thought of the confusion she had seen to the eyes of Mihael Zaichnevsky. She had held his friendship but not his love, but here he was before her again, in the guise of Tommy Bessford; she was still surprised at the resemblance, feeling that it was Mihael after all, that her womanhood had been given a second chance, yet knowing it could not be so. He had been full of face with the same hair, the same build, the same strength to his body Mihael had when they had met in Petrograd.

'You should grow a beard,' she said.

She bundled the corduroy and Lenin cap into her travelling bag and stood her full height, shaking her red hair around her neck and shoulders. She had brought from Moscow the dark serge costume and white blouse; she dressed and pinned a brooch to her blouse. She had brought too a shawl and placed the shawl around her head to frame her red hair. She knew her hair was not the same, it neither flared nor glowed. It was shorter and darker, but if her youth had gone she had gained in assurance.

She would not need to be taken by Tommy Bessford. She would take him.

She felt like a woman again in her costume and blouse, but she had been overwhelmed by fatigue and fell into his arms. He had been surprised how frail she was and he laid her upon the bed. He settled her fully dressed upon the blanket, taking the shawl from her head, letting his hand run down her hair, lying her on her back; but if she had fainted now she was asleep and he would sit by the bed till the light came through the yellow curtains. He left the room for breakfast and when he returned she was still asleep. It would be well into the afternoon before she would wake.

'Should I take you to Highhill now?' he asked.

'I want you to take me to London. I'm not ready for Highhill.'

'Why d'you want to go to London?'

The paper on the hotel room walls had been cheap and drab and the light through the curtains reminded Pauline of another room, with cockroaches upon pink curtains, the cockroaches running up and down the folds of the curtains. She had been startled and sat up, but she had seen only the gentle face of Tommy Bessford, less

417

harsh in the daylight, less anxious, not crushed like the features of Mihael Zaichnevsky, the hair across his brow, but without the disillusionment to his eyes.

'I'll tell you in the morning,' she said.

'It's past the mornin',' Tommy said. 'It's the afternoon.'

He lifted her into his arms but she was again asleep.

84

Binkie Fatherley woke in his cot-bed and listened to the silence of the village.

It had been the silence of the pit the day the waters had flooded the seams and killed the men, the silence of bank when he had returned in the ambulance tub, coughing putrid water, retching his stomach, the clouds scudding low over the headstock. It had been the silence of his downstairs room after the manager and Albi Birt had told him his eldest son had been killed in the pit not by water but by gas.

They had gone now to bury Ernie.

All of the village folk had gone to the funeral, as they had gone for the other men, and Binkie eased himself on the pillows, bandages tight around his chest where his ribs were broken; the bandage had been tight too around his dislocated shoulder. The fire had been built up and the room warm even with the door open. The range had been black-leaded and the bars across the fire swept clean but for a single stranger, a loose flake of soot that could not be dislodged.

Later Binkie would wonder if it had been a dream.

'I am your stranger on the bar,' she said.

She stood in the doorway dressed as a nurse, wearing a bonnet, blue uniform and black cape around her shoulders, the cape flowing red with its silk lining. She stooped because of her height, but she came into the room with all the cheerful bossiness of a professional nurse. She carried a parcel under her arm and laid the parcel on the table next to a vase of fresh chrysanthemums. She took off her cape and shaking raindrops upon the carpet she placed the cape on one of the pegs behind the door.

'Nothing's changed,' she said.

'You've been here before?'

'I was told how it would look.'

She settled on the cot-bed.

She lifted his eyelids to examine his pupils and checked the bandages to his chest and shoulders. She wore short sleeves, the sleeves trimmed white, the collar white too, and the dark hairs that ran up her arms were as dark as the hair that straggled under the bonnet and across her brow. She had no regular features, her nose crooked, her teeth too, but she smiled and tucked his clothes and straightened his pillows.

Binkie's shoulder had been uncomfortable, his ribs painful, his skin dull in the light; he shifted his buttocks but kept his eyes on the irregular face, the black hair across her brow. He decided it must be a dream,

419

but a pleasant dream he wanted to prolong, letting it run through his mind like one of those silent films they showed at the picture-house. The light fell white through the open door and the fire dropped in the grate, but neither disturbed his dream.

'We're all sorry about Ernie.'

'They say the gas got him.'

'But the water got you?'

'Only it didn't kill us like the gas killed him.'

'Will you miss him so much?'

'I had four sons. Now I've got none.'

'You lost Roger and Albert at Paschendale.'

'And my wife too. She died as surely as if she'd been shot by the Germans.'

'The Motherless Hun,' the nurse said.

'I've never heard of them.'

'And the Friendless Austrian.'

'I don't know about Austrians or Huns.'

'You have another son,' the nurse said.

'Dead and gone too, they say.'

'He sent you cards. *Zona di Guerra.*'

'Somebody sent us cards,' Binkie said.

'You should have faith.'

'Faith, you say? They're buryin' my eldest son in the churchyard and you talk of faith? When I came to this house it was full – my father, my wife, my bairns. I've never spoken to my father in years and now he's buryin' Ernie, as if he were his son, my wife died when her lads went to fight the war. Nobody saw Roland die – and nobody found his body. They never found Roger or Albert neither, but they're dead all right – like the rest of the Paschendale lads. Roland in Italy? Anythin' could have happened.'

'You've been left to wonder all these years.'

' I'm the only one left – and you talk of faith.'

'You used to have faith.'

'I saw one chapel burn and I built another.'

'Maybe you should pray to the Madonna.'

'There's a Church of Holy Mary down the road,' Binkie said. 'But I doubt she'll bring my lads back from the front or Bess from the grave or Roland from Italy. Or mend my shoulder and my ribs. D'you know how many years I've spent in this house? Twenty-six years. Only one tap of runnin' water and a closet over the cinder. I thought I'd see change in my lifetime, but there's no change I can see.'

'There'll be change when you recover.'

She took the parcel from the table and laid it on the cot-bed.

'I've travelled all the way across Europe to bring you this.'

85

'A pair of shoes?' he asked.

'Not a shoebox,' she said. 'Nor a pair of shoes.'

'Are you goin' to open it and show us what it is?'

'You gave Roland a ring before he left,' she said.

'I took it from his mother's finger.'

'He's worn the ring all these years. He has given it to another *famiglia* in token of his respect. The ring will be as safe with them as it was with him. I've brought you this – something he's proud of; something he prizes – because he wants you to know he loves you. Only you must promise you will honour this gift and treasure it – and keep it as you kept Ollie Lowden's token all these years.'

'You know about Ollie Lowden?'

'You must make the promise.'

'I promise on the bible if you want.'

'You don't believe any more.'

'I can only give you my word.'

'It has to be more sacred than that.'

She turned to the mantelpiece and ran her fingers among the medals and tokens and brass jugs and bowls till she found a thread bobbin with a needle in the bobbin. There had been Ollie Lowden's token and Roger and Albert's war medals, but no telegram from the Army Council, for he had buried the telegram with his wife. There had been no dust along the mantelpiece and as she returned to the bed with the needle the fire flared and flamed under the boiler.

'Let me prick your finger,' she said.

She had pricked his right forefinger before she had finished speaking, a sharp prick that brought blood to his skin, dark blood she ran across the palm of her hand, first one way and then another, so that when she held her palm to his there had been the sign of the cross.

422

'Roland once ran a red-hot poker through his hand in the blacksmith's shop,' she said. 'It left a sign of the cross. You see before me my hand – but you see Roland's too.'

She pricked her own right forefinger and held the finger in the air. She let the blood run down the inside of her finger, darting beyond the joints, so like his own blood, perhaps only lighter. She smeared the blood on the palm of his right hand as she had smeared the blood on her own. She made a cross with the blood and turned his palm towards him, kissing each finger, tenderly, respectfully, almost religiously.

'I have your blood,' she said. 'And you have mine.'

'You call that a promise?'

'A sacred oath,' she said.

She opened the parcel.

She removed the string and brown paper and soft white tissue that flowed around a leather satchel. Binkie could smell the freshness of the leather as fresh as teacakes and fadges; her hand moved into the satchel and she brought forward a silver medal she handed to Binkie. He took the medal with his right hand, the blood still warm to his palm. The medal caught the light, a proud medal, polished and revered, the silver cold, but if he had medals for Roger and Albert now he had a medal for Roland.

'The *Medaglio d'Argento al Valore Militare*,' she said.

'It's a funny lingo you have there,' Binkie said.

'The medal was awarded Roland a long time ago.'

Her hand had been lost again to the satchel.

She brought forward a leather scabbard she held as solemnly and carefully as she might a bible, the scabbard had jewels stitched into the leather. She balanced the scabbard upon her fingertips poised above his lap. She laid the scabbard in his lap upon the bedclothes. He looked at the scabbard without understanding, the leather smooth, polished as the medal had been polished, but meaningless, reluctant to touch it lest he enter another world. The scabbard had been as empty as his life had become.

He watched the jewels reflect the light.

'You've heard of Garibaldi?' she asked.

'My father took us to see him as a bairn.'

'When he visited Newcastle on his tours?'

'I was that young my father carried us on his shoulders.'

'When you think of this scabbard you must think of Garibaldi.'

'What's he got to do with Roland?'

'You must think of Roland too.'

She took the *Medaglio* and scabbard and replaced them in the satchel.

'You must keep these safe,' she said. 'So safe they can never leave *la famiglia*. That you have them must be known only to you. The scabbard and the *poignart* that it held shall one day be brought together, but the scabbard shall remain in *la famiglia* till such time as we are asked to give it back. Till it does – if it does – this scabbard and the Medaglia d'Argento shall be Roland's remembrance to you.'

She replaced the parcel on the baize tablecloth and produced from the folds of her uniform a leather wallet. She took from the wallet a syringe and capsule of colourless liquid. She filled the syringe and held the syringe to the light, the needle already dripping white. 'We call this a wonder drug,' she said. 'It comes from a wonder crop we never grow. It shall ease your pain and make you sleep. When you wake the pain shall be gone and you shall recover. Your past will be dead – but your mind and body strong.'

'You come from Italy, you say?'

'I didn't say,' she said.

'You know an awful lot about the family.'

She lifted his right arm and he felt the prick of the syringe as light as the touch of a fly, only longer, and when she removed the syringe she dabbed at the prick with cotton she had taken from the wallet. The syringe and empty capsule and cotton disappeared into the wallet and the wallet had been lost to the folds of her uniform. She took her cloak from the peg and swept it around her shoulders, fastening the cloak at the neck, looking out the doorway to the cold of the day.

She held her hands to the fire.

The soot flake had fallen now from the bar and she looked around the house for the last time at the fawny orange wallpaper, the brown-painted skirting boards, the brass fenders and tidies and kettles and pokers. She looked at the dish of fresh water that stood on a cracket, a towel placed beside the dish. She looked at the vase of chrysanthemums, the flower stems as green and proud as the baize tablecloth, the flower-heads white and chill like the light.

'Ernie would have liked those flowers,' she said.

Binkie began to dream that he and Bess and the children were on the cart being ferried across the river towards Highhill. The nurse had been with them. Yet he wanted to keep her in the real world; he wanted to raise his hands to hers; he wanted to lift himself upon the pillows. Though his mind might give the orders his body did not move and he began dreaming again, not the dream of the deputy's kist with the water rising, the taste putrid to his mouth, but the dream of happier days with Roland upon his knees before the fire, wearing his short'uns and Fair Isle jumper.

'Stay with us,' he said. 'Keep us company.'

'You ask too many questions,' the nurse said.

'Tell us about Roland,' he said. 'How do you know he's alive?'

'Because I'm his wife,' the nurse said.

86

Binkie woke to find Pauline Alyson standing over him.

He lay on his back looking at the ceiling, the door closed now, the village locked out, the light duller through the window, the heap ominous as scree rattled

426

towards the front door. His body felt weak and heavy, yet his mind had settled, filled with a gentle light; the worry of years had slipped from him and he felt comfortable. His shoulder and ribs no longer hurt. He smiled as he thought of his dream, crossing the river again. He sought to raise himself, but still his body refused to move. He turned his eyes from the ceiling, looking for the nurse but not finding her.

He settled again in the contentment of his dream.

'I dreamt Roland was alive,' he said. 'I dreamt his wife came all the way from Italy. She left us a satchel. It looked like a shoebox, but it was no shoebox; only there was a medal and a scabbard – all polished and smelly. The scabbard once held a dagger – only she called it somethin' else – and the dagger had somethin' to do with Garibaldi. She pricked my finger to make it bleed and she made me swear an oath; only I cannot remember what it was. It was like swappin' blood. And then she gave us an injection that put us to sleep.'

Pauline sat upon the cot-bed and raised him up.

She held his hands to the light, not disturbing the bandages, letting his body fall upon her shoulder. There had been no blood on his hands nor any sign of a pin prick to his finger nor puncture to his arm. There had been no shoebox or satchel, only the vase of cut-glass that stood upon the baize cloth. The sorrow of the day lay as heavily as Binkie across her shoulder and she felt for him a compassion she could not express. She held him close, letting her hands run through his hair, feeling the warmth of his body through the bandages across his chest.

'We'll have to do somethin' about Ernie's pigs,' Binkie said.

'I can look after your house,' Pauline said. 'I cannot look after pigs.'

'We'll gas-gun the lot.'

'And his allotment?'

'We'll sell it.'

'And the cups he won with his quoits?'

'They'll go the way of the pigs.'

'We really will start again?'

'We'll forget about the past,' Binkie said. 'It's as dead as that trip across the river all them years ago. I feel strong in myself – strong in mind and body – now who said that? It doesn't matter. We'll start again all right.'

Pauline let her arms drop from him and took the black scarf from her neck and draped it across one of the wooden pegs behind the door. She unpinned her black hat and placed the pins on the mantelpiece. Her red hair flowed around her shoulders; she had let it grow since she had returned from London, and it had lightened with the springtime. Her mouth had been small and closed, lines etched between her eyes as she frowned. She thought too much and her thoughts meant she walked with her head bowed, eyes upon the ground, and only when she uplifted her gaze did she see any future.

Any hope of a promised land.

'We'll have no fuss about the wedding,' she said.

'Your father can marry us in this room – and if you don't want your father we'll get a priest from the church. But there'll be conditions. You'll have to respect me – and what I believe. If you don't there'll be no wedding and no English revolution. And if there's no revolution all our people will suffer.'

'You can have any conditions you like, lass.'

'You promised years ago never to call me that.'

'I'll never do it again.'

'I want no mention of Bess or the lads. No dreams about nurses coming from afar with tales of Roland. I'll move in with you, but I'll keep my own house for painting, so that I can get away from you; get away from that cinder path and heap, the smell of pigs from the allotments; so that I keep something of myself to myself. You understand that, William Fatherley? I need to keep a part of me always for Pauline Alyson.'

'If that's what you want.'

'And there'll be no children.'

'You mean you'll not sleep with us?'

'I wouldn't marry you if I wasn't going to share your bed,' Pauline said. 'But child bearing isn't for me. You can have all the hugging and kissing you like, but there'll be no children. Those are my conditions, William Fatherley. If you want my body, you can have my body; if you want my mind so that we can fight together – change the world together – I'm yours. But if you want a family, to start again, if you want to prove you went wrong before, I'll walk out that door and never come back.'

'I need you here,' Binkie said.

'The medals must go too,' she said.

'Not the medals.

'You must keep them out of sight. At least out of my sight.'

'I'll never speak of the family again,' Binkie said.

'There'll be no ring either.'

'How will we be bound together?'

'We'll be bound by the revolution,' Pauline said.

87

The priest had pronounced them man and wife.

Pauline had worn a red costume with no concession to white other than a carnation to her lapel, the last carnation to be plucked from Ernie's allotment. There would be no loosely-hanging white dress with a ribbon around her waist, no white hat with matching ribbons, but with her uncovered head the light shone against her red hair. She was different from any one in the village, different from anyone in the world in the eyes of Binkie. She had worn red shoes, too, that had been made specially for her in the village, and there would be a red bag, but no lipstick added to the pallid redness to her lips, nor had there been rouge to her cheeks.

The red of her hair matched the red of her dress and made her complete.

Binkie wore his only suit, his collar starched and

tight, the yellow stud to the top of his shirt leaving an imprint upon his throat. He felt the collar so tight it hurt when he spoke his marriage vows, wearing a waistcoat with a watch and chain, the only possessions he had brought with him when he had come to the village. A narrow tie lost itself in the folds of his waistcoat. His boots were polished, the toes shining. There had been only the priest and Albi Birt and the colliery manager in the downstairs room, but outside the village folk had gathered upon the cinder, stretching down Slum Alley till they reached the street.

They had known when the marriage ceremony was over.

There had been applause followed by shouting and singing and dancing to the sawing of a fiddle. Pauline had wanted no celebrations but the village folk had different ideas; they filled the clubs and pubs and brought food and flowers that filled the doorway to their home and reached the window. The marriage meant a new beginning for the village; it had lost its sons to the war, to the pit, but life would go on. There would be other battles and they knew that Binkie Fatherley and Pauline Alyson would take the lead in fighting these battles.

They were still dancing when Binkie and Pauline retired.

As she slept Binkie listened to the fiddle and heard the shouting and thought of his marriage to Bess. He had told himself he would not think of the past, yet the past had been as clear as yesterday, so that not only could he see Bess he could see his mother too; she had been lying in the cot-bed in the corner. It had been a long time ago, but their conditions had changed so little; they were still oppressed and deprived. He had not achieved socialism in his nor anyone else's time. He knew he must devote the last years of his life to a cause greater than himself, greater than Pauline, that would give them respect and dignity.

He felt a presence in the room.

Had Bess come to condemn him, to wish him ill, or had it all come to pass as she had foreseen, as she had expected, and as she had wanted? Had his sons come to tell him he had failed them, letting them go to war or down the pit to be killed? Was it the nurse come to join him on the cart across the river? Had he been dreaming or waking? Or was it the spirit of the murdered woman or her hanged husband? Were they visiting their old home? Sometimes Bess would tell him of a white rabbit she had seen on the edge of the bed; other times a mist had filled the room and her mother would come through the mist. There had been no white rabbit and no mist, only the light through the closed curtain, the dying sound of the fiddle and the last shouting of the men.

He eased from the bed and went to the downstairs room.

He brought the cracket to the fire and sat as he had often sat with Roland on his knee, Roland in his short'uns, his Fair Isle jumper, his boots uncleaned, his knees dirty, the blonde hair unruly and uncombed;

Roland slim and bony, with no hint of the strength to come, both of them looking at the shapes the burning coal made, the flare of gases, Binkie stirring the embers with a poker so that there would be new shapes, new designs, fresh heat flaring from the flames.

Often he would rake the coals from the back of the fire.

Roland would examine the coals for fragments of broken glass or old lamps. Once they had found a penknife that had been lost to a conveyor belt and found its way down a hopper; that had been swept with the rest of the coal and delivered by the pit wagon to their door and flung into the coalhouse. Roland had been excited by the find. He had looked through the coal for another penknife, but there had been only the fragments of rubber from the conveyor belt or a length of slow-burning rope soaked in oil they called tarly-toot.

Binkie raked at the coals and pulled some of them from the back of the fire. The fire had been low, the grate full, there were no strangers on the bar, but the tumble of coal set the flames flaring, curling blue and red and blue again. He sought the odd splinter of pit prop or stone that could spit and spurt across the fire, thinking of Pauline in the bed above, taking the emptiness from the house, raking and musing till he saw something lying among the coal.

He pulled it closer to the flames.

Perhaps it had been a rat that had died and been hurried along with the coal and missed by men on the buttons, those who sat on the corners of the conveyor to keep the belt clear. He poked at the object with the rake, raising his head from the flames, remembering his dream; he set the rake aside and bent over the fire. He looked for a while at the object before leaning over and pulling away the coal. He hoped it was not a rat. He had always hated rats since he had killed them and cut off their tails and laid their tails on the table so they could be sold for a farthing a tail. It was not a rat.

It was a leather satchel.

He carried the satchel from the coal above the fire and dusted the coal from the leather. He settled on his cot-bed and looked at the satchel in the light of the flames. He pulled the satchel open and turned it upside down on his bed. A silver medal fell out but the other object, a leather scabbard, he had to pull from the satchel. The light of the flames caught at the jewels and the jewels danced and came alive. The medal lost its coldness, warm from the closeness of the fire, and he held the medal and looked at the scabbard and touched the leather.

He felt it comforting, reassuring.

He knew the nurse had placed the satchel where Roland had known he would find it because Roland had not forgotten how they had sat by the fire and raked the coals, but she had placed the satchel where only he would find it because, as she had said, this was a matter for the family, *la famiglia* as she called it, a matter for Roland and for him. They were all that was left of the true family. They were the last of the Fatherleys. The

434

medal and the scabbard, even Roland's existence, were to be their secret. He did not know why this should be, his mind could not fathom such mysteries, but he knew that this was so.

He noticed something else.

There had been a card in the scabbard, a *Zona di Guerra*, like the cards he had received from Roland when he had gone to the Front; like the cards he had received afterwards, mysterious cards he had not understood. This card he understood. Roland had written upon it with the same laboured handwriting he had used as a boy. Binkie lit a candle and brought the candle to the cot-bed; he pulled the card close to the candle. He could not read so well these days, the putrid water had done something to his eyes. There would be no more reading at the stapple bottom, but by holding the card close he could make out the words.

'I love you, dad,' the card said. 'I shall love you always.'

Binkie knew then his son was truly alive.

88

The barricades had gone up at Highhill after the great pit disaster.

They had gone up around the colliery institute and headstock and power station and brickflats and mechanics' shop and colliery yard. They had gone up across the two colliery entrances, the heavy wooden gates drawn closed, and they had gone up across the main road into the village. They had gone up around the officials' houses and the house of the colliery manager and around the drift mouth. The barricades stood as high as the sky, or so it seemed to the children, and above each barricade there had been raised a red flag.

Children had brought branches from oak trees and oak apples had rolled into the gutters; they had uprooted gorse, their ferns dark, their buds yellow. There had been timber cut from the forest and rolled through the streets. More timber had been taken from the colliery yards, tubs hauled to the top of the barricades; and if some of the barricades were lopsided, disjointed, they were ten feet thick and too high even for the children. They would stand by the sides looking up to the sky where the cloud drifted low and white.

The men on the barricades wore red armbands and had red stars stitched to their caps; their peaks were unfastened, the stars stitched across silver studs that had held the peaks. They wore their pit hessian, baggy coats and breeches, water bottles and bait tins by the side of the barricades as if they were a comfort. They looked grim and serious. The younger men carried pick handles and swung them gently, as if testing their weight; but there had been no violence in Highhill, for the village had been as one. Special constables sent from the valley halted their cars before the first barricade and returned as quickly as they had come.

Barricades had gone up in other villages.

Those villages Binkie and Pauline had visited many years ago, preaching their pithead gospel; those who had relatives lost to the pit disaster, those who had sent bus-loads to the Durham Big Meeting Day, who had heard Pauline Alyson; those who had read her book and pamphlets in the colliery institutes, those lodge secretaries and chairmen who had taken her into their homes.

The barricades went up and the red flags too.

Pauline had raised the red star on Bone Hill, the highest point in the village; she had illuminated the star from electricity she had run from the colliery. She had raised a white pole taken from the schoolyard and hoisted the star to the top of the pole. The pole would sway in the wind that rustled the tips of the fir trees; but the star had been well attached and if the pole swayed the star would shine night and day and be seen in other villages, its red twinkle drifting in and out of the mist or tainting the low cloud with its ruby shadow.

Pauline introduced the *subbotnik*.

This consisted of delivering soup to aged miners' homes, arranging a trap to take ill people to the hospital in the city, delivering poor relief to those too infirm to collect it themselves from the institute; delivering coal when none had been left in the coalhouse, the coal coming from the colliery hopper; bicycling messages from one village to another; even sand-stoning the steps of the aged miners' homes where the pensioners were so crippled with arthritis they could not get down on their knees.

There would be socialist burials too.

437

A child had died of diptheria and had been buried in a people's grave, a plot of land standing beyond the pitheap and allotments away from the graveyard. A red flag had been draped over the child's coffin and the Communist *Internationale* had been sung over its grave; the strains had been caught by the wind and tossed towards the houses. There would be no cross to mark where the child had been buried but a headstone had been erected, a kindly word written of the child, the symbol of a red rose cut into the stone. Red carnations would be scattered on the rough earth. Soon the grave would become a shrine for all those who believed in the revolution.

The institute had become the headquarters of the Highhill commune.

Poor relief would be paid from the library, passes would be issued, vouchers to be used in village stores, permits to leave or enter the village. An organising committee would work from the library, its members wearing red armbands; they would be the new Commissars of the People and their first task had been to change street names and pit seams. From this time forth there would stand in the village Marx Terrace and Lenin Avenue and Engels Street. The pit seams would be called the *Moscow Soviet*, the *Petrograd Soviet* or the *Kremlin*.

Even Slum Alley would become Zinoviev Terrace.

A new word had been drawn across the face of the institute above the doorway, obliterating the headstone that had indicated when the institute had been opened by the coal owners. There would be passes, too, to get in and out of the institute, white one day, red the other, and even Binkie and Pauline would not be allowed to enter without the right colour pass. The word across the institute had been inscribed upon a leather banner and painted in red letters: *Smolny.*

Revolution had indeed come to Highhill.

89

Binkie Fatherley led forty men to a sit-down strike in the pit that would last forty days.

'You'll be well looked after,' he said. 'I'll guarantee that.'

He led the men with full bait tins and bottles, bulging pockets and chests, carrying as usual their lamps and tokens but also dart boards and dominoes, cards and dice to while away the hours. The men had waited for Binkie in the pit yard so that he would be the first to step into the cage. He had walked past the colliery offices and looking down into the yard he had seen the sun upon their polished helmets, their scared faces pale in the sunlight.

They cheered as he walked past the office, holding his hands to his chest, not to withstand the pressure of books he had read at the stapple bottom but to contain the sandwiches and biscuits he had stuffed into as many spare tins he could carry. He kicked up spurts of dust, his helmet pushed back on his head. The men parted to let him through, still cheering and clapping, but the cheering and clapping ceased as he stepped onto the iron sheets before the cage mouth.

His boot studs scraped the sheets as he turned, slightly out of breath, holding with one hand his chest and lifting the other to rest on the iron frame of the cage. The cage had been used to haul not only men but tubs and there were small tracks in the cage to facilitate loading at the shaft bottom and top. The tubs were hauled along the engine plain from coal reservoirs fed by belts. They were loaded in pairs into the cage and once at the surface rolled off again and hauled to the screens.

The rails to the cage were shiny with use and caught the light. Binkie looked from the rails to the wheels of the colliery headstock that stood strong and proud against the sky, silent and motionless too, the winder men out of sight, ready to control the flight of the cage to the shaft bottom. The greased cables of the hauler glittered and the paintwork of the stock had been a dull red. Dust patches showed where the paint had flaked.

Binkie's gaze swept beyond the heads of the men to the sparse grass of an embankment, the officials' houses overlooking the colliery; he saw the sky a fragile blue, the clouds low and white, skimming from over the hill. He listened for the sounds of the colliery, the hiss of steam from the engine sheds, the clatter of coal down chutes, tools from machine shops, smoke from the chimneys; he waited to hear the rattle of tubs, the sound of unloading from the storehouse.

440

From the time of the pit disaster there had been nothing.

'There's nothin' to fear from gas or water,' Binkie shouted to the men in the yard below. 'The compressor will be kept on and the pumps too. We've brought canaries to keep you company. Keep an eye on them and you'll be all right – as long as you feed and water them! And you won't be fightin' on your own. You'll have the whole country behind you!'

Binkie smelt the air of the country.

The air had been fresh and unpolluted, not heavy with dust, not damp or fetid, stale and unhealthy, but clean and invigorating; not limpid with passing through galleries and air doors. He felt the cold iron to his hands and thought of the cold below, so that he felt indignation that men should work underground; that they should walk along galleries as hump-backed as rats, as blind as moles but for the candle-light from their helmets; that they should risk their lives in seams eighteen inches high, the weight of the world held from their shoulders by slim props.

The men had wanted better pay and conditions, not a penny off the pay not an hour on the day. They wanted no more blood on the coal, no more deaths by water or gas, no more injuries, no more nystagmus, no more pneumoconiosis. And no more coal owners. They had instead socialist communes and *subbotniks* and socialist burials. Their pickets would also wear caps with red stars and though they did not know it they would not leave the pit, they would not break the strike, because

441

pickets would prevent their departure.

Discipline would be revolutionary too.

'You'll be fed and watered like the canaries,' Binkie shouted. 'The doctor'll come down the pit to see how we're all getting on. There's a telephone if you want to call bank and we'll arrange for you to call your wives and sweethearts if you cannot stand the peace and quiet. And your mothers too, if you want tuckin' in at night. If we can hold out below ground the commune can hold out above.'

'What do we call this commune?' someone shouted.

'Little Moscow,' Binkie said. 'That's what it is – and that's how it'll be remembered.'

90

'There have always been Little Moscows,' the King said.

'The Foreign Office warned our Ambassador in Russia that Pauline Alyson would bring the bacillus of revolution to our shores,' Winston Churchill said. 'He allowed her to remain in Petrograd. Now we have Little Moscows in every coalfield in our country.'

Churchill had changed little since Pauline had pushed him under the train.

He had worn that night a homburger hat and shoes so polished the platform lights had shone from the toes; he had worn an overcoat with an astrakhan collar over his suit and carried a gold-knobbed walking stick. He had smoked a cigar he had puffed so contentedly his round face could hardly be seen beyond the blue smoke. In his audience of the King, he wore a more portentous suit, the waistcoat sitting more heavily across a gathering paunch; yet he carried the same gold-knobbed walking stick, the shoes as polished, the cigar as large, the ash thick and white and tipped into an ash stand at the entrance to Buckingham Palace where he had left his top hat and overcoat.

'Do you think it is right,' the King asked. 'To say there is a red reign of terror or that Pauline Alyson is a precocious Lenin? Or that the people of Highhill are under the heel of a knot of sullen, arrogant, hobble-dehoys?'

'The colliery manager and officials are prisoners in their own homes. They are surrounded by barricades. Men have gone on strike underground – heaven knows what they are doing to the coal owners' private property.'

'The *Official Gazette* calls Highhill a citadel of extremism under the red banner, clutching the hand of Communism. A spectre of a miniature Russia.'

'There is sedition, Your Highness. There is economic sabotage. Pauline Alyson has even organised the school along the lines of a Communist commune. There are breaches of our emergency regulations but no magistrate, no special constable can penetrate beyond the barricades. The respectable people of the village have been imprisoned in their own homes. The village is known far and wide as the reddest village in England.'

'A village of suspicion, of whispering neighbours – and of fear. That is what you say in your report to your King. But since no-one has been allowed in or out how do you know that?'

'The telephone works, sir. We are in touch with the colliery manager.'

'You say Pauline Alyson is in the pay of the Russians?'

'She brought with her from Russia a letter from Gregory Zinoviev. Zinoviev is chairman of the Third International – Pauline Alyson was and still is its Secretary. She is still a People's Commissar. She is a life-long member of the Bolshevik Party – a Communist with orders to infiltrate the Labour Party. The Zinoviev letter gives instructions to bring Communism to this country.'

'How do you know about the letter?'

'Pauline Alyson returned from Moscow with false papers. She sent a telegram to William Fatherley from Bergen. The telegram was intercepted and she was followed from the time she arrived on the Tyne. She came to London with the help of an accomplice and visited a bank known for its Russian connections. The letter was left in a safe deposit box but by divers means our intelligence services were able to open the box and photograph the letter.'

'There was money in the box?'

'Gold and bills of exchange,' Churchill said. 'Pauline

Alyson is using the gold and bills to finance her revolution. The gold is still coming in – from the Donbas miners, from the peasants' *soviets* – gold collected from the streets of Leningrad and Moscow. But gold all the same.'

King George V had received Churchill in an anteroom to his bed chamber; he had been dressed in silk pyjamas and a silk dressing gown and walked with the aid of a stick. He had been suffering from bronchitis, his chest tight, his throat raw with phlegm, his movements slow, his body weak from the bronchitis that had regularly struck him since childhood. The doctors had advised a foreign cruise but the King disliked travel even on the royal yacht. He had cancelled his official functions and settled himself in his bedroom reading state papers.

He had been writing in his diary when Churchill entered.

He had set his writing desk before the window so that he could benefit of the light but also the view of the Palace gardens. Tulips were in bloom, red and white, daffodils nodded their heads to the soft wind if not to him, and the grass lay deep and verdant around pools that had been set in hollows. '*I am anxious and worried about a national strike,*' he had written in his diary. '*I fear the consequences for my country of Fatherley's English revolution. I never seem to get any peace in this world. I feel very low and depressed.*'

The King intervened directly in state affairs.

He asked Cabinet Ministers to stay back after meetings of the Privy Council. He talked frankly with them, guiding them with his years of experience as monarch. He felt none needed more guidance than Winston Churchill, formerly Home Secretary now Chancellor of the Exchequer. He had not been consulted when Churchill had been appointed but had read of it in the newspapers. He had complained to the Prime Minister but it had been too late. Now he welcomed him in his ante-room. The King's beard had been trimmed, as grey as his eyes and hair, but the eyes were steady, never leaving Churchill's face.

'You are aware,' the King said. 'A hush has settled upon the country from one end of the land to the other?'

Full-fledged Communists who had been with Pauline Alyson at the Third Internationale had called meetings and claimed they represented a million workers. They mobilised the working class in every locality; they called for a National Congress of Action. The Durham coalfield had gone on strike, red flags flying at the pitheads. There were barricades and pickets and communes.

Before he had led his men into the pit, Binkie Fatherley had never attended more meetings. Not in all his days as lodge secretary, not in his visits to the Durham Federation at Redhills, not at colliery headstocks after he made his speeches; not at the chapel when he had been a lay preacher like his father. Not with the colliery manager to discuss face work and faults in the seams. There had been meetings with miners' representatives, meetings in other coalfields, meetings with industrial committees and action committees.

Men had downed tools and returned home in solidarity with the Highhill miners who had endured a great mining disaster and were now on a sit-down strike in their pit, supported by their womenfolk. They liked the idea of a commune with a red flag flying at the summit of their village and a building that had been converted into a *Smolny Institute.* Binkie Fatherley had lost three sons in the war and a fourth in the disaster.

Pauline Alyson caught the public's imagination with her corduroy suit and Lenin cap; her articles were being reprinted and so too was her book *The Red Sunrise.* She had been a militant suffragist who had almost died in Holloway Prison. She had been allowed out only on licence; she had been banished from London. She had been young and slim as well as a fiery revolutionary and not only had she caught the public's imagination, she had caught too their sympathy.

Not one industry but every industry had come out on strike. Trains and buses and trams stopped, some of the trains abandoned near the homes of drivers or footplatemen; four thousand London buses stayed in their depots, some abandoned by their drivers and conductors; and if the government declared there were private buses on the streets these were phantom buses. They were never seen. Underground trains had ceased to run and the docks had fallen silent.

Ships might arrive at ports but their passengers would need to disembark their own luggage, carrying wardrobe trunks and portmanteaus along the quayside to the customs sheds. They would be stranded outside the sheds unless they could find private charabancs. Even the goldbeaters' trade society had joined the strike, bringing out its three hundred members. Power stations had come to a halt but the strikers had ensured there would always be electricity for hospitals and bakeries and laundries.

'What do you propose?' the King asked.

'I propose that the South Wales Borderers and the Somerset Light Infantry march through the Durham coalfield, that they destroy each and every commune, pull down each and every barricade; that they haul down and burn every red flag. That they leave the Highhill commune to last – their destruction shall be total.'

'The national strike shall go on forever!'

'I shall deal first with the national strike. I shall crush the dockers and transport workers – and electricians. I shall call for counter-revolution through the *Official Gazette*. Only when we have crushed the workers, restored the authority of government and saved the constitution shall we make peace with the miners.'

The King coughed and his frame trembled.

He disliked his illness because it prevented him from leaving Buckingham Palace for Sandringham where he liked to shoot or Bognor where he liked to walk, or Balmoral where the highland air so invigorated him that he slept more soundly than in any of his other Palaces. His tone had become irascible, he was often querulous; sometimes he was filled with self-pity. Other times he could not be persuaded to make up his mind. A picture-house had been installed at Buckingham Palace to relieve his boredom.

He liked the intimacy of this ante-room.

He had passed many an hour reading newspapers, but though he had dismissed the flunkies and nurses who had followed him from the bedroom, they returned at the sound of his cough. The cough retched at his chest and reddened his face, his eyes protruded and stared at Churchill without seeing him. Churchill could not help his monarch, could not touch him, forbidden by protocol; his eyes ran along the gold inlays to the ceiling, bordering the walls, his audience drawing to a close. One flunkey handed the King his stick and another hovered as the King lifted himself from the sofa, his shoulders still trembling.

'I shall need hourly reports,' he said.

'We must save your throne, Your Majesty.'

'You must negotiate with William Fatherley,' the King said. 'Not destroy him.'

'And Pauline Alyson?'

The King began coughing again and his nurses led him into the bedroom.

91

'Why did you let the men into the pit?' Rosemary Rutland asked.

'Why are you feeding them and giving them drink?'

'I'm doing it for Roland Fatherley.'

'Roland's dead and gone,' the colliery manager said.

'Not according to his father.'

Binkie had come to see Rosemary before he had led the men into the pit. He had thanked her for getting poor relief for the village and setting up soup kitchens on every corner, offering free credit from her shops for as long as the sit-down strike lasted. He had never before set foot in her house, but he knew Roland had been a frequent visitor; he wondered if she had seated him where Roland had sat. There would be no whisky for Binkie as there had been for Roland.

'A couple of things,' Binkie said.

'You want to talk about Roland?'

'I thought he should've stayed in the village and married you.'

'He wanted to marry Pauline Alyson.'

'He had his own ideas,' Binkie said. 'And so he left.'

'To be killed in a country he'd never set eyes on.'

'I want you to know,' Binkie said. 'He's not dead – he's alive somewhere. I know no more than that – and he doesn't want me to know, but he's alive all right. You shouldn't worry your head any more.'

'And the second thing?'

'Look after Pauline when I'm down the pit.'

Rosemary had the grace of a village matriarch.

She wore a twin-set and double row of pearls; she fingered the pearls absent-mindedly. Her blonde hair had silvered, there were dark stains to her brow, and though she still walked with the limp she was hardly conscious of it. She had bought the first car to travel upon a village road; she found it eased the strain to her leg and she had been able to visit other villages and other shops. She had been allowed to pass the barricades and delivered messages to the Miners' Federation in Durham. She had the respect of the village, she had their admiration, and she would become in their eyes a legend in her time.

'We've formed a distress committee with the women's guilds,' she said. 'Teachers and shopkeepers and chapel superintendents. We have a sub-committee of grocers and lodge officials. There are the soup kitchens and boot repair shops.'

'All the same, if you could keep an eye out for Pauline. She's a true revolutionary. She's been to Petrograd and Moscow. She's seen revolution. She's been on the winnin' side. I'd sleep better in the deputy's kist if I thought you and the colliery manager would watch out for her.'

'I'll speak to the colliery manager,' Rosemary said.

The manager's house stood apart from the village beyond the railway line and embankment and welfare field and allotments; a two-storied house of solid stone, the windows filled with pools of shadow. He enjoyed his garden and from his bedroom window, depending on the season, he could see tall torch-like lupins, violet and pink, that graced the pathway from his house; he could see the rustling tails of the laburnum in a grove beyond the lawn, often the blossom tarnished, the nectar sucked out of the honeycomb petals.

Rosemary would walk with the manager to the centre of his lawn where she could see the first summer roses, dew still nestling in the cups of the leaves, the blossom already bursting from their buds, minute flies picking at the red among the green. Now she found the manager kneeling against the wall of the house; he had planted a new kind of climbing ivy and already the tentacles were hooking themselves into the mortar cracks. He had been kneeling to see how the ivy had been getting on; already it stood three feet tall, the young leaves showing their green faces to the sun.

He had kissed her hand and brought her into the house.

'The pit disaster has destroyed me,' the manager said. 'If the men want a sit-down strike why should I stop them? How can I stop them? They have pickets with red stars to their caps; they've blocked the drift mouth and closed down the headstock. They've kept out the special constables. The coal owners accept there's nothing I can do.'

'It's costing me nothing to supply the village,' Pauline said. 'The money comes from London by bills of exchange. I take the bills to my bank in Durham and they're converted to money.'

'You don't know where the money's coming from?'

'It's feeding men, women and children.'

'Especially the men in the pit.'

Hot food had been sent down twice a day, at ten o'clock in the morning and ten o'clock at night; stews and soups and hot-pots, tea sent down in canisters the size of samovars; and between the hot meals, between soups laced with brandy and stews stiffened with rum, there were sandwiches cut by family who waited at the bank top.

In the pit there had been comfortable palliasses of straw and choppy – hay feed for the ponies – and blankets to keep the men warm, as they bedded down in old boardrooms, on belts and landings, above loading points; some had bedded down in a disused pony stable in old workings. The stable had been near a downcast shaft where the air was fresh, their sleep had been deep and invigorating, and if they could not rid either themselves or the pony stables of the sweaty tang of manure, if their pillows were hard, their palliasses bumpy and uneven, they were settled.

'I'll keep them going as long as I can,' Rosemary said. 'It'll be hard over forty days and nights.'

'Pauline's issued a proclamation,' the manager said. 'She wants the men to work, not for a living, not to hew coal, but to keep their minds and bodies occupied. She calls it a *subbotnik*.'

The men would clean faces, stone-dust ways, white-wash walls, repair belts, clear out old boardrooms. They had even sent to bank for more whitewash and stonedust. Some of the younger men had wanted to clamber on faces and hew with picks; they had wanted to manipulate the hopper, but the pickets had seen to it that no damage would be done and the men did not get out of hand

'We have to watch Pauline Alyson,' the manager said.

'Pauline Fatherley now,' Rosemary said.

'She's kept her maiden name.'

'Call Pauline Alyson what you like.'

'All the same,' the manager said. 'We have to watch her.'

'That's what William Fatherley said.'

'We'd better watch her for his sake,' the manager said.

92

He and Binkie had both been young and in love with the pit but from a different perspective. Binkie loved the men and if the manager loved the men too he loved the drift and shafts and rolleyways and coal faces, the life that emerged from the pit and spread across the village, that became effervescent, belligerent, tempestuous even, life running through every street into every home. He and Binkie had grown old together but they had not grown old gracefully. Conflict and confrontation and now death in the pit had seen to that.

Rosemary had once asked the manager why he had never married.

'You see, Rosemary, it's like this. The pit never stops. Even when I'm walkin' around the grounds or talkin' to you on the phone – or takin' a ride in your car – there's men workin' underground. Always there's things to be done and things to worry about. I worry about the Brockwell seam – with its fault – they call it *The Kremlin* now, by the way. I worry about a runaway set – about new timber props we've just put in.'

'Do you worry about Alma?'

'I worry about Alma as much as I worry about the pit.'

Alma had been the manager's sixteen year old daughter.

Her body had filled out and her eyes were as dark as her hair; her long unspoilt fingers had a way of running down the side of her cheek. As a child she had strong legs and long dark hair she wore in a plaited pigtail; she had prominent teeth but these had mattered less as she had grown into her teens. Her father kept her at home. He knew she would need protection from the world. She would never be able to keep up the life of a pit wife, even though she could make dresses and repair clothes and do his washing and cooking and keep clean his house.

Alma had been simple in the head.

She had gone to school but she had been easily confused. Her father taught her to read and write, but she had grown apprehensive in the noise of the schoolyard; she had been confused by the classroom with its desks and chairs and boards and books; the teacher had stood so close her long skirt had touched her cheek. She had returned home crying. Her father had taught her arithmetic but she had been content to stay at home and clean his brasses.

She came into the room with tea and freshly-baked teacake and wearing a woollen hat.

'You like me woollie hat?' she asked.

'I love your hat,' Rosemary said.

Alma had knitted a fine woollen hat of rainbow colours. After she had cleaned the brasses, she had knitted or darned or sewed, making dresses and hats, her long fingers at work; she had seamed too and grown to be a fine dressmaker. She liked making woollen hats of many colours: panels of red and green and yellow with a pom-pom on top. Alma liked pom-poms and would make several a day. At night she would throw them from her bedroom window and the gardener found them next morning.

'Do you think her mother will be back?' Rosemary asked.

'Will anyone be back?' the manager.

'Do you think she knew she was simple?'

'She knew her head lolled as a baby. She's my child – my responsibility. I've done the best I can for her – I'll always do the best.'

456

Alma's mother had been the village milliner.

She had befriended the colliery manager but they had never married. She had abandoned her daughter and left the village to live her own life. She had wanted to be an actress and singer, casting off her shyness. She had created her own dancing troupe and toured other villages where the troupe played to packed houses. She introduced sword-dancing. Her troupe had no proper swords, only bed lets with ends wrapped in cloth, but she had been so successful they were able to buy proper swords of Sheffield steel.

'No news from Barbara?' the manager asked.

'She's in Palestine.'

'And married, you say?'

'Others say – she never told me.'

'You're still waiting for Roland?'

'Nor Tom either,' Rosemary said. 'The War Office declared him officially dead.'

They walked again in the garden and Rosemary could see the poplar trees the manager himself had planted, held erect with ropes and canes, a slight wind stirring the slim foliage. There were fruit trees besides the poplars, apple trees with drooping branches, cherry trees that never yielded fruit, nut trees rising like iron from the ground, the sun shining with promise on the stained grub-eaten leaves. Sunlight shone through the trees upon another lawn where a disused well stood at the centre encircled by crazy-paving. The well had been filled and in the earth pansies had been planted.

'You're free to marry?' the manager said.

'Who would I marry?' Rosemary asked.

'You and I are of the village, Rosemary. It's my life and yours. The village will survive Binkie's English revolution. We'll still be here when it's all over. Isn't companionship turning to love worth marrying for?'

'I think only of Pauline Alyson.'

'Perhaps we should think of ourselves.'

'You should think of Alma.'

'The time will come when Alma too will be of the village.'

'Who will look out for Pauline?' Rosemary asked.

'The one to look out for Pauline Alyson is Grandfather Ernest Fatherley.'

93

Grandfather Ernest had taken to wandering the village.

He looked like a prophet of old, bent almost double, shrivelled by age. He had long ceased shaving and his beard had been long, his hair white and thin and plucked by the wind. He wore an old mackintosh, dirty and scuffed, and would stand before the chapel he and Binkie had built so many years ago. Some of the slates were gone from the roof. He surveyed the chapel windows and recalled how they had been inset with such care.

He had raised his voice against the barricades.

He would commandeer a trap and tour the barricades;

he would stand in the seat waving his stick and call the barricades a blasphemy, a challenge to the state that would bring retribution to the village. The men on the barricades laughed but were uneasy; they looked beyond the barricades down the road where nothing had been seen other than the car of Rosemary Rutland and the traps Pauline had sent to tour the villages.

The men did not believe tanks or armoured cars would come up the hill to attack them, but though there were no newspapers there had been the wireless that brought news of warships on the Tyne and troops disembarking. Children standing by the barricades were afraid of Grandfather Ernest, not so much of his language, his imprecations, but the sight of one so poor, so wild and so threatening.

Pauline Alyson had stopped by his old miner's home.

'You'll not convert me to that revolution of yours,' he said.

'You were for the war and I was against it,' Pauline said. 'You believed in Lord Kitchener and I didn't. I never bothered you then. Why should I bother you now?'

'You weren't in the family in those days.'

'You had a fine service for Ernie.'

'But you didn't let me marry you.'

'That was your son's wish.'

'You've moonstruck my son,' Grandfather Ernest said.

'William understands there must be equal rights,' Pauline said. 'Equal liberties, equal enjoyments, equal

459

toil, equal respect, equal share of production. No more Lord Kitcheners urging men to war. No more governments to oppress miners and dockers and railwaymen and transport workers – men and women both equal.'

'We live in Highhill – not paradise.'

'It'll be paradise when we sweep away the ruling classes. If we nationalise the land and give it to the farmers – what do you think the farmers would say? If we nationalise the mines and gave it to the pitmen? If we took over the docks and gave them to the dockers? Don't tell me what the owners would say – tell me what the workers would say.'

She had brought soup to Grandfather Ernest.

She had set aside her corduroy suit and Lenin cap and dressed in the finery that her mother had sent years ago when she had first come to Highhill. She had stored her belongings in her cottage by the sand quarry but though she kept her paints there, her brushes and easel and canvases, with Binkie leading the sit-down strike she had settled in the family home. She slept in the cot-bed, using the upstairs room to change.

She had brought the soup in a small milk urn.

She had been so gentle she had impressed even Grandfather Ernest. She was after all his daughter-in-law and she had done something no Fatherley had done; she had crossed his thresh and settled before the fire. She had made him tea and poured soup and served him in his rocking chair; he might have resisted pneumoconiosis, he might have surmounted a hacking cough, but he could not surmount old age. His strength had been ebbing, each day a greater effort to commandeer the trap, to stand upon it, to shout his scourges at the men and children.

'There's more people in the chapel now that I've denounced your barricades and your heathen funerals. The Highhill people don't want to follow you. They think William's down the pit to be out your way. They wonder how long the food'll last – and the poor relief. They knew where they stood with the coal owners. The people still fear me because I'm a man of God.'

'That's why Vladimir Illych banned religion.'

'I'm o'er old to read history books.'

'I'll stay with you till you're settled,' Pauline said.

There had been nothing in the house to remind him he was a man of God who had united the village when the pit disaster had struck. The back window looked out upon slanting fields where cows strolled among tussocky grass and nettle clumps; the fields flanked the colliery line, settled upon a cinder embankment. But if there had been nothing to remind him he was a man of God nor had there been anything to remind him of his wife or his other children. Grandfather Ernest might be a man with a future but he had nothing to remind him of his past.

She wrapped a blanket around his shoulder.

She made him comfortable as he smoked his clay pipe before the fire. He had a row of clay pipes on the mantelpiece and as he smoked he let a finger tip dab at the silver cap to the glowing tobacco; he controlled the glow and sucked at the stem of the pipe, feeling contentment with the smoke to the back of his throat. He laid his pipe aside to take the soup, settling the bowl in his hands, feeling the warmth of the bowl rising like the warmth that came from the fire.

'I'd rather settle myself,' Grandfather Ernest said.

'It's nice being close to William's father.'

'I was never that close to Bess.'

'You were close to her sons.'

'That's why I did the funeral service for Bess – and the funeral service for Ernie. Her lads at the front were dead and everybody knew they were dead. Everybody knew I should do the service – even Roland said I should do it before he went to Italy.'

'They say you spoke so often of hellfires and damnation the village people mended their ways. Your strong sermons brought good to the village. They say you were a force against evil. Were you a force against evil, Grandfather Ernest?'

'I'd like to think so.'

'Have you heard of revolutionary truth?'

'Not that I can think on.'

'It's means to an end,' Pauline said.

She helped him from his rocking chair to his bed.

She settled him for the night, taking soap and water and bathing his face and neck, letting her hand run the cloth from the bowl down the white hairs of his chest. She fastened the buttons to his night shirt, but there had been no electricity to the home and she lit candles and an oil lamp, and placed the candles and lamp so that the light reflected upon the bed.

Grandfather Ernest kept his eyes on Pauline.

He had become so weak he allowed Pauline to settle him and could hardly raise himself upon the pillow; only when he coughed did he rise on his elbows and lean over to spit mucus into a bowl by the side of the bed. His eyes were filled with distrust, malignant, not softened by her kindness; yet his body had weakened, the strength leaving him, his thoughts wandering, sleep overtaking him. He struggled to keep his eyes open but failed in the struggle.

Pauline glided around the bedroom.

Her red hair fell around her shoulders as she brushed and tidied and placed objects in better order on the lace strip that lay on the dressing table. She did not look at Grandfather Ernest, but kept her hands busy, her back turned, the shoulder padding to her dress making her shoulders square. She did not smile, her mouth tightly set, two spots of red high to her cheeks, her eyes as cold as her lips, the skin to her throat yellow in the light of the lamp.

She turned and came to the bedside.

There had been a harshness to his breathing; he had fallen asleep on his back and she turned him over gently so that the breathing became less harsh. His old face clung to the pillow, the beard straggled, lying above the sheets, but she settled the beard and smoothed his silver hair and running a hand across his brow she felt it cold. An ice sweat clung to his skin. She removed the pillow and settled his gnarled hands beneath the covers;

she blew out the candles and extinguishing the oil lamp she drew the curtains.

She kissed him three times, on each cheek and on the forehead.

'You're closer to the family than you think,' she said.

She suffocated Grandfather Ernest with the pillow.

94

Binkie Fatherley had returned to bank on hearing the news of his father's death.

'I'm sorry about Ernest,' Albi Birt said.

'He'll not be spittin' on my door step again,' Binkie said. 'Nor tellin' our men to take down the barricades.'

'He was your father, all the same,' Albi said. 'He might have died of old age, but he brought your family from Bedlington. The two of you built the Methodist chapel. Them were the good years. The village'd take it badly if you didn't go to his funeral.'

'The revolution cannot stop for a funeral.'

'They can for socialist ones.'

'I could do with a bath and my back scrubbed,' Binkie said.

On the day he had taken the men down the pit they had clambered up the iron steps to the headstock, waiting patiently for the opening of the cage gate. They had stood in their fustian breeches, shabby coats and canvas-thick shirts; their faces had been starched white, their lips dry and flecked with spittle. He had seen comprehension in their eyes. They understood why the battle had to be fought. Once in the pit the first impulse of the men had been to avenge those who had lost their lives in the pit disaster. They had wanted to set about the cutters, sabotage the belts, damage the pumps, pull the props from the faces, tamper with the fan that circulated the air. They had wanted to dismantle a cutter and send it to bank as a gift for the manager. Their tempers had cooled in the cold and they had slipped into as many woollens as they had brought with them.

Binkie had told them he wanted the public's support not its hostility.

He had placed more pickets around coal faces and told Tommy Bessford to act as his special liaison between the faces, wandering from one district to another to gauge the mood of the men, carrying messages, listening to complaints, relaying these back to Binkie. He knew that a sit-down strike was not the best of strikes; fears were like shadows that enlarged themselves in the reflection of a light, minds began to wander, to take on eerie thoughts. The cold attacked feet and despite the welter of garments moved up through the body like ice in the bloodstream. Darkness and damp were everywhere and so too was loneliness; the loneliness a man feels when he is not with his wife, not in the heat and sweat of his social club, the comfort of a bed to ease his aching muscles.

Even the warmth of a bath.

'You cannot go back down the pit,' Albi Birt said.

'I want to be with my men.'

'There are more men that need you in London.'

Albi had stayed in the village after the pit disaster.

'It makes sense, William,' Pauline said.

She had come into the billiards room in the institute and taken William's hand.

The billiard tables had been covered with tarpaulin; maps of the village and pit had been laid across the tarpaulin. There were red and green pins on the maps. The red showed the barricades throughout the village, the green the deputies' kists in the pit where the forty men had made their homes. Blankets had been sent down as well as food and drink and the men would sleep in the kists or landings or stapple bottom. The red pins showed, too, where barricades had been erected at the pit head and drift mouth; barricades that would stop special constables getting in should they return to the village.

They would also stop the people from getting out.

'We've got to pull down the Union Jack from Westminster,' Pauline said. 'We've got to chase the King from Buckingham Palace.'

'We want somebody in London,' Albi said. 'Winston Churchill's brought battleships up the Tyne and landed two battalions of infantrymen. They've been dashin' off the battleships with steel helmets and rifles and equipment. They say he's goin' to march them all the way to Highhill to smash the barricades and the strike. There'll be blood on the barricades and blood in the pit if he has his way. That's why you need to be in London.'

'The soldiers are all sons of the working class,' Pauline said. 'They'll not shoot their kith and kin.'

'Kith and kin, you say?' Albi said. 'Bullets don't know anythin' about kith and kin – especially when they're bein' fired.'

'They won't be fired,' Pauline said.

She had entered the billiards room quietly, unobtrusively, dressed in her corduroy suit, wearing her Lenin cap with the star stitched into the front. She gave Albi three kisses, but they were cold kisses and for a long while Albi would remember their coldness. Could she really be her mother's daughter? Had this been the young woman he had saved in London and brought to his flat? She took the cap from her head and shook her red hair around her shoulders.

'It makes sense for you to go to London, William. You can take over the strike committee – give them backbone. They don't believe in the dictatorship of the proletariat – that they can pluck power like blossom from a cherry tree. You understand, William. You can make them understand too.'

'Where can I stay?'

'You can stay at my flat,' Albi said. 'It's not as clean as when Mary Alyson looked after it, but I'll get you on the strike committee of the Trades Union Congress. There'll be no trouble about that. You'll be from the Miners' Federation – another miner fightin' for the

467

lads – the man who brought them out on strike in the first place.'

Vladimir Illych Lenin looked down across the billiard tables from Pauline's partially completed portrait she had begun in her cottage studio. He sat in a single chair, his legs crossed, his beard a faded russet, his bald head catching the light; his chin had been uplifted, his eyes penetrating, his hands loose across his knees, his fingers long. He wore a brown suit and waistcoat, a high collar with a brown tie; he looked more like a country solicitor; but if there had been anger to his eyes there was anger to his body, a tension that lay coiled seeking to leap out from the portrait.

On the walls to the billiards room there were sketches of Leon Trotsky and Gregory Zinoviev; sketches, too, of her mother copied from the frontispieces of her books, taking her from youth to middle age. Albi Birt's portrait had been lost to the green walls; it sat above the brown scoreboard, no light catching his features, noticed by none of the People's Commissars who came and went. He found it odd to be so close to Mary Alyson, hanging together as they did upon the walls of the billiards room in the colliery institute.

Pauline had set up an easel in a corner of the room.

She had made a drawing of a colliery banner and worked from the drawing upon a silk canvas; she used oil paints to dab at the silk stretched taut on a wooden frame. The paints were set upon a tressel table and she had brought in a high stool for comfort; the smell of paint had been fresh to her nostrils. She worked to capture the spirit of the commune and she recalled the cartoon of a woman holding a scarf she had sketched for the suffragist movement.

She sat on her stool and watched through the open door as printing presses were brought into the institute, small presses capable of turning out proclamations and handbills and even a broadsheet newspaper. Mechanics from the pit had volunteered to work the presses. The handbills and proclamations would fill the Durham coalfield; they would be found on billboards throughout the county. There would be Pauline's own newspaper entitled *The Clarion*. She understood she had to empathise with her fellow *communards* if they were to succeed.

'It's time you wrote your name into the history books, William,' Pauline said. 'No longer need you hide your lamp under a bushel. As Vladimir Illych left the *Vyborg* and crossed the *Liteiny Bridge* for the *Smolny* so you must take a bus to London. No more lackeys to capitalism! No more exploitation! Besides, we've planned it all – we've got it all worked out.'

'I'll need you with me, Albi,' Binkie said.

'As long as you do the work.'

Albi had never recovered from Mary Alyson's departure to India. His wife had hanged herself in the cupboard of her colliery home; they said she had taken her life from loneliness. The love that he had felt for his wife had long since extinguished, the friendship with Mary had been like an almond tree that never blossomed. They had been tragedies too many for Albi, but he knew there were more ahead.

'Who'll look after the men down the pit?'

'We've already got somebody in the pit,' Pauline said. 'We've got Tommy Bessford.'

'I didn't know Charlie's son had it in him,' Binkie said.

95

The strike committee had worked out of Ecclestone Square.

'A socialist springtime at last,' Binkie said.

There were cherry trees on each corner of the Square, the trees in bloom, the cherry blossom pink and proud, not yet scattered upon the pavement. Pigeons fluttered above the cherry trees, making for window boxes in the servants' basement quarters; chestnut trees stood tall, their white phlox as proud as the cherry blossom. There were flowers too, tulips and daffodils, red and yellow, primulas and grape hyacinths, small and bright and blue, all weaving a carpet of many colours around the lawns.

'Bess used to like talk of a socialist springtime.'

'The Russian revolution was completed not in spring but in October,' Pauline had said. 'Remember – only Vladimir Illych knew what he was about. So it is with you. Others might argue and talk – but you are for revolution. You are for uniting the working class – for sweeping away bureaucracy and establishment.

You are for destroying capitalism and its structures. If
you take your eye from this goal – if you lose yourself
in detail – the chance will be missed.'

The strike committee worked from the home of the
Trades Union Congress.

The building stood tall and colonnaded, the door black
and polished, an old gas lamp above the door converted to electricity. The lamps to the Square had
also been converted, but even if there were no coal
being produced fires burned in every grate, keeping
the rooms warm against a spring chill. Smoke idled
from the chimneys above the Square, arrogant and
defiant; the building had been painted a rich cream,
the door-knocker polished. The door had been opened
for Binkie and he had been ushered inside and into the
room where the strike committee was meeting.

'Seems more like the Winter Palace than the *Smolny*.'

'They've got good telephones,' Albi said. 'You'll
need them, if nothin' else.'

'I don't think much of yon chandelier.'

The ceilings were high, the corridors long, plush
carpets running along the marble; the chandelier above
their heads shimmered gold in the evening. Binkie
came from a house without electricity; he wished to
overthrow the government and rid Buckingham Palace
of its King; he paused in the doorway as if it were indeed
the Winter Palace with the Czar still in residence. He set
aside his romanticism. The strike committee had been
waiting, they had settled themselves in, and this was
where he must work.

471

'This is not a general strike,' he said. 'This is a revolution!'

He set up an organisation committee to handle hundreds of queries that came from every part of the country. He found there were office boys but no messengers or despatch riders, and if Albi had praised the telephone system there had been but a single telephonist operating a switchboard with a few telephone lines. Binkie learned that whilst there might be a grand scheme of things detail was all. He organised communications with pitheads, with communes, with action committees so that his revolution would indeed be run from Eccleston Square.

'I've heard the strike committee wants sport and entertainment to keep the lads busy. I want workers' defence groups. I want barricades and pickets. I want Lenin caps with red stars. I want policemen hit over the head with bottles. I want the Horseguards removed from Buckingham Palace.'

'Steady on a bit,' Albi said.

Binkie organised a joint transport committee to issue permits for essential transport; he wanted to starve the bourgeoisie and wreck the state. The permits caught too the strikers, cooperative stores needed permits but even when they had been issued the stores had received nothing but soap. Beer could not be delivered nor newspapers, and buses would be commandeered to run food. Even the bus that had brought Binkie from Highhill would run provisions from Eccleston Square to Battersea. A blackleg driver had tried to pick up a load of frozen mutton at a London wharf. He had been brought before the local strike committee.

'This is one for you to sort out,' Albi said.

Binkie had gone to the wharf.

He found the strike committee meeting in a rag-and-bone shop, the ceiling low, the room dirty, the committee sitting around a tressel table hardly visible through their own tobacco smoke. The strike committee were meat handlers by trade and the smell of meat and tobacco, of rags and crushed bone being stewed to glue, made Binkie flinch. There had been but a single light in the room, its white shade casting shadows to the four corners. The blackleg sat under the light like a man due for the condemned cell.

'What should we do with him, Binkie?' Albi asked.

'Shoot him!' Binkie said.

'We've got no guns.'

'Drown him in the river. We've got to show an example.'

'An example to who?' Albi asked.

'Who do you think,' Binkie said. 'Winston Churchill, of course.'

96

Churchill had called for military parades in London and other cities and armed convoys to deliver food; he had wanted a tent city in Hyde Park where milk and bread would be sold. He had been over-ruled by the Cabinet and some said the King, but Albi had taken Binkie to the Foreign Office quadrangle in Whitehall where stood a queue of people four deep before a wooden hut.

They had edged into the courtyard through a narrow portico.

'What are they doin'?' Binkie asked.

'Churchill has them signin' up.'

'Signin' up for what?'

'Special constables – volunteers. You name it – they'll do it.'

'They're all workin' class.'

'Enemies of the people – as Pauline might say.'

'It's the wireless,' Binkie said. 'It's broadcastin' all Churchill's appeals.'

'They're askin' people with private cars to give lifts to them that have none,' Albi said. 'It's spreadin' false information about men returnin' to work. It says you ordered one man shot and another drowned. All you did was dock his strike pay and send him home. It says enginemen and firemen are back to work – and there's food ships unloaded in river mouths all around the country.'

'All that's lies,' Binkie said.

The wireless had been a new-fangled contraption.

It had been no more than a crystal set that often worked with the bedstead for an aerial and a stove for an earth; the crystal set gave the news to those who lived in the country where Churchill's *Official Gazette* did not circulate. There would never be a pitman on the wireless or a member of the strike committee; nor a relative from Highhill who had lost a loved one in the pit disaster. Householders without a crystal set would crowd into the home of someone who had, the news getting through like the mails of old.

Binkie had not planned for it and did not understand.

'They recorded the Prime Minister sayin' how much he admired the miners, no way would he lower their standard of livin'. He was a man of peace. He said nowt about Churchill and the warships on the Tyne. We should smash the wireless station instead of sittin' on our backsides under that fancy chandelier.'

There might be no buses or trams but there had been plenty of traffic, bicycles, cars, ponies and traps and even governess' carts. Binkie had seen a four-wheeled bicycle on its way to the City of London. These were civil servants and clerks who had no sense of working class solidarity, no spirit of comradeship; they were on their way to work because they thought the revolution was fun. Some car drivers had put up printed notices inviting anyone who wanted a lift to ask for one. Others carried destination boards as if they were omnibuses.

'Should we shoot them all?' Albi said.

'One at a time,' Binkie said.

He paused before a Fleet Street bookshop to rest his legs.

He neither smoked nor drank but he ate at the wrong times so that he put on more weight than his legs liked to carry. He would walk from Albi's flat to Ecclestone Square. If he slept little he talked much; so much his voice became hoarse and he rasped from the back of his throat. There had been pain to his legs, but he ignored the pain. He treated it as of no account, except when the muscles tired and he settled himself on the ledge of the bookshop.

City workers might block the Street with their traffic but they ignored two working men in cloth caps and boots who had paused before a window. In the window were the works of Mary and Pauline Alyson, books and tracts carrying their portraits, larger portraits set in either side of the window; in the centre of the display stood the latest edition of *The Red Sunrise*. Young lads pushed past the two men, shouting good-humouredly, making their own way to the City. They were bound to be late, bound to have nothing to do when they got there.

They were happy all the same.

'The country's quiet as a mouse except for this lot.'

'We're winnin',' Albi said. 'Isn't that right, Binkie?'

'The pits are out, the trams have stopped, there's no buses on the road. Despite what the wireless says the docks are quiet and there's no food circulatin' without our passes. All we need is another push – a big push – a stormin' of Parliament or Buckingham Palace – and even Churchill will be gallopin' to the Channel.'

'I wish we had him gallopin' now,' Albi said.

97

'You're supposed to smoke a cigar,' Binkie said.

'It's a weakness like brandy,' Winston Churchill said. 'I have a strong constitution – I can put up with both. You must tell me about yourself, William Fatherley. You were against the war – yet three of your sons went to fight in your name.'

'I've always been willin' to shoulder a rifle to fight for the workin' class – but not for the enemies of the workers.'

'Your sons didn't think so.'

'Two of them paid with their lives. The third is somewhere in Italy – but lost to me and the village.'

'Your fourth son was killed by gas.'

'He died quicker than from any bullet.'

'What do you know of Pauline Alyson?'

'I married her, if that's what you want to know.'

'She's secretary of the Third International.'

'She's a Communist, I grant you that. We're all Communists now in Highhill – that's why we're called Little Moscow. It's a village on a hill but it cannot be hid like a candle under a bushel. We've socialised our people; they live on a higher plain. They know what they want and how to get it. That's why the revolution started – and that's why we'll win.'

Churchill led Binkie into an office looking out upon

Downing Street. There were yellow curtains to the window but no carpets on the floor; the parquet had been polished and shining. The light from the broad window fell across a desk holding a green lamp and on the desk stood a telephone and a box of cigars. This had once been the Colonial Office where Lord Nelson had met the Duke of Wellington for the first and last time. It was now the office of the government chief whip, sparse as the office should be, since the chief whip worked in the House of Commons.

Churchill had lost the leanness of his earlier years, as he had lost the gold-blonde to his hair; his jowls had begun to fall and there had been more flesh along his jaw. A thickness had developed around his waist and a heaviness slowed his movements. If he had lost the gold-blonde his hair had become thinner, only the odd strands across his crown, the strands grey turning to white. There had been a thrust to his jaw, a tilt to his face, so that his blue eyes looked beyond Binkie rather than at him.

'Why did Pauline Alyson raise a red star above Highhill?'

'The red star's a symbol of our movement – a movement that will destroy capitalism and build a new Jerusalem. We want to banish poverty and crime. All them things come out of capitalism. We're goin' to share in a great cooperative commonwealth. That's why the red star glows in the night – why I'm proud of the people of Highhill.'

'Your revolution is an alien conspiracy engineered

by Pauline Alyson as an agent of Vladimir Illych Lenin. She is a tool of the Soviet Union – as Russia now wants to be called.'

'We want a people's democracy,' Binkie said. 'There'll be no place for the likes of you or the King when the capitalist order is destroyed.'

Binkie wore the dark suit he had worn for his wife's funeral so many years ago. It had been his only real suit, that he had worn again for his wedding, but he had cleaned his boots so that the toes shone back at him, hearing the sound of the tipped heels and toes as he had come down Horseguards Parade towards Downing Street. Churchill had wanted him in for a cup of tea. The great Winston Churchill had wanted to meet Binkie Fatherley. The sun had been higher in the sky and the socialist springtime had been as close as the daffodils in Green Park.

'Pauline made a promise to Vladimir Illych,' Binkie said. 'He wanted one more revolution before he died. She made him a vow there would be an English revolution – Binkie's revolution, if you like – that it would start and finish at Highhill. We'll not be distracted now. She'll keep her promise to Vladimir Illych – and I'll keep my promise to her.'

'A promise built on Moscow gold.'

'The Kaiser's gold was good enough for Lenin.'

'You know your history, Fatherley.'

'The men'll hold out – gold or no gold.'

'There'll be no more Russian gold for Highhill. No more bills of exchange from Pauline Alyson. We know

479

your wife tours the pitheads in Durham giving out gold sovereigns. We know she receives messages telegraphed to different post offices in the coalfield – messages from Moscow that go to other strike committees. All that will come to a halt. An Order-in-Council has ordered the interception of all messages from abroad passing through post offices.'

'You'll never break the national strike committee.'

'We've issued warrants for their arrest. We've told the committee they must bring their so-called revolution to an end or face imprisonment for sedition. You'll be arrested too, William Fatherley. You might not end in Holloway like your wife but you might end up in Durham. Only there'll be no forced feeding for you – hard labour, I should surmise. No remission for good conduct. Once you step out of the front door you'll be arrested.'

'The strike committee will never accept that.'

'The strike committee are upstairs negotiating with the Prime Minister. They have indicated they will abandon their revolution. Their general strike will be called off. The order will go out from midnight. Civil commissioners will take over and special constables will move into all factories where there are strike committees. Poor relief shall stop at midnight. Our troops on the quayside in Newcastle will move through the Durham coalfield, taking down barricades, restoring order.'

'And the men at Highhill?'

'They will leave Highhill till last.'

'The men are on strike in the pit.'

'The mines inspectorate will want to know how the great pit disaster happened. Do you know, William Fatherley? Was it an accident or sabotage? The dramatic event Vladimir Illych called for? The mines inspectorate will want to know and if there has been sabotage we shall want the culprits – or culprit – brought to trial. The mine will be sealed. Coal will never be worked at Highhill again.'

'The strike committee will never negotiate behind my back.'

'Not even Albi Birt?'

'Not after all these years.'

'Have you heard of the Zinoviev letter?' Churchill asked.

98

'What do you mean?' Binkie asked.

'Instructions from Gregory Zinoviev, Chairman of the Third International to Pauline Alyson as secretary and counter-signed by her. Ordering that there should be first a pitman's strike followed by a national strike; that all factories by brought to a halt – by acts of sabotage if need be – that food supplies should be interrupted, barricades built the length and breadth of the land. That there be insurrection and sedition. That the government and King be deposed. It is all in the letter.'

'Nobody signed a letter like that,' Binkie said.

'Pauline brought the letter from London when she returned from Petrograd – or Leningrad, if you prefer. She travelled with a man called Tommy Bessford. Do you know him? He comes from your village. They stayed at the King's Cross Hotel – before you were married, of course. She went to the Gorinsky Bank in Cambridge Circus – a Russian bank that handles Russian affairs in this country. We have our people in the bank, of course – that is why we were able to photograph the letter in the vault.'

'You told this to Albi Birt?'

'He is a Member of Parliament. He has sworn an oath of allegiance to the King. He immediately called the strike committee to Downing Street to inform the Prime Minister that the strikes were over, the putative revolution finished. He told the Prime Minister he had never wanted revolution – only better worker conditions. He said Pauline Alyson turned your head.'

'What will you do with the letter?'

'A full protest shall be made to the Soviet *chargé d'affaires.* I shall tell him the Zinoviev letter is a flagrant violation of international agreements. Full publicity shall be given to the letter and our protest. The nation must see what saboteurs we have in our midst.'

Binkie Fatherley looked at the telephone on the desk.

He thought for a moment he had been back in the deputy's kist waiting a call from bank. Or on the stapple bottom, taking a call from the colliery manager at four in the morning, telling him to get a message to the under-manager and the men in the maintenance tub. Perhaps he was in the billiards room at the institute waiting for a call from another pit. Only when he raised his eyes from the telephone and saw the unrelenting blue of Churchill's eyes did he remind himself he was in Downing Street.

'The pit lads'll never call off their strike,' Binkie said.

'The miners will have to accept the terms of the coal owners,' Churchill said. 'Union lodges shall be disbanded, Highhill colliery shall be sealed. Never again shall mining communities be allowed to become hotbeds of revolution. The bacillus of Pauline Alyson shall be swept from the system.'

Binkie rose from the chair.

He felt his legs weak, the thigh muscles tired from the walk across Horseguards Parade, not rested by his long repose in the chair; he swayed and rested his hands against the desk top. The miners had been betrayed again, but this time by one of their own. The revolution had been betrayed too, but its spirit would live on. Pauline had created Communist cells up and down the country in factories and trade unions; she had set up committees of action on factory floors and factory newspapers had been printed. Printing presses had been installed, rudimentary presses but with enough striking workers to print them. All this could never be fully dismantled. The bacillus might be subdued but never eradicated.

Winston Churchill knew this.

He had reorganised coastal trade and distributed food around the coast when it could not be delivered by road or rail; he had brought back to life ancient mills to grind corn. Local brewers had supplied the yeast. A shuttle of destroyers around the coast had supplied the great bakers where millions of loaves were baked. The coastal system might have become obsolete or semi-obsolete, but it had worked; he had broken the strike and the revolution. He had fed the people. The barricades and the passes and the authorisations had been defeated.

But not the will of the men.

The revolution might have been betrayed, but its time would come as surely as the sunlight through the window. Churchill understood this as he stood too, thrusting his hands behind his back so that his coat-tails rose and fell. His eyes met those of Binkie Fatherley and their gaze held; they were indeed the same height. They might come from different backgrounds, understand different histories, but their eyes said there had been neither victor nor vanquished.

They were equal as men and they would meet again.

'Remember this, William Fatherley,' Churchill said. 'Yesterday's friends are today's enemies and today's enemies are tomorrow's friends. When this is over the coal industry must be put on its feet. And the country, too – never forget the country. The day will come when I will need you and you will need me.'

'What will happen to Pauline?'

'She will escape for reasons of state. She helped the British Ambassador in Moscow. She spied on Vladimir Illych Lenin – though perhaps Lenin used her to spy on the Ambassador. What they call a double agent. She will fight to live another day, as you will too if you go out through the back door and take your battle bus back to Highhill. There'll be no arrest, no charge, but if there's further mischief in Highhill even I cannot help you.'

'Pauline's all right – no matter what?'

'We shall want a proper examination of the causes of the pit disaster.'

'And the revolution's at an end?'

'Peacefully or otherwise. Soldiers begin marching through the Durham coalfield at dawn. It's up to you, William Fatherley.'

99

Tommy Bessford stood before Pauline Alyson.

He smelt of the pit, a fustian coldness that seeped from his clothes; a smell of damp and staleness. He wore a muffler and pulled his cap down across his heavy, coal-dusted brow; the white buttons to his hessian shirt had been tightly fastened, like lips that would not open; he had thrust his hands deep into his breeches. They were stiff from cold. He had done no pit work but coal dust lined his eyes and lips and ears; the coal dust to his eyes had been irritating and painful, their corners inflamed with a dark conjunctivitis.

'I grew a beard for you,' he said.

Except the beard had been ragged and uncouth, not dark like his hair, half-grey half-black, coal dust deep into its roots so that he looked dishevelled. He had met Pauline at the drift mouth and, holding a lamp above his head, he had led her to the deputy's kist. The kist had been freshly whitewashed to keep the men busy and some of the whitewash had fallen across the desk that stood against the kist wall. A calendar had been pinned to the wall and to the left by a notice-board stood a green-painted medical box bearing a red cross in a white circle.

'This is my *Smolny*,' he said.

Men in the kist had moved out with a nod that matched their stiffness; they joined other men sitting around transformers and compressors or against empty tubs, feeling the iron cold to their backs; men with faces that were black and shrunken by their days in the pit. At least they had been fed and watered. They had blankets against the cold, their enthusiasm had been lost to the darkness, to the dampness, and to their fear of water and gas.

A canary perched on its cage bar.

The canary had been better fed and watered than the men. A single light without shade hung by its flex from the kist roof. The light had been a brittle pearl and the canary sat on its bar, as discouraged and forlorn as the men, with no song to its throat, its yellow coat covered with coal dust. Its hooded eyes were barely open, and with its wings closed it appeared so frail it might already be dead.

The canary stirred when Pauline entered the kist.

'Even the canary cannot stand much more,' Tommy said. 'There's no more hot food – only sandwiches and cold water. And the men are sick of sleepin' on palliasses.'

'We'll bring the men to bank soon,' Pauline said.

'Then what'll we do?'

'We'll flood the pit.'

'Why do you want to flood the pit?'

'The coal owners will seal the pit when the strike's over. Not another ton of coal will be won. We'll flood the pit so there'll be nothing for them to take – no winding gear or tracks or props. I want the pit ponies out first and then the men. And the canaries. But when the men are gone we'll put out the fires that keep the pumps working.'

'My father'd not like me destroyin' the pit.'

'He's been dead and gone long enough.'

'All the same, it was his pit, his and the lads – he wanted us to work here rather than go to the Army. He worked his bargains and kept his face clean. If the pit's flooded there'll be no work for the men when the strike's over.'

'There'll be no work when they seal the pit.'

'My father would turn in his grave.'

'You must flood the pit,' Pauline said.

'There's no law that says we have to flood the pit.'

487

'Revolutionary action.'

'Like that business of revolutionary truth?'

'Churchill wants to investigate how the pit disaster happened.'

'You know how it happened.'

'I know water and gas killed the men. But how did the water flood the seams? Who set the shot that blew the old workings and let the water through? Who said there was no gas in the pit and the flood would only be a little flood?'

'There'd never been gas in Highhill.'

'You set the shot, Tommy Bessford, because you knew I wanted to start a strike. You knew I wanted a revolution on the back of the strike. I wanted to light a flame to light the world. You took the shot and blew up a district and flooded the pit.'

'You wanted a dramatic event.'

'Not a dramatic event that killed the men and killed William's son. That almost killed William. Is that why you fired the shot at four in the morning when you knew William was on the stapple bottom? Were you so jealous that you wanted to kill him?'

'You married him 'cause you felt sorry for him.'

'Because you killed his son.'

'You killed them all, Pauline. You know that.'

'You must flood the pit to save yourself.'

'Save you – you mean.'

'I'm a sister of the revolution. Our struggle has just begun. The revolution cannot fail. I will not allow it to fail. After we've flooded the pit we shall seek a truly dramatic event – an event that will shake the nation. An event that will bring all working men and women together so that they storm Westminster and Buckingham Palace. That will halt Winston Churchill with his battleships and his troops.'

'What do you have in mind?'

'We'll blow up Durham Cathedral!'

100

'How d'you think you can do that?' Tommy asked.

'With the same shot you blew up the old district.'

'It'll take more than shot to blow up Durham Cathedral.'

'The act will be sufficient. There'll be shock throughout the coalfields – throughout the country. Everywhere there's a strike committee, a committee of action. They'll see miners fighting in the heart of their coalfield. They'll never believe the strike committee in London. You must help me, Tommy Bessford. It's the last thing I shall ask.'

'You mean it's over between us?'

'It was over the day I married William Fatherley.'

'You'll not get away from us that easily,' Tommy said.

He led Pauline out of the kist beyond the tubs along a short path to a narrow staircase that led to the top of the hopper. The passage between the rock wall and belt had been narrow, the way rocky and uneven. Her hand rested first against the wall and then against the belt. She felt the hopper as she stumbled, her lamp tumbled between her legs, and Tommy paused and returned the lamp so they could go on again.

They moved up a sharp incline connecting two seams along ways where there had been no light, the air dank, water dripping from the roof, the going worse, the mud reaching to their knees. Finally the light from their lamps played upon the dampness of a wall, as if they had been walking along an alleyway looking for an exit, only to find a cul-de-sac. There had been an aperture no greater than eighteen inches cut into the left of the wall.

Tommy removed his cap and his hair fell across his brow.

'This is the mothergate,' he said. 'It comes out the other end as the tailgate. This is the bargain we worked for my father, may he rest in peace. We always think of him – me and my brothers. If you want to know what your revolution's about, it's about poor souls like us creepin' into this seam and workin' the coal whilst the coal owners talk about markets and the union talks about fewer hours for more pay.'

'I'm glad you've shown me where you work.'

'I want to show you more than that.'

Tommy pulled her close and she felt his roughness against her.

She felt too his manhood strong beneath the hessian and her own instinctive feelings rose within, a tingling to her nerves, an excitement reaching to her face so that she felt her cheeks flush, a warmth to her cold lips. He held her roughly, not like William often held her, not like a lover for there had been no tenderness, but as if she were his to dispose of, like a colliery wife.

There had been no confusion to his face, no uncertainty as there had been at the King's Cross Hotel. There had been traffic all night long before the Hotel, the window had not properly closed, and they had heard not only the lorries along the camber but the shunts and groans of freight trains from railway sidings, the throaty hiss of steam from the engines, the steam wraithing from the station so that Pauline could taste it upon her lips and tongue through the partially open window.

A street light stood slim and spindly before their room, its light strong through the thin curtains, catching the brass bedstead and fawn wallpaper, casting white reflections around the water jug and dish on a sideboard. The only heat had come from their bodies and the sound of their breathing had been lost to the noise of the traffic.

Pauline had dominated Tommy Bessford as Mihael Zaichnevsky had dominated her in Petrograd.

She had seen the confusion to his eyes as she had pushed him down onto the bed and loosened the buttons to his shirt and let her white fingers pause among the dark hairs to his chest. She had settled on top of him and pulled his shirt from his shoulders, the shoulders strong but cold, the muscles stronger to his arms, stronger than the muscles of Mihael Zaichnevsky, but there

491

had been no peasant smell of the earth, rather the smell of the pit village, its allotments, leeks and pigs and pigeon crees.

She had taken Tommy as she had wished to take Mihael in Moscow; only it had been too late, the strength had gone from his body, his nerves shattered. She thought of Winston Churchill the night she had pushed him under the train, the same steam wraithing the platform; she thought of the *traktir* and how Mihael had followed her through the snow. She had submitted to his will in Petrograd, but she had taken Tommy Bessford and been satisfied.

Her will had become her own again.

Now Tommy Bessford pulled her down into the mothergate. A pit prop cracked and blue post fell across her shoulder. She had often been told stories of the narrow seams, how timber needed to be safe, stone properly canched; how the floor might heave towards the roof, the dull coal threading the canch. At least this seam had been dry, no dampness, no mud, only a cold that rose around her from the depths of the earth, a cold like none she had known even in Petrograd or Moscow, devoid of air, of feeling, of character.

'You opened the buttons to my shirt once,' Tommy said. 'You can open them again.'

'You'll flood the pit for me?'

'If you make love to me here,' Tommy said.

'And you'll give me the shot for the Cathedral?

'My father would be pleased at least.'

492

'Anything for the revolution, Comrade,' Pauline said.

101

'You can betray me!' Pauline said. 'You cannot betray him!'

She flung her arm towards the portrait of Vladimir Illych on the wall above the billiard tables. She had thrown her Lenin cap upon the floor, scattering in a single sweep of her hand the red and green pins that had lain across the maps on the tarpaulin that covered the tables. A pile of red and white passes and telegrams and instructions from the strike committee in London and poor relief forms lay across another billiard table. She flung these too and papers and passes and forms flew around Binkie's shoulders.

'I never betrayed you, lass. It was Albi Birt who betrayed the revolution.'

She flung billiard chalk at his head, but the chalk missed and smacked against the scoreboard.

'I meant to call you Pauline.'

'You believed the Zinoviev letter as Albi Birt did.'

'They had the letter from Gregory Zinoviev – and your signature on the letter.'

'Did Churchill show you the letter?'

'He read it to Albi Birt.'

'*Read to Albi Birt!* There's many a man – and woman

493

– been shot for less in the *Lubyanka*. I told you never to take your eyes off the goal. That goal was revolution. I told you never to trust any of them. You let Albi Birt and the strike committee out of your sight whilst Winston Churchill flattered you in Downing Street.'

'He was goin' to send in the troops.'

'You mean he appealed to your vanity.'

'He was goin' to march them through the coalfield.'

'All those on the strike committee will end up in government service with government pay. Albi Birt will finish his days with a knighthood. Churchill has tricked you once – but never let him trick you again. Our revolution is not over if we do not believe it's over.'

'What do you want us to do now?' Binkie asked.

'Who owns the institute?' Pauline asked.

'It belongs to the men.'

'We shall seal the institute. It will be our monument to the revolution – we'll even keep the *Smolny* sign. The passes and maps and forms and instructions. And the paintings. Vladimir Illych shall stay on that wall till the time comes for him to be taken down. That time can only come when the revolution succeeds. We shall keep Gregory Zinoviev and Leon Trotsky – but not Albi Birt. I shall drop that down the pit shaft. Another generation shall visit this institute and see how it might have been but for his class treachery.'

'Will it be a tomb or a museum?'

'It will be a beacon for the future – like our red star on the hill.'

'What will we do with the star?'

'We'll store it here – for the next time.'

'Will there be a next time?'

'For you or for me – or for other Fatherleys? The time will come when there is no Parliament and no Buckingham Palace – and no King. We commit ourselves this day for a generation – for a century if need be. It will be the wish of the Fatherley family.'

'We'll never be shot of the King in my lifetime.'

'There will be other lifetimes.'

'A citizen Fatherley runnin' the country. That's worth many a socialist springtime.'

The printing presses stood idle at the back of the institute and the doors to the library were closed where poor relief had been distributed. The King had signed an Order-in-Council banning poor relief for the families of men on strike; he had signed another preventing banks from paying out money to support the strike. He had intervened on the side of the government. He and his dynasty had become enemies of the people. How long would it take before the ultimate confrontation?

The word *Smolny* still ennobled the front of the institute but the men had gone. Those who had brought messages, those on their *subbotniks*, those who hung around the doorstep, grass strands between their teeth; those who played cards, or in Pauline's words were as lazy in this world as they would be in the next. They had taken the excitement with them, the nervous energy, the sense of achieving, of changing the world, so that even the daffodils on the borders to the institute had curtsied and bowed.

495

Now their heads dropped and the institute was empty.

'I'll bring my sons' medals and the scabbard.'

'What scabbard?'

'The scabbard they'll come for one of these days. We'll seal everythin' in the institute till somebody – sometime – comes for it. Churchill thinks we're defeated, but he knows we'll be back. He knows he can defeat the revolution but never destroy it.'

'We're not defeated yet,' Pauline said.

102

The candle-lit procession had moved from the colliery headstock.

The night had been cold but the air still and the candles glowed like fireflies as the village people made their way out of the colliery yard up the bank beyond the institute to the fields that led to the drift mouth where the striking men would return to the surface. They had spent their forty days and nights. Forty men had gone down the cage with Binkie and forty would return. There had been no slinking back to the surface, seeking to circumnavigate the pickets, no allowance for sickness or rheumatism.

The procession had been silent.

As silent as the day when it had walked from the colliery headstock to the chapel for the funeral services of those killed in the pit; as silent as the procession that had made its way from the chapel to the graveyard behind hearses pulled by dark-coated horses bedecked in black, black bridles, black pom-poms around their ears, yet the horses striding forward with their heads in the air, as if proud of the moment, proud to be taking part, proud to be as one with a sad pageant of people united in their mourning.

As silent as the moment when coffins had been lowered into their graves.

The men who came from the pit were hardly recognisable to their womenfolk. Their faces were blanched, their skin pinched at the cheeks, and despite streaks of dried mud yellow stains were prominent around their eyes; their eyes were almost closed with fatigue, their veined lids listlessly drooping. The candle-lit procession did not break ranks but the men who came up the drift mouth slipped quietly into the arms of their loved ones, with relief rather than love, with weariness rather than affection.

Their ordeal was over.

They had left behind the compressors, the pumps, the tubs and the hopper, deputies' kists and the landings and the shaft bottom where they had slept, but they had left too a part of their lives, a part of their souls. Few would ever be the same again. They would go to their graves remembered as those who had held a sit-down strike at Highhill colliery as other would be remembered for war-time service. They had fought for their dignity, for proper conditions, proper pay and proper respect.

They would be punished for their rebellion.

'You did a good job, Tommy, son,' Binkie said.

'I'm goin' back to turn off the pumps and compressors.'

'The safety officer'll do that.'

'Do you think I don't know my own pit?'

Tommy Bessford handed a yardstick over to Binkie. It had been a symbol of his authority.

He had removed his cap and in the candle-light his hair had been a sullen caked black, the black deep to his brow and cheeks, the corners to his eyes still red with conjunctivitis, the corners angry and irritated by coal dust. Tommy had shaved off the beard he had grown for Pauline. He had used water taken from old workings and the edge of a pen-knife; the skin to his cheeks was as rough-hewn as the coal. He had been taller and rounder than Binkie had remembered.

They did not look each other in the eyes.

'I'll come back with you,' Binkie said.

'There's no need for that.'

'Me and your father grew up in this pit. He had high hopes for you, Tommy, as he had for the rest of his lads. He'd have been proud how you left your bargain clean and how you and your brothers worked as a team. He'd be pleased for us to come with you, I know that.'

'My father appreciated you puttin' our young'un into the blacksmith's shop when Roland left,' Tommy said. 'He'd not be pleased the way things have turned out. Water and gas in the pit. Men dead. Now the owners wantin' to seal the pit and me floodin' it to destroy their property.'

'They'd destroy it all the same.'

They would raise the brickflats, dismantle the engine sheds, the joiners' sheds, the machine shop, the electrical shop, the storehouse, the keeka's office, the weigh cabin, the time cabin. They would tear the wheels from the headstock and with the wheels the cage; they would remove the winding gear and the landing. They would strip the shaft of its timber and the seams of their picks, their conveyors, their girders and their pumps; even the fan that circulated the air. They would take the tubs and tracks from the rolleyway and would clean out the pony stables and deputy's kist.

They would leave nothing but the cold, the dark, the dust and the damp.

They would not rest till their destruction had been complete, till the heapstead was stripped of its coal chutes and hopper, the power station raised to the level of the brickflats. The houses too would be destroyed, uncouth houses of white brick standing row upon row to the colliery headstock and heap. Slum Alley would be the first to go where Binkie had brought up his family. Could so much be destroyed at a single stroke? Did it all mean so little? Could they be so discarded like worn-out tools?

If the colliery died the village must die with it.

'The rats'll be first out,' Binkie said.

'You'll find everythin' you need in there,' Tommy said.

499

'What's this? What do I need?'

'Speak to Pauline,' Tommy said.

He handed Binkie a haversack he had brought from the pit.

'You're the last one out,' Binkie said. 'Now you'll be the last one in.'

'I'll shake your hand at least,' Tommy said. 'For my father's sake.'

'For your own sake, lad,' Binkie said.

Binkie held him firmly by the hand and elbow.

'There never were any hard feelin's,' he said.

'Not between the families.'

Tommy turned and walked away from the candles.

He left behind the procession and stumbled across sleepers and rails, avoiding the oiled rope that heaved the set. The oil had been thick, the rope rusting, but he had looked at neither, keeping his head down, his eyes on the dark orifice of the drift mouth. A silence had fallen on the procession and in the silence they heard the dullness of his hob-nailed boots across the sleepers and rails.

Binkie watched him go.

He had envied Charlie Bessford and the loyalty of his sons; they had never let him down, never gone behind his back. He understood Bessford honour as bookmakers and bus runners and pitmen who respected their pit even if they did not love it; they had been proud of their bargain work and how they kept their coal face clean. Tommy would indeed turn off the pumps and compressors. He would let the air go sour and stale

500

and the pit flood. The flood would not be sudden as the pit disaster, but come slowly from old workings, the water rising steadily till the seams and rolleyways were filled.

Binkie knew Tommy would never be back.

He would die in the old workings.

His body would never be found.

103

Durham Cathedral stood stark and sombre against the night sky.

Binkie and Pauline had taken their own trap and made their way with the haversack to Durham City. There were few lights in the City, but they made out the Cathedral and castle and the bridges across the river; the night had been too dark and they could not see the river meandering beneath the bridges. They had paused on a crest of the road, green fields and a coppice of pine trees behind them, and they could smell the pine as well as feel the cold. They had hitched their horse to a tree by a trough below the coppice and they could smell the wild flowers and shrubs around the trough.

The wind stirred and they felt its chill.

'We should make love here,' Pauline said.

'What do you mean – make love here?'

'It's every woman's fantasy to make love on the grass.'

'We're not here to fantasise. We're here for revolution.'

Pauline nipped his ear with her small teeth.

'You're doing something for me,' she said. 'Let me do something for you.'

They lay on the cold grass with the pine needles to their backs, looking for a break in the cloud that would show the moon. Their horse had found the trough and dipped its head deep into the water; they heard its snuffle and satisfied whinney, but it did not stray from the tree. Even when the clouds did break there had been little moon and only a scattering of stars like dust thrown across the sky. The cold began to edge through their clothing but the smell of the grass was sharp and exhilarating.

'You should go to the House of Commons,' Binkie said.

'I hate Parliament. My mother hated it too.'

'You can have Albi Birt's seat. He's on his last legs, poor Albi, class traitor and all. To think I saved his life on the railway line. He thought everythin' could be arranged by a speech in Parliament – but he's made many a speech without much happenin'. If you took his place you could make it happen.'

'My mother wanted me to be the first woman Member.'

'Instead you went to Petrograd.'

'And came back to marry you.'

'Only you went to London and the Russian bank.'

'Gregory Zinoviev wanted to turn industrial unrest

into class war and armed insurrection. How else could we have our revolution? And how could the revolution be sustained without gold? It's called working class solidarity.'

'There'll be votes for women soon.'

'But who won the battle – me or Terry Kenny? Or my mother who gave out white feathers in Hyde Park in return for the Prime Minister's pledge?'

'Mebbes, in the end, the women won.'

Binkie had taken the haversack from the trap and hoisted it upon his back.

He had felt a tremble to his legs and wondered if the tremble came from fear or the sudden weight of the haversack. There had been an ache to the backs of his thighs since the pit disaster, that he had felt in London, but as he had ignored it then he would ignore it now. Pauline adjusted the straps to the haversack so that it balanced evenly across his shoulders. As they walked towards the City they heard the echo of their boots from the houses on the opposite side of the bridge.

The echo followed them to the Cathedral.

Binkie walked up to the door.

The tremble had gone from his legs, he no longer felt the cold; his heart beat against his chest as hard as that of any felon beating at the same door for sanctuary. How many had been allowed in and how many had sailed into exile? He took the haversack and laid it by the side of the door. It had been well-packed and kneeling over the haversack Binkie had taken out bobbins of shot and long tapering matches.

503

He looked at the wall by the right of the Cathedral.

He probed for weaknesses in the plaster around the bricks. He took a hammer and chisel from the haversack and chipped at the plaster near the hinges; he stood his full height and probed to find other weaknesses in the plaster above his head. He knelt to find more weaknesses near the base of the door. Each chip of the chisel, each blow of the hammer, had been like the sound of a footstep on the shale behind him, echoing back from the Cathedral walls.

The more he chipped the louder became the step, as if a man were walking towards him. He looked over his shoulder. There had been only the darkness and in the darkness Pauline's restless shuffle as she waited by the tree. Beyond the tree and the shale pathway stood the entrance to the castle as dark as the Cathedral, cloud drifting low, but still no sign of the moon to lift the darkness.

He removed the bricks from around the hinges and, pushing his arm into the wall, settled the pitched cotton of the bobbins as deep into the holes as he could. He followed the fuse of each bobbin out of the wall so that the fuse hung dull and grey and hostile in the darkness. He replaced the bricks and was left with six fuses from six bobbins, four around the hinges, one above his head and the other at the foot of the door.

He stood back upon the shale.

He looked at the bronze door that had stood since ancient times.

'I cannot do it,' he said.

Pauline had moved from the tree to his side and before he had time to speak another word she had lit a long tapering match; the spurt of the head, the lick of the flame, caught the whiteness to her throat and the red to her hair. She worked quickly, the flare of the match yellow to the palm of her hand. She lit each fuse till all six were lit and smouldering. She let drop the tapering match and, taking Binkie by the hand, she turned and ran back to the tree.

'I was born with the match girls,' she said.

104

They held the ceremony in the courtyard of Durham prison.

Warders lined the walls of the prison yard, but when the gates were opened the men came quietly, respectfully. They were led by Pauline Alyson, dressed in her Moscow costume of dark serge with a white blouse and brooch and modest red hat to match. Her red hair had been tucked beneath the hat and only wisps of dull fire showed to the back of her neck. The men parted to stand by the walls, but there had been no hostility between them and the warders. They stood at ease but alert as the men removed their cloth caps and placed them in their pockets.

The City noise carried through the open gates.

Seagulls wheeled from the river, drifting in from

the coast, but hovering curious above the yard, before swooping into back streets in search of scraps. There had been the monotonous sound of trams and the irritated toot of car horns as drivers drove slowly behind the trams. Voices carried from the racecourse where other men had assembled as if it were Durham Big Meeting Day. The river meandered silver and above the racecourse, above the City, stood the Cathedral and castle.

Four men carried the new Highhill colliery banner through the prison gates and marched slowly forward till they stood at the centre of the yard. They held the banner firmly, the feet of the wooden poles implanted in leather holsters they held around their shoulders. There had been no wind but a slight breeze rustling across the prison ramparts would be enough to catch at the silk and lift the poles. The men were all veterans of other marches, holding other banners, and they held the poles tightly and close to their bodies.

Binkie had been brought from his cell by a single warder.

The warder walked ahead of him and respectfully opened the prison doors that led to the yard. He stood six feet tall but walked with a round-shouldered stoop. He had a sandy-grey moustache and grey eyes that were attractive but sad as if they were a prism for his life's experience. He wore a new warder's uniform, stiff and overtight; his boots were as polished and shiny as the rim to his cap. Binkie followed his broad back as he opened the last door leading into the yard.

'It's a big day for you, sir,' the warder said.

'Nobody ever called me *sir* in my life,' Binkie said.

'Mister Fatherley then.'

'Nor that either. I was born William but they call me Binkie.'

'Because of the stone in the pit,' the warder said.

'Saved by the bink, they used to say.'

'It's not every day you're presented with a banner.'

Pauline kissed Binkie three times the Soviet way.

She had come forward and linked his arm and they had gazed at the new colliery banner she had made in a corner of the institute, or *Smolny* as she still called it; the richness of the colours were stark against the stone of the prison ramparts. There were on the banner Vladimir Illych Lenin and Pauline Alyson and Binkie Fatherley. On the banner were blazoned the words from one of her mother's books: *'We take up the task eternal, the burden and the lesson.'*

'We gave the old banner to the Donbas miners,' Pauline said. 'They sent it to the Kremlin and it will be lodged in their Hall of Fame.'

They walked around the prison yard as warders and men stood silently around the wall. The wind ruffled the silk of the banner and it swayed against the sky. The gold spear-shaped tips of the poles caught the sunlight, but the four bearers did not sway, their caps firm across their brows, their gaze ahead as if on parade, standing to attention, their legs slightly astride, their feet firm upon the cobbles.

'What is sedition anyway?' Pauline asked.

507

'I looked it up in the prison library,' Binkie said. *'Conduct by word or deed or writin' that directly tends to raise discontent and dissatisfaction among the King's subjects. Or brings hatred and contempt upon the government of the day and the laws and tendin' to public disorder.* You see, I've even had time to learn it by heart.'

'You're the one who should be Member of Parliament.'

'Only when I get out of here.'

The judge had sentenced Binkie to two years' imprisonment but not hard labour; he had lost a son in the great pit disaster and three to the war, two dead and another missing presumed dead. That had been punishment enough for one lifetime, but an example must be made; others must understand that the path to revolution was also the path to prison. Hatred and contempt for the government there had been a-plenty, public disorder too, and for this Binkie had been sent down.

There had been a muffled explosion when Pauline had blown the Cathedral door; they had felt its force as they reached the tree. The force ripped through the foliage and leaves and twigs fell upon them; shale scattered in a cloud of red hail and smashed into the castle windows, splintering the glass. Plaster and mortar from the door had fallen around the tree and there had been smoke too, black and heavy, rolling over them to make them cough.

They had not gazed upon their handiwork but ran towards the steep pathway leading from the Cathedral.

Bricks had exploded, the hinges had blown, the door had slumped but remained intact. Binkie knew the fuses should have been longer, but fragments of haversack and pitched cotton found by special constables after the blast proved that they had been the property of the Derwent Valley Iron and Steel Company, that they had been allocated to Highhill colliery.

Who had blown the door?

'Tommy Bessford,' Pauline Alyson testified.

'And where is he now?' the judge asked.

'He died in the pit.'

'Why did he die in the pit?'

'He died of remorse.'

Pauline declared to the court that when Tommy had returned to bank after the sit-down strike he had brought the haversack with him; he had declared it contained shot and pitched cotton. He had wished to create a dramatic event to assist the revolution and he had taken a trap to Durham and tried to blow the Cathedral door. He had returned with the trap to the village and descended into the pit through the drift mouth.

His father had loved the Cathedral from his days at the Durham Big Meeting and Tommy had been filled with remorse. He had turned off the air and compressors. He had wandered down among the old workings till he reached and pushed open the door to a small gallery not the size of a kist; he had felt to his face the full strength of the fan as it whirred before him. He had let the force of the air clash shut the door and swaying on his heels, feeling the rush

509

of air to his chest, he had taken the cap from his head. He had set down his yardstick and lamp and settled down to die as the air soured and water rose around him.

How did she know this?

Because she and Binkie Fatherley had led a search party into the pit to look for Tommy Bessford; they had retraced his steps, but as the air soured and the water rose they had abandoned their search and returned to the surface. He had survived the great pit disaster, the causes of which would now never be known; he had worked in the pit all his working life; his father and brothers had worked alongside him. Now he had died in the pit. There would be no socialist burial let alone a Christian one.

'How do I know this is the truth?' the judge asked.

'There are others who can testify,' Pauline said. 'William Fatherley himself – others who made up the search party; those who had heard Tommy Bessford talking on bank before he left for Durham in the trap with the haversack. All those who were in the candle-light procession.'

'You call this truth?'

'Revolutionary truth,' Pauline said.

'And what is that?' the judge asked.

'The same as any other truth,' Pauline said.

'Thomas Bessford died as he lived,' the judge said. 'That is in the pit. He had been inspired by those such as William Fatherley who by their seditious acts have brought his life to a sad and desperate end. I am satisfied that he extinguished the fires that had made the pumps and compressors work and so damaged the pit. The owners can only seal those dark orifices and transfer the work force to other collieries. William Fatherley – you might not be expected to pay for such a death and such damage – but you must pay for sedition.'

Pauline Alyson had not been charged.

105

'The red star came down and the barricades too,' she said.

'There was nowt for the civil commissioners?'

'Nor for Churchill's armoured cars. The soldiers marched up the hill with fixed bayonets as if they were on the Somme. They thought they might be machine-gunned and fanned out when they reached the barricades. There was no-one on the barricades, no-one in the streets, the shops were shut by order of Rosemary Rutland, and the clubs too. Talk about a deserted village. By then the pit had flooded.'

'I'm told the Miners' Federation have made us President for life,' Binkie said. 'Inside these prison walls I'm chairman of the library committee.'

The prison had its own workshop, its own chapel, visiting room, bathing facilities and library; his fellow inmates had indeed elected him chairman of the committee. He would be treated as a special prisoner and would wear a uniform with broad yellow stripes down the trouser legs and around his chest. It reminded Pauline of her own uniform in Holloway Prison, with its broad chocolate-coloured arrows. She linked Binkie closer and let her cheek rest against his shoulder.

'Now we've both seen the inside of a prison,' she said.

'I sew a few mailbags too.'

'You must read,' Pauline said. 'You'll have plenty of time for that.'

'I'll think too. We have to be shot of the King. He signed the Orders-in-Council that got rid of poor relief. He stopped you puttin' the money around that stopped the hot food to the men in the pit. He stopped the telegrams. We'll get rid of the King in his Palace all right.'

The King had authorised Churchill to set up voluntary committees to organise the supply of food and fuel and water, sanitation and gas and electricity; he had organised transport and communications. The voluntary committees had organised distribution and control. There had been no compulsion, no requisition, but there had been enough noble-minded citizens to heed their King and take on the burden.

For Pauline the revolution had failed because the national strike had failed; the men had followed trade union rather than political leaders. The trade unions had no ideology, no concept of the lives they had wanted for their members. Power had not fallen into the gutter as it had in Russia; it had stayed in Parliament and Downing Street and Buckingham Palace. Vladimir Illych had wanted to cleanse the world of the ruling classes, cleanse the world of the rich, but the ruling classes and the rich – fleas and bedbugs he would call them – were still in power in England.

'Vladimir Illych wanted the King to bring the Czar and his family to England,' Pauline said. 'He gave me a message for the British Ambassador. The King refused. The Czar and his family were shot. There might have been blood on the barbed wire of the Somme, blood on the coal, but there's blood on the King's hands too. His own kith and kin, as you would say.'

'Never trust a King,' Binkie said.

'Nor will we ever again.'

'The day will come when we're no longer comrades,' Binkie said. 'We'll live in a Republic. We'll all be Citizens in a free country joined with other countries across Europe to Russia.'

'We've already made a start,' Pauline said. 'We're setting up a medical aid society in the village. To fight pneumoconiosis and tuberculosis. We'll bring in our own doctors. The shopkeepers are all chipping in – and Rosemary Rutland too. She married the colliery manager.'

'Some of the men are leavin' for Canada?'

'Others are staying to organise concerts and a choir. Clothes are being donated to children. Some of the men have found coal outcrops on the surface – they've dug the coal and sold it in the city. The houses won't come down yet – except your house, of course. They say the whole of Slum Alley's over-run by the pit heap.'

'The village is like a flame,' Binkie said. 'It shall never die.'

Binkie inspected the banner again and nodded to the four bearers.

The bearers moved from the centre of the prison yard to the prison wall and eased the poles from their holsters; they controlled the banner through its ropes, dipping the spear-headed tips. They rested the banner against the wall. The prison gates opened and the bearers marched from the yard into the street; other men followed and there were cheers and applause from those outside who had not been allowed in. During the whole of Binkie's trial they had waited outside the assize court and settled by the river on the racecourse. There had been free drinks offered by the Miners' Federation and fires burned along the racecourse like camp fires.

Now the men would return to their pit villages.

'I almost forgot,' Binkie said. 'It's all the com-motion.'

'What have you forgotten?' Pauline asked.

'I've a message for you.'

'What do you mean – you have a message?'

'It came from one of the warders. He got it from the outside – from comrades in another country. It's for you, right enough. He says to be sure to pass it on. A friend of yours has been killed in Russia. A man called Mihael Ziachnevsky. He was deliverin' messages for Leon Trotsky – that's what the message says; don't blame me. He was arrested and shot.'

Vladimir Illych stared back at Pauline from the colliery banner.

'He was never a true revolutionary,' Pauline said.

'Sounds a bit like Tommy Bessford to me,' Binkie said.

106

'I've brought you a book,' Pauline said. 'You'll not find it in the library.'

She handed Binkie a book without a cover, the pages stained damp, almost fetid; the corners of the pages had been wrinkled and curled upon themselves. He felt the dampness and, as he did in the pit, he slipped the book into his shirt so that he felt the pages against his chest. Pauline kissed Binkie three times, on each cheek and brow, lifting herself on her toes, letting her hands run through his hair, receding now, his forehead pallid in the light, the lines deeper and more corrugated.

'Read the book when I'm gone,' Pauline said.

The warder came to lead him back to his cell.

'I've wanted a word with you, Mister Fatherley.'

'You're still calling me Mister?'

'A form of politeness, if you like.'

'There's manners even in prison.'

'I was with your sons when they died,' he said.

They climbed through the prison to Binkie's cell.

'I've always wanted to meet you and shake your hand and tell you how it was for your sons. They were brave lads, both of them, but it was Roger that took Paschendale, single-handed you might say. He got under the German barbed wire down a culvert filled with water. He came up behind them. He blasted the blockhouse door with a Mills bomb and charged inside. He took thirty prisoners. Then he upped and off to take the ridge into Paschendale village.'

'What did your say your name was?' Binkie asked.

'Serjeant Amis, sir. I'm only a warder here.'

'And you were sayin'?'

'Albert set up his own machine-gun post and raked the Germans till they turned tail and made it easy for our lads to go up the ridge to get to the village. He found Roger with a German cigar, large as life you might say, and one of them looks to say he'd had a prile at brag. I said old Binkie'd be proud – and you would be proud, I can tell you – just to see him sittin' there in that old broken down house with the Germans gone and their tails between their legs.'

'How did it all happen?'

'Roger got shot on the way back. It was nothin' really – nothin' like them other poor buggers. I seen

516

one man with his face half shot off. Roger had a bullet through the thigh. We got him to a casualty station and settled him down with Albert by an ambulance wheel. I went to get a doctor or a nurse. I came back with a nurse. It turned out to be Rosemary Rutland's daughter. This bomber came sneakin' out of nowhere, just like the Germans, sneakin' across in the half-light when the battle was over and the men were havin' a cigarette.

'The Germans dropped three bombs. One fell on the casualty station and killed everyone inside, includin' the surgeon and the poor bugger with only half a face. It was as if God had sent the plane over to put him out of his misery. The second exploded in a ditch and covered everybody with mud. Another hit the ambulance. There was nothing left of the ambulance and no sign of Roger or Albert. They'd gone all right. At least they'd gone in each other's arms. The last thing Roger did was put his arms around Albert. I saw it with my own eyes. They'd laughed like men and they'd died like men – but they were like twins in the end.'

'I had their medals on the mantelpiece.'

'I didn't fancy comin' back to Highhill after the war. Barbara Rutland didn't fancy comin' back either. She'd fallen out with her mother over somethin' or other, she never did tell me. We got ourselves married and I enlisted for Palestine. We've been there ever since, guardin' the Jaffa Gate, so to speak, but I've always wanted to come back to you and tell you what happened, but Barbara says to stay put, we're happy where we are.'

'What brought you back?'

'I had to come back with the revolution and all. I come from Highhill too, but you'd not remember my mother or father; they weren't pit folk, you see. Barbara stayed workin' in a hospital. I can go back to her one day mebbes, but we were good for each other; we saw each other through bad times. Now the bad times are behind us. I carried messages in the revolution, but when it was over the only job I could get was in this prison. You're the first prisoner I've had to look after.'

Binkie had followed the guard up the spiral staircase.

His cell stood on a floor in the higher reaches, away from the common prisoners. The cell had been similar to the cell Pauline had occupied in Holloway. A stone floor and barred window, four bars to the window, but the window frame slanting so that Binkie had turned his bed. The light would bathe his face and waken him in the morning, white to his closed eyes. A dish and jug of water stood on the trellis table in the corner and his bunk had been low against the wall.

Binkie had taken as many books as he could carry from the prison library. The books lay on the floor and against the wall and upon the wooden shelf next to the dish and jug. He read with full concentration. He read rapidly because he loved knowledge; he read to catch up on time he had lost after the pit disaster, lying on his cot-bed beneath the stairs; he read to clear his mind, to see the future clearly. As clearly as he could see the sky through the bars beyond the glass window once he had cleared the dust from the window.

He heard the door close to his cell.

He felt the dampness of the book to his skin and pulled out the book by its spine. He read the heading. It was the book on socialism by William Morris he had been reading when the waters had struck: *Socialism is no dream but a cause. Men and women have died for it, they work in the mines; they are excited by it, ruined for it. Believe me,* William Morris wrote, *when such things are suffered for dreams the dreams come true at last.*

An envelope fell from the book's pages onto the floor.

He picked up the envelope and tore it open; there had been a single note from Pauline, the ink black and long dried. Binkie read the note and looked through the cell window. The last of the procession had crossed the cobbles outside the prison walls and made its way through the narrow gate and beyond a pill box that stood by the gate. He wondered how long the banner would stand against the wall before other prisoners came to carry the banner into the prison and place it in the library. The banner would stay with him till he completed his sentence.

He looked up to the square of sky.

There had been no cloud, the blue pale and frosty, but Binkie knew if he waited long enough cloud would melt the blue. Only what manner of cloud? An odd white wisp that floated over the Pennines, a lazy cloud with nowhere to go and nothing to do; or a dark cloud filled with a hint of rain? It might be a cloud deep-throated with thunder, lightning sharp and violent in and out of the chasms. Or it might be a gentle welcoming cloud filled with hope and optimism.

Binkie again read the note.

'I'm expecting a baby,' Pauline had written. 'I think it's twins!'

Two lives snuffed like candles, he reflected.

Two others about to begin.

'There'll be a Citizen Fatherley one day,' he said.